MASTER WARRIORS

A BattleMech, the single most formidable fighting machine ever made by man, is not invulnerable, especially when confronted with another 'Mech. A MechWarrior has been trained in simulators and the harsh school of combat until he's very good at what he does. But the opponent may be better. Equipment, skill, and courage may improve the chances of surviving, but they cannot always save you. Sometimes it's just a matter of luck, and that luck can run out. . . .

BATTLETECH #4
WOLF PACK

BATTLETECH.

#4

WOLF PACK

ROBERT N. CHARRETTE

A ROC BOOK

To the Tuesday night gang at Eagle & Empire.
It's been really scary.

ROC
Published by the Penguin Group
Penguin Books USA Inc., 375 Hudson Street,
New York, New York 10014, U.S.A.
Penguin Books Ltd, 27 Wrights Lane, London W8 5TZ, England
Penguin Books Australia Ltd, Ringwood, Victoria, Australia
Penguin Books Canada Ltd, 10 Alcorn Avenue,
Toronto, Ontario, Canada, M4V 3B2
Penguin Books (N.Z.) Ltd, 182–190 Wairau Road,
Auckland 10, New Zealand

Penguin Books Ltd, Registered Offices:
Harmondsworth, Middlesex, England

First published by Roc, an imprint of New American Library,
a division of Penguin Books USA Inc.

First Printing, April, 1992
10 9 8 7 6 5 4 3 2 1

Series Editor: Donna Ippolito
Cover: Bruce Jensen
Interior illustrations: Earl Geier
Mechanical drawings: Earl Geier

Part 1

3053
INTERMIX

1

My name is Brian Cameron. I am a MechWarrior of Wolf's Dragoons.

I would like to say that I am only a simple soldier, but my friends tell me that my attempt to tell this tale makes me more than that. Perhaps they are right. Perhaps not. I only know that I find it necessary to record certain events, to make an account of matters that affected my life and those of all others who wear the uniform of Wolf's Dragoons. In doing this my hope is that those who come after will profit from the mistakes and experience of those who went before.

I do not pretend to omniscience, but my effort is honest. For those events occurring where I could not see and for words spoken where I could not hear, I rely on the integrity of my witnesses and my own sense of the affair. I have tried to be true to the heart and mind of the speaker, at least as true as any outsider can be about another person. I have spoken with all—well, all but one—of the persons from whose viewpoints I shall tell this tale. They have told me their piece of the story and answered my questions about their feelings and motivations. I am confident that they have spoken true, at least so far as they see the truth. Who but the Creator can know the ultimate truth?

As I said, my name is Brian Cameron. For the first seventeen years of my life, Brian was all the name I had. Of course, I had a unit nomen, but that is merely a useful designation, not a true name. I will not digress to recount the trials of my youth for that would only further delay the telling of my tale. In the Dragoons, we believe that hesitation is death on the battlefield. Lacking the life-and-death incentive of battle, I have tarried overlong.

I offer my apologies.

By the end of February in the year 3053, only ten of us still remained in our sibko. The rest had failed in one testing or another and had been assigned elsewhere. We were all nervous as we assembled on the review field at Tetsuhara Proving Ground for the announcement of the results of our final testing. The tension would have been bad enough had we been merely awaiting the scoring for our final MechWarrior assignments, but it was made unbearable by the fact that we also awaited the results of the Honorname Trials.

I knew I had succeeded in my last trial, but I thought my score was low enough to have cost me ranking. I felt assured of a slot in one of the line units, certain that my skills were sufficient. Still, I was nervous. Like my sibs, I had then entered the Honorname Trials. We were all part of the genetic heritage of the Cameron honorline and thus honorbound to compete when eligible. Though we were all young for our ageframe, some of us held hopes that the compensatory adjustments would give one of us a chance. I had not considered my own performance in the trials to have been particularly stellar.

Thus, I stood stunned when the rankings scrolled onto the screen situated above and behind the reviewing stand where our training officers sat in solemn array.

My name and nomen was at the head of the list. I had done what no one else in my sibko, no one else in my ageframe, had managed. I had tested out and earned the privilege of bearing the Honorname of Cameron for my generation. The unit assignments would not roll onto the screen for minutes yet, but I didn't care. I was happier than I had ever been.

Several mates of my ageframe crowded near as I stood staring at the posting board. I could see in their eyes the disappointment at their own performances. Jovell, an older contender who had outscored me in all battlefield categories, swallowed his pride and was the first to offer the ritual greeting to the newly Hon-ornamed. I could not suppress my grin of pleasure as I returned his greeting. The way he stiffened told me I had offended him, but I was lost in my own spinning world of joy and relief. I didn't give a moment's thought to his true feelings as he turned and shoul-dered his way through the crowd. There were too many others who wanted to congratulate the new Cameron.

Many of the others displayed honest pleasure in their greetings. We all face the same trials and, if we have made the maximum effort, there is no dishonor in not being first. We were all part of the Dragoons and a success for one Dragoon is a success for the others. But as pleasant as it was to receive the congratulations of agemate strangers, I was overwhelmed by the ec-static reaction of my sibs. Each had wanted the Cam-eron name for him or herself, but they hid any disappointment they felt. They smiled and laughed and pummeled me on the back, refusing to address me by anything other than my full name. *Brian Cameron.* A sib had won the name and we all shared the honor. The moment was electric and I was afire with pride. But I was secretly ashamed as well. I doubted I could have been so honestly and openly cheerful had it been Carson or James or Lydia rather than me who won the name.

My crowd of well-wishers parted and revealed a tall black man moving toward me. It was no less a per-sonage than Colonel Jason Carmody. The multiple decorations of his dress uniform combined with his snowy hair and age-lined face to mark him as a successful warrior, one skillful enough to have survived. Carmody was one of the old cadre, one of the original confederates of Jaime Wolf himself; he had plied his trade for longer than my sibs and I had been alive. Once, Carmody had commanded all of the Dragoons' aerospace assets. He had retired after an injury in an action over Capella, only to be recalled to serve as commander of our homeworld of Outreach after the death of Colonel Ellman. Carmody's post made him commander of the Home Guard and also put him in charge of the Dragoons' training program. It was in that last capacity that we had come to know his iron hand.

He had always been a stern and distant figure, a source of authority, discipline, and rare praise. Now he had left the reviewing stand and come to stand before me. I went to rigid attention as his eyes swept me from head to toe and back again before he spoke.

"I greet you, Brian Cameron. You have earned an Honorname. Earn honor for your name."

His speaking the ritual greeting made it real in a way Jovell's words had not. This was my commander speaking; his voice was authority. I could only whisper, "Seyla."

The grim visage softened. "You so resemble him that it's almost like seeing a ghost."

I knew I resembled my Honorline's founder, but then all my sibs did to some degree. I had never thought the resemblance especially remarkable. I knew that age and memories can cloud eyesight, so I only smiled and bowed my head, acknowledging the colonel's remark. When I raised my head once more, I realized that the shock of having Carmody come to address me directly had blinded me to the two other Dragoon officers accompanying him. I could say that I was too excited, but that is no excuse. I should have noticed them at once, for I knew both by sight although I had never spoken to either. They were the Camerons.

The older warrior was Major Alicia Cameron. Though not the first to earn the name hallowed by our founder William Cameron—that honor had gone to Malcolm, who had died on Luthien—she was the line's eldest, having earned the name in a replacement contest held after Malcolm's death. The younger, Captain Harry Cameron, was the second-generation Cameron. He had held his name since the first contest for his ageframe, beating William Cameron's own blood son. Though he had been a Cameron longer, he deferred to Alicia.

"I greet you, Brian Cameron. My brother Malcolm and I welcome you to the family."

I had to lick moisture onto my lips before I could say, "I am honored."

She smiled, but it was not like the warm smiles of my sibs. "You have shown yourself capable of the honor. You have not earned it yet."

Harry chuckled at her remark, then said, "I greet you, Brian Cameron. I welcome you to the family."

Fearing another blow to my newfound pride, I tried what I hoped would be a safer reply. "I thank you."

He chuckled again. Something had changed in his attitude, but I couldn't read him clearly. I would have to learn, though; they were my family now. I suspected that they would be reserved toward me for some time, for although they knew my scores, they didn't know me. I felt that I was not done proving myself.

Colonel Carmody broke the awkward silence by demanding my codex. I took the tags from around my neck and handed them over. He inserted them into the reader that he wore at his belt and tapped in some instructions. He nodded as he read the screen.

"Very well then, MechWarrior Brian Cameron." He snapped the reader closed and handed back my codex. "A Dragoon must always be ready to move. Have your gear to Pad Twenty-two by 1730."

I was surprised. New MechWarriors get a furlough,

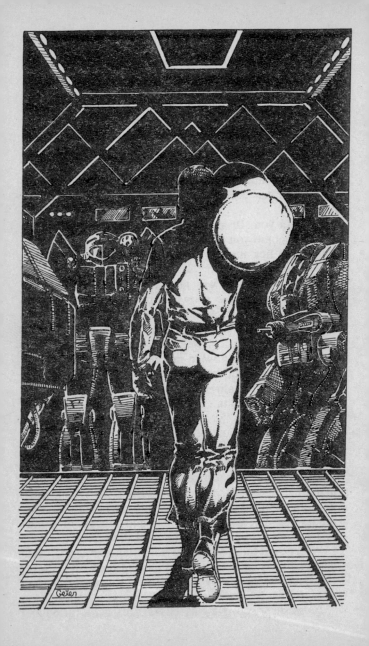

but it usually took place on Outreach. Did earning the Honorname rate an offworld vacation? "Why, sir? I—"

"You have orders, MechWarrior. You are to report to Colonel Wolf aboard the *Chieftain*. You have been assigned to his staff as an aide."

I must have stammered out another question, but I really don't remember. I do know that Colonel Carmody said some more, but I don't remember his words, either. They were meant to be encouraging, I think. My memories of the next few hours are equally jumbled, a whirl of congratulations and celebration. Carson and Lydia made sure I was at Pad Twenty-two by 1720.

After they left, I stared up at the giant DropShip *Chieftain*. Its huge ovoid shape screened half the stars twinkling in the sky of Outreach's chill winter night. I can still recall the awe I felt. And still feel the dread that colored it. It was not the *Overlord* Class DropShip that stirred those emotions, though. It was what awaited me inside.

I was to serve at the side of Jaime Wolf, legendary commander of Wolf's Dragoons. He was known throughout the Inner Sphere as the finest—a consummate MechWarrior, strategist, and tactician who for years had confounded his enemies and been a boon to his friends. He had led us through the fire and out again more than once, always keeping the Dragoons not just alive, but ready to fight. He had made us the premier mercenaries in the Inner Sphere. We sibs called him the Wolf because to us he was the archetype of the fierce ruler of a pack, at once a father, a guardian, and a leader.

If I did my job, I would be noticed. Immediately. And even more immediately, if I failed. Thoughts of Founder William flashed through my head. He would be proud—as long as I didn't botch up. If I botched in the Wolf's sight, there would be no honor for me. I'd disgrace the name, and the family would petition for my displacement. I would lose the right to bear the Cameron Honorname. Then where would I be? No one in the Dragoons would want to take in a disgraced no-name.

To be a warrior is to know fear and, knowing it, to press on. Though I was not so anxious to meet fear and laugh in its face, I shouldered my duffle and walked unfalteringly up the ramp.

2

Once, so I am told, the Inner Sphere believed Wolf's Dragoons to be simple mercenaries. The spheroids knew that the Dragoons had sources of supplies and materiel beyond those of ordinary mercenaries, but most pundits ascribed the Dragoons' bounty to control of a secret cache left behind after the fall of the Star League some two and a half centuries ago. A secret Star League cache. Many merc companies had found just such treasure; it was assumed by most that the Dragoons had been even luckier and uncovered a major find. Of course, everyone now knows that there was no cache.

The Dragoons had never been simple mercenaries. When they made their entrance into the annals of Inner Sphere history nearly five decades ago, they were on a mission of reconnaissance and evaluation for their masters among the far-distant Clans. Their Clan fellows would probably have considered the Dragoons' vintage equipment merely second-rate, inferior cast-offs good only for barely acceptable warriors, those of insufficiently pure genetic heritage or too wild for their fellows of the ruling caste. To the militaries of the Inner Sphere, however, the Dragoon supplies and equipment were pearls of technical treasure the like of which had not been seen since the golden age of the Star League.

Jaime Wolf and his Clan brother Joshua were the

leaders of that mission, having been promised legitimacy as a reward for success. Their assignment was to learn the strengths and weaknesses of each of the Great Houses of the Inner Sphere, signing on to serve them, one by one, as the mercenary regiment Wolf's Dragoons. The Great Houses, or the Successor States, as they had become known after the collapse of the Star League, were the mighty star empires that ruled over human-occupied space.

At first, the Dragoons met with success, both as warriors in the Inner Sphere's battles and as spies for the Clans from which they had come. Somewhere along the line, loyalties and sentiments began to change. Dragoon records are not specific on the point, but I believe that the change directly resulted from Joshua Wolf's death at the hands of a rival faction within the House of Marik, rulers of the Free Worlds League. From that time on, Jaime Wolf served as sole leader of the Dragoons, contrary to the dual command structure the Dragoons had inherited from Clan Wolf. Though still hiding their origins, the Dragoons continued to operate in the Inner Sphere, earning a fearsome reputation as the best, most honorable warriors since the time of the Star League.

That reputation took a blow when Jaime Wolf himself revealed that the Dragoons had originally arrived as spies for Clan Wolf, and by extension, for the whole body of the Clans, who were at that moment invading the Inner Sphere. The Dragoon name became a curse in mouths of desperate and frightened people everywhere. Who could blame them? Jaime Wolf admitted that he had been a member of Clan Wolf, the same Clan that had raced ahead of its fellows, gobbling up Inner Sphere worlds like the legendary Norse wolf-beast Fenris. As the Clan hordes drove implacably toward Terra, even the protestations of friendship with the Dragoons by the leaders of the Inner Sphere could not ease the hostility of the common people.

It was not until the siege of Luthien, capital of the Draconis Combine, that spheroid opinion began to shift back to a favorable view of the Dragoons. Hanse Davion, lord of House Davion and de facto ruler of the still new Federated Commonwealth, a marriage-spawned amalgamation of his own Federated Suns and the Lyran Commonwealth, ordered the Dragoons and other mercenaries to assist the besieged Combine. The move shocked many people, especially those who believed that centuries of mutual hatred would prevent cooperation between the Federated Commonwealth and the Draconis Combine, even in the face of so grave a common threat as the Clan invasion. After the Dragoons played a key role in checking the Clanner flood at Luthien, the ordinary spheroid began to believe that we had truly split from our past and joined our fate to that of the Inner Sphere. Once again, the Dragoons and Jaime Wolf had become heroes.

In the old days, Jaime Wolf used to play a game with those he had never met before. When the Wolf's face was not well-known, a visitor would be ushered into the presence of a number of Dragoon colonels. Jaime Wolf would be among them, but no sign would be given, no names exchanged, until the visitor had reacted. I am told that people usually mistook one of the other colonels to be the leader of the Dragoons. A comment, I think, on the inferiority of the average spheroid. But the faces of galactic heroes eventually become seen and remembered by grateful people everywhere and so the Wolf's game is no longer played.

I thought about that test as I entered the Wolf's DropShip. I knew that I would not have failed as so many others had; but then, I am a Dragoon. We are trained to look beneath the surface and sense a person's strength. I would have no need to recognize the chiseled features and the iron gray hair and beard. I would not need to know of his short stature and lean physique. Jaime Wolf would be unmistakable, his inner strength easily sensed by a true warrior, even if his appearance were not familiar.

But the days of games were long over. The Dragoons had fought hard, grinding campaigns, not the least of which was the siege of Luthien. Though the ruling lords of the Great Houses expressed their belief that we were wholly a part of the Inner Sphere, we knew where we stood. We had turned our backs on the warped traditions of the Clans, but we had still not become assimilated into the ways of the Inner Sphere. We were our own breed, standing alone in a hostile sea of stars. Only the planet Outreach was ours, and we would hold it by any means in our power. Sibkos such as my own were proof of our resolve. As we say in our ceremonies, the Dragoons will stand until we *all* fall.

The guard who met me at the head of the ramp checked my orders before summoning an ensign of the ship's complement. She led me through the maze of corridors to a small cabin, where I dropped off my duffle. There were three other bunks; I was too junior to rate a private cabin. A short ride on a personnel lift brought us to the main deck. Standing amid their transport cocoons were the ship's complement of BattleMechs, their giant shapes casting fantastic shadows. Flickering among the shadows were the lights of the techs working to refit or repair the huge battle machines.

I had hoped to be ushered onto the upper decks, the Wolf's den. Sibko rumor reported the off-limits portions of the *Chieftain* as a place where instruments of various decadent pleasures existed side by side with the most advanced combat-command technology. My disappointment at being unable to confirm those legends was drowned in a rush of excitement. I would soon come face to face with the Wolf himself.

Grouped around a table in the central open space, Dragoon officers huddled over a tactical briefing table.

In the reflected light of the holotank, the washed-out tone of their flesh lent them an eerie resemblance to ghosts. Jaime Wolf was seated at one end of the table, listening to his commanders talk over some problem.

The ensign nudged me and I was suddenly aware that she was holding out to me the packet containing my orders. I took it from her and she left without a word. With no reason to delay, I approached the table and handed the packet to the Wolf.

He looked up at me, taking the bundle and tossing it onto the table without a glance. His face was familiar, but that made it no less terrifying. This was the man who had held the Dragoons together through nearly fifty years of travail. His strategic sense and tactical genius were legend. Who could stand in his presence and not feel awe?

"Welcome aboard, Brian," Jaime Wolf said. His gray eyes were penetrating, clear and deep as glacial ice. I imagined that he could see into my soul and read it as easily as a datascreen. Not daring to speak, lest I embarrass myself by stammering, I only nodded and shook the offered hand. As I did, something moved in the depths of those clear gray eyes and the Wolf's expression shifted slightly for the briefest moment. Disappointment? Had I failed already? "You'll need to know everyone here if you're on my staff."

He introduced the other officers. They were all heroes, each a veteran of at least twenty years with the Dragoons. At the time, I barely noted them. But to tell the tale fairly, you must know who was there.

Colonel Neil Parella was the only combat commander present. My first impression of him was colored by his somewhat slovenly manner of posture, speech, and dress, but I had heard that life in the field is somewhat more relaxed than in the training cadres. Who was I to criticize? The battle ribbons and the patches of units defeated by his regiment that decorated his combat jacket told the tale of a successful warrior. I had heard rumors he'd had a drinking problem as a junior officer, a flaw that would have been unforgivable in a senior officer. But he had obviously overcome that; he was commander of Gamma Regiment, after all.

Colonel Stanford Blake, a dapper man of advanced middle age, was the head of the so-called Wolfnet, the Dragoons' intelligence operation. He had served in Wolf's Command Lance as intelligence officer until moving up to his current post. Of all of them, Blake alone actually seemed pleased to see me.

The oldest of the four in attendance on the Wolf was Lieutenant Colonel Patrick Chan. I knew from the archives that he had earned even more decorations than Parella, but Chan did not wear them on his uniform. Like Blake, he wore a MechWarrior's simple undress blues bearing only his rank insignia and the wolf's-head shoulder patch of the Dragoons. He no longer held an active field command, serving instead as Colonel Carmody's second-in-command and head of the BattleMech Operations Command.

It is not rare for Dragoons to wear patches signifying former affiliations, but I was surprised to see an infantryman's patch on the uniform of Major Hanson Brubaker. He was even shorter than the Wolf, a slim ferret of a man, hardly the sort one would expect to be a groundpounder. Then I noticed the Special Recon Group patch and understood. In his current post, Brubaker had moved on to reconnaissance operations of another sort; he was head of the Contract Command, the branch of Wolf's Dragoons that handled negotiations, recruitment, and public relations.

Introductions over, the officers fell back into conversation. The topic was not a tactical operation, as I had thought, but seemed to concern the details of a contract. I had never been very attentive in civil affairs classes, a failing not uncommon among Mech-Warriors. Only now did I feel the lack. Colonel Blake must have noticed my confusion. He leaned over and smiled. A trifle indulgently, I thought, but amicably.

"Kantov's Battalion of Gamma Regiment is up before the Mercenary Review and Bonding Commission for violation of contract."

"Ain't true," Parella objected from the depths of his sullen slump.

"House Marik alleges otherwise," Blake continued. "They have a substantial amount of evidence. The commission's judgement will likely be in favor of House Marik."

"It can't be! They're Dragoons," I blurted out, drawing the attention of the other officers to myself.

"Can and is, tinspawn," Chan said harshly. "Kantov's goons are guilty, and a blind ComStar acolyte could see it. You're out of the sibko now, boy. You'll be seeing a lot of things that can't be, but are. I've always said the metal womb freezes brain cells. You tinspawn are all alike. Why, I remember . . ."

"Ease off, Pat." Blake's voice held a note of tiredness, as if Chan's complaints were an old and worn-out story. "The boy's ours. He hasn't had Clan ed-com."

Chan shook his head. "Real world's the only real education."

"Give the kid a break, Pat. You were young once, too." Blake's smile was easy. "He'll learn."

"He'd better learn fast."

I tried to make my voice firm. "I will."

Chan only stared at me, his face expressionless. Long ago his troops had dubbed him Old Stone Face. I wondered if it was age that had made his features so craggy and foreboding or if they had always had such an austere cast.

Brubaker punched my shoulder, rocking me from my rigid stance. "Don't let the old goat get to you, Cameron. He is a fine example of ed-com himself. A fine example of its failure, *quiaff*?"

To my surprise, Chan ignored Brubaker's remarks and turned to Colonel Wolf. "I still say showing up for the trial will be bad for public relations. Let Kantov rot. We don't need to have Jaime pulled into this."

Brubaker snorted. "So you say. You haven't dealt with the public since you took over 'Mech ops. I leave those problems to you, so why not leave the relations problems to me? It is vitally important that Jaime stand before the commission. As leader of the Dragoons, the Colonel is the ultimate commander of the unit in question, a personage required by the commission to attend. This is the first time the Dragoons have been called before the commission for a violation and if the Colonel does not appear, he will give credence to all the rumors that the Dragoons backed the new commission for our own convenience. Our detractors will have ground for their claim that the Dragoons helped set up the commission to protect themselves. Or our commanders."

Chan waved his hand in dismissal. "I've already heard your arguments."

"But you obviously did not listen."

"That's enough, gentlemen. The Dragoons have enough enemies; we don't need to fight among ourselves." The Wolf's voice quieted his subordinates the way a sudden peal of thunder overrides the drumming of a storm's rain. "I would appreciate concrete suggestions on how to deal with this Marik problem. If you haven't anything useful to contribute, you're dismissed."

There were no more outbursts after that. The discussion of the problems inherent in the commission review proceeded in orderly fashion. But the more I heard, the more distressed I became. I had dreamed of following in Founder William's footsteps and serving the Wolf personally. Now it seemed that my first service would come as he and the Dragoons stood trial.

3

The hulks of the shattered BattleMechs lay strewn across the terrain like giant corpses. Foamed titanium-alloy bones glinted from within dark, gaping wounds in their armored shells, and shreds of myomer pseudomuscle hung gray and limp like strands of decaying flesh. Bits of exposed metal stained the 'Mech surfaces with streaks of rust resembling old crusted blood. Wheeling overhead, a raven shape cruised the old carnage.

From his position in the belly of a gutted *Thunderbolt*, Elson Novacat watched the aerial visitor and grinned. He could have brought it down easily with a shot from his laser, but there was no point. The aircraft's sensors wouldn't be able to detect him among the hulks of the destroyed 'Mechs, and firing on the spotter craft would only give his position away.

The destroyed 'Mechs had belonged to a House Liao strike team that had hit Outreach in some kind of vengeance raid while the combat regiments of Wolf's Dragoons were off defending Luthien during the Clan siege. The Capellans must have thought they would have an easy time against the old men and children the Dragoons left behind, but they had been proven disastrously wrong. The victorious defense forces had stripped the Liao raider 'Mechs of useful equipment and left the shattered hulks to rust in the field. Had the battlefield been in a more public place, it would have served as a warning. But this was "the other side of the mountain," a place where only Dragoons and specially privileged people were allowed to come.

Elson had to admit that the Dragoons had not fallen prey to the profligate tendencies of the Inner Sphere. Even dead, these BattleMechs continued to serve. Training exercises were sometimes held here, with the fallen 'Mechs re-armed to serve as pillboxes. Knowing that, he had searched for any with active weapon systems, finding none. These machines were all impotent hulks. But even as hulks they provided excellent cover, and cover was life for an infantryman, even when he wore an Elemental battle armor suit.

An Elemental's battle suit might look like a 'Mech to a civilian, but only if the civ had no reference for scale. The suit had a bulky, humanoid shape, made bulkier still by the backpack missile launcher. The boxy launch ports thrust up above the dome of the helmet assembly gave the armor its hunched shoulders. The left arm, non-human in proportion, terminated in a three-fingered power claw, while the right hand, when not fitted into a weapon assembly chosen to suit the mission task, had a reinforced glove of more human arrangement. Though similar in appearance to a BattleMech, the three-meter-tall armor suits barely topped the knee of the smallest 'Mech. Elemental suits carried only a single reload for their short-range missile launchers and, once the SRMs were expended, they had only limited anti-'Mech armament. Though offering a trooper the best protection and movement capabilities short of a vehicle or 'Mech, a battle suit could not make him a one-on-one match for even the lightest of 'Mechs. But then, Elementals didn't operate one-on-one against 'Mechs.

When he was sure the spotter was out of range, Elson left his refuge and called his Point together. The other four troopers in the Point called the unit a "squad," but that was because they were spheroids and Dragoon kids. Their archaic nomenclature was only a minor annoyance.

"Think we were spotted?" Jelson asked. He was Point second, a position he held only because of the lack of challengers.

They'd have known. "Neg," was all Elson said.

"I still think we should be laying for them in the pass with the rest of the platoon." That came from Killie. She was spheroid through and through, even though she had the build of an Elemental—a small one. Though she rarely complained about staying suited, she always questioned everything and was far too free in expressing her own ill-informed opinions.

"But that's where they'll expect us." This from Vorner, the over-eager Dragoon kid.

"So what?" Killie laughed. The sound was harsh over the suit comm. "It's the best defensive terrain around. No clear lines-of-sight beyond fifty meters. Perfect toad terrain."

Toad! If Elson had not been sealed into his suit, he would have spat. Some spheroid 'Mech jock had dubbed Clan Elemental infantry troops "toads" the first time he'd seen them come bounding toward him across a plain. The Clanners had been executing a rapid closing maneuver, using their jump packs for all they were worth. Those Elementals had been moving their suits with precision and grace, and all that free-birth jock could think of was hopping toads. The name had taken hold among the spheroids, even among their own battle-armored infantry. The unity-forsaken fools used the name for themselves. They had no pride.

His anger suddenly seemed pointless. He was among Wolf's Dragoons now. How could he expect better?

The spotter's presence meant the enemy would be arriving soon, too soon for Elson to allow his Point to engage in idle speculation and futile questioning of his commands. He cut off the discussion and dispersed his Point among the hulks, selecting their positions for maximum coverage of what he estimated to be the opposition's most likely route. He returned to the *Thunderbolt* and climbed atop its torso. Scanning the horizon, he caught a flash of light. He keyed the magnification circuit up to ten-power. Sure enough, a slight dust cloud. He had sent the Point to ground just in time. The enemy was coming.

He slapped an optic-link sensor onto the *Thunderbolt*'s hull and dropped down out of sight, letting the 'Mech's bulk shield him from the scans of the approaching BattleMechs, as it had from the spotter. He kept watch through the optic link.

The enemy was a single lance, all light 'Mechs. The heaviest was a model he had seen recently for the first time, a humanoid 'Mech body with an almost canine silhouette to its head assembly. It took Elson a moment to remember the designation . . . *Wolfhound*. The others were classic Star League designs, two stilt-legged *Locust*s and one more humanoid 'Mech, a *Wasp*. They moved in a diamond formation, with the *Wolfhound* in the lead and a *Locust* on each wing. From the *Wolfhound*'s position in the formation and its significantly superior mass, Elson guessed that it must be the lance commander's machine.

The 'Mechs slowed as they approached the old battlefield, cautious of the danger the broken terrain offered. That was wise. A misstep among shifting rubble could throw the machine off balance, perhaps overloading its gyros. A pilot in such a predicament would have to work hard to keep the mighty battle machine from crashing ignominiously to the ground. Such a fall rarely destroyed a 'Mech, but could severely injure a pilot, even if the damage was only to his pride.

Patient as a Nevtonian spiderlion, Elson waited. One by one the BattleMechs entered the old battlefield. They were moving slowly, cautiously. But their concern was only for the terrain—a mistake that would cost them. Elson let them reach what he judged to be the center of the 'Mech graveyard before rising from cover.

He painted the trailing *Wasp* with his laser, marking his Point's primary target. Triggering the short-range missiles in his suit's backpack, he gave the order to open fire.

The rockets roared from his launcher, rocking him for the microseconds it took the thrust of their engines to force them free of the launcher. Feeling the heat wash over his helmet as the missiles streaked toward their target, he was pleased to see twin smoke trails rising from four other locations almost simultaneously. His whole Point had launched on the target.

Booms followed flashes and smoke blossomed around the *Wasp*, but before it was obscured in the growing cloud, Elson saw one of his shots impact the head. Though he knew the shot would not penetrate, he relished the knowledge that the 'Mech jock would be hurt. But there was no time for exultation. He needed to be gone before the the the *Wasp*'s companions could react.

He concentrated on reaching his second position safely. Dodging to maximize cover from the alerted BattleMechs, he could not see the other members of his Point. The lack of return fire from the enemy 'Mechs encouraged him. The Point must have taken the 'Mech jocks by surprise.

Safe in cover, he risked a look around. His position only allowed him to see one of the other Elementals. Killie. She was flashing him the signal, pumping her arm up and down four times to indicate that all Point members were in position.

He checked on the 'Mechs. The *Wasp* was down. That was good. Very good. In fact, better than he had dared hope. It meant his Point had a chance at another. The other 'Mechs had halted. No doubt they were working their scanners overtime, trying to find whoever had struck down one of their number. Elson grinned savagely. They would find out soon enough.

The *Wolfhound* remained stationary, apparently on overwatch, as the two *Locust*s spread out to search. They gave wide berths to the dead 'Mechs, almost as if they expected one to spring up and throttle them like some revenant from a grave.

Caution in these circumstances was smart, but the lance commander was not as smart as he thought. Elson was ready for the jock's reaction. Recalling his Point members' assigned positions, he made a quick estimate of how far off they might be. He recorded his new orders, compressing them for transmission before he screeched out a burst to his Point. He had to keep it short to prevent the enemy 'Mech pilots from locating his position.

"All suits, vector on *Wolfhound*. Three minutes to firing position. Concentrate on right arm. Screech in two if unable to comply."

He waited ten seconds, then moved out.

Mark: one minute, twelve seconds.

He crouched and waited behind a dismembered BattleMech arm. From off to his left came the sizzle of a 'Mech-mounted laser. There was no explosion or further fire—the warrior must have been spooked, firing at shadows. No fire had come Elson's way, so he knew his passage through the rubble had not been spotted. The *Wolfhound* was still standing motionless, watching its lancemates.

Mark: two minutes.

The Point's frequency was silent. Still the *Wolfhound* had not moved. Things were progressing better than expected.

Mark: three minutes.

Elson popped from cover on a short burst of his jump jets, just enough to clear the debris. Launching his last salvo of SRMs as he landed, he bounced again, heading for new cover. The rest of the Point was attacking, too, bursting from cover, firing, then scrambling back. This volley was more ragged than the last.

The *Wolfhound* reacted at last. It spun on its left leg, lifting the right and rocking forward into a step as it raised its laser arm. Elemental missiles impacted that arm, its shoulder, and the 'Mech's chest in thunderous cacophony. The *Wolfhound* swung its right arm, the snout of its Setanta laser a hungry maw. Lambent energy leapt out to bathe Vorner's battle armor as he sprang for heavier cover, then beams from two of the 'Mech's chest-mounted lasers struck the ground to either side of him. The 'Mech jock had fired all his weapons, obviously wanting to eliminate the Elementals he had spotted. Too bad he wasn't a better shot.

Elson fired his own laser, a poor thing compared to the gigawatts of energy the Setanta heavy laser could kick out. But he was a better marksman than the 'Mech jock. He placed the beam directly on the shoulder housing already cratered by three of the SRMs. Two other thin beams speared out. One hit the chest, but the other also caught the shoulder.

The *Wolfhound* emitted a high-pitched whine. Its laser dropped, the glow fading from the energy coils. The damage inflicted by the Elementals' attack had rendered the 'Mech's primary armament useless.

Elson grinned.

"Fade," he ordered his Point. They had done their job. All they needed do now was lie low and survive.

Elson felt a savage joy when he saw how accurately he had guessed the 'Mech jocks' reaction to the attack. Even though they knew that this particular Point of Elementals had spent all their missiles, the jocks couldn't know whether there might be more Points hidden among the destroyed hulks. Even if they wanted to fight, the 'Mech jocks still had their own mission, which was not to destroy annoying infantry.

The lance was almost down to half-strength and their lance commander obviously did not want to lose more.

The *Wolfhound* pulled away, accelerating through the graveyard without regard for caution. The two *Locust*s followed. Speed would let them escape the Elementals. The 'Mechs raced away in the direction the lance had originally been moving.

Elson thought the rapid retreat was the lance commander's best decision in the entire encounter. As the 'Mechs reached the foothills, he wondered if they would have any better luck against the rest of Harold's Star.

Elson hauled himself up onto the half-buried *Crusader* behind which he had taken cover. Sitting on its chest, he let his legs dangle into the empty cavity that had once held a missile launcher. The fighting was over. For now.

Twenty meters away Vorner was kicking one of the shattered 'Mech hulks in frustration. He popped his lid, squirmed out of his battle armor, and promptly proceeded to transfer his aggression to the suit. His kicks had no effect on the Elemental armor.

Elson laughed. This trial was over, especially for Vorner. He had lost, tagged dead by the *Wolfhound*'s laser. Infantry didn't get second chances like the 'Mech jocks did. It might have been better for Vorner if the 'Mech's laser had been allowed to fire at full strength.

In the distance Elson could see the *Wasp* rising to its feet, the umpires having released their electronic lock on its controls. Doubtless the 'Mech jock was even more upset than Vorner. 'Mechs were not supposed to lose to Elementals.

The crunch of gravel told Elson that someone was approaching from behind him. He did not bother to turn around.

"One Elemental for one 'Mech. A good bargain, *quiaff*? Well done, Candidate Elson."

Recognizing the voice, Elson hitched his legs over the side of the 'Mech and dropped to the ground to

face Colonel Griffith Nikkitch. Elson stood to attention. Respect was due to the rank, even if the colonel
lost points for not using Elson's last name.

Nikkitch was an ordinary infantryman and well into
his fifties, but neither circumstance was necessarily a
disgrace. He wore battle honors and still stood
straight. Though large for the ordinary run of people,
Nikkitch did not have Elemental blood. Even when not
wearing his battle armor, Elson towered head and
shoulders over the officer who stood before him. Waiting until the colonel was craning upward to stare into
the suit's faceplate, Elson said stiffly, "My duty, Colonel."

Nikkitch did not seem fazed by Elson's manner even
though it verged on disrespect. It was also to the old
man's credit that he was not bothered by the faceless
bulk offered by Elson in his battle armor. "I suppose
you're wondering why you rate the Infantry Ops commander for your umpire."

"Not my concern, Colonel."

Nikkitch scowled. "It ought to be. Why'd you split
your Point off from the Star."

"Cadet Captain Harold had failed to appreciate the
battlefield, sir."

"Blunt." Nikkitch turned and surveyed the rest of
the Point as they gathered. He half-turned back toward
Elson. "And you saw something he didn't?"

"I was wearing battle armor while he was still
learning to spell the word in his sibko, sir."

"Clan wisdom says the new generation is superior
to the old."

"Clan wisdom says the young shall be guided by
their elders, sir."

Nikkitch nodded, his lips pursed. "And Harold
wouldn't listen to you. Said he'd worked this field before and knew the best ambush spots."

The accurate description made Elson wonder if the
colonel had listened in on the Star's strategy session.

"I had scanned the field maps before the exercise, sir."

"I know," Nikkitch said, revealing that he had taken an interest in the Star's planning. "What are you trying to prove, Elson?"

"I am a warrior, Colonel."

"Bondsman."

Elson bowed his head. The motion would not be seen outside the suit, but it helped him control his anger. He reminded himself that his status as bondsman was only temporary. When he felt he was controlled enough to speak calmly, he said, "As you say."

"I've seen your codex, Elson. You're not trueborn. Why are you so hot about this? Speak candidly."

"I may have been freeborn, but my blood is warrior blood. I earned my rank in Clan Nova Cat. I proved that I was a warrior."

"So you resent having to do it again, *quiaff*?"

"Aff. Yet I am bondsman to Wolf's Dragoons, taken in fair combat. I will fulfill my obligation."

"But nothing's going to keep you from being a warrior again?"

"I must be true to my heritage."

Nikkitch harrumphed. With a gesture, he included the rest of the Point in the conversation. "Well, you'd all better hope the rest of the Star does well without you. It's the whole unit score that will count the most. Your Point's score may be high, but it won't cut it if the rest of the Star botches up. Or loses because they're under-strength. Infantry has to work together."

Elson did not care for the rebuke. He had made the right decision. "All arms must work together, sir. And all arms must take advantage of their strengths, applying them in the best way possible."

"True enough." Nikkitch slowly turned to face him. "Your codex shows high aptitude in strategy. I suppose you want to be an officer?"

"I will serve as my abilities warrant, sir."

"We shall see."

That ended the impromptu review.

It was almost a week before the scores were posted. Elson had achieved a high enough score to make warrior rank and, to Elson's surprise, so had Harold. Once Elson had led his Point away, Harold had reconsidered Elson's advice and spread his unit out, extending the gauntlet through which the BattleMechs had to run. The result had been the effective elimination of the lance through accumulated damage from Elemental harassment.

Elson was summoned before Colonel Nikkitch.

"Harold has acknowledged that it was your strategy that allowed the unit to succeed. Does that surprise you?"

It did, but Elson refused to admit it. "Harold is honest when he sees no advantage in being otherwise."

Nikkitch shook his head, somewhat confounded. "Are you always so blunt?"

"I beg the Colonel's pardon."

"Forget it." The colonel indicated that Elson should sit. Seeing that the chair before the desk was both large and sturdy enough, Elson did so. The colonel waited a moment, no doubt judging Elson's state of mind, before continuing. "I am very impressed with your performance, Elson. Far more than I expected to be, considering the Nova Cats' showing on Luthien."

Elson damped his anger. The colonel was obviously intending to make some kind of point. Why could he not do it without gratuitous insults?

"Elson, the Dragoons are building their own force of Elementals. You are well aware that we are short of experienced commanders who know how to handle such a force. We need experts. You have advanced faster than any of the other bondsmen we took on Luthien, proving that you are an expert." The colonel paused, obviously awaiting a reaction. Elson presented the same stone face to praise as he had to insult. Nikkitch's face flashed with a brief expression of annoyance. "Would you be willing to work with me on organizing Dragoons Elemental units?"

"Does this mean I will not be given a command?"

Nikkitch smiled slyly. "Afraid you won't see battle?"

Elson gave him the stock answer. "In battle there is honor."

"Dragoon commanders do not have a reputation for sitting in camp while the grunts do the fighting."

"Then there will be a command?"

"Yes. And more, if you want it. You have potential, Elson."

"Then I accept. Bargained and well done." He stood and offered his hand.

Nikkitch laughed as he took the hand. "Bargained and well done, then. The formal ceremonies will be at the end of the month, but let me be the first to welcome you to the ranks, Elson Wolfson."

Elson released his grip. *Wolfson* indeed!

Nikkitch's eyes narrowed. "Now what?"

"I earned the name Novacat when I was inducted into the ranks of Clan Nova Cat's warriors. Though I have been accepted into your ranks, I will not surrender that honor."

Nikkitch sighed. "I'd hoped you would try to fit in. That name isn't going to make you any friends among the oldsters."

Elson replied with a contemptuous stare. What the "oldsters," the original Dragoons, thought of his name was of little consequence to him. They harped on Clan Wolf's feud with the Nova Cats, but that was waste heat. What did it really matter to them? They were all freeborns who had proven the trueborns' opinion of their kind. Had they not turned their backs on the heritage of the Clans? Had they not turned traitor to Nicholas Kerensky's dream?

Let Elson's name remind them of what they had spurned. It mattered little that he himself was free-born. He had earned his honor, won his name as a warrior. That had been his first step in proving the worth of his genes. He had shown these Dragoons that he was worthy of a warrior's name. Now he would show them that he was worthy of more.

4

The duly appointed panel of the Mercenary Review and Bonding Commission filed into the chamber. The first three members were stern-faced, properly somber. The fourth and last to enter, Colonel Wayne Waco, looked smug, as if secretly pleased about something. Yes, it was *that* Wayne Waco, the one whose Waco Rangers claimed a blood feud with the Dragoons. His presence on the panel was unavoidable. Under the new commission rules, an inquiry panel must always have a mercenary commander as one of its members, and Colonel Waco had come up in the rotation. The Dragoons had already used their one veto to disempanel the Draconis Combine representative. Despite the Dragoons' presence at the siege of Luthien, Colonel Jaime Wolf still maintained that the Dragoons were feuding with House Kurita, the rulers of the Combine. Unlike the Rangers, the Clan-born Dragoons understood real blood feuds just as well as the neo-samurai of House Kurita. A Kuritan on the panel would have been more damaging than the sour old leader of the Rangers.

Even with the Wacko Ranger, it seemed that the panel would be sympathetic to the Dragoons. Both Great House representatives belonged to factions that very much desired the Dragoons' good will. Baron Humfrey Donahugue of House Davion had been one of the negotiators of the contract that had brought the

Dragoons from the Combine to the Federated Suns back in 3028, at the start of the Fourth Succession War. He was as much a friend of the Dragoons as any employer could be. The other House representative was Freiherr Rolf Bjarnesson of the Free Rasalhague Republic. With Rasalhague almost completely under Clan domination, the FRR government was seeking aid and friends wherever anyone would stand still long enough to listen.

The panel was chaired by the obligatory ComStar official, one Merideth Ambridge. I didn't know what her official title was. A year ago calling her an adept would have been proper, but ComStar was going through changes. Most of the members we met nowadays were touchy about the use of the mystic titles they had formerly insisted upon. Whatever her title, Ambridge seemed fair and open-minded during the hearings. She called the session to order with a tap on the touch pad at her place, making the recorded sound of a gong to peal from hidden speakers.

"Let the representative of Wolf's Dragoons stand before the panel," she said.

Colonel Jaime Wolf rose from his seat. If he was intimidated by the august assembly and its solemn demeanor, he gave no sign. He walked smartly to the open space before the table and came smoothly to attention. Age had done nothing to diminish his military manner. Indeed, as he raked his gaze across the panel, it was more as if they were the ones on trial. Even the ComStar official flinched as the Wolf's eyes touched her.

"Colonel Wolf," she said hesitantly, "we did not expect to see you. This complaint involves only one battalion of Gamma Regiment."

"If it involves a single Dragoon, madame, it involves me."

"Been saying that for years," Waco sneered.

The Wolf ignored him. He had been doing that for years as well.

Ambridge cleared her throat. She spoke haltingly, nervously. "Then, we must presume that you stand to accept the judgement of this commission. The unit commander of record signed the document agreeing to abide by the recommendation of the panel. By coming before this panel, you are personally assuming this obligation."

"That is correct."

"If you're willing to take the blame, it'll apply to the whole lot of you murderers." Wacko Rogers looked like a hunting cat about to pounce. If he'd had a tail, it would have been twitching.

"Colonel Waco, you are out of order," Baron Donahugue said. The fat old diplomat seemed outraged. "The judgement applies only to the unit cited and its immediate commander."

Both Freiherr Bjarnesson and Waco started to speak, but Ambridge rapped her touch pad. The gong drowned out their words. When quiet returned, she spoke.

"Despite the esteemed Colonel Waco's manner, he is partially correct. Colonel Wolf, you do understand that the recommended sanctions are intended to apply only to the unit involved and its commander? And that by stepping into Major Kantov's place, you will take any punitive obligations onto the Dragoons as a whole."

"I do."

"You need not do this, Colonel," she said. "Major Kantov was the officer in charge. He is the commanding officer of record, according to the complaint."

Next to me Kantov shifted in his seat. I could smell the stink of nervous sweat rising from him. Out in the center, before all eyes, the Wolf never wavered. "He is a Dragoon and, therefore, under my command," was his response.

Ambridge looked uncomfortable. It didn't take a scientist's genes to figure out that the judgement had come out against the Dragoons. Even Kantov could tell.

"Very well, then," Ambridge said.

"A moment, Madame Chairperson," Baron Donahugue said quietly. Ambridge turned to face him with a raised eyebrow. "I should like to ask Colonel Wolf a question. Off the record, of course." She nodded assent and he turned to the Wolf. "Colonel, I applaud your loyalty to your troops, but I should think you might want to reconsider."

"That's no question," Waco snapped. "Don't try to talk him out of it."

The baron shifted in his seat as if to disassociate himself from Waco. "I apologize to the commission. The esteemed colonel is correct; I did not pose a question. I shall do so. Colonel Wolf, will you not let Major Kantov stand for his own actions and receive this judgement?"

Beside me, Kantov began to squirm.

"The unit bore the Dragoon name and colors," Jaime Wolf answered. The baron clearly didn't understand why the Wolf was doing this, but the slump in his expression showed that he recognized the Wolf's response as a negative. I wasn't surprised by the baron's confusion. He was a politician, not a warrior. Politicians don't understand taking responsibility.

Ambridge waited until the baron nodded before rapping her touch pad again.

"It is the finding of this commission that the mercenary unit known as Kantov's Battalion of Gamma Regiment of Wolf's Dragoons is guilty of breach of contract. Additional charges of insubordination, improper use of civilian facilities, theft, and cowardice in the face of the enemy have also been substantiated. In this matter, the employer, the Duchess Kaila Zamboulos and the House of Marik, have been found to have operated within the bounds of normal expectations and practices.

"At the beginning of arbitration, both parties agreed to be bound by the commission's findings. The commission has determined a reasonable compensation. Let the record show that Colonel Jaime Wolf stands as commander of the defaulting mercenary unit. Do you still agree to be bound by the findings, Colonel Wolf?"

"In the name of the Dragoons, I do."

Kantov sighed heavily. He looked relieved, as if he were off the hook. His reaction was noticed by most of the panel, but Colonel Waco was the only one who didn't seem annoyed. Ambridge had to visibly compose herself before continuing.

"Those gathered here will be the first to hear the decision of the commission, but you shall not be the last. ComStar will broadcast the findings and post them at all our Blessed Order's stations. Let the light of truth illuminate our lives."

She paused to draw breath.

"Now hear the unanimous decision of the commission.

"The payment bond placed in the care of ComStar by Duchess Zamboulos will be forfeited in full by the Dragoons. All monies and goods rendered for services shall be restored to the duly authorized agents of the duchess or the government of the Free Worlds League. Further, additional compensation in the amount of one hundred million C-bills shall be paid to the complainant. These funds shall be gathered by a ten percent deduction from all mercenary incomes of the unit in question, which by Colonel Wolf's acceptance of responsibility, shall be taken to be Wolf's Dragoons in its entirety.

"The officer responsible for the unit is placed under hiring ban for one year. Should he actively participate in a contract, either as a field commander or in a staff function, the ban shall be made permanent and he shall be declared a war criminal under the Ares Conventions, at which time the plaintiff may undertake civil or criminal prosecution at will.

"If the unit and officers in question refuse to abide by these findings, the commission recommends that the signatories of the Mercenary Review and Bonding Commission Compact place the mercenaries under ban. These stern recommendations are in accordance with the response to a grave situation.

"Colonel Wolf, do you accept the findings of this commission?"

"Madame, the actions of any mercenary affect the reputation of all mercenaries. Though Wolf's Dragoons has long held a reputation for honest and distinguished service to our employers, our performance in this most recent contract has been dismal. This is not the way the Dragoons will conduct business in the future. What happened with Kantov's Battalion has happened. Nothing can change that. The commission has conducted a fair and impartial enquiry into the affair and has reached a reasonable verdict. I can do no other than accept the judgement."

His voice was firm and calm, but I thought I detected an undertone promising that the issue was not yet closed.

"Thank you, Colonel Wolf," Ambridge said. "I declare the proceedings closed."

The commission members filed from the room through the same door by which they had entered. As the Marik party headed for the main exit, their chief counsel approached Jaime Wolf.

"It was not our intent to involve you personally, Colonel Wolf. I hope you do not hold this against the Free Worlds League or the noble House of Marik. We only wished justice."

The Wolf responded softly, "You've gotten justice, counselor. You'll get more."

The counselor stiffened. "Is that a threat, Colonel Wolf?"

"A promise."

The counselor might have taken the Wolf's word as directed at him and his state, but I could see where the Wolf was looking. His eyes were on Kantov. Jaime Wolf ignored the counselor's mumbled leave-taking. When the room had emptied of all but Dragoons, the Wolf beckoned Kantov to him.

"Kantov, you're from the Inner Sphere, but you've been with the Dragoons long enough to understand some of our less public customs."

"Sure do, Colonel. And believe me, I'm grateful. Those prissy diplos got snowed by the Marik sissies. Might have been different if that Wacko wasn't pouring venom in their ears, too. I really appreciate your standing up for us."

The Wolf cut off the torrent of words.

"Do you acknowledge the Trial of Grievance?"

"The what?" Kantov went pale beneath his swarthy skin and dark stubble. I smelled his sweat again. "You can't mean—"

The Wolf smiled tightly.

"As the challenged, you may choose to fight augmented or not. With our age and size difference, Dragoon custom will allow me to appoint a champion if you decline augmentation. But I assure you that if you select augmented combat, I will not demand BattleMechs of equivalent tonnage. You may use your *Awesome*."

Kantov's *Awesome* was an assault class machine. It would outweigh the Wolf's heavy *Archer* by twenty tons. Twenty very significant tons that would give Kantov an advantage.

"When you have made your decision, tell Lieutenant Cameron. He will inform you of my choice of battlefield. Until then, stay out of my sight."

"Hold on, Colonel," said Colonel Parella, commander of Gamma. He sounded annoyed. "Ain't you overreacting a little?"

The Wolf turned to face him. I would not have wished to be the object of that stare. "Your own place is not so secure, Colonel. Had you done your job, this problem would never have arisen."

"You gave us all leave to run our regiments as we saw fit."

"I have been known to make mistakes," Jaime Wolf said coldly.

Parella's eyes narrowed. "Well, I think you're making one now."

"Do you, Colonel Parella?" The Wolf hesitated for the briefest of moments. "You may be right."

Turning on his heel, Jaime Wolf headed for the exit. I followed.

"Colonel Wolf." My voice was hesitant and soft. I was confused, but hoped he'd think I just wanted to keep the words private. "I don't understand why you're taking Kantov's punishment, then challenging him. If—"

"You need to look at the bigger picture, Brian. I have a lot more concerns than one regiment's problems. Even if I wanted to, I couldn't sort out Gamma's problems even if I beat the stuffing out of its members one at a time."

"Then why the trial? Kantov's a lot younger than you and his *Awesome* is more than a match for your *Archer.*"

The Wolf laughed. "Don't worry, Brian. There won't be any fight."

"You mean that was all for show?" I was more confused than ever. If the Wolf's challenge was supposed to show people that he didn't really approve of Kantov or his actions, his timing was off. There hadn't been any audience but Dragoons.

Jaime Wolf shook his head. "The challenge was real enough. When I said that there won't be a fight, I meant that Kantov won't be around by the time of the trial.''

I stopped walking, shocked. It couldn't be. Would the Wolf would have some agent eliminate Kantov? Noticing that I was no longer at his side, he stopped and turned to me.

"It's nothing underhanded," Colonel Wolf said, apparently divining the direction of my thoughts. "Kantov is a coward. He'll run rather than fight.''

I was relieved that my fears that the Wolf was less than I thought him were mere imaginings. I remembered the tenets of his books on strategy and tactics, especially those teaching that one must know his enemy well. The Wolf was the master at knowing his enemies, an impeccable judge of men. If he believed that Kantov would run, Kantov would run. My faith in the Wolf's honor restored, we walked on.

The Wolf had another surprise for me. "As soon as Colonel Blake finishes his review of the commission's report, have him forward the list of dismissals along with his recommendations on replacements to fill the open slots in Gamma.''

"Dismissal? Replacements?''

"The bully boys in Kantov's Battalion had their chance. Those who weren't a party to the battalion's actions condoned them. The rot must stop with them. If the Dragoons aren't beyond an employer's reproach, we're no better than a bunch of pirates, and I won't lead a bunch of bandits. The Dragoons are better than that. We have to be.''

I was stuck by the fervor in his voice. "You say that as if you have something to prove, Colonel.''

"There's always something to prove.''

We exited the hall to face the assembled reporters.

5

The Wolf was proven correct; there was no Trial of Grievance. Kantov disappeared from his barracks and a week later Colonel Blake's sources reported him outward bound on a JumpShip headed for the Capellan Confederation. Kantov had found himself a new home with Olson's Rangers, a mercenary regiment more than happy to have an ex-Dragoon, even a disgraced one. From what I'd heard in the common hall, Kantov might actually raise the Rangers' level of morality. Several of Kantov's cronies left Outreach as well. Most headed for Capellan space with Kantov, but a few grabbed slots in the first unit that would take them. Within two weeks none of the people on my dismissal list was still on Outreach.

I was glad, and not just because it meant fewer discharge files for me to handle. The Dragoons were well rid of them. But we still had to deal with Kantov's legacy.

At first, the Wolf took his exile from combat well. He threw himself into work he said needed to be done. The sentence of the commission didn't prevent him from dealing with Dragoon business operations. When the Wolf wasn't doing business, he was overseeing the training facilities, adjusting class strategies, and reviewing the progress of almost everyone taking instruction on Outreach, from the transient spheroids to the training sibkos. He also spent a lot of time with the scientists and the teachers.

I spent most of my time shuffling requisitions and proposals. Though I told myself all of it was important, I must confess that I paid more attention to the Blackwell communiques. I was a young MechWarrior and Blackwell Corporation was now our primary weapon supplier—and new technologies are, after all, far more interesting than personnel transfers, grade rankings, and spare-part requests. I didn't understand a lot of the technical specifications for the new factories, but I appreciated the capabilities of some of the new machines that would be coming out of those factories. If I couldn't fight, at least I could keep up on the state of the art.

The Wolf himself wasn't working, but the Dragoons certainly were. They needed to be. The commission's penalty meant we needed a lot of contract business to maintain the cash flow that Jaime Wolf demanded. He spent a lot of time within the marble-sheathed walls of the Hiring Hall. His attention to the organization of Dragoon contracts made sense to me. Having combat units spread over half the Inner Sphere made coordination vital. What I didn't understand was why he spent so much time glad-handing the unaffiliated mercs who came to Outreach.

Their motivation was much clearer. They wanted the Dragoons' seal of approval on their units. Despite the commission's verdict, it had done little to diminish the Dragoons' reputation among the hireling soldiers of the Inner Sphere. If anything, our reputation improved. Maybe they thought us more human; they certainly saw that we were willing to admit to our mistakes and then rectify them. Whatever their reasons, the other mercs came and Jaime Wolf saw them.

Those he approved were added to the Dragoons' recommended roster alongside such longtime subcontractors as the Black Brigade and Carter's Chevaliers.

Sometimes I thought the Wolf wasn't as discriminating about the honor of those mercs as he might have been. I tried to be fair; after all, they were not Dragoons. But my worry over those units was nothing compared to the disgust I felt about some of the ragtag collections of MechWarriors that set up shop outside the Hall. They were Kantov's kind of people, and were using the draw of the organized contracting to offer cut-rate deals to prospective employers. I didn't understand why the Wolf permitted them onplanet. They drew customers away from our operation and those the Dragoons sponsored.

"Unavoidable," the Wolf said when I asked him. "We need an open city for open commerce. Keeping them out would be discriminatory and lose us our reputation for fairness. As long as they pay their rent, they can stay. But they'll never see the other side of the mountain."

"The other side of the mountain" was where the Dragoons trained, the greater continent on Outreach where once the old Star League had held its Martial Olympics. It was also known as the "Outback" to distinguish it from the "World," the smaller continent where we did our public business. The Outback had other uses now, not all of which I can tell you. Outsiders only visited it under escort. Even orbital overflights were forbidden under pain of attack. If Outreach was our home, the other side of the mountain was our private quarters.

Of course we of Jaime Wolf's Command Lance got to the other side of the mountain, but not often enough. The Wolf's Command Lance was a reinforced lance of six BattleMechs that was structured for combat as well as staff functions. But with the Wolf's undesired furlough, we were all sidelined. Still, no one in the Dragoons goes very long without a chance to sharpen combat skills. Periodically the dullness of cityside duty was relieved by a training exercise.

Such exercises gave me an opportunity to get used to my new *Loki*. At sixty-five tons, it was a far larger 'Mech than I had ever piloted. Had it been a standard combat configuration, I probably wouldn't have had any trouble. It was the equipment installed so that I could perform my duties as common officer that complicated the situation. My *Loki* had an extensive suite of communications and electronic gear, making it more functional for regimental command in a mobile battle than most spheroid command centers. If a spheroid comm officer were ever to observe its compactness and power, he would probably die of envy.

I often found myself wondering how well Founder William would have handled the machine. As one of the original Dragoons, he would have understood OmniMechs far better than any of my generation or the adoptees. OmniMechs were Clan tech and, therefore, new to us, but the Dragoons had few of them as yet. To be allowed to pilot one was a privilege and an honor. I intended to be worthy of it.

I can say without pride that my skills in the 'Mech increased with each session. If only I had been as confident of my skills outside the machine. As comm officer I handled an immense load of signals. For weeks I confused call signs and the units to which they belonged. With the Dragoons changing unit compositions and organizational structures on what sometimes seemed a daily basis, a certain amount of confusion was inevitable. I understood some of the restructuring, but other arrangements were clearly experimental. Occasionally, I suspected that the Wolf made some of the changes just to relieve his own boredom. Maybe he enjoyed watching me make mistakes.

At least the Wolf was patient with me. I never rated extra duty more than twice a month. Other members of his staff were not so lucky. He drove them increasingly harder, always finding fault with their performances. Perhaps his frustrations owed as much to his inaction as to any failings on the part of his subordinates. Looking on, I often thought the staffers didn't deserve some of the chewing-out they got.

They say a good commo officer is invisible, a transparent filter for his commander. Maybe so. I know there were times I felt like a mechanical fixture in the command center. Increasingly, that was the way Jaime Wolf treated me. Over the months I seemed to have become for him little more than an extension of the radio, laser, optic, and hyperwave commlinks spanning the distance between him and his troops. Wanting to be a good commo officer, I told myself not to worry, to take that kind of treatment as a compliment. I told myself that I didn't mind, and I believed it until the day he first called me William.

I was shocked. And frightened. Had the strain become too much for the Wolf? I had heard that old people sometimes lived in the past, seeing their surroundings as some other time or place and speaking to those long dead. Was the Wolf so old that he was falling prey to such a weakness of the flesh? He had become snappish, another trait they say is common to the old. I didn't know what to think. Warriors do not normally have long life spans, and I had had little experience with old people.

I sought out Stanford Blake, with whom I had come into extensive contact in our common service to Jaime Wolf. The senior intelligence officer had been helpful, more times than I could count, and I had come to rely on him when I was confused. Though he was older than me by far, I found him a good companion. He had an easy manner and had even told me to call him Stan, as long as there were no customers around.

That day I found him studying the reports from Alpha Regiment's deployment in a raid on Brighton in the St. Ives Compact. The Capellans had offered a premium on the contract, paying for the entire regiment's services when the mission profile required no more than a reinforced battalion. Stan had told me that he suspected the Capellans had misrepresented the situation. Epsilon Regiment was pulling garrison duty on Relevow, a system only a jump away. The Capellans were renowned for their deviousness, and I suspected from the communiques I had been ordered to route to his console that Stan was trying to find some hint that the Capellans were setting up a sucker punch.

"Any sign of trouble?" I asked as I tapped on the divider that separated his desk from the main ops floor. Even in my agitated state, I knew enough to be respectful of my superior's concerns.

"Nothing yet," he murmured absently. He waved me in without looking up from his datascreen. I waited, unwilling to interrupt his thoughts. After scanning a few more documents, he flicked the screen to hold, leaned back in his chair, and gave me a grin. "What can I do for you, Brian?"

"You've been with the Wolf since the start, haven't you?"

"Yes." Stan surveyed me thoughtfully. "What's happened now?"

His easy recognition of my agitated state bothered me, perhaps unreasonably. I heard the defensive whine in my voice as I spoke. "Who said anything happened?"

"You did," Stan said, far too cheerily. "Whenever something happens that you don't understand, you open with some variation on that line about 'since the start.' Why don't you sit down and tell me what happened?"

I sat.

"Is it something about Jaime?" he asked.

"Not exactly. The Wolf—"

"Stop calling him 'the Wolf.' "

I sat back, surprised. "It's what everyone in the sibkos calls him."

"Well, they shouldn't be doing it either. But we can't

very well issue an order for them to stop. Around here, where he can hear, call him Colonel Wolf or just Colonel. That was good enough for William.''

"But I'm *not* William!''

He was taken aback by my sudden vehemence. "So that's it.''

"What?''

"I've been waiting for this to happen.'' Stan shook his head slowly, a sad smile on his face. "In some ways I'm surprised it didn't happen sooner.''

So, I concluded, he shared my worries about the Wolf. My fears had been justified. The Wolf was old, more than seventy years, maybe close to eighty. He was older than than any other commander in the Dragoons. And now it seemed that he was finally succumbing to the cowardly leeching effects of age. I didn't know what this portended. If the Wolf was failing, what would happen to the Dragoons? Most people seemed to expect that his blood son MacKenzie would take over the Dragoons. But MacKenzie Wolf was not his father. He lacked . . . something.

"What are we going to do?'' I asked in a whisper.

Stan shrugged. "Ignore it.''

I was shocked. Stan's callous attitude was more disturbing in some ways than the Wolf's failing. "How can we?''

"It'll pass. You're doing William's job almost as well as he ever did. That would have been enough. But your resemblance to him makes a slip almost inevitable. I'm surprised I haven't done it myself. Don't worry, you'll make your own mark soon enough.''

"My what?'' I felt my face flush. I had misunderstood Stan's remarks. While I was fearing senility in the man who still held the Dragoons in his hands, shaping them as a potter does clay, Stan had seen the truth. I had been *too* good at filling the founder's shoes. My only failure had been interpreting a slip of the tongue as evidence of a slipping mind.

As all the oldsters liked to remind me, I was still young.

"You'll get over it, Brian. We all grow up having to deal with other people's pasts, needing to be ourselves instead of some imposed image of perfection—or even the image of our blood fathers. Didn't you know what you were headed for when you entered the Honorname competition?"

"I guess I didn't."

"But you're learning now, aren't you?"

I nodded.

"Don't be afraid of growing up; it's the only way to be yourself instead of someone else's idea of what you should be." His serious expression melted into a smile. He laughed. "Now if we don't stop this philosophizing, we'll get reclassified right out of the warriors. That's something I'm not ready for. Did you get a signal from Beta command yet?"

Stan's sudden question reminded me that I was a warrior, too. I suppressed my feelings and anxieties and sat up straight.

"Routed through to your commdeck at 1130. Colonel Fancher reports no action on planet since the initial skirmish with the planetary militia. She is expecting bridgehead defense complete by dawn local. She will upscale patrolling at that time."

"No reports of Kurita activity on the continent?"

"Neg."

He frowned. "Hard to believe the Snakes aren't squirming all over Beta."

"Intercepted Combine signals suggest aerospace activity behind the near moon. I appended the intel report to Colonel Fancher's report."

The frown twisted into a wry grin. "Interpretation is supposed to be my job."

"No interpretations, Stan. I just reported the signals and source codes."

"If they're forming back of the moon, they may be planning a counterdrop. Flash an alert to Fancher."

"In addition to the relay of the intercept?"

"No, I guess not. Alicia will reach the same conclusion I have." Stan laughed. "William would have cleared the relay first."

Even though he was doing it humorously, he was still comparing me to the founder. I hid behind formality. "Facilitating command's work is my job, sir."

He laughed again. "And you do it well. Thank you, Brian."

I found his good cheer infectious. My feelings about being called by Founder William's name seemed suddenly childish. I was doing my job. *My* job. And doing it well. Stan's praise wasn't the Wolf's, but it still made me feel better.

6

To Dechan Fraser, the gardens were all the more marvelous for the fact that their wildness was so artfully derived. Each bush was chosen, planted, and trimmed for effect. Here was a tangle of shrubs and wildflowers that might been a jungle on any other planet if one did not recognize the lonely blooms of Kiamban fire lilies; there was a slice of Alshain where a clump of slender rock suggested the spires and minarets of that planet's capital. During his years in the Draconis Combine, Dechan had learned to appreciate this artistic tradition wherein a place, or rather the mood of a place, was suggested by shape, silhouette, and shadow. He had even begun to understand how it was that some of the greatest architects of these oases of peace could be warriors.

The Combine was dominated by House Kurita, and the Kuritans maintained a warrior tradition in the style of the ancient samurai. Like those ancient samurai, the best and brightest of the Combine were both redoubtable warriors and subtle artists. This garden, designed by Takashi Kurita, was a part of that tradition. Takashi was the Coordinator of the Combine, its absolute ruler and embodiment of the mythical Dragon. Although he left the military aspects of governing to his son Theodore, the Gunji-no-Kanrei, Takashi had been a formidable MechWarrior in his youth. He was still a MechWarrior, having only recently led his elite guards into the crucial battle against the Clan invaders in their siege of Luthien. But Takashi was also an artist. The garden was a subtle expression of humanity's imposed control over nature's chaos, as well as an insistent but equally subtle statement of the Coordinator's dominion over all the many worlds of the Combine.

The path led Dechan down into a dell and across an arched wooden bridge. The burble of the stream below him was a hushed, comforting sound as he walked up the slope and around the mossy hump of a knoll studded with boulders of pink quartz. Twisting around the mound, the path continued. Dechan moved slowly, reluctant to leave the calm of the little valley. Then, turning the corner, he saw something that stopped him in his tracks.

Though startling, the massive bulk of the Battle-Mech did not at first seem out of place. Its hulking, mostly humanoid shape was framed within an arch of branches whose leafy shadow dappled the machine's gleaming blue surface. Gold trim highlighted segments of the 'Mech's armor and outlined selected fittings. A golden stripe wrapped around from the heavy launcher housings that gave the machine its characteristic, hunch-shouldered profile, then dipped into a vee down the sloping front of the center torso. It was an *Archer*, a seventy-ton BattleMech designed primarily for fire support, but a formidable fighter in other roles as well.

Dechan didn't need to see the red disk with the black wolf's-head on the left thigh to recognize the 'Mech. Though the markings didn't quite match his memory, the differences were unimportant. He had no doubt whose *Archer* this was supposed to be: Jaime Wolf's.

So, he thought, there must be truth to the rumors that Takashi was once again becoming obsessed with the Dragoons.

Takashi's messenger had told Dechan to take this

path, which meant the Coordinator had intended for him to see the *Archer*. If Takashi had summoned Dechan because of his former connection with the Dragoons, why not also invite Jenette? Dechan had assumed that the Combine's Internal Security Forces were well-satisfied that he and Jenette had long ago severed all ties with the Dragoons. But if Takashi was hunting the Dragoons once more, perhaps even the ISF's assurances would not be protection enough.

Would Theodore help? Dechan and Jenette were supposed to be members of his *shitenno*, his inner circle of advisors. But could Theodore protect them from his father if the Coordinator decided they were Dragoon spies and insisted on their deaths?

The threat was ironic.

Years ago—more years than Dechan cared to remember—he and Jenette had gone with Michi Noketsuna on the trail of the Kuritan warlord Grieg Samsonov. Samsonov had been a principal engineer of the events leading to the near annihilation of Wolf's Dragoons in 3028. Michi, seeking revenge for the death of his mentor, Minobu Tetsuhara, had led Dechan and Jenette against the warlord and then on a trail that was to lead eventually to Takashi Kurita. Jaime Wolf had approved and detached the two MechWarriors from regular duty. The trail was long and twisty but had come to a sudden, abortive end after a chance encounter with Theodore Kurita. The then-young Kanrei had convinced Michi that his samurai honor required him to forego his vendetta and to work instead with Theodore to save the Combine from the impending threat of invasion by its neighbors. Publicly, Dechan and Jenette had gone along out of fellowship and became advisors to Theodore's newly reorganized army. At the time, Stanford Blake had called it a coup for the Dragoons, a golden opportunity to spy on their old enemy, Takashi Kurita. Dechan and Jenette had dutifully filed their secret reports on the changing military capabilities of the Combine, each time risking their lives for the sake of Wolf's Dragoons. They had been good spies, constantly awaiting the move Jaime Wolf would make to end the feud with Takashi so they could finally return home. But the call never came.

Then the Clans had appeared.

Ignored, possibly forgotten, Dechan and Jenette received no word via Wolfnet for more than four years. And when Wolf had found it necessary to contact Theodore, he had used others, contrary to Dechan's understanding of his and Jenette's place in Dragoon-Kurita relations. And for all his protestations that Dechan and Jenette were trusted advisors, Theodore had not taken them to the meeting on Outreach in which Jaime Wolf had briefed the Kanrei and the other leaders of the Inner Sphere on the Clan threat. Hellfire, Dechan didn't even learn of the meeting until a week after Theodore left. Jenette's comment was that it was all politics, part of the game. He had retorted that her faith in the Dragoons was too blind, that Jaime Wolf must have asked Theodore to leave them behind. They didn't share a bed for a week after that.

But that had been almost a year ago and with still no contact with the Dragoons, even Jenette's iron faith was wavering.

Following the path, Dechan passed between the widespread feet of the *Archer,* his eye caught by some small tablets that lay clumped on either side of the stepping stones. The tablets had writing on them. Crouching to look closer, he saw that each slab bore a name. Most of the names he didn't recognize, but some he did. They were all Kurita warriors who had fought against the Dragoons. The presence of one name especially surprised him, more for its prominent place than for its presence.

Minobu Tetsuhara.

Tetsuhara had been the Kuritan officer assigned to act as liaison with the Dragoons during their contract with the Draconis Combine. He had admired the Dragoons and learned much from them, enough that when he received orders to destroy the mercenaries with regiments he had raised on their model, Tetsuhara had nearly succeeded. Though caught in a conflict of *giri*, his duty to the Combine, and *ninjo*, his human feelings for his Dragoon friends, he had followed his orders like a good samurai. And, like a good samurai, he had committed *seppuku* to atone for his failure. Tetsuhara and Jaime Wolf had become close friends. That friendship was as much a part of the Dragoon/Kurita feud as the treacherous behavior of Warlord Samsonov, who had been Tetsuhara's superior. The hunt for Samsonov had connected Dechan to Michi Noketsuna, Tetsuhara's protégé, and that friendship had brought him into House Kurita service.

How much did Takashi know?

It would be ironic if he and Jenette were to be denounced as spies now. Could Takashi believe that the deaths of two forgotten Dragoons would affect Jaime Wolf? Did he think he could use them as pawns in prosecuting his feud? What a laugh! The Dragoons didn't need Dechan and Jenette. They had given up their feud, had begun to treat it with the contempt they showed Waco's Rangers. A feud no longer exists when only one side takes it seriously. Dechan and Jenette had been abandoned, discarded as unimportant to Jaime Wolf's plans, just like his blood feud with House Kurita.

Now Dechan was on his way to a private meeting with the Coordinator of the Draconis Combine, the lord of House Kurita, and he had been deliberately reminded of the supposed blood feud.

Did the Kuritan code also call for *seppuku* by forgotten and impotent spies?

Dechan straightened and tugged his uniform back to

order—his Kuritan uniform, which he had worn longer than he had the garb of a Dragoon. So where did his loyalties lie now? He looked down the path, glimpsing a small portion of Unity Palace, the imperial palace, through the trees. That was where his future would be decided. There was no point in turning back.

Dechan drew nearer to the palace.

The guards kneeling on the veranda were in their ceremonial armor, wide-mouthed stunners cradled in their arms. Staring impassively ahead, they did not move at his approach. They might have been statues, save that he could see them breathing. As his foot touched the boards of the veranda, a *shoji* panel slid open behind the guards. A beautiful woman in traditional kimono and full make-up bowed to him. He returned the bow, and she led him into the hall.

The doorway to which she guided him opened into a room redolent with the scent of jasmine. Across the wide chamber, a man in a dragon-figured kimono sat on a low chair. His white-haired head was bowed over a sheet of rice paper, his face concealed. He held a brush in his right hand. Like the guards outside, he did not move as Dechan approached.

Two meters away, Dechan stopped, unsure. He had heard rumors that Takashi had more than once ordered the death of someone who failed to observe proper protocol. What was the proper protocol? Waiting was usually safe.

He waited.

The man suddenly moved, dipping his brush into the lacquered ink tray and brushing ink in strong, sharp strokes onto the paper. He gave a tight, affirmative nod and grunted to himself. Laying the brush down, he turned to face Dechan.

Takashi Kurita's face was as familiar to Dechan as it was to any citizen of the Combine. He knew the scars, the firm line of the jaw, and the penetrating gaze of the ice blue eyes. Unfamiliar were the age lines, but

Dechan could sense the vigor of Takashi's spirit. The man was still dangerous. The Coordinator inclined his head to his visitor, and Dechan bowed deeply in reply, then knelt.

"Ah, *Tai-sa* Fraser." The Coordinator's slight smile was lopsided, as if one side of his face refused to co-operate. "You honor an old man by your visit."

Dechan swallowed, made nervous by Takashi's self-effacing opening. "The Dragon is ever strong," he responded.

Takashi chuckled. "There is little need to be formal, Fraser-*san*. We are just two old warriors here. Feel free to speak as one old friend to another."

Dechan was immediately on guard. Though he was one of Theodore's *shitenno*, relations with the Kanrei had always been formal. For all his years in the Combine, he had never been on intimate terms with any member of the Kurita clan, least of all the Coordinator. But it would be an insult to contradict Takashi. "I am honored by your grace, Takashi-*sama*."

The Coordinator's smile remained. Dechan had chosen the right course. They talked of the weather and Dechan praised the garden, traditional Kurita small talk. Dechan had almost relaxed when Takashi quietly asked, "How is your old friend Michi Noketsuna?"

Dechan stiffened, knowing that the Coordinator could not miss his reaction but unable to control it. Michi had sworn to kill Takashi for his part in forcing Tetsuhara to commit *seppuku*. "I have not spoken with him in years, Coordinator-*sama*."

"Yet you are friends. Was he not responsible for your coming into the Dragon's service?"

"I made my own decision, Coordinator-*sama*." Did Dechan dare believe that the Coordinator didn't know about Michi's vow? Takashi's next words dashed that hope.

"Had you not agreed to aid him in his vendetta, you would not have made that decision."

Dechan searched the Coordinator's inscrutable expression. Was this an attempt to incriminate him? Should he lie? He decided against that. If the Coordinator knew of his history, he would know the lie. "That is correct."

"And do you still aid him in that vendetta?"

"I serve the Dragon."

Takashi's eyes narrowed. His voice was harsh as he said, "You serve my son."

"Your son serves you and the Combine both, Coordinator-*sama*."

"Which says nothing of you," Takashi said quickly. More calmly, he continued, "You have learned our Kuritan indirection reasonably well, Fraser-*san*. Do not think to delude me. Do you stand with Noketsuna?"

"He has forsaken my friendship."

"Have you forsaken his?" Takashi leaned forward as if avid for Dechan's answer.

Dechan felt a drop of sweat trickle clammily down his side. Frankness had to be the safest course here. But how could he give honest answers to the Coordinator when he was not sure he *had* any answers? "If you mean, would I aid him in killing you, I think not."

"You are not sure? Where is your loyalty, Fraser-*san*? Where is your honor if you do not fulfill your oath to aid him?"

"I was young when I swore to help Michi achieve his goal. I am older now. Times have changed, needs have been superseded. A true samurai understands when he must subordinate his honor to a greater honor, and the threat of the Clans overpowers any one person's needs. Michi himself was willing to set aside his vengeance, back in the thirties, when your son Theodore persuaded him that the Combine needed the service of all her samurai. Then the threat was only the Federated Commonwealth, a mere inconvenience compared to the danger posed by the Clans. How could he think of disrupting the Combine now?"

Gèin

Takashi leaned back in his chair. "Then he has abandoned his vendetta?"

"I believe so. He has not been seen in the Combine for almost two years. But, as I said, I have not communicated with him for much longer than that."

"Communicated? You draw a distinction." Takashi grunted. "When was the last time you spoke with him?"

"We've met only once since the end of the war with Davion. I knew he didn't want to be warlord anymore and asked him to join the Ryuken. He said that he was not worthy, that he had failed as a samurai and would retire from the world." Dechan paused, remembering the pain of that meeting. "He also told me to stay out of his life."

"Yet you persist in your friendship. That shows loyalty, and misplaced loyalty is dangerous. Where is he now?"

Wishing he had another answer, Dechan replied, "I don't know."

"What would you do if I told you where to find him?"

"I don't know that, either."

"You are honest. Not subtle enough to be a Kuritan, Fraser-*san*." Takashi gestured to the writing desk. "For your years of service to the Dragon, I grant you the reward of life."

Dechan looked at the desk, wondering what was written on the scroll. He made no move to take it. Whatever the trial had been, Dechan had passed. But with Takashi's next words, Dechan realized that a new trial had begun.

"Before you came to the service of the Dragon, you were a member of Wolf's Dragoons."

Honesty had saved him before. "I have never hidden that fact."

"A warrior must not hide his affiliations. No one in the Inner Sphere can deny that the Dragoons are redoubtable warriors and, as such, worthy of respect. You fought by their side in the past, but you did not fight by their side when the Clans came to Luthien. Why was this?''

Dechan had wondered about the answer to that question himself. "I was fighting with the Ryuken."

"You have shown me you are a man who values loyalty. Your record with the Ryuken shows you are a warrior of considerable merit. The Ryuken was only raiding; the true battle was on Luthien."

Dechan was angry. Takashi's badgering reminded him of the shame he'd felt then. The Dragoons had returned to the Combine, but without a word to him. If they had called for him, he would have left the Ryuken, who didn't really need him. But, once again, no word had come from the Dragoons. He knew Takashi would hear the anger underlying his words as he said, "I was not called."

"*So ka.*"

Takashi seemed satisfied. Dechan cursed him for finding satisfaction in another man's shame.

"Yet you still harbor loyalties to the Dragoons."

Takashi's statement was a truth Dechan avoided admitting to himself, the reactor that fueled his pain. Admitting any loyalty to the Dragoons in the presence of the Coordinator could be lethal. "I have done nothing to undermine the strength of the Dragon," he said, the lie amid the truths.

"That is not at issue," Takashi said, dismissing the comment. The Coordinator fell silent, leaving Dechan to wonder what the issue was. Takashi sat and Dechan knelt. The room was silent for many minutes. Finally Takashi spoke, his voice dreamy.

"How would you characterize Jaime Wolf, *Tai-sa* Fraser?"

"He is a fine commander."

"Fine? That is all you can say about a man who

obviously inspires such loyalty in you that you hate him for it?''

''I don't hate him.''

''Don't you? He abandoned you and your wife. For years you worked as his agent, watching me and mine. Yes, I know. The ISF is diligent and not half so foolish as some people believe. How often have you wondered why Wolf did not use you to convey his subversive invitation to my son? How often have you pondered the stain on your honor that his distrust brings you?''

Stunned by the Coordinator's revelation of knowledge, Dechan stammered, ''I don't—''

''Your quarrels with your wife say otherwise,'' Takashi snapped. ''Do not call me a liar!''

''*Gomen kudasai*, Coordinator-*sama*. *Shitsurei shimasu.*''

''Your apology is that of a Kuritan, but you are not Kuritan. You are only forgiven because you are a barbarian and it is expected that you will speak like a barbarian. Still, you are a warrior and a warrior does not lie.''

Takashi turned away, pondering something. At length the tension bled from his shoulders. ''A warrior's honor is his life. If he has no honor, he has no need for life. What is your place in the feud between Wolf's Dragoons and my House?''

''I have no place in it. I thought the feud had ended when the Dragoons helped defend Luthien.''

''A safe answer, but no less untrue.'' Takashi laughed harshly. ''If I ordered the Ryuken units you have so carefully trained to attack Outreach, would you lead them?''

Dechan swallowed to loosen the knot of fear in his stomach. That the revivified Ryuken might be used against the Dragoons had always been his greatest nightmare. ''I would ask you to reconsider.''

Takashi stared in Dechan's eyes. ''And if I did not?''

Dechan was distressed to realize that the years had

sapped his fear of one day being ordered to lead a military action against the Dragoons. He was suddenly unsure of what he believed in. "I don't know."

"You obviously face a conflict. Another brave man who served me once faced a similar conflict. The Dragoons were involved in that as well. That honorable man followed his orders, then committed *seppuku*. Are you as honorable as he, Dechan Fraser?"

Did Takashi refer to Minobu Tetsuhara? "I am not samurai."

"I could make you samurai."

"I am . . . was a Dragoon. We have our own code of honor."

"Is your honor worth your life?"

"I . . . Sometimes."

Takashi smiled his half-smile. "Does Jaime Wolf believe this as well?"

Dechan was confused. "I don't know."

Standing, Takashi took a deep breath. "Wolf is the leader of his Dragoons, secure in his place as any *daimyo* lording it over his samurai. He understands the demands placed on a lord. This is so, *neh*?"

"I believe so."

Takashi nodded sharply. "I believe so, too. You may not understand the problems of a ruler, but Wolf does. The Dragoons are his fiefdom, and there he is ruler. I do not envy him.

"Once I was the undisputed ruler of the Draconis Combine. The state and the army were mine to command. Now my son has taken some of that power from me. He rules not only the army, but no little portion of the state. He is a man in the prime of his life, while I sink toward old age. With each year I see more of my contemporaries pass from the stage of the drama that is the Inner Sphere. Even Hanse Davion is gone now. With the Fox dead, what other Inner Sphere lord is a worthy opponent? My day is passing."

Takashi seemed older suddenly, which disturbed

Dechan somehow. "You are still Coordinator," he said.

Fire flashed in Takashi's eyes. "Do not coddle me! I am not a dodderer to be pandered to. I am not so weak-willed that I intend to lay down and die. I am samurai!"

Dechan thought it advisable to say nothing. He bowed low, hoping that he was not being foolish in taking his eyes off the Coordinator.

"A samurai cannot die if his honor is stained," Takashi stated with what sounded like religious fervor.

"The Coordinator's honor is clean. You are the hero of Luthien. The charge of your Izanagi Warriors finished the Clan attack."

"Did it?" Takashi snorted. "What part, then, was played by Wolf's Dragoons and the Kell Hounds?"

"They were merely part of the forces fighting to save Luthien."

"They are mercenaries. Mercenary scum! For them to have participated in the defense of the capital of the Draconis Combine diminished the honor of House Kurita." Takashi stalked to one side of the room and threw open the screen, staring outside. "There is only one thing that can wash away such a stain. Do you know what it is?"

"Blood." The answer to everything.

"Your understanding ennobles you. I am pleased to see that there is some little honor in the Dragoons."

Dechan was angered by the slight, another sign that his Dragoon loyalties still tugged his emotional strings. Defiantly, he said, "Enough for you."

The Coordinator smiled. "So I had hoped."

For the first time, Dechan looked outside. He saw what Takashi stared at so raptly, the blue and gold *Archer*. Dechan didn't understand what the Coordinator was seeing as he stared at the 'Mech, but he knew now that the rumors of Takashi's obsession were more than that. Not sure which of his loyalties prompted him, Dechan felt the need to know the Coordinator's mind.

"Forgive my impertinence, Coordinator-*sama*, but may I ask a question?"

A slight wave of Takashi's hand was his answer.

"Why is that BattleMech in your garden?"

The Coordinator was silent for so long that Dechan thought that he had misinterpreted the hand signal, that it had not been permission to speak. Dechan rose, assuming he had been dismissed. Just as he was about to pass through the door, he heard Takashi speak, so softly that Dechan wondered if he had been meant to hear.

"The Fox is gone now," the Coordinator said. "All I have left is the Wolf."

7

As Subhash Indrahar listened to the conversation between the Coordinator and the Dragoon spy, his brows drew together with worry. Once Takashi had nearly destroyed the Combine with his obsession to destroy the Dragoons. Now with the Clan invaders encroaching, the Combine could no longer afford to humor Takashi's samurai honor. Once his old friend would have seen that as clearly as Subhash did, but as the years passed Takashi seemed to grow weaker in mind as Subhash grew weaker in body.

Touching the controls on the arm of his powered support unit, he sent the chair wheeling across the room. The door slid open just in time for his chair to continue on without stopping. As he entered the command center, Internal Security Force agents snapped to attention all around the perimeter of the chamber. The technicians and special agents at their consoles barely glanced up, however; they had work to do. All was as it should be.

Despite his concern, Subhash almost smiled. The cogs in the great machine that was the Draconis Combine whirred on. Nothing must interfere with the functioning of this great machine of state. If someone, even a Coordinator, were to become sand in the gears, the sand must be removed and the gears re-greased.

Subhash cut smartly around a corner and slowed to a stop at the station of a red-haired man wearing the black uniform of an operations agent. The man's uniform was clean, but so rumpled it looked as if he had recently returned from action. The agent looked up from his console as the powered chair rolled to a halt with a soft sigh of brakes and a whiff of volatilized rubber. He straightened, coming to as much of a formal stance as he ever did.

"*Ohayo*, Subhash-*sama*," said Ninyu Kerai-Indrahar.

"Attend me," Subhash said, spinning the chair.

They entered a transpex-walled conference chamber. As Subhash rode to the central console, Ninyu engaged the anti-listening devices. The room now secure, Subhash began to speak.

"What were you working on?"

"The last batch of dispatches from Dieron. Gregor reports things are shaping up there as you expected."

Feared would have been a better word. For all the ancient rivalry between House Kurita and House Davion, it had been House Steiner and their Lyran Commonwealth that had most hurt the Combine in the last generation. The Commonwealth's successes, even before joining with the Federated Suns to become the Federated Commonwealth, had bred a new generation of hatreds. Those animosities now smoldered on the Dieron-Skye border.

The appointment of the new warlord of Dieron was one of Subhash's rare failures. Takashi, having learned of his son Theodore's machinations in the Dieron Military District, had insisted on personally choosing the new warlord. His choice of Isoroku was most regrettable. The young fool had Kurita blood, all right—all the bad parts. He saw military glory as the road to rulership of the Combine and dreamed of supplanting both Takashi and Theodore.

Even so, the situation might have been managed had not the Federated Commonwealth appointed Richard Steiner to command in the Ryde Theater. Richard was the son of Nondi Steiner, one of the Commonwealth's great military heroes of the last generation. Steiner had made little secret of his desire for revenge against House Kurita, no doubt believing this would make him more popular among the masses. He was most certainly going to need a heavy dose of popularity should he ever attempt to achieve his more secret goal of wresting the rulership of the Federated Commonwealth away from the Davion line and gaining it for his own House.

For all the intensity of Inner Sphere rivalries, they were not the greatest threat to the Draconis Combine in these latter days. Despite the ComStar Treaty of Tukkayid, which forbade the Clans to advance rimward toward Terra, the Clans still threatened Combine star systems spinward and anti-spinward. Even the most cursory study of that treaty revealed that its terms did not prevent the invaders from expanding their grasp within the Inner Sphere, so long as they approached no nearer to Terra. Such a solution might be satisfactory to ComStar, but it left much of the Combine, including the capital, at risk.

The Combine was not the only state at risk. Much of the former Lyran Commonwealth was beyond the treaty's boundary and also wide open to predation by the Clans. The Federated Commonwealth could not ignore such a threat to what was now its economic heartland. Any clear-sighted ruler could see that this was no time for military adventurism. Subhash hoped that young Victor Davion realized the foolishness of continuing to prosecute the old Davion-Kurita rivalry while the two Houses currently faced a greater common enemy. Indeed, the director fully expected Davion to follow his father's recent policy of demilitarization along the Combine's border with the Federated Commonwealth. But the Prince was young and not securely in control of his state. Already there had been incidents.

"The combination of the aggressive Isoroku Kurita and the equally belligerent Richard Steiner is volatile," Ninyu concluded.

"Correct. However, we may have a more dangerous situation developing."

"This is new, then?"

"No." Subhash rapped his fingers on the arm of his chair. "Unfortunately, it is old."

"Takashi."

Subhash was pleased that his protégé was so astute. If only the son of his now-withered loins were so competent. "Your reasons?"

"I saw that he had called for the former Dragoon." Ninyu consulted his watch. "An appointment that might be over by now. Barely. Now I speak to you and find you agitated."

Subhash smiled. Yes, far better than his bumbling son. "The Coordinator is dwelling on the past."

Screwing his face into a frown, Ninyu said, "I thought you said that letting him build that *Archer* would settle it."

Subhash sighed. "The infallibility of the Director of the ISF is only credible to those who do not live in reality. Those of us involved in the great game know infallibility does not exist, only skill and fortune."

"And the first often produces the second," Ninyu finished for him. He shook his head and frowned. "If the Coordinator is focusing his attention on those damned mercenaries again, it will be trouble. His obsession almost cost us the Combine during the Fourth Succession War. Had it not been for Theodore's brilliant strategies on the Lyran front and the limited Davion presence on the Federated Suns front, we would have been crushed. But the Coordinator had his priorities. As it was, we lost too many star systems. We should have been able to halt the Lyrans and take systems from Davion."

"The past only lives in the mind."

"And the heart, adopted father. I sometimes think you forget emotions."

"I never forget them, adopted son." Subhash chuckled. "I merely control them and put them to use. A skill you must practice, if you wish to succeed me as director."

"I shall," Ninyu said, laying his hand on the back of the powered chair. "I have the strength."

Subhash frowned. "The director rules by his wits, not his arms or his legs."

"I'm sorry, adopted father. I did not mean to . . ."

"It is forgotten," Subhash said, amused by his protégé's honest embarrassment. "You are not at fault for the weakness of my body." He wheeled the chair out from under Ninyu's hand. "I am still director. No one will take that away from me."

"Not as long as I live, adopted father."

"Is your commitment to the Combine as strong, adopted son?"

"Stronger."

Subhash sensed his heir's sincerity and was pleased. There would be a sure hand to guide the Combine after he was gone. Takashi had already agreed to the papers of appointment. It was only a matter of time before Theodore did. How could he refuse to accept his old battle comrade, one of his *shitenno*?

But the directorship of the ISF meant nothing if there was no Combine to guide and to perfect. And should the Combine fall, the strongest force for order in the universe would disappear, a result totally abhorrent to him. And so Subhash would continue to do what needed to be done, as he had all his life. As long as he still breathed, he would fight to see the Combine endure against all enemies, internal and external.

"Your concern is obviously for Takashi," Ninyu said. "Is the Coordinator's instability increasing?"

"That is still unclear. His lapses become ever more difficult to cover up."

"We will do what must be done."

"Yes, we will. The Combine must be strong and unified in this time of trial." Subhash felt Ninyu's resolution. That was good. Strong and implacable resolve would be imperative. But a journey could only be made one step at a time. "How is the Coordinator's new *kendo* partner doing?"

Ninyu seemed hesitant to speak, reluctant after the earlier reference to Subhash's failing body. Subhash had once been Takashi's *kendo* partner. Their sessions had offered the director many opportunities to influence the Coordinator, but now Subhash had to discover other such opportunities, making his influence on Takashi less than it had once been. Still, the *kendo* was good for Takashi and Subhash made a point of arranging only the best partners. Before they were coordinator and director, they had been friends. They were still friends, when being coordinator and director did not get in the way.

"The Coordinator says he enjoys his matches with Homitsu-*san*," Ninyu said. "He also says that he thinks Homitsu is holding back, but he is confident that Homitsu will prove challenging once he understands that the Coordinator does not wish to be coddled."

"Very good." Subhash smiled. He truly hoped Takashi was enjoying the matches; there was so little joy in being a leader. "That is most satisfactory."

8

Each of the Hiring Hall's towers stood twenty stories tall and the domed central area was itself ten stories. Its architecture was bold and open, the better to serve the image of Outreach as a planet where anyone could come to hire mercenaries. The Hiring Hall is, deliberately, the most prominent building in Harlech, the capital and principal city of Outreach. It was a public relations decision to make it tower over Wolf Hall, the multiacre complex that served as command headquarters for the Dragoons. We might be the best, but Jaime Wolf's program required us to demonstrate, rather than lord, our superiority over the others in our trade. And proof was saved for where it counted, on the battlefield.

I spent a lot of time at the Hall.

As the months wore on I became accustomed to my place at the Wolf's side. He must also have become more accustomed to me for he called me William less and less frequently. I was pleased, feeling that I was carving out my own place. But I knew I had yet to face the real test. Combat is only the briefest part of a soldier's life, but it was where I would truly prove my worth.

The Command Lance was busy even though we were not in action, which, I suppose, made the Wolf's suspension from combat less of a trial than it might have been. It was harder for Hans Vordel and his Bodyguard

Lance. In the old Dragoons, Hans had been the Wolf's bodyguard, a member of the Command Lance. Though an excellent warrior, he showed little aptitude for anything beyond BattleMech combat.

When the Dragoons first came to Outreach in 3030, we were in bad shape after the Fourth Succession War. Many feared that Takashi Kurita would take advantage of our weakened condition to mount a strike that would destroy the Dragoons completely. Meeting in council, the Dragoon colonels had demanded that Jaime Wolf form a Bodyguard Lance. The Wolf had insisted that such a move was unnecessary, but the colonels had overridden him in the vote. Hans had been detailed to select the best warriors, and he selected them from among several ageframes, on advice from Stanford Blake. I suppose the idea was to create a continuity of experience, balancing the faster reflexes of the younger generations with the battle experience of the older. Whatever the reasoning, the team consistently garnered superlative scores in testing. Hans worked hard to maintain his lance's edge.

I believed that the combination of different ageframes had an additional benefit, but I'm afraid it was a personal rather than a professional one. For the newest member was of my ageframe and, like me, the product of a sibko.

Her name was Maeve.

If I tell you of her alluring beauty, her midnight hair, her slender, feline grace, you will think me besotted, thrall to a young man's hormones. No one, you will say, could be so fair. Perhaps you would come to distrust anything I tell you. So instead, I will speak only of her prowess as a MechWarrior. That can be verified by the records; though her selection for the Bodyguard Lance should be proof enough of her skill. There is also documentation of her accomplishments as a commander later in life. Additionally, I can also attest to her sharp tongue and quick wit, and also be found honest. There are recordings. Any one of those areas would make her stand out, so accept my evaluation that she was exceptional.

She was my first love.

To her, however, I was simply the comm officer, a mere fixture in her military life, only taking on importance when messages were to be given or received. My tongue betrayed all my efforts at casual conversation, so our exchanges were strictly business. Somehow, I was able to speak to her when she was just another Dragoon, but beyond that I was hopeless. I hadn't been so backward with my sibs. That was how I knew I was in love.

I remember clearly her first day on duty. She had drawn late shift along with Sergeant Anton Benjamin and so had joined the Command Lance near the end of our standard duty rounds. The Wolf was completing some business at the Hiring Hall, a subcontract for the Black Brigade. When he was finished, we met our new lancemate outside the conference room, where Maeve and Anton waited to relieve Hans and Shelly Gordon. I know I heard Maeve's name, but after that not another word of the introduction registered in my brain.

I was too busy trying to think of some way to talk to her as soon as I went off duty, but my thoughts didn't want to work. We all left the building together, Stan placing himself between her and me. I thought about how near the command lounge was to the Wolf's office. The bodyguards often relaxed there when Jaime Wolf was busy in residence. This slowly forming plan suddenly slipped from my grasp at a shouted call.

"Colonel Wolf!"

Much to my annoyance, the Wolf stopped and turned at the sound of his name.

The man approaching us was short, but not so short as the Wolf, or even Maeve, for that matter. Despite the coolness of the weather, he wore only a Mech-Warrior's cooling vest and shorts. Perhaps he wished to show off his muscular build. I wondered what Maeve thought of him. Spheroids were often impressed by such macho posturing, but I hoped that a Dragoon would have higher standards. The MechWarrior thrust out his hand as he stepped up to Jaime Wolf.

"Colonel, I wanted to say thanks. I just found out that it was your word that cinched it with the St. Ives contractor."

"Captain Miller, isn't it?" Wolf said as he shook the man's hand.

"That's right. Call me Jason."

"Glad we could help. I always like to see a reliable unit get a contract. Too many defaults give all mercenaries a bad name."

"Don't they just." Miller grinned. "We all have to stick together or the Houses will eat us alive."

Grinning back, the Wolf said, "I'll count on you the next time Takashi's on my tail."

Miller looked startled for a moment. Apparently deciding the Wolf was joking, he laughed and said, "You got it! The Twelve Pack and the Dragoons against the Snakes. Done deal!" There was an awkward moment while everyone stood looking at one another. "Well, I just wanted to say thanks."

"You have, Captain. I wish you success on your contract."

They shook hands again and we proceeded on, leaving Miller on the steps of the Hall. The Wolf dropped his jovial manner as soon as Miller turned his back. I watched Maeve's brow furrow. When we were far enough away that her voice wouldn't carry, she said, "I don't see why you do it, Colonel Wolf. I mean, helping other mercs get contracts. These other guys cut into our business." She tossed her head back, sweeping an errant lock out of her eyes. "They'll never be Dragoons."

"Some might," Jaime Wolf smiled indulgently. "Some have. There was a time when we needed warriors and we took in Inner Sphere mercs. We couldn't get soldiers fast enough any other way.''

"But we took only the best," she said defensively. "We tried."

She was clearly still unsatisfied. "But this business with the Hiring Hall and all these other mercs. The Dragoons are at full operational strength." The Wolf's eyes narrowed slightly at that comment and I knew he didn't agree. I had thought we were up to strength as well. Maeve didn't notice. "We don't need anybody to take up the slack."

"Not every contract is a Dragoon's contract."

"Agreed. But I checked the board today. There were at least three suitable openings and we weren't bidding on any of them."

The Wolf looked at her thoughtfully for a moment, then said, "There were other outfits that needed the work more."

"Are we a charity?"

Stan answered for the Wolf. "Don't forget, we get a cut of any contract made through the Hall."

"We're not merchants!" Maeve shouted, real passion in her voice. She must have come from one of the more protected sibkos.

Yelling at Stan was as bad as yelling at the Wolf. It was no way to start a tour of duty. I didn't want to see her transferred out just when I'd met her, so I was relieved to see that the Wolf was feeling indulgent.

"Aren't we?" he asked. "We sell our services, and fighting isn't the only thing we do. We'll take our money where we can find it."

Maeve screwed up her face and looked away.

"Listen, Maeve. You're too young to have been there and the teachers don't always give the sibkos the hard facts. So listen up; I don't want this kind of display in front of the customers."

Her voice was small. "I understand, Colonel."

"No you don't. But I want you to." He waited until

she looked at him again. "The Dragoons started helping other mercs find contracts just after the Fourth Succession War, when we were in too bad a shape to accept any contracts of our own. Besides, the Dragoons had always done some subcontracting, hiring other mercs when we didn't have available forces. I don't think there was anyone in the Inner Sphere who didn't know that we had been mauled in the fighting. We didn't have the military resources to guarantee anything. All we had was our rep for knowing who was good. The Dragoons needed to rebuild, and rebuilding costs money. We had Davion's promises to make good our losses while under contract to him, but that wouldn't have brought us up to strength, even if he had come through with all the money he promised."

"The text says we lost over fifty percent effectiveness on Misery."

The Wolf nodded somberly. "A cold evaluation, but true. Money could replace the machines, but the warriors were gone forever."

"We were hard up," Stan added. "We played on what rep we had. By brokering good contracts, we made a lot of friends among the Inner Sphere mercs."

"Why not just take in the best mercs we could find and patch together a provisional regiment to be hired out?" Maeve asked.

"A patchwork regiment wouldn't have been able to keep up the rep," Wolf said, shaking his head. "And we didn't have the strength to put together a pure Dragoon regiment. We were all too tired. Even if we had gone out selling our services, who would have protected Outreach and the families?"

"But we had Davion to protect Outreach," Maeve protested.

"The political situation was still in turmoil. We couldn't rely on Davion, only ourselves. As soon as things settled down a bit and we had a chance to catch our metaphorical breaths, Natasha Kerensky took the Black Widow Battalion into the field.''

Benjamin spat. ''Bloodnamed bitch!''

''I will have none of that kind of talk, Mister,'' the Wolf snapped. Benjamin mumbled an apology, which the Wolf ignored. ''Natasha followed her conscience when she left us to return to Clan Wolf. We had chosen our own way long before. We're on our own.''

''Is it true that they put Natasha on trial and found the Dragoons innocent of treason to the Clans?'' Maeve asked. ''If they did, we could go back.''

Stan snorted. ''There's more to life in the Clans than legal verdicts. We made our choice when we ignored the ilKhan's last summons.''

The Wolf nodded agreement. ''We've seen other ways besides Clan ways now. We can't go back. It just wouldn't work. At best, we'd all end up dead in trials or be declared bandits. We're better than that.''

Maeve wouldn't let it go. ''What's to keep us from ending up as somebody's lap dogs like the Horsemen?''

''Only ourselves. As long as I have any say in it, the Dragoons will never be anyone's bought dogs,'' the Wolf said with steady conviction. ''We will make our *own* way here in the Inner Sphere. Even if it means submitting to questioning from junior officers.''

Maeve had the good grace—and the good sense—to keep her mouth shut after that. We proceeded to Wolf Hall and, unfortunately, the Wolf had a full night's work for me. Hans and Shelly were back on duty by the time I stumbled bleary-eyed from Jaime Wolf's office. I went to my bed and dreamed of Maeve.

9

Near the horizon we could see the BattleMechs of the Spider's Web Battalion racing over the ridges. Mac-Kenzie Wolf, Jaime Wolf's blood son, was leading his unit against the flank of the Jade Falcon position. From our over-watch position on the slopes of Ziggilies Mountain, we listened to the soft thunder of explosions and watched the distant flashes of manmade lightning.

This was Jaime Wolf's first day out from under his year of suspension. The Command Lance had landed on Morges, on the border of Clan Jade Falcon's occupation zone, coming in at dawn over the top of Ziggilies Mountain. Beta Regiment and Spider's Web Battalion were already onplanet, having been hired by the Federated Commonwealth for a counterstrike against the Jade Falcon occupying force. The Falcons were looking to expand their occupied territory and the Dragoons were to help stop them. FedCom units were engaging the Falcons on their own, but the Dragoons would provide added punch to make sure the Falcons went home, and went home bloodied. It was the hottest contract the Dragoons had underway. Naturally, the Wolf wanted to be in for the kill.

I had no doubt that Jaime Wolf was happy to be here.

"That got their attention," he said. Reconnaissance had reported that the Falcons were engaging the Spider's Web with significant forces. The Jade Falcon commander would soon see that the ante had been upped. "Brian, give aerospace the go. The Falcons will start dropping reinforcements soon. Let's give them a warm welcome."

"Aerospace on the way," I responded as I received acknowledgement from the command ship in orbit. "Major Baracini is promising them a bumpy ride down."

"That's a promise he'll keep."

Maeve cut in. "Brian, tell them to let some through. We don't want those aerojocks hogging all the fun."

She laughed lightly, clearly relishing the coming combat. Though I was eager, too, to be honest, I must also admit to feeling some trepidation. Should the Jade Falcon reinforcements arrive in significant numbers, the fighting would be deadly. The Dragoons would not get off easily.

The Wolf gave the order to move out of our positions. Taking care on the treacherous slopes, the BattleMechs of the Command and Bodyguard Lances picked their way down toward the plain. The vector we followed would take us to a new position about four kilometers behind the lines, and from there we would be able to see the battle progressing. We had covered only half the distance when Alicia Fancher, the Beta commander, put in a priority call.

"Delta call, Colonel," I relayed. "Beta reports a Jade Falcon breakthrough twenty klicks north of Josselles."

"Map feed," he ordered.

"In process."

I reviewed the feed on my monitor, trying to guess the Wolf's response. The Falcon attack had pierced Beta's right-flank defenses and threatened to drive a wedge between the Dragoons and the FedCom forces. Worse, the command center coordinating the operation was in Josselles. If the Falcons succeeded in reaching it, they would disrupt our attack. With our coordination shattered, they could turn on the FedCom troops and waste them while holding us off. The map plainly showed that Beta's 'Mech forces could not intercept the Falcons in time to prevent them from reaching the command center. No one had expected the Clan force to mount a counterthrust so swiftly.

"Vector on me." The Wolf turned his *Archer* in the direction of Josselles. "Brian, sound Code White."

There were other orders as well, but I was soon too busy to contemplate their importance. Handling the volume of comm traffic inherent in a multiregiment battle is a full-time job. Try adding to that the task of piloting a BattleMech traveling at fifty kilometers per hour over rough terrain and see how much time *you* have to consider tactical subtleties. I was shocked back to the immediate field when Vordel's *Victor* took the first round of fire.

The *Victor* rocked under the impact of a volley of long-range missiles, but kept moving, twisting right, then left, to throw off the enemy gunner's aim. Raising its right arm, the *Victor* fired its Gauss rifle with a crack that ripped the air. Then the rest of the Bodyguard Lance joined in. Missiles screamed downfield, the smoky billows of their exhaust trails lit with bright blue flashes of particle projector bolts.

Then I saw Maeve's *Thunderbolt* take a brace of heavy laser hits. Missiles struck all around her, raising dust and hiding her from view. My heart stopped as chunks of fused armor blasted free of the obscuring cloud in a rain of shrapnel. The pulsing of her 'Mech's arm-mounted Blackwell 20 laser told me she had survived the attack, even before her *T-bolt* cleared the cloud of steam and smoke. The armor of the 'Mech's right arm was shredded and I could see the gleam of its internal structure. Craters from missile hits pocked the sloping chest, but the *T-bolt* moved with undiminished speed. I began to breathe again.

A Star of five enemy BattleMechs, three *Thor*s and two *Mad Cat*s, emerged from the treeline, racing for the cover offered by a razed town. Not Josselles; we were still several klicks north. The Falcon 'Mechs fired as they moved, no doubt hoping to slow us and gain the protection of the rubble and burned-out buildings, while simultaneously denying it to us. Once behind the buildings, they could fire on us as we moved through open fields to close with them. And we would have to close, for their weapons generally out-ranged ours. If we attempted a long-range duel, I knew that the other 'Mechs of their detachment would already be moving through the trees, racing past toward Josselles.

The Falcons must have been confident, and who could blame them? Intel had reported that most of the Jade Falcon BattleMechs onworld were second-line models, 'Mechs similar to Inner Sphere designs but equipped with Clan weapons, engines, and electronics. Such machines were dangerous enough, but this Star consisted of OmniMechs, battle machines as superior to Clan second-line models as those models were to most Inner Sphere 'Mechs.

Omnis were one of the Clans' great advantages, and the Falcons knew how to use them. In our two lances, we had only three Omnis.

The radio waves crackled with challenges from the Clan warriors. They were calling for single combat, 'Mech against 'Mech. Clan honor, Inner Sphere suicide.

"Ignore the challenges," the Wolf ordered. "Bodyguard Lance concentrate on the lead 'Mech. Command Lance to direct all fire at the trailer."

Maeve protested, wanting to duel her opponent. Hating the necessity, I overrode her circuit. The Wolf had given his orders and she was out of line. Concentrated fire might let us bring down one or both of the target Omnis and thus even the odds.

Despite her protest, she followed the Wolf's orders.

The *T-bolt*'s laser sent iridescent gouts of energy into the leg of the lead Falcon 'Mech, a *Thor*. Her shots placed right on target, a hole punched through by her lancemates. The *Thor* stumbled, then righted itself, but only for a moment. As the seventy-ton machine's weight came down on the the injured leg, the foamed titanium bones gave way. The *Thor* toppled. A second *Thor* leaped past as it fell, continuing the Falcons' charge for the ruined town.

The Command Lance wounded its target, a *Mad Cat*, but the Omni kept moving. Our attack hadn't slowed the Star and we didn't have time for a second round before the leading Falcons reached cover. It seemed obvious that we were going to have to go in after them and that we'd take damage doing so, possibly even lose some of our 'Mechs. I hoped Maeve's wouldn't be one of them.

The situation suddenly worsened as Hans announced, "Star at four o'clock."

A new Star emerged from the woods, charging toward our flank. The Falcons had laid a trap, drawing us into a commitment, then hitting us from two sides. The first Star's Omnis reached the town and I could hear their jeers overrunning the open frequency.

The shouting changed its tone when those Omni pilots found *our* trap.

The Jade Falcon *Thor* that had taken the lead passed through the outer fringes of the town without being molested. His pilot took up position on the edge of town and opened fire on Anton Benjamin. The Omni's massive autocannon roared with a staccato beat, revealing itself as an ultra model that could pump out twice the normal volume of fire for a weapon of its class. The *Thor* mercilessly pummeled Benjamin's *Black Hawk*, gouging armor and shredding myomer pseudomuscle and titanium structural members with almost equal ease. The *Black Hawk* went over backward and stopped moving, smoke rising from the savaged torso.

That's when we sprang the trap.

Dragoon Elementals emerged from hiding, launching SRMs at deadly point-blank range. Caught by surprise, the Falcons took heavy damage. One, a *Thor*, rose on a column of superheated air, trying to escape the Point of Elementals swarming over it. The Elementals dropped free, using their own jump packs to land safely. Scurrying back to cover, they sniped at the Omnis remaining in the town.

The escape of the airborne *Thor* was like a signal for the rest of the enemy Star. The surviving Omnis pulled back from the Elemental-infested buildings. The *Mad Cat* that had been Bodyguard Lance's target never made it out. The remaining three enemy 'Mechs cut wide, trying to avoid our fire. We poured it on and the second *Mad Cat* went down. The surviving *Thor*s escaped with heavy damage.

When the first shots from the second Star began to land around us, the Wolf ordered us into the town. He wanted to put the buildings between us and the fresh Star. So did I. We took more hits until we got under cover. Shelly's *Ostsol* had an arm blown off when its torso was ripped open. Shelly ejected from her crippled machine, and we were down to six effectives, all damaged.

The Falcons got cautious. Maybe they thought we had a lot more in the town than we did or maybe they were just showing the standard Clanner's dislike of close-in fighting. They would be well aware of what the Elementals could do in close.

To whittle us down, they started a long-range bombardment. We replied as best we could. The Wolf himself scored hit after hit with volleys from his *Archer*'s missile launchers.

When our ammo began to run low, reducing our long-range firepower, the Falcons reacted as if they knew we were low. They began to move in, circling more like wolves than their namesake. They kept up a murderous barrage while staying out of the Elementals' range. The least battered of our Omnis, Kara's *Loki*, got mired in a collapsed building while moving to cut off a thrust against our flank. Unable to maneuver, she was little more than a pillbox. The Falcons shifted away, leaving her out of the battle. Franchette's *Rifleman* got caught and went down while shifting from an exposed position. Maeve's *T-bolt* went into heat overload and shutdown. Ignoring the Wolf's order, she stayed inside, trying to restart her engine.

The Falcons ceased their attack, giving me respite to run the comm channels and take a real look around to find out why. The heavy radio traffic and the smoke rising from the forest to the east told the story. Beta's reserves had arrived. Our intercept of the Jade Falcons' spearhead had slowed them down enough for FedCom conventional forces to throw up a roadblock and slow the Falcons further, long enough for Beta's reserves to interpose themselves. The counterthrust was checked; even Omnis were not invincible.

The Falcons withdrew.

We survived.

Carrying our dispossessed pilots in the jump seats of our functional 'Mechs, our lances reached Josselles. The Wolf dismounted at the Dragoon command trailer, leaving his 'Mech to be reloaded and repaired by the mobile tech unit. I helped Shelly out of my *Loki* and made sure she got medical attention before following him there. I wanted to see how Maeve was, but I had my duty. The battle was not yet over.

The trailer didn't have the facilities of the *Chieftain*, the Wolf's command DropShip, but it was well-supplied and adequate to its task. Colonel Fancher was at a forward post, but Martin Reed, her executive officer, was there and already in conference with the Wolf. I went to the comm deck and transferred the

link from my *Loki* to the center. Reports flooded in.
The battle was shifting decisively in our favor, but it
flickered on for hours like a smoldering fire.

Sometime during the night, Maeve showed up and
brought me some rations. I ate at my console while
she rubbed my shoulders. Her touch reassured me that
she was glad we had survived. At the time, it was
enough.

I suppose the return of MacKenzie Wolf and his
company commanders marked the conclusion of the
battle. The Spider's Web had secured its objectives and
pulled back for refit. All across the front, the Falcons
were retreating. Fancher was able to disengage Beta
and move into reserve mode as backup for the Fed-
Coms and the Fourth Skye Rangers. There'd still be
fighting, but the campaign had been decided. The
glory, what there was of it, of kicking the Jade Falcons
off Morges would go to the F-C troops. The Dragoons
in the trailer were all exhausted, but there was still
work to do. The morning shift came in, but the off-
duty techs and officers couldn't seem to muster enough
energy to go to quarters. Exhausted and half-awake,
they slouched in spare corners, where they slurped coffee, gnawed ration bars, and kept one eye on the
screens and holotank.

Dawn light spilled into the trailer and a man entered. He was obviously of the Clan Elemental bloodline, for he barely fit through the door. He also looked
unfairly rested. I guessed him to be Elson, commander
of the infantry Star involved in the trap, because I
vaguely remembered having sent an order for him to
report to the trailer.

Elson moved between the closely packed rows of
consoles with a deftness that I found surprising. How
could such a mass of muscle move with such assurance
and delicacy? Even when one of the commtechs suddenly backed his chair into the Elemental's path, the
big man stepped around and through the narrowed

passage without contacting the chair or slowing his pace. He halted just outside the ring of Command Lance personnel around the main holotank, settling into a relaxed but ready stance that I suspected he could maintain for hours.

He didn't have to wait long. Jaime Wolf froze the holo display and turned. Smiling, he held out one hand to the infantryman, who dwarfed him.

"You did a good job today, Captain Elson."

The Elemental seemed unmoved by the Wolf's praise, but shook his hand and answered politely. "Thank you, Colonel."

"You seem to be living up to Grif Nikkitch's advance billing. He's a hard man to please."

"For an infantryman," MacKenzie Wolf added.

Most of the MechWarriors around the holotank laughed at Mac's joke. It was not sycophantic laughter; we were all MechWarriors. We didn't really understand how someone could be willing to go into battle without the advantage of a 'Mech. As 'Mech pilots, we did not think it demeaning to make a joke at an infantryman's expense. It was common knowledge that they made uncomplimentary remarks about us as well. It was just the way things were. Elson seemed totally unmoved.

"The Colonel wished to see me," he said tonelessly.

"I did, Lieutenant." Jaime Wolf folded his arms across his chest. "I am given to understand that you have ambitions beyond commanding a Star."

"I will serve as I can, Colonel."

"Well, I'm going to give you a chance. Think you can pass the tests for Trinary command? Are you ready to command three Stars?"

"I am a warrior. I will do my best."

"And that will be good enough?"

"I am good enough." Elson paused. To me it

seemed that he was going to add something more than
the simple "sir" he tacked on as an afterthought.

"Very well, then." The Wolf nodded. "But we're
not on Outreach today and I need a Trinary commander today, Brevet Captain Elson. Stick around. We
have a briefing in thirty."

"I serve, Colonel," Elson said. He touched his fist
to his forehead and, lowering his arm to waist level,
bowed over it. The action was a formal, ritual acceptance, out of place in the relaxed atmosphere of the
field command center.

Jaime Wolf returned his attention to the holotank.
He was into his third replay of the day's action when
Stanford Blake decided it was time to move on to other
business.

"Colonel, the Hall has posted a signal."

"They know our availability as well as I do."

"They thought, and I agreed, that you might want
to give this offer some consideration." Stan slipped a
data disk into the tank's console. Contract specifications appeared in a window that opened over the min-
iature display of the battlefield. I couldn't read the
words from my angle of vision, but I knew what they
said. I'd seen the signal. Stan waited until the Wolf
looked up. "As you can see, House Kurita is offering
a contract for two regiments to go against the Nova
Cats on Meinacos. The spec doesn't include their
compensation offer. I guess putting a price on a military operation is some sort of violation of their samurai honor, but the Hall's got all the details. They're
offering nearly double our usual rates and full salvage
rights."

The Wolf was silent. MacKenzie spoke for him.

"Tell them we decline."

Stan slammed his fist into his thigh. "Don't you
think this has gone on long enough? I was there, too,
but I'm willing to let it go."

"We're not," Mac said firmly.

"I thought we were going to run this operation economically," Stan said angrily. "Kurita is offering double our standard rates. How can we afford to ignore that?"

Mac started to respond, but the Wolf held up one hand. The son deferred to the father. "Even if it weren't Kurita, it would be a hard-luck contract. Meinacos is close to the district capital at Pesht. There'll be hard fighting."

"The Dragoons never backed away from a hard fight before," Captain Winnie Harding said. She was an adoptee, a spheroid who had been deemed good enough to join the Dragoons after Luthien. A former battalion commander in House Steiner's Skye Rangers, she'd given that up to serve as a company commander in MacKenzie Wolf's Spider's Web Battalion. She was still learning her way around the Dragoons. "It's because it's the Snakes, isn't it?"

No one saw the need to answer her.

Stan sighed. "Jaime, this can't go on. For somebody who can turn his back on his heritage, you've got a strangely strong grip on the past."

"It's a practical decision."

"Practical! I'll tell you what's practical! Practical is living with the reality that we've got to support more military assets than any *five* planets with the resources of *one*. We need well-paying contracts. You've just spent a year out of combat to heal the precious reputation of the Dragoons and preserve the Mercenary Review Commission's rep for impartiality. You've made a lot of speeches about impartiality and fairness. No favorites, you said. The Dragoons are for hire, to the best contract. What happened to equal and unbiased services to all Houses and all political units?"

The Wolf glared. It was a display of emotion he wouldn't have allowed himself if outsiders had been present. It was the same license that let Stan shout at his superior. Though we were among Dragoons, Jaime Wolf said nothing.

Stan turned to me and asked softly, ''Brian, whose name is on the contract as sponsor?''

''Theodore Kurita.''

Stan returned his attention to the Wolf. ''You see, Jaime? Not Takashi, Theodore. The Kanrei, who you invited to Outreach.''

Elson stepped forward, eclipsing one of the light panels. His shadow fell across the holotank, cutting between Stan and the Wolf. ''Leave Wolf alone, Colonel Blake. This is feud.''

''Feud be damned!'' Stan turned on the Elemental. ''This is business. We can't claim to be unbiased if we refuse a contract from one of the Houses. We can't afford to pass up lucrative contracts just because somebody connected to the customer has a history with us. Unity! If we did that all the time, we'd have nobody to work for.''

Unimpressed by Stan's fervor, Elson shook his head slowly. ''It is a point of honor.''

''Look here, Elson—''

''Let it go, Stan.''

''Jaime . . .'' Stan's appeal faltered as he saw the adamantine resolve in the Wolf's eyes. He paused a moment, then rallied, prepared to launch his appeal on a different tack.

''I said, let it go,'' the Wolf said softly.

The intelligence officer took a deep breath and let it out slowly. Then he shrugged and walked across the trailer to his console. Jaime Wolf returned to studying the local tactical reports. I looked at Maeve to see how she had taken the exchange, but she was disappearing beyond the massive bulk of Elson, heading outside. Elson stood passively, a thoughtful expression on his face. It might have been business as usual.

But I could feel the unresolved tension.

10

Most people think a warrior with a small build is worth little in a brawl, where the ability to inflict and endure punishment is usually paramount. The small fighter's lack of reach and mass are definite disadvantages in such a fight. If he's to survive, a small warrior must be fast and skilled. Maeve was that, especially the latter.

We were back on Outreach and I was just rounding the corner on Herrara Street in Harlech, when I came upon Maeve standing over an opponent, presumably the aggressor, who was on the ground. Downed he might have been at the moment, but he had four friends. The drunken laughter I had heard as I approached rattled down to an awkward stop.

"Tinspawn bitch," one of them growled.

"He asked for it," I heard her say. "Why don't you take him back to quarters and let him sleep it off?"

"Freeborns don't take orders from your kind anymore." The speaker's voice was slurred, but he moved fast enough.

Maeve ducked the punch, but her counterstrike was ineffective. Either the man was too drunk to feel the pain or else his big frame absorbed all the energy she could generate from her off-balance kick. He spun on her and she had to scramble to escape his grasp. One of the thug's companions clipped Maeve on the ear as she dodged. I saw blood spray.

I ran toward them.

All four were circling Maeve, but they were either too drunk or too absorbed to hear me coming. But Maeve had. She gauged my strategy and took advantage of it. Just as I came up, she struck out, opening herself up to the big one. Oblivious to me, he tried to grapple her.

I tucked into a ball as I launched myself into the back of the big one's knees. I imagined the surprise on his face as he got hit, and wished I could see his expression as we collided. We went down in a tumble, but I had enough momentum and he landed mostly off me. Wanting to slow him down, I cracked his knee hard as I pulled myself free from under his legs. When I was on my feet again, I saw that it didn't matter; he was heaving his guts up. We wouldn't have to worry about him for awhile.

Maeve had taken down her target, but had not taken him out. Unfortunately, he had dropped her to the pavement as well. Her attackers were closing on her as she pushed herself onto her hands and knees. The thugs had their backs to me, their problem. As I went by, I kicked the woman. She whuffed and collapsed, groaning as she joined her big companion in decorating the sidewalk.

"Two left," I said, moving into the freeborns' view. "Even odds. Still want to play?"

One of them risked a look over his shoulder, maybe to see if there were more where I came from, or maybe to check on his companions. The noise they were making should have told him their state. The other kept his eyes on us. The expression on his bloodied face told me Maeve had taught him to keep his eyes on her. I could have blind-sided his nosy partner, but I gave them a chance to answer my question.

The nosy one gulped and shook his head. The two freebirths backed away. The two still on their feet helped the exterior decorators up, and the four of them managed to rouse their leader enough that they only had to half-drag him away into the darkness.

"Nice timing, friend," Maeve said. She tossed hair back out of her eyes and got her first good look at me. "Brian!"

I was pleased to see her expression of relief change to one of gladness. "It looked like you needed help."

"They lost the first bid and upped the stakes." She shrugged and winced. "They were drunk enough. No real threat."

"The medical center is down the street. I was headed there anyway."

"Don't need a doc," she said, rubbing the side of her head. She looked surprised to find blood on her fingers. "I would have handled them."

"Sure." I offered her the medpack from my belt. "Sure."

She smiled sheepishly as she took my offering. "Thought you were on duty tonight."

"Things were slow." I made a point of looking elsewhere while she tended her cuts and scrapes. "You fought well."

"Good reflexes," she said with a shrug. Then she smiled, a twinkle in her eyes reflecting memories of other times. I wished I could have been a part of those times she seemed to recall with such pleasure. Then the moment was gone and she returned to the present. "They should have known better, but everyone thinks they're better than the ones who tried before."

That didn't sound good. "You've been attacked before? The Wolf should be told."

She shook her head.

"Not his business. Not my style." She laughed, but she couldn't hide the concern in her eyes. "Come on, Brian. You're not a spheroid. You grew up in the Dragoons like I did. You ever go crying to your sibparents when another sibko gave you an impromptu test behind the barracks?"

"Of course not. It wouldn't be honorable."

"Or smart." Her expression demanded agreement and I complied with a nod. She shrugged again. "That's all that happened here. A few freebirths thought they were better than me just because they've got blood parents. I was just educating them."

"They didn't seem to be grasping the lesson too well."

"I guess it was a large class for just one teacher. I'm glad you came along."

Her smile melted me. "So am I."

"You said you were headed for the med center? The Wolf ordering up a new crop?"

"No. Not that. I was . . . I was just . . ." I found myself wanting to tell her the real reason I was going to the med center, but her offhanded remark had struck too close to the truth and I was wary. I wanted to tell her, to share with her, but I was afraid. I tried telling myself that it was the scent of her in my nostrils and the heat of her nearness on my skin that made me so unsure of myself. I wanted to believe that she would understand, but I couldn't be sure. I'd never met anyone who had understood, but then, I had never told anyone outside my sibko about what I did, and I hadn't even told all my mates. James would have laughed his derision. Maeve might scorn me the same way.

"Just what?"

Her eyes that had been steel when turned toward those who would harm her were clouds of soft gray now. They made me believe that she cared. Fearing that I might have misread her, I throttled up my courage.

"I was going to the wombs."

Her brow wrinkled briefly in puzzlement. I quailed.

"Why?" she asked quietly.

"It's where I go when I have to think."

There. I had said it. She could taunt me now. Better I had told James; I could have punched him. Waiting

for her scorn, I realized my eyes were closed in anticipation of her harsh words. Wouldn't a warrior react
harshly to someone who still ran back to where he had
been birthed whenever he was troubled?

"Me, too," she said.

I looked at her. Her face was expressionless, tran-
quil. The pools of her eyes were cool depths. I could
have drowned in them. The heat of my embarrassment
was quenched. I was only too happy to agree when
she asked if she could come along. I hadn't been sure
I wanted to be alone, and I was not about to pass up
the chance to spend some off-duty time in her company.

The womb halls were mostly dark; all the scientists
having returned to their quarters for the night. Only a
skeleton staff was on duty and they stayed at their
monitors, leaving only to take their breaks in the
lounge. We walked the corridors unchallenged. I knew
our close connections to the Wolf were enough au-
thorization for our presence, but had anyone noticed
us, we would have been reported. I didn't want that,
and I didn't need to ask Maeve if she agreed with my
clandestine approach. Her stealthy tread as we neared
the building had told me that she knew the unwritten
rules concerning night visits to the wombs.

We made our way to the visitors' gallery outside
chamber 17. Beyond the transpex was my birthplace.
Or so I had decided. We were never told which of the
womb chambers had been ours. If the particular gallery made any difference to Maeve, she never said.

Through the transpex we could see the iron wombs
in the chamber. It was night cycle, but we didn't turn
on the lights. We didn't need to; the chamber had light
enough for our purposes. Most of the soft illumination
came from the floor strips marking the aisles with dots
of amber. The wombs themselves were firefly structures of monitors and status lights. There were no red
lights. All was calm, quiet.

For a while, we sat without saying anything, content to soak up the peace of the place. Haltingly, we began to talk. At first we spoke about the little matters of our work, like returning to quarters after a contract or the problems of explaining to a tech how your 'Mech just *feels* wrong. Low-key shoptalk. She told a funny story of how a sibmate had gotten himself a year's worth of extra duty and that got us onto how our sibmates were doing. From there we moved on to growing up in a sibko. I guess it was almost inevitable, given where we were.

She was a delight and I hoped I didn't bore her. I was startled to notice how close together we were now sitting on the bench when she surprised me with a sudden shift of topic.

"You said you come here when you need to think. I don't think you wanted to relive your childhood. That's best done elsewhere and with your sibmates. What were you coming here for?" She rushed on before I could answer. "You can tell me to shut up, if you want. If it's business and you can't talk about it, I'll understand."

"No, it's all right. It's not business. Or at least not exactly." I knew my smile was lopsided, but I hoped it was reassuring. "I saw an old communique today. About the gene pool."

"You know your parents?" She was eager, excited by the possibility. Obviously our talk had brought such speculation to the front of her mind. She had told me that hers was an unnamed sibko and now it seemed that she had transferred her own hopes of learning her parentage to my situation. In her eyes I saw unfeigned joy for what she believed to be my good fortune. I had to disappoint her.

"No, not that."

"Don't you want to know?" Her own longing was naked in her voice.

I was embarrassed.

"I've always known mine. I was of the William Cameron sibko."

"Right. I forgot. You're not a no-name like me."

There was pain in her voice. I reached out to embrace her, give her the human warmth that helped wash away that loneliness. She didn't move until I touched her, then she started. I pulled back and she turned her shoulder to me.

"You'll earn an Honorname," I said awkwardly.

Her voice was tiny. "I want my own."

I understood that. Compared to her, I was lucky. I knew my parents, knew I was the seed of an Honorname bloodline. Even if I hadn't won the name, I could carry the knowledge of my heritage with me. But I had won a name. Unity! I must have sounded condescending to her.

I dropped my arms to my side and turned my face to the window. Beyond the transpex, the rows of iron wombs marched into the darkness in their immobile ranks, their inner warmth hidden within the chill metal. New life was stirring there in the core of those wombs that looked so hard and nonhuman. The children born of them would face lives full of fighting. Some would know their geneparents, as I did. Some would have no idea who had provided the sperm and egg from which they grew. All would grow up dreaming of earning a name. Some, a very few, would succeed in doing so. Many more would die.

And why?

To fill the ranks of Wolf's Dragoons.

And why?

To be ready for the renewed assault of the Clans.

Jaime Wolf had determined that the Dragoons would be there to oppose the return of the Clans in their drive toward Terra. His official reasons were on record in the private Dragoon annals. The sibkos had been full of rumors that hinted at hidden reasons. I heard even wilder speculation once I left the sibko and had free encounters with spheroids. Correct or not, speculation didn't change truth.

The Dragoons were renegades from the Clans, the people who had developed the iron wombs. Most of the oldsters, the Dragoons who had been among the Clans, were freeborns. They had been born of human parents, and some had even grown up in real families. That parentage, derogatorily known as freebirth, had made them second-class citizens, looked down upon by the so-called trueborns who had gestated in the iron wombs and grown up in sibkos. The irony tore at my guts. Here on Outreach the Dragoons had turned to the iron wombs to save themselves as a group, much as had the followers of Nicholas Kerensky, founder of the Clans; the so-called renegades were walking the path of those against whom they'd rebelled. The sibkos were to fill out the ranks and make the Dragoons the elite warriors of the Inner Sphere. Like Clan warriors, the sibkin would become the Wolf's soldiers. They would be educated and trained from birth to be the best. Soldiers without parents, the elite of Wolf's Dragoons.

Like I was. Like Maeve was.

The children birthed of the wombs were our brothers and sisters, even those with whom we shared no genetic heritage. We were all a family. If the Wolf's plan worked, we would be more closely knit, better-trained, and more cohesive than the Dragoons had been when they had first come to the Inner Sphere, fresh from their Clan training.

"Brian?"

I grunted a reply. Very eloquent.

"I'm sorry," she said.

"You don't have anything to apologize for."

"I know you were trying to help."

"I . . ."

"Can we just forget it?"

"Sure." What else could I say?

"You started to tell me why you came here to-night."

"In the sibko we were told that the Dragoons take care of their own."

"Unity of mind, unity of purpose," she quoted.

"The communique I saw was addressed to the scientists. It was about an addition to the gene banks."

"A new Honorname line?

"No. New genes."

Maeve's eyes went wide. "What do you mean?"

"Do you remember when the leaders of all the Inner Sphere came to Outreach? The Wolf was supposedly warning them of the threat of the Clans. He told them of our origin among the Clans and our repudiation of that allegiance. He offered them anti-Clan training and intelligence. He even had them bring their heirs so the new generation would be ready to fight the Clans. The House leaders got training and information all right, but they paid for it in a way they will never know."

"You said new genes."

"That's right. The Wolf ordered genetic samples taken from all the heirs while they were having full medical evaluations. During those examinations, each of the children of the House lords was asleep. I hope they had pleasant dreams, because while they slept, they were leaving something of themselves behind. They're all in the genetic banks."

"The Wolf added spheroid genes to the pool?"

I couldn't tell if she was shocked or just surprised. I nodded.

"Even Kurita genes?"

"Aff."

She was quiet for a long time. "But he kept it secret."

"Aff. A commander must keep some secrets. It's not just a part of the mystique, it's a necessary tool in maintaining unpredictability. Secrecy is as much a part of war as particle projection cannons and blood. A lot of what the Wolf does is secret. He wears one face in public and another in the command center.''

''Like any good officer.''

I hoped that was all. ''It's more than that. I wish I knew what.''

''Maybe he's afraid that the adoptees will have a problem with his decision,'' she said thoughtfully. ''They don't like the sibkos. I think they really do think we're not quite human.''

''Maybe they're right.''

''You know better,'' she said, touching her hand to my face.

She sounded like Lydia. My sibsister had always had a comforting word when I had not done well in a test, but Lydia rarely offered physical comfort. Maeve's palm was hot on my cheek. I tried to ignore the contact, but it burned its way to my brain. I mumbled, ''Do I?''

She turned my face to hers and stared into my eyes. Her other hand dropped between my legs.

''You're human enough for me,'' she said.

And she was human, too.

═══ 11 ═══

If I hadn't been thinking about the previous night, I might have reacted faster. Maeve, too, must have been dulled by our late night, for she was just as slow. Then again, maybe it wasn't a fault in us, but I still don't believe it. We should have been more observant. *I* should have been more observant.

As the Dragoons equipped more infantry troops with Elemental-style battle armor, people dressed in battle suits were an increasingly common sight in the streets of Outreach. The equipment of war is not out of place in a camp of warriors, and Harlech, as the capital of Outreach, was certainly that. On this particular day, this particular battle suit bore Dragoon markings, which was as it should be; Dragoon policy prohibited any but our own on the planetary surface. Battle suits were still not commonplace in the rest of the Inner Sphere, so we had no reason to suspect that this wasn't one of ours.

Still, I was disturbed to see the battle-armored infantryman lounging against the concrete barrier wall screening the side entrance of Wolf Hall. At the time, I put my unease down to thoughts that the soldier might be the big thug who Maeve and I had fought last night; he had been big enough to be an Elemental. Now I realize that I was dimly registering that the battle suit's markings were definitely Dragoon insignia and tactical signs, except that they were out-of-date.

Wolf Hall was the command center for all Dragoon operations, and it housed business offices for all senior officers. Today was paperwork day for the Wolf, and that meant time in the office. He would be there and we were very nearly late. Jaime Wolf didn't like his staff to be late.

The sun felt warm after the chill of the tube station as we walked toward the small door in the east side of the building. The entrance was inset in the wall, the only shade in sight on that sunny morning. Maeve was passing through the scanners in front of me when I heard a groundcar pull up. I looked over my shoulder and watched the car stopping near the stairwell that we had just left. The flags on the car's fenders marked the vehicle as the Wolf's. I was relieved; we had arrived before he had. Then I thought again. Experience had taught me that the Wolf must be having a bad day if he wasn't an hour early. A bad day for the Wolf was a worse day for his staff.

I had no idea how bad the day was going to be.

As the groundcar doors began to open, the Elemental shifted from his position at the concrete barrier. He emerged from behind the creogan bush at the end of the fence, his weapon leveled. The snouts of the multibarreled antipersonnel machine gun built into the suit's right arm were dark with ominous promises of destruction.

It was too late to shout a warning. Wolf was out of the car and turning just then to see his danger. I reached for my pistol, a futile gesture because the weapon could never penetrate the battle armor. But I had to do something.

The Elemental opened fire.

His first shot went just ahead of the Wolf's groundcar, tearing up concrete beyond it as the heavy slugs impacted. With the next shot, the Elemental corrected his aim and sent fire ripping along the front fender of the car. The car's driver, who had been walking around the front of the vehicle, was cut in two. Grotesquely, her legs took another two steps after her torso hit the ground. Then the Elemental poured fire into the car, and shrieking metal shrilled.

I could see the Wolf crawling along the pavement, keeping the car between him and the Elemental. I guessed that he was headed for the stairs down to the tube station. The concrete would provide better cover than the groundcar. I was terrified to see that he left a trail of blood. He had been hit, whether by weapons fire or some of the shrapnel generated from the car I couldn't tell. He needed help.

If I ran to help him, I would be killed.

Leveling my pistol at the Elemental, I pulled the trigger and sent impotent slugs to patter against his bulbous chestplate. They were no threat, but I got his attention. I ducked back into the building as he raked the entrance with fire. The walls were thick enough to protect me.

I had bought some time for the Wolf.

Maeve crowded me as I blocked the door.

"What in hell's happening?"

"Elemental firing on the Wolf." I shoved her back, in case the Elemental changed his line of fire. Knowing nothing better to do, I changed the magazine in my pistol.

The door guard pushed his way past us. He had faith in his armor and weapons, but the Elemental cut the man down the moment he appeared.

Outside, the firing subsided.

Troops would not be long in arriving, but would they be fast enough to save the Wolf? Was it already too late? I risked a look. The Wolf was nowhere to be seen, but his blood trail led to the stairwell. He had made it!

The rogue Elemental was rocking from side to side as if trying to see through or into the burning ground-car. I guessed he was unsure of his handiwork. I

thought to draw the rogue's attention again to give the Wolf more time to escape, but before I could move, Jaime Wolf showed himself. The Elemental spotted him, too, and sent a burst at him. The Wolf ducked, fast enough that slugs sprayed concrete shards over the sidewalk but missed him.

The rogue started to run toward the stairwell in ungainly strides. Four meters from the conflagration that separated him from his quarry, he cut in the suit's jump jets and arced into the air.

It was what the Wolf was waiting for.

A tight stream of water under high pressure burst from the stairwell, catching the Elemental square on his portside backpack launcher. Twisting backward under the impact, he lost control of his flight. The jets smashed him down into the pavement. He toppled onto his back, moving spasmodically as if dazed.

Then Jaime Wolf appeared at the top of the stairwell, fire hose in hand. He fought the stream down and directed it at the Elemental, setting the suit to spinning on its back as a child might toy with a tortoise. The rogue flailed his arms, apparently unable to regain control of the suit.

I rushed to the guard's station and opened the commlink to call for Elemental support and a medical team. As I directed the arriving security forces, Maeve slipped outside and scooped up the fallen doorguard's rifle. She set herself in stance and started firing in short bursts, seeking the weak spots in the battle suit as it rotated.

It took only two minutes for the Elementals to arrive, a five-man Point plus Captain Elson. With brutal efficiency, the Point pounced on the rogue, who was too disoriented to fight. They cracked him out of the suit. Maeve must have found at least one crack in his armor, for his right arm was bleeding. Except for that he seemed unharmed. The medical term arrived shortly afterward and rushed a gray-faced Jaime Wolf off to the med center. The would-be assassin went in a second ambulance, but he received less solicitous care.

Stanford Blake handed me my commnet headset as he brushed past me to join the group of officers gathered around the untenanted battle suit. Several senior officers were present, including the Home Guard commander, Jason Carmody, Hamilton Atwyl, the aerospace commander, and Hanson Brubaker of Contract Command. Elson, the helmet of his battle suit rocked back to expose his head, stood with the officers. His remaining men—two had gone with the Wolf and one with the rogue—were still sealed in their suits. The pair moved away to hold their own conference. I spent a few minutes linking to the commnet and assuring various commands that all was under control before joining the officers. I left a channel open to the med center frequency.

"Suit's Nova Cat style," Stan announced. He looked puzzled.

I looked at Elson. He was stony-faced and silent, but his skin had flushed a bright red. He had been a Nova Cat once and still bore their Clan name as his own surname, just as Jaime Wolf bore the Wolf Clan name. Neither was a member of his original Clan anymore. Was Elson feeling embarrassment that his old Clan would try this assassination attempt, or was it because they failed? Or did his apparent response mean something else?

Jason Carmody kicked the empty suit's arm. It barely moved, but the impact was enough to make the two thick fingers and the opposed thumb of the left gauntlet quiver and uncurl slightly. He shook his head slowly.

"Don't they know we've been repudiated by Clan Wolf?"

"They must know, Jason," Stan said. "Maybe they don't care. Maybe it doesn't matter to them because we helped beat them on Luthien. We know they over-extended themselves on Tukkayid to prove that Luthien was an accident. All they did was end up getting soundly beaten again. Not to mention that losing the Battle of Tukkayid is the reason the Clans have had to promise to hold their invasion at bay for fifteen years. We've given them enough reason for hate by ourselves; they don't need the old feud with the Wolves.''

"Can't be a feud with us. There was no declaration," Brubaker pointed out.

Stan sighed. "Be serious, Hanson. We aren't living in an honorsong. Nova Cats aren't the only ones calling us bandits. Nobody has to declare feud with bandits.''

"But the ilKhan hasn't proclaimed us bandits," Hanson protested.

"And he won't," Carmody said. "He's a Wolf himself.''

"*Maybe* he won't," Stan corrected. "He's got a lot more to worry about than the welfare of a bunch of runaway freeborn warriors.''

Carmody looked unhappy at Stan's assessment. "Maybe this is an attempt to punish the Dragoons for betraying the Clans.''

Several of the officers agreed with that theory.

"How much do you think the Nova Cats would have bid for that privilege, Elson?'' Atwyl asked.

"I am no longer a Nova Cat warrior.''

"So what? What do you think?''

"I never participated in such a bid session.''

"Fat lot of good you are,'' Atwyl snapped. He let out his frustration by kicking the unoccupied battle suit. "I think Jason put his finger on it. The Cats would love a scheme like this. They ace Jaime and they make a double score. They get revenge on the Dragoons for Luthien and at the same time they get to embarrass the Wolves by cleaning up their mess for them. They'd raise their stock with the other Clans and that's something they need to do, especially after Tukkayid.''

''Maybe we can learn something from the Elemental.'' Carmody sounded hopeful.

The messages filling my right ear gave me the unhappy duty of destroying that hope.

''Med center reports the Elemental DOA. Bit off his tongue and drowned in his own blood.'' To the chorus of questions, I added the more important news, ''The Wolf is stable. Prognosis is good.''

''Any word from MacKenzie?'' Atwyl asked anxiously.

''Unity, Ham! The message only just went out.''

''I know, Stan.'' Atwyl frowned. ''I'll be happier if he's back here until Jaime's up and around. Somebody's got to ride herd on this bunch.''

There was general agreement, but I was surprised to note that some of the officers seemed less than enthusiastic. I made a point of checking Elson's reaction, but when I looked for him, he was gone. So were his Elementals.

12

MacKenzie Wolf arrived on Outreach two weeks after the attack on his father. The trip would have taken longer had not Colonel Atwyl diverted some of the Dragoons' JumpShips from their regular duties and put them into place to create what the spheroids called a command circuit. A sequence of JumpShips was put at his disposal all along his route to Outreach. Instead of having to stop and wait while his ship recharged its interstellar drives, MacKenzie was able to transfer his DropShip from JumpShip to waiting JumpShip. The multiple transfers made the trip to Outreach relatively brief, but there had still been more than enough time for everyone to devise a favorite theory concerning the identity of the would-be assassin.

Some theories had more adherents than others. Clan assassin, pick your Clan. Spheroid revenge. Interference by the reactionary faction of ComStar. A first strike by the majority faction of ComStar. A simple rogue. Even a renegade Dragoon. The last was especially popular with spheroid Dragoons who wished to believe that we were led by a cabal of manipulative Clan puppets. I had formed no opinion; I was waiting for the evidence to come in. I was, however, troubled by the outcome of all this wild speculation.

Within days the leading theories seemed to have become ossified into rigid, almost political, positions. Arguments had erupted, even a few fights, between proponents of one theory or another. It began to seem that one could know the theory favored by a Dragoon by knowing which was his favorite among the factions that appeared to be developing within the Dragoons.

I found the division and acrimony unsettling.

In the sibko, I had been raised to believe that the Dragoons were one big family. Without knowing your genetic parentage, you could call any Dragoon from an older ageframe a parent and any of the same or a younger frame a sib. I had really believed that as a child, and that belief had made living in a sibko easier to bear. And why not? With every Dragoon either a parent or a sib, concern and caring could be found anywhere within our ranks. I was learning that life in the Dragoons, like life anywhere, I suppose, wasn't that simple. If we were a family, we weren't getting along very well.

I began to see the attack on Maeve as a symptom of a malaise afflicting the whole Dragoons, rather than an isolated incident. Once I had thought such differences merely the stuff of good-natured jibes. Now I saw a deeper source, a true rancor. I began to see that the Dragoons had families all right, families within families. Some seemed on the verge of feud.

Spheroids distrusted the oldsters, and sibkos held them in contempt for it. Those born of natural parents looked down on those of us who had been born of the wombs. And Clan bondsmen had nothing good to say about anyone else. I do not mean to suggest that everyone with a particular background felt exactly the same; they did not. But there were groups who nurtured those who shared their sentiments. Some were more open about it than others, but none were above recruiting more of their own kind. Each day, it seemed, the huddled heads in one corner or another grew in number.

I tried to tell myself that my fear of factionalism was paranoid. We were all Dragoons, loyal to the Wolf.

This outbreak of acrimony was merely a sign of stress. Worry for Jaime Wolf's health had made everyone edgy, distressed. When he was recovered, all would be well.

I hoped that I wasn't fooling myself.

During the weeks of Colonel Wolf's confinement at the med center, I was in almost constant attendance on him. That was how I came to be there whenever his family, his blood family, came to call.

Of course, I knew Marisha Dandridge. She was co-ordinator of sibko socialization, and I had seen her often during my early life. She had always been warm and, during my younger years, I believed that she was especially fond of me. Early in my third training frame, I had dreamed that I was in love with her. Then I learned that she was the Wolf's wife and I was filled with the sort of unformed terror that only a twelve-year-old can conjure. Our relationship changed overnight. I don't think she ever knew.

Marisha was Jaime Wolf's second wife. Though she was from a younger ageframe, her passionate feelings for him were evident. Uncomfortably so at times, for me, that is. Jaime Wolf certainly approved. A different sort of emotion was reflected in the two children she had borne him. There was an easy intimacy between the children and parents that I had seldom seen outside a sibko. Even in a sibko, I had never observed such depth of caring. I told myself that my flustered embarrassment was due to my old crush or my obvious intrusion on their privacy, but I knew better.

They were a blood family. I felt out of place.

But my duty was to be at the Wolf's side, except for brief times when he or Marisha requested privacy. In those weeks at the Colonel's side, I saw who came to visit him and who did not. I saw who was comfortable in his presence and pleased with his recovery, like the oldsters, and who seemed to harbor uncertainties. I felt sure that he noticed all that and more, but he remained cheerful and friendly to all who came.

It was halfway through morning visiting hours and I was in the midst of the morning status report when MacKenzie arrived. Business was shunted aside as the younger Wolf greeted his sire with great affection. I stood back out of the way; the report could wait.

MacKenzie and his father were close, just like the rest of the family. Seeing MechWarriors of such different ageframes display so much affection still seemed odd to me at the time. They might have been sibkin. Once MacKenzie had assured himself of his father's condition, he kissed and embraced Katherine and Shauna, his wife and youngest child, before greeting his stepmother and stepsibs.

"Where's Alpin?" MacKenzie asked.

"He said he had maintenance duty." Katherine's usually open expression was damped down, hardening the lines of her angular face. I knew she suspected the truth that I already knew from the duty rosters: MacKenzie's son had no maintenance duty this morning. All the 'Mechs in his lance had received operational certification yesterday.

MacKenzie frowned briefly, then turned to his father with a smile. "Even in bed you keep the Dragoons hopping, Dad. Can't have operational MechWarriors without operational 'Mechs. I guess I didn't need to rush back. You've got everything under control. Maybe we should get you attacked more often."

"Not funny, Mac," Marisha said.

"Sorry."

There was quiet for a moment. Feeling uncomfortable, I tried to leave but the Wolf stopped me.

"Where do you think you're going, Brian?"

"I thought . . ."

"That you'd get light duty just because this hellion is back home? Unlikely."

"Nice try, though," MacKenzie added. "It sounded like the morning report."

"It was," the Colonel confirmed. "But it's also routine. I think you've got something else on your mind, Mac."

MacKenzie nodded. Sitting on the edge of the Wolf's bed, he said, "I've been reading the reports and theories, Dad. They all lack something."

"Go on."

"Well, the facts don't fit exactly."

"You're being vague."

Sighing in frustration, MacKenzie slapped his thigh. The sound was loud. "This whole thing is vague."

"Life's not all open field battles." The Colonel reached out a hand to his son. "Work it out. Start with the most obvious."

MacKenzie bowed his head. Marisha shepherded her daughter-in-law and the children from the room. I wanted to go, too, but a slight shake of the Colonel's head gave me my orders. MacKenzie seemed to find where he wanted to start.

"The soldier in that battle suit was clearly not of the Clans' Elemental genetic line."

"Implying an Inner Sphere source," Jaime Wolf prompted.

"But Hanson says the pilot could have been a free-born not of an Elemental bloodline."

"And, therefore, a good choice for a dishonorable assassination attempt."

"Dad, I was just a kid when we left the Clans, so I don't really know them. But it just doesn't feel right to me. The Dragoons are out of their culture now. The Clanners might think us bandits, but they don't go around assassinating bandits. They wouldn't think it worth the trouble."

I had even less personal knowledge of the Clans and I wasn't one of those who doted on the Dragoons' Clan heritage, but I agreed. Still, I knew others held a different view. Ominously, some of those others were the Dragoons' newly acquired bondsmen and warriors. Those former Clansmen seemed to believe that the Dragoons had sullied or even betrayed their Clan heritage. They did not believe the Dragoons to be completely divorced from Clan society. Many of them voiced support for the theory that the Elemental had been sent by one or another of the Clans.

MacKenzie shook his head. "The suit does have Clan tech."

"Good thing he didn't know how to use it all," the Wolf said.

"A very good thing."

"And?"

"And that's why I don't think he was Clan."

"I agree."

"Do you know who sent him, then?"

"No. Does it matter?"

"Unity! Yes!" MacKenzie leaped to his feet. "They need to be taught a lesson."

"In time. We need to know the student before we can hold class." The Wolf smiled slyly. "I'm in no hurry."

"I just want to do something. I don't want anybody thinking they can strike at the Dragoons, especially at you, with impunity."

"You think you can do better?"

"Oh no." MacKenzie laughed wryly. "You're not catching me that easy. I'm not ready to take over the Dragoons yet."

Father and son laughed together, but I couldn't join in. MacKenzie's last statement was the one thing many of the factions agreed on. I had heard too many voices saying exactly what Mac just had. The Wolf's son was a good field commander; few questioned his competence. But watching him struggle with the problem of this assassination attempt, and knowing that the master of the Dragoons had to deal with more than just battlefield problems, I feared that those who thought him unready were right.

Fortunately, Jaime Wolf had survived the attack and would soon be in the command chair once more.

====== 13 ======

"I have read your records and concede that Anton Shadd was a man worthy of renown. His actions at An Ting proved that, but it means little; Shadd is no Bloodname."

Elson Novacat was larger than the man he disdained. That in itself was no matter for pride. Size was simply his genetic heritage, a part of what made him suitable to be an Elemental. This Shadd was born of a freeborn Elemental as Elson had been, but Shadd's father had abandoned his genetic heritage to take up a MechWarrior's hot seat. For all that this smaller man had won a Dragoon Honorname, he came from a lineage that had turned its back on its genetic calling.

"Shadd is an Honorname," the smaller man stated defiantly, his dark eyes flashing with anger. "It is better than a Bloodname."

"Your so-called Honornames are but shadows of the truth. Had I wished your *name* for my own, I would have won it easily," Elson said simply. The pup needed to be put in his place. As the highest-ranking Elemental in the Dragoons, he had been one of the Trial supervisors for this infantryman's Honorname. He had seen the results and knew he could have bested this newly named Pietr Shadd's scores. Therefore, Elson's statement was no boast, but Shadd apparently took it as bluster.

"Big boast for someone who insists on naming himself after a pussy."

Officers around the room tensed, no doubt fearing that this confrontation verged on physical violence. Elson ignored them. He and Shadd were both bigger than anyone else present. If it got physical, the damage would be done well before the gathered Mech-Warriors, aerospace pilots, and staff officers could interfere. If they acted quickly enough, the best they could do would be to save Shadd's life by getting him prompt medical attention. But Elson had no intention of letting matters go that far. A brawl anywhere in Wolf Hall, let alone in the conference center, would undo all he had worked for. This was a time for words, not actions.

"I earned my name in honorable combat," he said softly.

Shadd was not mollified. He raised his voice. "Some name. The Nova Pussies get whipped by Dragoons as easily as by Wolves."

"Mine is a name won in the old ways. I know *The Remembrance* of the Nova Cats. Theirs is an honorable lineage, invulnerable to your words. Can you say the same?"

"I haven't any interest in Nova Pussy glory songs."

Elson was becoming annoyed. Louder than he intended, he said, "I learn your history. It is expected."

"Yeah, it *is* expected from losers."

"You have no concept of honor," Elson barked.

"Wake up. You ain't in the Clans anymore. We don't need their lopsided honor here. You're an adoptee now. If you don't get with the program, you'll get left behind."

Elson sneered. "As you have left your heritage?"

"I'm not a Clanner," Shadd said. He seemed to be proud of his lack. "I'm a Dragoon, born and bred."

"As you say, freebirth. You have no place questioning the honor of the trueborn."

"You're freeborn, too."

Stung by the reminder, Elson felt his resolve to avoid violence slipping. This honorless pup was insolent and needed to be shown the error of his ways. Shadd must have sensed Elson's shift of intent for he came subtly on guard. Elson held back, surprised; he had not expected Shadd to be so alert. The moment's delay and the opening of the door brought matters to a sudden halt. Out the corner of his eyes, Elson could see MacKenzie Wolf at the head of the arriving officers.

Elson took a step back, ceding the field. Shadd smiled, but there was the raggedness of relief in the breath he drew. Enjoy your little victory, Elson thought. It is only a skirmish, not the war. There will be other times, he promised himself.

"What's going on here?" MacKenzie demanded.

"Nothing, sir," Shadd replied.

MacKenzie's expression showed he did not believe Shadd's words. "Pretty loud nothing if I could hear it in the corridor."

"You say nothing's going on, Elson?"

"It is unimportant."

MacKenzie's eyes narrowed. He took a deep breath and straightened his shoulders. "We're all Dragoons," he said, sweeping his gaze from Shadd to Elson. "You got that? *Dragoons.*"

Elson felt MacKenzie's gaze linger longer on him than on the born-and-bred Dragoon. It was a sign of who had the power here, and another sign of how the Dragoons had drifted from the true path. But Elson understood honor, even if they did not. He endured MacKenzie's stare, listening compliantly as the officer continued.

"We're not *this* because of where we were born, or *that* because we trained somewhere else. We're Dragoons, first, last, and always. That's what you became when you put on the uniform. You're not Clanners anymore. You're not just hire-ons or sibkin. You're

Dragoons.'' MacKenzie walked the room as he spoke, pacing back and forth behind the holotank. "I don't care if your family has lived in the Inner Sphere since before the fall of the Star League, or if your ancestors shipped out with General Kerensky. I don't care if you're blood-born or sibkin. I don't care if you signed on after Misery or after Luthien. Young or old, greenie or veteran, you're all Dragoons and I expect you to act like it.

"They used to say that the Irish of Terra always fought among themselves because they could find no other worthy opponents. Such indulgence is something the Dragoons can't afford. We've got plenty of enemies, not the least of which are the Clans. They're sitting out there behind the Tukkayid line now, but they won't stay there forever. We've got to be ready. And we will be. The Dragoons will hand them their heads, because we'll be good enough. *You'll* be good enough. If you forget what you were and be what you are. Dragoons!" He leaned on the holotank. "You got that?"

In the midst of the ragged chorus of "Yessirs!" Elson answered, "I hear you." He wondered if MacKenzie would understand the difference.

Jaime Wolf and I arrived in time for the end of MacKenzie's little speech. It seemed an awkward way to open the Wolf's first formal appearance since his injury. The strained atmosphere relaxed somewhat as the Colonel went around the room, greeting the officers and accepting their good wishes. We were settling into our places for the conference when the side door opened to admit a group of late arrivals, including Maeve.

I had seen little of her for most of the month since our night at the wombs, and then it had been only on business. She hadn't returned my calls. I warmed at the sight of her, then my heart fell as I saw that the rumor I had heard was true. Instead of her bodyguard leathers, she wore the uniform of the Spider's Web Battalion, MacKenzie Wolf's unit. Upon his return to Outreach, Mac had relinquished command to John Clavell, which moved officers up and opened a slot. Maeve must have requested the position, passed the command test, and won the slot. I had not seen the request in the usual communiques, so I could only assume that she had somehow arranged to keep it from me.

What had I done wrong?

I had no more time to ponder my problem. The Wolf called the meeting to order, and I was soon too busy running the feeds to the holotank and keeping the flow of information current and matched to his needs.

At his command, I opened a secret file on the OmniMech production facilities that Blackwell Corporation was administering on the other side of the mountain. I knew about the file but had never seen its contents. Ordinarily, I would have been as fascinated as the other 'Mech jocks to see the progress at the facility, but I wasn't paying any attention. My mind was on Maeve as she watched the display with an avidity I had dreamed she might hold for me. Somehow she had come to stand beside Jaime Wolf, a last chance to be his bodyguard, I suppose. Stanford Blake had to poke me when I missed the Wolf's cue to change the display.

Having opened with the good news, Colonel Wolf launched into his plans for the Dragoons' future. We had spent many hours preparing this pitch, hours I might have spent with Maeve if I hadn't been so obsessed with being a good comm officer. Colonel Wolf intended to integrate the disparate elements of the Dragoons into a new tradition, a tradition of and for the Dragoons. It was a good plan, although Stan had expressed some reservations about its feasibility in the face of the enemy. I believe the Wolf spoke eloquently, he always did. There might have been arguments; I don't remember.

I drifted in shattered hopes and fallen dreams. I vaguely remember MacKenzie chiming in to bolster his father's arguments, and sensing something shift in the flow of conversation. It bothered me, but not as much as my lost love.

There was a break in the meeting and Jaime Wolf took the opportunity to congratulate Maeve on her new command. I watched the two of them. The former bodyguard was of a size with the man she had protected, but the size of a pilot didn't matter when BattleMechs fought. It didn't matter at all now. She was going elsewhere, and someone else would have to protect the Wolf. Stupid considerations. That seemed appropriate; I felt stupid. Unable to think straight, I sat and did nothing. Somehow her eyes never looked my way. If they had, I would have . . . what? I don't know. I know I stared when she left with MacKenzie's executive officer.

Her DropShip was to launch in two hours. As the arguments started, I knew I wouldn't be able to leave before then. Someone wanted the allocation of OmniMechs altered, while someone else questioned the new organization for the regiments. There were protests about personnel assignments. Officers argued over the structure of the Elemental units, but everyone wanted Elementals attached to his command, whatever the level. The loudest arguments came over the new sibkos and the revised training regimens. It all flowed past me. Later I was able pick up many of the details by reviewing the tapes, but at the time I heard nothing but a mournful babble.

She never said goodbye.

Part 2

3054
OLD FEUDS

14

Colonel Jaime Wolf had noted the dissension among the Dragoons, had noted that his reforms were not having the hoped-for effect. Factionalism was still growing and each faction had its own agenda. Sometimes it seemed that the Wolf and his closest officers were the only ones who viewed the Dragoons as a single entity.

And as always now, the threat of the Clans loomed on the horizon.

The original Dragoons had been strangers in a strange land, an odd-man-out effect that had bound them closer together than their military structure and on-campaign situation could have done alone. The trials they had faced in their wanderings through the Inner Sphere, especially the fierce fighting on Misery, where the Kuritans had nearly destroyed them, had brought the survivors even closer together. Those who had endured, whether Clan-born or spheroid, considered themselves oldsters now.

One might have thought that the threat of the Clans would become the source of similar trials and bonding, that the mere anticipation of the Clan threat would have been enough for the factions to want to iron out their differences. But so far only the oldsters and a few others had seen the need for complete Dragoon harmony.

In a bid to simultaneously promote harmony and

improve our military position, the Wolf had devised a plan. Carefully chosen personnel were assigned to a special, secret mission.

Out in the Periphery lay a cold star named Bristol, ringed by barren planets. It isn't on any of the Inner Sphere's star charts—it's so far away from habitable systems that a rickety spheroid JumpShip would be lost if something went wrong with its drives. But Bristol is on the Dragoons' charts.

Before the Dragoons' entry into the Inner Sphere, they had marshaled in the cold space around Bristol. Their original mission called for them to pass as Inner Sphere mercenaries, but covert recon missions had shown them that Clan intel had made a few mistakes. Some of the Dragoons' equipment was well beyond what was available to even elite units of the Great Houses of the Inner Sphere. Using such hardware would have raised uncomfortable questions, if not murderous greed. Jaime and Joshua Wolf, co-commanders of the mission, had decided to leave some of their equipment hidden at that cold star. Advanced JumpShips and DropShips, BattleMechs that had been only prototypes when Kerensky's people had left the Inner Sphere, and early Clan electronics and weaponry went into mothballs. I think that even then, the Wolf brothers must have foreseen the possibility of a break with the Clans. Creating the supply depot made practical sense in any case. As it was, the Dragoons created stir enough with the quality and designs of the equipment they didn't hide away.

Now the Dragoons needed whatever edge we could get. Our once-secret Clan origins were now public knowledge. We no longer had to pretend, but we did need strength. The cache at Bristol would give us some of that.

The mission had to remain secret from the leaders of the Inner Sphere, however. With the Clans on their doorstep, they would have been more covetous than ever of what we would be bringing back. But the ships and machines were ours. They were to be our ace in the hole, our last resort should we be threatened by angry employers. If we survived the threat of the Clans.

The voyage into the dark had another purpose as well, a subtler, perhaps more important purpose. MacKenzie Wolf was named first among the officers in command of the mission, and his council was carefully chosen from among the factions. On the voyage to Bristol, MacKenzie would have the opportunity to forge a rapport with the men and women who would become his hard core of commanders.

Besides the necessary technicians and scientists who would restore the cache ships and their cargo to working order, there were representatives from all the Dragoon combat arms and most of the support arms. Non-combat personnel would go along also to provide a microcosm of the Dragoons. Isolated and in pursuit of a common goal, the group would come to know one another better, to learn that they shared a common goal and needed one another to accomplish that goal.

Jaime Wolf had concluded that much of the factionalism within the Dragoons was because the various groups were not familiar enough with one another. He knew that shared trials united even the most disparate groups. This mission was intended as an opportunity to end prejudice and replace it with respect.

The DropShip *Orion's Sword* would be the flagship of the small fleet. It was a reconfigured *Overlord* Class ship, massing nearly ten thousand tons. Fully loaded for a combat mission, it could carry two companies of BattleMechs, six aerospace fighters, and a battalion of infantry and their support vehicles. Even without the ship's own firepower, that was a force more than sufficient to raid a defended planet. Although invasion was not the *Orion's Sword*'s mission, she carried her full complement. The other three DropShips in the fleet had full complements as well. The DropShip fleet would be carried via a command circuit through various uninhabited Federated Commonwealth star systems, finally meeting up with the JumpShip *Talbot* for the final leg of the journey into the Periphery. The official reasons for the military force were caution: no one knew what had happened to the cache, and long-term, deep-space operations were likely to feature prominently in future Dragoon operations. The Wolf felt sure that his ploy would not work if his real reasons were known.

I was on the bridge of the *Orion's Sword* conferring with the signals officer when MacKenzie Wolf arrived on a kind of conducted tour of the ship with his family. Katherine hung on his arm as if reluctant to let go of him. Shauna, their daughter, wandered around inquisitively, poking into things until techs shooed her away. She would be one of those MechWarriors fond of tinkering with their equipment if she didn't test into the tech class. Alpin followed the group at a distance like a tall, glowering shadow. Even though there was no chance of immediate action, he wore his cooling vest and pants rather than a Dragoon jump suit. His left shoulder was tattooed with a garish Clan Wolf crest, by which he proclaimed his sympathies with those who romanticized the Dragoons' Clan origin. His usual sour expression lightened occasionally when he spotted some bit of Clan tech captured on Luthien that had been incorporated into the *Orion's Sword*.

"It's a wonderful ship," Katherine was saying to MacKenzie as they reached the comm station. "I'm very proud of you."

Alpin snickered. "The heir gets all the good toys."

"That's out of line, Alpin," MacKenzie said.

"Jaime didn't pick your father just because he's family," Katherine chided.

"Yeah, sure." Making a show of indifference to his

parents' words, Alpin wandered away to examine the captain's chair.

Katherine leaned close to MacKenzie. "It isn't that, is it?"

"No," Mac said with a shake of his head. "Dad wouldn't do that. Why do you think I spent all that time in Beta Regiment under another name? Dad named me first among officers for this mission because he thought I was qualified enough to lead it, and unseasoned enough to need this sort of milk run."

"There's a rumor running around the compound that this is some kind of test. To see if you can glue some of the factions together."

"If it is, he hasn't told me about it."

"Be careful."

Mac smiled at Katherine and patted her arm. "We're not going into battle. We're just going to pick up some equipment."

She looked unconvinced. "You know I worry."

"Well, you worry too much," he said and kissed her.

"You give me cause."

Mac laughed softly. I thought there was a sadness in the sound. "Worry about Alpin. He gives you as much cause, and me even more."

They both looked at their son. Alpin had abandoned the captain's chair and was trying the fit of the military commander's couch. Mac sighed. Relinquishing his hold on his wife, he walked over and placed a hand on Alpin's shoulder.

"I'm going to have to get down to business soon." Mac's loving gaze took in the rest of his family. "I don't want you to go, but it's time."

Alpin threw himself out of the chair. "You could have gotten me an assignment on board. I could've commanded one of the lances."

"I didn't think it appropriate. Besides, your mother will need you."

Clenching his jaw, Alpin stared at the ceiling. When he looked at his father again, there was rage in his eyes. "Why are you shielding me? Your father let you be a warrior."

"I'm not—"

"I'm as good as you ever were."

"Alpin . . ."

"I don't need this." Shrugging his father's hand from his shoulder, Alpin stormed to the lift. He stabbed the call button, then slammed the panel with his fist when the door did not open at once.

Mac stared forlornly after his son. Katherine came and stood by his side. She raised a hand and began massaging his neck muscles. The tableau held for almost a minute until Shauna came dancing up, insisting that her parents come see something she had found. Still staring at his son, Mac resisted her for a moment before giving in. Then parents and daughter moved to the far side of the bridge.

I watched the angry son.

The lift door opened and Alpin charged through, directly into a mountain of an Elemental.

Elson.

Although tall himself, Alpin had to crane his neck to look up into the face of the man he had crashed into. "Get out of my way!"

Elson laughed. "You are not cleared for this mission and that should be 'get out of my way, sir,' Lieutenant."

"You're a groundpounder."

"And you are a high and mighty MechWarrior who cannot see rank insignia. I could teach you, but you would not like the lessons. However, I can see that you have already had some trouble today and I will be lenient. You are fortunate that I am in a good mood."

"I don't care what kind of mood you're in. You're in my way."

"Which is where I will remain until you explain

yourself. I will not have this kind of behavior on my ship.''

"It's not your ship; it's his," Alpin snarled. He tossed his head back to indicate his father.

Elson looked over Alpin's head in the direction indicated. The tip of his tongue appeared between his lips and moved slowly back and forth.

"And he is your problem?"

"He's my father." Alpin muttered something under his breath. "Yeah, you could say that he's my problem."

Elson nodded slightly. "I see."

"I doubt it."

Elson folded his huge paw of a hand around Alpin's shoulder. "I can understand your anger. He is not much of a warrior."

"He's a good officer," Alpin snapped defensively.

"Oh, a very good *Dragoon*."

Peeling Elson's hand off, Alpin sneered. "You're a Dragoon."

Letting his hand fall to his side, Elson said simply, "I was a Nova Cat."

Recognition dawned on Alpin's face as he took a step back. His tense stance shifted and his entire manner changed.

"You're Elson!"

The Elemental smiled.

"I've heard a lot about you. You were born in the Clans, weren't you? I mean, *quiaff*?"

"Aff."

Alpin shot a glance at Mac and smiled as he saw his father engaged in conversation with one of the ship's officers. "*He's* not going to need you for a while. Maybe I could buy you a brew and you could tell me what it's like. Being a Clan warrior, I mean."

"My Elementals are secured and I have a little time." Elson wrapped a huge arm around Alpin and drew him into the lift. "There is much I could tell you about the honor road, and I can see that you are some-one who will understand.''

The lift door closed, cutting them off from my sight and hearing, but they didn't leave my mind for some time.

15

MacKenzie's group had been gone for a month when the ambassador from the Draconis Combine arrived at Gobi Station above Outreach. At first we all thought it was just another job offer from Theodore Kurita, albeit one carried by a fancy messenger. When Ambassador Kenoichi Inochi, the head of the Kurita mission, refused to speak to anyone other than Colonel Wolf, suspicions were immediately aroused. For by then we had learned the origin of the rogue Elemental.

Careful analysis had shown that the assassin's battle armor was indeed of Nova Cat origin, though the assassin had not been as big or bulky as a typical Clan Elemental. That might suggest that the man was not a Clanner, but it wasn't proof; not all Elementals are of the Clan-bred phenotype. On the other hand, any Clanner not of the Elemental phenotype who had won the right to wear battle armor would have to be a highly competent soldier. Wolf's would-be assassin had barely been able to control his suit. The real evidence, however, came from the modifications made to allow the smaller man to use the suit: they were all of Inner Sphere manufacture.

We knew that the Combine had captured a number of battle suits from the Nova Cats when Hohiro Kurita had tricked them on Wolcott, and many more after the battle of Luthien. Most of the modification components in the assassin's suit were of Combine manufacture, making House Kurita's realm an obvious choice as a starting place for the search. Our lack of agents in the Combine made progress slow, but the assassin was at last tentatively identified as one Ken O'Shaunessee. Lifted Kuritan ISF files identified O'Shaunessee as an agent of the Dofheicthe clan, an hereditary organization modeled on the ninja of ancient Terra. Wolfnet had failed to uncover any record that the man had received battle armor training, but they were able to place him on New Samarkand, the planet where the Kuritans had set up the training facility for their newly formed Elemental-style infantry units.

When intel's final report was circulated, only the stubborn clung to theories of a Clan origin for the assassin. Though Wolfnet could not determine who had actually ordered the attack, it seemed likely that Takashi Kurita had decided it was time for Jaime Wolf to die, honorably or not.

Now a Kuritan was knocking on our door, and the Wolf was intrigued.

A reception was laid on for the ambassador. It was no more than we would have done for the representative of any of the Great Houses, but far more than had been done for any Kuritan since before Misery. The hall was decorated in the Kuritan style and certain pottery was displayed prominently near the guest of honor's seat. I thought it too subtle a touch: this ambassador was unlikely to recognize the work of such a minor artist as Minobu Tetsuhara, however much fame he had achieved as the Kuritan commander on Misery.

Ambassador Inochi arrived dressed in formal Kuritan style. He wore a tailed waistcoat of blue silk so dark that it looked black over gray pin-striped trousers. A cummerbund of iridescent *daigumo* silk circled his waist, and spats of the same material covered the tops of his shiny black shoes. He was a slender man and walked with a limp—acquired in combat, to judge by the medals and ribbons on his chest. Several of the decorations indicated action on the Davion-Kurita border during the Fourth Succession War. Likely that his unit had fought us, then.

If Ambassador Inochi recognized the pottery, he gave no sign.

As he and his party made the requisite small talk for hours, I wondered how they could do it, but was even more amazed that Jaime Wolf was easily a match for them in this game. I'm told that earlier in his career, he had been more direct. With age comes restraint, I expect, but there are those who think that politeness and circumlocution are signs of weakness.

It wasn't until ten in the evening that Inochi announced that he had brought a message from Takashi Kurita, Coordinator of the Draconis Combine. Some of the Dragoons around me expressed surprise; they must have assumed that Inochi was Theodore's man. The Wolf never batted an eye.

"You do not seem surprised, Colonel Wolf," Inochi said. "Perhaps you learned of my mission during the long weeks that I spent traveling here to Outreach."

The Wolf smiled blandly. "Perhaps your message will be more surprising than your sponsor."

"Perhaps it shall, Colonel-*san*." The ambassador inclined his head. "The Coordinator is a man of honor. He has a long memory."

"As do I."

"This he understands." He held out a hand. A kimono-clad aide shuffled up and handed Inochi a scroll of rice paper. Tying it shut was a black ribbon sealed with the dragon's-head symbol of House Kurita. "The Coordinator is well aware of your command of Japanese, yet he has composed this message in your language. It is intended as an honor."

The Colonel made a formal bow. "I accept the gesture in the spirit in which it is offered."

The ambassador bowed back, a wry expression on

his face. I suspect that he recognized the ambiguity of Colonel Wolf's words, and that he appreciated it.

"The Coordinator's message begins with a poem:
Glorious sunset;
Blossoms on an autumn wind,
A warrior's life."

The Wolf straightened and drew in on himself. For more than a full minute he was silent. Inochi waited patiently, silent as well. Apparently the rest of the message had to wait for the Wolf's response to the opening poem. People had begun to shift nervously when, at last, the Colonel spoke.

"Sun and moon, brothers.
Evening light shines like spilled blood;
New day, the wheel turns."

The ambassador bowed deeply. "I see that my unworthy fears that the Coordinator misunderstood you are groundless." As if on cue, the aide brought out a message pouch from his kimono and handed it to the ambassador. Inochi bowed and offered the packet to Colonel Wolf. "This contains the formal challenge, as well as a personal message from the Coordinator. Shall we be able to work out the details soon?"

Colonel Wolf accepted the package, but his reply was cut off by the arrival of Stanford Blake. Stan wore his undress uniform, rumpled from travel. He must have come straight from the spaceport upon hearing that the Wolf was entertaining a Kuritan embassy.

"What's going on?" he asked as he bulled his way through the people separating him from the Colonel. If Stan was aware of the ambassador, he was deliberately ignoring his presence.

Halting Stan's charge with a raised hand, the Wolf said to the ambassador, "Please excuse my officer's lack of courtesy, Inochi-*san*."

"Courtesy be damned," Stan snarled. The sudden apparent reversal of the Wolf's policy had obviously made Stan forget his usual decorum. "I want to know what's going on."

Jaime Wolf turned to him and said calmly, "Takashi Kurita has just offered me a duel to the death."

"And Colonel Wolf has accepted," Inochi added.

Turning to face the ambassador again, the Colonel said, "Your pardon, Inochi-*san*. But I fear you have misunderstood me. I had only intended to acknowledge your Coordinator's offer."

The ambassador's face darkened. "Then you refuse?"

"I acknowledge." The Colonel shrugged. "To do more at this time would not be proper. I have responsibilities, and must gauge the balance of duty and honor. Surely you understand that this is a matter that will take some thought."

Mollified, the ambassador said, "I understand." He bowed. "I will be honored to convey your response as soon as you have made your decision."

"There won't be any duel," Stanford announced.

Inochi gave Stan a look of distaste. The Wolf addressed the ambassador. "It's not Colonel Blake's decision."

"Jaime!"

"Not now, Stan." The Wolf never took his eyes from the ambassador. "I am sure that you will understand if I retire now, Inochi-*san*. Please feel free to remain and enjoy our facilities."

With formal politeness, the Colonel took his leave and departed the room. The ambassador must have been expecting him to perform some sort of private meditation, for his face took on a puzzled expression when the senior officers present filed out after the Wolf. Inochi returned Stan's glare with a smile that never touched his eyes.

From among the transmissions that were continually passing by my headset commo unit, I picked out a public-band announcement. Recognizing its importance, I hurried after the officers. I reached the conference room before they had all settled into their customary places, and skirted the wide table to halt at the Wolf's side and stammer out my discovery.

"Colonel, there's a public announcement going out that Takashi Kurita has challenged you to a duel."

"He's pushing it." Stan was angry. I felt sorry for his operatives; Stan's thunderous arrival made it clear that they hadn't warned him of this.

"Just bull," Carmody ventured. "The old Snake's just blowing waste heat."

"He's samurai." That came from Neil Parella, commander of Gamma Regiment. "He can't say things like that in public if he don't mean it."

"Who says it's public, Neil? What if the report is for our ears only?" Carmody turned to me. "What about it, Brian? What kind of distribution is that announcement getting?"

"It's on the ComStar network. The broadcast tag says the message is going out all over the Inner Sphere."

That brought curses from most of the officers. Jaime Wolf sat quietly in his chair, leaning on one elbow. Above the hand that hid the lower part of his face, his eyes were thoughtful.

Stan addressed him, but spoke loud enough so that all present heard his words. "Reject the challenge and Takashi loses face. It would be a major insult. We'll never work for the Combine again."

"Isn't that what we wanted anyway?" Kelly Yukinov asked. The Alpha Regiment commander looked around the gathering, soliciting support.

Carmody slammed his hand on the table, as if that settled matters. "Then there's no point in worrying about it. Ignore the old Snake."

"What about Dragoon honor?" Hanson Brubaker objected. "Duel is a proper way to end a feud. Kurita is walking the honor road. If the Colonel ignores the challenge, is he fit to call himself honorable?''

The Wolf ignored the implied insult. Carmody rose to his defense.

''You weren't at Misery. You don't understand.''

Brubaker frowned. ''I understand honor.''

''Honor?'' Carmody laughed. ''The Kuritans claim they understand honor.'' Turning to the Wolf, his voice took on an imploring tone. ''It's another trap, I tell you. Jaime, ignore the Snake.''

''Who can ignore honor and live with himself?'' Brubaker asked as he stood. His face was suffused with blood and his carriage was stiff. He seemed ready to challenge Carmody, or perhaps the Wolf himself.

''Sit down, Hanson,'' Stan said. ''We're talking Kuritans here, not honor.''

The arguments went on for more than two hours before Colonel Wolf finally dismissed his officers. He announced no decision. On and off over the next two weeks, further arguments erupted. The Wolf listened patiently, never rising to any bait tossed before him. He let his advisors dispute at will. Given their head, they beat the subject to death; their opinions never changed, only solidified. Sometimes the Wolf just seemed tired, bored with it all. Other times he was fiercely alert. At those moments he seemed to be waiting, as if wanting someone to make a specific point. When no one did, he seemed disappointed, yet remained almost perversely unwilling to lead the discussions.

The Kuritan ambassador grew impatient, but each note he sent was returned with a polite refusal of an answer. Despite repeated requests, the Colonel would not meet again with Inochi. Then word came that MacKenzie's mission was successful—they had found the cache. As if that settled matters, the Colonel cancelled the afternoon conference. Smiling at some secret pleasure, he said to me, ''Now there's only one piece of old business.''

He sent for the ambassador from the Draconis Combine.

=== 16 ===

Standing on wide-braced legs, Elson surveyed the bridge of the *Hammer*. The DropShip was not as large as *Orion's Sword*, but being an infantry assault ship, it was more suited to his preferred kind of warfare. He was also pleased to note that Captain Brandon and her crew seemed more efficient than those serving aboard *Orion's Sword*. At least they chattered less as they went about their duties. Perhaps his transfer here would not be so bad after all. Command anywhere was better than having to stand in the shadow of a barely competent officer like MacKenzie Wolf.

The sigh of the lift doors and then the sound of footfalls behind him announced a visitor to the bridge. Elson recognized the step as Captain Edelstein's. The man was of a Dragoon sibko, one of those stressing the size and physical skills necessary for Elementals. He reminded Elson a little of Pietr Shadd, though he lacked the insufferable man's grace. Though Edelstein had a touch of the Elemental bloodline, his lumbering walk marked him as inferior to one of pure Elemental lineage. Still, he was a passable warrior and an adequate Trinary commander, despite some lack in personal initiative.

Edelstein stopped behind Elson, just out of sight, then stood there waiting. Elson let him wait for nearly two full minutes while pretending intense interest in the DropShip's status monitors. Only when he heard the soft rustle of Edelstein shifting slightly from foot to foot, a signal that the man was losing patience, did Elson finally speak.

"You wished to speak to me, Captain Edelstein?"

"Yes, Major Elson."

The catch in Edelstein's voice told Elson that he had caught the captain off guard. Satisfactory. "What is it?"

"I wanted to make sure that you understood that I harbor no ill will toward you."

"Why should you?"

"Some might think I would resent you taking over command of the *Hammer*."

"I have military command in my position as Elemental leader and strategic command as a member of the Council of Officers. Operational command remains with Captain Brandon. Do not misstate the chain of command."

"The *Hammer* is an assault ship, sir. That makes military command the real command. Leastways that's Dragoon doctrine." Edelstein moved around so he could look Elson in the face. "That was *my* job until MacKenzie Wolf had you transferred here. I wanted you to know I don't resent it. In fact, I'm pleased. I'd hoped to get a chance to serve directly with you. Wolf might think he's shuffling you off to the sidelines, but we think he's got his head screwed on wrong."

"We?"

"The troops, sir. We all think you're the best officer to hit the conventional arm since Anton Shadd."

The comparison didn't bother Elson. He actually found it flattering, making the smile he offered Edelstein quite real. *Anton* Shadd was a hero, unlike the Elemental imitation who had won the right to bear the name. "Thank you, Captain. I appreciate the thought, but MacKenzie Wolf was within the rights granted him by his father."

"Scuttlebutt says you were also within your rights when you spoke out."

"Yet 'Mech jocks rush in where groundpounders fear to tread."

"Damn right." Edelstein nodded his head vigorously. "He had to go and dash off a message to his father as soon as the cache fleet was sighted on deep scans. Puling bloodbirth. Always looking for a parental pat on the head. What a weakling."

"I gave him my advice, but he chose to ignore caution."

"That's his right," Edelstein conceded. "But he shouldn't have embarrassed you by laughing off your concerns about the count of the ships. 'One too many?' " Edelstein whined in poor imitation of MacKenzie's voice. " 'Just a record error.' He should have taken your advice to investigate before pumping a message back. MechWarrior's false pride, that's what it is. Power fantasies."

"Not all 'Mech jocks are seduced into believing they are gods because of the apparent power of their machines," Elson offered in a charitable tone. "Perhaps he really believes it is a record error."

Elson didn't know what MacKenzie really believed, but he thought it unreasonable to assume that a contradictory count of ships was insignificant. Too much exposure to the faulty science of the Inner Sphere, he supposed. For all that they spurned their heritage, Wolf's Dragoons was unlikely to incorrectly account for war material. That sort of accounting was burned deeply into a Clanner's genes. Edelstein wasn't to be pacified. "I just wanted you to know that there are those who think that Wolf, whether he turns out to be right or wrong about the ships, was wrong in the way he treated you."

"That is comforting."

The comm officer, calling across the bridge, ended their conversation.

"The *Orion's Sword* reports that she is ready to detach from the docking collar."

"Stand by stations," Captain Brandon responded. She addressed the infantrymen. "You might want to take seats, Major Elson, Captain Edelstein. The *Talbot*'s not the youngest JumpShip in the fleet, and her docking collar releases are not always smooth."

"I will be fine, Captain," Elson replied.

With a longing look at an empty crash couch, Edelstein said, "As will I."

Brandon shrugged. "As you wish."

The ship shuddered slightly, then pitched to port. Edelstein lost his balance and landed on his rump, but Elson remained standing. It took quite an effort to maintain his balance without shifting stance, and almost as much to keep the strain from his face. But he was rewarded by the whispers he heard all around him, admiring his skill. Let them think it was easy, that was part of the image. Image was just one of the things a successful commander needed.

"The *Orion's Sword* is away," the commtech reported.

"Very good, Mister Jones. All stations return to normal duties."

Elson gave Edelstein a hand. When the embarrassed captain was back on his feet, Elson took a step closer to Captain Brandon's couch.

"Captain, can we observe the flight of the *Orion's Sword*?"

She shrugged. "How about it, Mister Jones?"

The commtech's answer was the brightening of the main viewing screen. Stars burned in the distant night of space, but the lower-left screen was bright with the pockmarked face of the planetoid above which the cache fleet orbited. Stretching across the arc of the planetoid was the *Talbot*'s spine. None of the Jump-Ship's cargo of DropShips was visible because the *Hammer* was docked in the collar closest to the bow.

At the end of the *Talbot*'s long spine was the globe of its main hull, a dark silhouette against the bright polygon of the sail that collected solar energy to recharge the ship's interstellar jump drive. The bright, irregular dots in the distance were the cache ships and the asteroidal debris among which they were hidden.

"She's coming across now," Jones reported.

The lumpy ovoid of the *Orion's Sword* slowly intruded from the screen's left, eclipsing the view. Flares of light erupted in irregular rhythm along her flanks as her maneuvering thrusters nudged her around the *Talbot*'s spine and clear of the sail. Safely distanced from the JumpShip, the *Orion's Sword* fired her aft thrusters and started on an arcing course that took her around behind the sail. She disappeared from view, but Elson could follow her trajectory on the orbital-path monitor. The *Orion's Sword* was headed directly for the largest concentration of cache ships.

"Glory hound."

"That remains to be seen, Captain Edelstein," Elson said softly.

They waited for the *Orion's Sword* to emerge from the blocking zone of the *Talbot*'s sail. "Captain," Jones said, voice pitched higher than normal. "*Talbot*'s bridge reports movement among the bogies."

"Has the *Orion* got it?"

"Neg. She's screened from us by the sail and the bogey's running behind what should be"—Jones paused to consult a secondary screen—"the *Alexander*."

Brandon tapped the keys that routed the line to the *Talbot*'s bridge and directly into the captain's earpiece. She listened, running her tongue over her upper lip. Elson found the display of nervousness unprofessional. "Are you planning to detach to take up a support position, Captain Brandon?"

"Those are the orders from JumpShip."

As he had expected. "Patch me through."

"This is space ops, Major Elson."

That was expected as well, but Elson was unfazed. "As a member of the officer council in command of this expedition, I outrank all aerospace commanders except Colonel Atwyl of the *Talbot,* who is also a member of the council. Are you disobeying an order?"

Brandon's tongue appeared again. She shrugged. "Talk all you want. Patch him through, Mister Jones."

"Thank you, Captain," said Elson with a thin smile.

Brandon grumbled, but Elson noted that she did not halt her preparations for undocking. She would learn.

"Colonel Atwyl, this is Major Elson Novacat aboard the *Hammer.* I understand you have given orders that we undock and take up a position supporting the *Orion's Sword.*"

"I'm busy, Elson," Atwyl replied tersely.

"Acknowledged. May I remind you that Colonel MacKenzie Wolf specifically ordered that his be the only DropShip detached from the *Talbot* until contact with the cache ships was achieved?"

"That was before we had a bogey."

"It was a specific order. In that connection, I point out that there is no evidence of imminent threat to warrant a legitimate disobedience."

Atwyl's sigh buzzed as static on the commlink. "That bogey might—"

"And it might not," Elson said sharply.

"I don't like taking chances."

"Which is exactly what you are doing with your career by disobeying an order. Even Colonel Jaime Wolf subjected himself to discipline." Elson was pleased at Atwyl's lack of response. Time for the next step. "The *Orion's Sword* will clear the sail shortly, correct?"

"Ten minutes."

"And there will be another estimated twenty for transit time to the cache orbit. That is more than enough time to communicate with Colonel Wolf and let him make his own decision.''

Atwyl thought it over for a few seconds before replying, ''Very well.'' Then he added, ''Captain Brandon, keep the *Hammer* ready for departure.''

''Aff,'' Brandon acknowledged.

''Sound strategy, Colonel,'' Elson said.

Turning to the screen, Elson watched the almost unchanging picture for half of the ten minutes. He checked the orbital monitor and smiled. Though hardly an expert in aerospace tactics, he understood the uses of cover and the necessity for subterfuge when dealing with a larger opponent. The enemy would be waiting out there—if indeed there was an enemy.

The *Orion's Sword* had barely cleared the shadow of the jump sail when energy beams lanced out from among the debris belt. Silent flowers of light burst from the side of the *Orion's Sword*. The comm crackled with a nearly garbled voice. ''Warning only, claim-jumpers. These ships are ours. Stick around and you'll get worse.''

''This is Wolf Dragoon ship *Orion's Sword*, MacKenzie Wolf commanding. You are trespassing on Dragoon property. If you do not leave immediately, you will be considered looters.''

''Frak,'' was the reply over the comm. The bogey made a more substantive response by firing again.

Elson spoke as the bogey's beams raked the *Orion's Sword*. ''*Orion's Sword* is under fire, Captain Brandon. I order you to detach the *Hammer* immediately and take her in on a vector that will provide us a rapid approach to the bogey.''

Atwyl's order to do the same came half a minute later, but Elson was already giving his Elementals orders to suit up.

Edelstein was grinning.

''Gonna save the wolf cub's ass.''

''We are going to do our duty. Recovery of the cache

ships is our prime mission. If that involves the sacrifice of MacKenzie Wolf's pride, so be it. He could be
losing a lot more.''

Edelstein nodded, his grin growing wider. ''Be a
shame if the looters got him, wouldn't it?''

''I would not cry.'' Elson shrugged off his contem-
plation of the irritating MacKenzie and what might
come from this interplay of orders once the action was
over. Until then there was a fight to be fought. ''Have
First Star report to the shuttle bay. All other Stars pro-
ceed to boarding stations. Drill Beta.''

''Aff, Major Elson.''

As Edelstein raced to the lift, Elson called after him.
''The shuttle team will pursue the bogey. Boarding
parties are to secure the hostile ships. Assignments at
your discretion. If MacKenzie Wolf proceeds with his
plan, he may need help. Some of the looters may have
boarded the cache ships and be laying traps.''

''Aff,'' Edelstein affirmed as he stepped into the
lift.

''I will lead First Star.''

Edelstein flashed a salute as the lift doors closed.
Elson swept his gaze around the bridge. He admired
the way each of the spacers attended to his or her task.
He was pleased that his crew was efficient.

Almost too efficient. The *Hammer*'s detaching
caught him off guard. Though he managed to stay on
his feet, the feat lacked the grace of his previous performance. This time no one noticed, which was good.
A true commander had to maintain his dignity.

Calmly, he walked to the lift and called for the car.
There would be more than enough time to don his
battle armor.

17

"Hey, Homi-*kun*. You in or not?"

The Japanese man looked up from the book he had been reading. A dark patch covered one eye, but the other glittered in the wan light of the barracks. "Call me, Homitsu, Mosul, or do not speak to me."

Mosul stepped back, hands held up in a placatory gesture. "Damp the heat, pal. Just trying to be friendly."

"The bodyguards of the Coordinator are supposed to be warriors, not courtiers. One is chosen for the Izanagi Warriors for one's skills, not one's personality."

"Ain't that the truth," Mosul said. "Look, you want in on the pool on how long it'll be until Wolf rejects Takashi's challenge? There are still slots open in the eighth week. Prime territory."

"I prefer not to gamble." The Japanese man closed the book and stood, turning his back on Mosul to stash the volume in his footlocker. Task finished, he straightened and looked around again. Mercifully, Mosul had returned to his cronies. Taking his uniform jacket from the hook beside the bed, Homitsu slung it over his shoulder and moved toward the door. He needed some air.

The pundits in the barracks believed that Jaime Wolf would ignore the Coordinator's challenge. He was an honorless mercenary, after all. Who could seriously expect mercenary scum to understand honor?

Homitsu had no interest in wagering on when Wolf's response would come. Having some experience of Jaime Wolf, he believed that the troops were wrong. If he were to bet at all, it would be on Wolf's accepting, not rejecting, the challenge. The odds-makers would give him long odds, and a handsome killing would go a long way to supplementing the dwindling reserves of cash he had hoarded for so long. But betting in favor of Wolf would only attract attention, the last thing he wanted or needed now. Money wouldn't matter soon anyway.

Very soon, if he was right about Wolf.

Karma.

He paused for a moment outside the storage building to be sure no one was observing him. Satisfied, he entered. Even to his night-adjusted eyes, it was dark inside. He crossed to the place of concealment by memory alone and opened the compartment. Removing what was within, he turned on a low-power lamp and set to work. The light was dim; it would not penetrate to the outside. The sounds were soft; they would not attract the attention of anyone passing by.

Some time later, he hefted the blade. It felt right, well-balanced for all its straightness. This sword was not a *katana*, the samurai's sword. That would be inappropriate. He held the blade before him, edge up, and raised his other hand above it. Opening the palm of his free hand, he released the feather that had nestled there. In the motionless air of the dark chamber, the feather drifted lazily downward, barely hesitating at the moment the gleaming metal of the blade split it neatly in two. Once Homitsu would have smiled, taken pleasure in the keen edge he had crafted. Today, his expression remained serene.

A sword was a tool.

As he was a tool.

Cold and hard.

18

Plugged into the commander's feed onboard the shuttle, Elson's battle suit kept him updated on the sensor-input from the bridge. The *Hammer*'s vector permitted it information unavailable to the other Dragoon ships. Hidden in the shadow of the planetoid was a JumpShip, Scout Class, by the readouts. The ship must have been the transport for the looters whose DropShip had fired on *Orion's Sword*. As the *Hammer* moved in its direction, the bogey JumpShip vanished, traveling faster than light to some other star system before the Dragoons could close, abandoning its DropShip to the Dragoons' mercy.

Elson was disgusted at how little loyalty the spheroids showed. But he also knew that if the JumpShip was as tattered as the DropShip lurking among the cached Dragoon ships, running was its only chance at survival. Not honorable, but understandable. Did the people aboard the abandoned DropShip applaud their comrades' decision?

The *Orion's Sword* continued its cat-and-mouse game with the looters' DropShip, each shifting angle forcing the bandit more directly into the path of the *Hammer*. The looter did not manage to score again on the Dragoon ship, but neither had *Orion's Sword* been able to get a clean shot. Soon it would not matter.

"Coming up on release," Captain Brandon reported. Her voice was terse, businesslike.

"Containing barrage only, Captain," Elson replied in like manner. "I want to board her intact."

"That wreck's so beat up, I won't guarantee it surviving a near-miss, let alone a direct hit."

"Then do not hit it."

"Unity! Your shuttle could drive through their hull without taking damage. It's not worth risking the troops."

"Your assessment is noted." Elson flicked off the channel to the DropShip bridge and watched the shuttle's monitors. In seconds the release warning lit. "Red light on."

"Troopers strapped in," reported Clair, his Point second. Elson checked his harness; it was secure. Either Brandon would follow his orders or she would not. He would soon be too busy to deal with it for a while. Eyes on the unlit "go" light, he murmured, "Stand by."

The light flashed on and the shuttle intercom crackled as the pilot reported, "We've got green light."

"Launch," Elson ordered.

His mild annoyance at the pilot's unnecessary announcement vanished, replaced by more immediate concerns as the craft lurched and he was rocked back in his harness. After the gentle tug of the DropShip's regular acceleration, the boost of the shuttle was a sudden, merciless, and implacable foe, but he fought it, pitting his strength against its. Futile, but exhilarating. He comforted himself with the thought that soon he would face real foes.

Attitude jets fired, twisting the craft on a corkscrew course. The maneuver simultaneously separated the shuttle from the DropShip and made it a more difficult target. The shifting motion and stresses of acceleration also brought nausea and giddiness to the passengers. The status monitor on Trooper Four, Harmon, flashed red as the sensors in his suit logged him as unready. He had not been able to control his stomach and had fouled his battle suit's recirculation system. The computer had locked his acceleration harness; Trooper Harmon would not be part of the boarding party.

Confused by the *Hammer*'s barrage or else just plain incompetent, the looters' gunners were too slow. The shuttle slipped past their erratic fire without taking the slightest damage. The pilot might be talky, but he performed well. With one last violent rotation, the aerojock dropped his craft into the looters' fire shadow. Within the safe zone, inaccessible to the DropShip's weapons, the shuttle pilot profligately burned reaction mass to match velocities before the looter pilot could blast away.

The grapples launched, making the shuttle shudder. As the pilot reported success, Elson's Point second called out the vector to the nearest airlock on the DropShip. Metal groaned as the slack was taken up and the pilot's skill at matching velocities was shown to be less-than-perfect but sufficient; the lines held. Then the shuttle's airlock opened and the Elementals were out of their harnesses, floating across the shuttle cabin and into space.

The jump to the DropShip was minimal. Scrambling along the hull, Elson led his troops straight to the hatch. He worked the lock, counting the thumps as the members of his Point landed around him. He waited another half-second after the third set of thumps before remembering that Trooper Four was out for this excursion.

The lock was only big enough for one battle-armored trooper at a time, so he climbed in first. He could have blown the inner door, but that would have compromised the DropShip's atmospheric integrity, an unnecessary tactic at this time. The outer door slid shut and he was alone.

The battle suit's atmosphere sensors flickered messages on his display as oxygen hissed into the cramped space around him. If they had been quick enough, there would be no problems. If not, he would be the first into battle.

He thrust the suit's right arm through the crack as the inner door started to slide open. The machine gun fitted to the arm swirled its barrels, at speed and ready. Unnecessarily. There were no targets; this staging area leading to the main hold was deserted.

Elson stepped out of the lock and locked his boot magnets onto the floor before hitting the controls to recycle the airlock. Releasing the magnets, he pushed off, heading for the door that gave access to the main hold. On landing he locked down again.

The area beyond looked deserted; as yet the crew had not reacted to his intrusion. The telltales on the bridge would alert the crew that the lock had been activated, tipping them to the location of their unexpected visitors. Assuming their equipment worked, he reminded himself. The interior of the ship looked more worn-out than the exterior, and his atmosphere sensor reported high concentrations of waste-product gases in the air.

The first crewmember arrived, floating through the doorway just as Elson's Point second was exiting the lock. Elson didn't bother with a weapon. He clubbed the man down. The crewman cartwheeled under the sudden impact. Elson reached out with the suit's manipulator claw and tugged him through the opening. Dead or unconscious, the looter made no sound as the three tines of the claw cut into his flesh, but his body thumped loudly as it struck the far wall.

Fire from somewhere in the main hold caught Clair as she advanced to join her commander. Slugs splattered impotently against her battle armor or whined away in frustrated ricochet. When she loosed a short burst of her own, the firing stopped. Joining Elson at the entrance to the hold, she waited with him until the third Elemental was in the airlock before advancing.

The boarding action was anticlimactic, the looters

offering minimal resistance. Within twenty minutes
Elson was in command of the bridge and using the
DropShip's comm to inform the *Hammer* of his suc-
cess.

Relaxing, he popped his carapace. The air was every
bit as foul as his sensors reported, but it was nothing
he hadn't smelled before. Unpleasant but not dangerous. Leaning against the captain's couch, he listened
to the chatter between the Dragoon units. MacKenzie's
ship had grappled the *Alexander* and he had sent a
party aboard, where they were meeting resistance. The
Hammer was completing the maneuvering necessary
to send her last boarding parties into the fight aboard
the *Alexander.* Fortunately the looters had not activated the *Alexander*'s weapons.

With Elementals soon to be involved aboard the
cache ship, Elson saw little to do but wait. Edelstein's
troops would deal efficiently with unarmored looters.
If the scavengers had infested any other ships, their
turn would come. There were too many ships for the
Elemental troopers to deal with at once; they would
mount their sweep operation only once they encountered immediate resistance.

Clair joined Elson on the bridge to report that resistance from the DropShip crew had ceased. A check of
the ship's computer showed all crew accounted for.
This battered hulk was his. Elson's part of the job was
done for the moment.

With the help of his Point second, he linked his suit
comm to that of the captured DropShip, which let him
listen in on the tac channels aboard the *Alexander.*
MacKenzie Wolf was leading his team against the looters. Not surprisingly, they were calling for Elemental
support. The 'Mech jocks and techs were neither
trained nor equipped for close-in combat; the free-fall
conditions would only further reduce their effectiveness. They would need help, zero-gee-trained help.
Edelstein had assigned a full Star to the boarding ac-

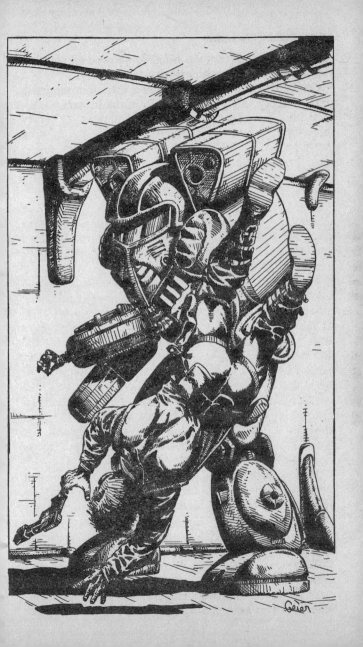

tion. Visual feed from the *Hammer* showed all shuttles returning from depositing their loads.

On the link through the *Hammer*, Edelstein reported unexpectedly heavy resistance from the looters.

19

When Colonel Wolf announced his decision, the arguments stopped, at least where he could hear them. New arguments erupted, but they too were reserved for times and places where the Colonel could not overhear. Many people seemed to think the Wolf had made the wrong decision, but I was coming to understand that the decision would have met opposition, no matter how he'd decided. I thought about telling the Colonel all I was hearing, but in the bustle of imminent departure, the grousing came to seem relatively unimportant.

Lydia stopped by Wolf Hall. She'd been away on a contract and I hadn't seen her for several weeks. The last time, we'd spent the night in each other's arms, consoling each another for the loss of Carson. A mercenary's life is not without hazard and, as good as the Dragoons are, we do take losses; Carson was the first of our sibkin to die in battle. That night had made me see Lydia—who had formerly seemed so standoffish—in a different light. I should have been happy to see her again, but her first words set my emotions on a different path.

"Is it true about the Wolf?"

I frowned. My sibs had often tried to squeeze me for information or used me as a rumor-buster, but never before had one come to me while I was on duty. That kind of harassment usually came from others.

"I'm on duty."

She wouldn't let me concentrate on my work. Tugging my head around, Lydia stared into my eyes. "Brian, this is important."

"So is my duty," I said, removing her hand.

She rolled her eyes and sighed. "If you'd only answer me, you'd be back to your duty by now."

She was right, of course. Thinking that she would leave once I'd confirmed the rumor, I said, "It's true."

Taking in my words, her expression became dreamy. She sighed. "An honor duel. Just like in *The Remembrance*."

Not exactly. The tales of honor that made up so much of the half-history, half-epic poem that was *The Remembrance* were simple, clear-cut stories. Real life wasn't like that, especially life in the business end of the Dragoons. But then, I couldn't expect Lydia to know the complexities of the situation; she was posted to a combat unit. "No cares beyond a good soldier's cares," she'd said on that night we'd cried over Carson. She'd said that was enough for her.

"He'll win, of course," she said confidently.

"Takashi Kurita is accounted one of the greatest MechWarriors of the Inner Sphere."

"He's an old man now," she said with a shrug.

"So's Jaime Wolf," I pointed out.

She laughed, dismissing the issue. "But he's the Wolf. You'll be going with him, won't you? What an honor. I wish I could be there to see the Wolf kill the old Snake."

I found myself wishing I could share her confidence. She was living in a child's world, surrounded by dreams of glory and honor, in which the great hero always slays the villain and right always triumphs. I had dreamed those same dreams. Much as I wished them to be true, I had grown to doubt them. Seeing them in her eyes made me uncomfortable.

"You'll be leaving soon, won't you?"

I nodded.

"I'm off duty for the next thirty-six," she said with a smile. "Maybe tonight we could . . ."

She left the invitation hanging, unwilling as ever to actually voice it. I forced a regretful smile and said, "I've got a lot to do."

Patting my arm, she said, "Ever faithful Brian. You do your duty." She started to leave, but turned suddenly. "James is in town, too," she said. "You find the time, look us up. Sibs always got to be there for sibs, *quiaff*?"

I nodded agreement, but wondered if that were so. Certainly I missed my sibs; we had seen so little of each other since my posting to the Colonel's staff. Things just weren't the same. Each time we gathered, my former sibmates seemed different, less—I don't know what. Maybe less informed. Had being Jaime Wolf's comm officer changed me, or had it only opened my eyes? As much as I missed my sibs and others of my ageframe, I had come to know that their narrow, comradely view of the world was not the only one. James would have said I'd been corrupted, blaming the spheroids.

I thrust those thoughts away and tried to concentrate on the report I was writing. But the words wouldn't come.

Soon I would be leaving Outreach again, but this time was different. It wasn't just because I had never been to the Draconis Combine. This was not a combat ticket or an inspection tour or a commercial-relations junket. We were responding to a challenge from a blood enemy. And if Colonel Carmody was right, we were walking into a trap.

The Wolf didn't seem to believe it was a trap, though. Or if he did, he didn't care. He had refused to allow a major force aboard the *Chieftain*. There would be only a single lance of BattleMechs: his *Archer*, my *Loki*, Hans Vordel's refitted *Victor*, and

Franchette's new *Gallowglas*. We had a skeleton staff, mostly Kurita specialists that Stanford Blake had insisted upon, but we were not equipped for battle. Luthien, the Kuritan capital world, was garrisoned by at least five BattleMech regiments. If it came to a fight, we would be overwhelmed.

I could not help but wonder whether the Wolf was planning to return to Outreach.

Two days later, my fears were only enhanced as I watched the emotional farewell between Colonel Wolf and his family. They all came to see us off. Even Alpin showed up, though he stood to one side with a band of bondsmen with whom he'd been keeping company. James and Lydia were there to bid me goodbye, and I discovered I was not as ready to part with their company as I had thought. Difficult as the leave-taking was, we did not make a public display of it. We had said our real goodbyes the night before. For all his public show, I thought Jaime Wolf must have done the same with Marisha Dandridge last night.

I envied Jaime Wolf's blood family. Theirs was a closeness different from the family of the sibko. It might not be better, but I thought it must be, if only because it was the form of affection and closeness that the Wolf chose. I found myself scanning the assembled crowd for a face that could not possibly be there. The adopted Clanners would deride me for it, but I searched for one warrior in particular, a short, raven-haired MechWarrior named Maeve.

How often had Jaime Wolf felt the pain of separation?

I watched the small man who had led the Dragoons for so long give his wife a last kiss, then stride away up the ramp. He was an old man, older perhaps than any other living Dragoon, but though the gray had conquered his once-jet black hair and beard, he was unbowed by the years. He had seen it all and done it all. Freeborn, he had won his way into the Wolf Clan's warrior caste and been given a greater command than any ever entrusted to a freeborn warrior. Years later, he had abandoned his mission in the belief that the way of the Clans was flawed, possibly wrong. He was a man of unyielding principle. Now he was on his way to a duel with the Coordinator of the Draconis Combine. Whatever the outcome, it would be sung in a new verse of the Dragoon *Remembrance,* another chapter in the legend of Jaime Wolf.

The boarding klaxon sounded and I hurried up the ramp.

20

"Fire two levels down. Second and Fifth Points down the core lift shaft. Third Point hold in engineering. Fourth with me," Edelstein ordered. As the Elemental Points deployed, Elson followed their movements by their tactical chatter. Occasional sounds of combat interrupted, but he was pleased. His Elementals were performing with precision to clear the *Alexander* efficiently. From the echoes of fire occasionally overlaying the communications, he judged that his troopers were showing proper restraint and using minimum force. It would not do to destroy what they had come after.

But something about what he was hearing began to nag at him until he realized what it was: Edelstein was dispersing his team wider than was either necessary or prudent. The boarding party from *Orion's Sword,* except for the group with MacKenzie Wolf, was gradually moving further away from the core sweep team of the *Hammer*'s Elementals. Elson had thought Edelstein a better tactical commander than that.

Returning to the shuttle, he recalled his Point. Battle armor cleared and ready for duty, Trooper Hanson welcomed him aboard. Elson ordered the man back into his restraint harness, then pulled himself up to the cockpit. After scanning the datascreens, he spoke to the pilot.

"Estimated time to *Alexander.* Direct course."

"It'll take me a minute to calculate."

"In that case, launch." Elson turned to head back for the passenger bay. "You can figure it out on the way."

He ignored the mumbled acknowledgement. The Point was strapping in when he climbed back into the bay. He took his own seat as the pilot cut power to the grapples and fired thrusters to adjust the shuttle's attitude. The main engines fired and the shuttle began its trip to the *Alexander*.

As they made their final approach, the tac channel between Edelstein and the *Hammer* erupted in bursts of static and the sound of small-arms fire. Elson urged the pilot to make the landing quickly. As he started to undo his harness, the pilot complied. Jolted by the hard contact, Elson was thrown free from his seat and slammed into a bulkhead. Only the protection of his battle suit prevented him from being harmed in all but dignity. Grabbing a grip iron near the hatch, he re-oriented himself. As soon as the docking confirmation light lit, he slammed his suit's fist into the airlock hatch release. The panel arched up and he slid through, leaving the rest of the Point to follow as they would.

He had been aboard ships of the *Alexander*'s class before and had a good idea where Edelstein was. He launched himself across the deck, bounced off the far wall, and darted down a supply shaft toward the lower levels. Unfamiliar with the ship design, his Point was slower. He left them behind.

Edelstein's channel was silent.

Elson found Fourth Point exactly where he expected them to be. There had been a battle and the Point had obviously come out on top. Bodies and spheres of spattered blood were floating everywhere in the zero-gee environment. Most of the bodies wore Dragoon uniforms. Elementals were dragging looter bodies out of the path of the corridor and securing them against convenient surfaces. Edelstein was bent over another corpse, and it wasn't until the Elemental captain straightened up that Elson saw that the man had been bending over the lifeless body of MacKenzie Wolf.

"What happened?"

Edelstein's suit went rigid. "The looters ambushed us, sir. I warned Colonel Wolf that we shouldn't advance too quickly through this stretch, but he insisted. I asked to lead, figuring the battle armor would provide cover for the troops behind us. The looters figured it out, too. They let us pass, then opened fire. We scoured them out, but it was too late. They killed MacKenzie Wolf and his men in their crossfire."

Edelstein made his speech so quickly and smoothly that it almost sounded rehearsed. Elson would have liked to look the man in the eye, but Edelstein was sealed in his battle suit, his face invisible behind the dark, vee-shaped viewport. Elson looked around the corridor, assessing the damage. It might have been as Edelstein said; it might not.

Nova Cats had no love for Wolves, trueborn or freeborn. He wouldn't mourn Wolf; mourning was reserved for the death of true warriors. MacKenzie was merely a true Dragoon, a traitor to the heritage of the Clans. If the looters had shot him down, it seemed like cosmic justice that an attempt to profit from the Clans' heritage had been the death of the man.

But if MacKenzie's death had been contrived, it could not have been the act of a single man. Elson found that fact significant. These Elementals might be more loyal to him than he had suspected. The possibility was important because one must always adapt to the circumstances that battle brings.

"*Hammer*, this is Elson. Medical teams to this location." He switched frequencies. "*Talbot*, Elson for Colonel Atwyl."

"Atwyl here. What's going on, Major Elson? We've been getting a lot of breakup in transmissions."

"Nothing good, Colonel. I believe we need to call a meeting of the officer's council. Colonel Wolf has been killed."

After a moment Atwyl said, "Acknowledged," and no more.

No orders, just an acknowledgement. Elson unclenched his teeth. Someone had to take control. "I suggest we meet aboard the *Talbot* one hour after the *Alexander* is declared secure. I also suggest that we keep the deaths quiet at least until then."

"Acknowledged."

Elson cut the channel. He was irked by Atwyl's ineffective response, but satisfied in other ways. There were opportunities here. And there was work to be done before the meeting on the *Talbot* if he was to take advantage of those opportunities. Meanwhile, other matters were even more pressing.

"Are there any wounded?"

"Not a one," Edelstein reported.

"Your troopers are the only survivors of the ambush?"

"Correct, sir."

As he had suspected. "Finish securing the ship."

"Yes, sir. We'll have it all cleaned up before you take command, sir." Edelstein saluted and led his men away.

Elson didn't think it would take very long.

Searching the chamber, Elson deliberately looked for any sign that MacKenzie Wolf and his men had not been killed by the looters. Everything he saw fit perfectly with Edelstein's account of the event. The only thing out of place was the excessive force used on the last looters, but that could be ascribed to the rage of men who had just seen their commanding officer gunned down.

Considering his conversation with Edelstein before

the boarding, Elson noted that he would have to be
very careful around the man. Edelstein was most efficient. He would be a useful, if dangerous, tool, but
with such dedicated men, Elson knew he could accomplish much.

21

The stars watched from their places high in Luthien's night sky. They, and the ghosts drifting along the streets, were the only ones to note the passage of the dark-clad man. He moved with a fluidity that would have surprised those who knew him as Taizo Homitsu. That MechWarrior never ran. He even walked with a slight limp.

Homitsu entered the storage facility and emerged moments later. The black duffel bag slung over his shoulder looked no fuller than before, but the ghosts knew it carried his long-hidden tool.

Hurrying down the street, Homitsu fretted. This was not the time he would have chosen, but his hand had been forced. Jaime Wolf was coming to Luthien. There was still work to do, things to be prepared.

Two blocks outside the compound he stopped. His breathing had become unsteady, which annoyed him. This was no time for mortal failings. Taking cover in an alley, he leaned against the wall to catch his breath. The calm was slow in coming, but come it did. At this point, haste could undo him, and he was determined to fulfill his vow, whatever the cost.

Composed, he leaned away from the wall. Ready again, he moved on. He was silent, one with the night. His passage went unremarked. The stars above watched, but they told no one. The ghosts were quiet.

Who could stop the man who did not fear death?

* * *

Dechan Fraser was familiar with ghosts, for so many haunted his dreams, but their visits were no less disturbing for that. The ghosts of Misery were the worst, and they were the ones who came to him tonight.

He slipped from the bed, surprised that Jenette hadn't been wakened by his thrashing. Or had his thrashing also been part of the dream? He crossed the hardwood of the bedroom floor, the polished boards cool and firm under his feet. Sliding open the screen, he looked out across the garden.

Luthien's stars twinkled in the predawn sky, a last hurrah before morning. Many of those stars had their own planets. For the worlds of those systems, each star was a sun whose burning light made day, while, here, each of those stars was no more than a single twinkling among the many lamps of the night.

Once Dechan himself had been called a rising star among Wolf's Dragoons, but now, other than the ghosts, how many Dragoons remembered him?

In the distance he could see the dark patch among the city lights that was the imperial palace. Takashi Kurita slept there tonight, satisfied. Ambassador Inochi had returned with word that Jaime Wolf had accepted the duel, and the late-night newscast had made much of the story. But Dechan Fraser had received no advance warning from Theodore or any of the Kuritans he knew. No warning had come from Dragoon agents, either. Once again, Jaime Wolf was coming to Luthien and Dechan was in the dark. He wondered if Michi knew about the duel. If he did, would he be pleased or annoyed?

Dechan didn't know his own mind; how could he predict the reaction of his old friend?

If, indeed, Michi had been his friend and not just another manipulator. It seemed that everyone used Dechan when it was convenient and forgot him when other matters demanded their attention. Everyone except Jenette. She had been as loyal to him as he to her. Yet she slept on, undisturbed by his doubt and anger. It was a burden he didn't wish to lay upon her.

He was still staring out the window when she awoke and crept up behind him to give him a sleepy hug.

"Up early," she said, kissing the back of his neck.

"I thought I'd see the sunrise."

She slid around him and draped his arm around her waist. "It's a beautiful one," she said, resting her head on his shoulder. "You should have awakened me."

"I didn't want to disturb you. You looked so peaceful." He kissed her hair. "There'll be other mornings."

"But never another today." She nestled closer. "We could start it off right."

He felt her hand caress his belly and move downward. His body responded before his mind, but when he kissed her, he let himself fall into her love. For a while at least, the rest of the world went away.

22

The *Talbot*'s conference room was crowded with every off-duty officer who could squeeze in. There were a fair number of ratings as well, all anxious to hear the Council of Officers. Their presence would prompt caution and even keep some arguments from entering the discussion, but, by Dragoon custom, this could not be a closed session. Elson could see that the presence of observers bothered some of the older Dragoon officers, especially Colonel Atwyl. Their nervousness reassured Elson that encouraging the lower-ranking Dragoons to attend had been a good strategy.

Elson also saw many of his Elementals scattered about the periphery of the chamber, their presence easy to spot because they stood head and shoulders above the crowd. He had not ordered them to come, but they had, spacing themselves judiciously around the conference room. He did not think it a coincidence that one stood near each of the other council officers. The precaution was probably unnecessary, but he was pleased that his men showed such initiative.

Content to listen through the preliminary debates, he sat back. The air was warm, and the laboring climate-control unit chugged faintly as it tried to compensate for heat generated by bodies in a quantity far exceeding the room's rating. He let the heat soak through him, loosening flesh and easing the passage of blood. He was calm, content to smile at Hamilton Atwyl as the rest of the council argued.

The first step involved adding a seventh officer to the council. Gilson's nomination of Edelstein was well-timed. The 'Mech jock presented her arguments well, just as Elson had rehearsed her. His seconding of the nomination brought rousing approval from the crowd. Atwyl pushed another two names onto the list before Brandon spoke from the crowd and demanded the roll call. When the balloting was over, Edelstein was confirmed by a final vote of four to two.

Returned to full strength, the council moved to its other business, the election of a new first among the officers. When Elson's name was the first put forth, Atwyl seemed ready to do battle. Then, after Captain Brandon confirmed Gilson's spirited account of the first minutes of the encounter with the looters, someone in the crowd began to chant Elson's name. Gradually more and more of the spectators took up the shout.

Amid the din Atwyl called for order and slowly got it, but his spirit seemed to have diminished in the heat of the general response. He spoke about the deep-space nature of the mission and the importance of having a commander who was trained in and understood the intricacies of such missions. But his argument was flawed and easily seen to be so; the mission's first commander, MacKenzie Wolf, had been a Mech-Warrior, not even an aerojock, let alone a deep-space commander. The increasingly restive crowd was quieted when Jessica Sedano, captain of the DropShip *Havelock,* stood and nominated Atwyl. Gilson, at a nod from Elson, seconded and immediately called for a decision. Only Sedano and Shankar, the aerospace flight leader, stood by Atwyl. Elson was named first officer of the council.

The news was broadcast throughout the JumpShip and her attached DropShips, as well as to the prize crews aboard the cache ships. Before the crowd in the conference room dispersed, Commtech Ishora entered the chamber and bulled his way through the crowd to the open space around the council table. He hesitated for a moment, then seemed to recollect the new order. Addressing Elson, he said, "A message from Dragoon command, Major."

"Colonel," Edelstein corrected. The first among officers was always a colonel, if only by courtesy.

"I'm sorry, Colonel Elson," Ishora stammered.

"It's all right. I'm not used to it myself." Elson took the flimsy and held it before him. He didn't need to read it; he had done that when Ishora had first brought it to him yesterday. Fortunately, the commtech was one of Elson's backers; the contents of the message might have tipped some of the wavering officers in the wrong direction. But now the message was his to announce, and his to interpret as necessary.

"Dragon command announces that Colonel Jaime Wolf has taken ship for Luthien. He is responding to a challenge from Takashi Kurita." He let the murmuring die down before adding, "The Coordinator has proposed a duel to the death."

There were shouts of disbelief and delighted cheers. Elson stood like a rock as the crowd washed around him, babbling excitedly. Some speakers expressed the opinion that Wolf had made a mistake, but they were in the minority. Most of the mission crew seemed glad to hear the news, although it was clear to Elson that their reasons for cheer were varied. The largest group, mostly younger Dragoons, were elated that the old Snake was going to get his, but some were simply relieved that the end of the feud with Kurita was at hand. Most of the latter were older Dragoons and their blood kin. They were the ones Elson needed to address.

He raised his hand and waited until the crowd noticed him. Hushing noises from those nearest him damped the sound, eventually quieting the gathering.

"Do you think this will end it?" he asked, pitching his voice to carry to those in the corridor outside the room. Some of his listeners nodded, but most only looked at him curiously. "I may not be native to the Inner Sphere, but I have studied its people. Those observations have taught me that, among all the peoples of the Successor States, the Kuritans are most like the Clans, especially in matters of honor. Even if Colonel Wolf kills Takashi Kurita, this feud will not end."

"If they are honorable, they will let it end," Atwyl said.

"You have not been attentive to the details, Colonel. The message from headquarters contains no indication that this duel is a surrogate for the feud. By all appearances, it is a matter of personal honor, one man settling matters with another—a Trial of Grievance. Therefore, the Kurita clan will not be bound by its outcome."

"I disagree," Atwyl stated. "With Takashi dead, Theodore will rule. He understands how destructive this feud has been and can be. He's no fool."

"Theodore Kurita is accounted a fine commander," Elson conceded. "But he is a member of the Kurita clan. Does not their honor code insist that a man may not live under the same heavens as the slayer of his father?" Atwyl reared his head back. He seemed about to say something, but Elson gave him no opportunity. "You know it is so. If Wolf wins, Theodore Kurita will be obliged to kill him. If Wolf dies, Takashi will be rid of the one man he believes has kept him from eliminating the Dragoons entirely. Win or lose, Wolf has put his personal honor before that of the Dragoons. Among the Clans, that is cause for dismissal."

There were objections from the crowd that the way the Clans was not the Dragoon way, but along with the protests were murmurs supporting Elson. Not enough to sway things, but enough to satisfy him that he had increased his base of influence. For now, that would serve. It was a long voyage back to Outreach.

"We can stand and talk or we can do our jobs. There are ships to reclaim for the Dragoons," he said. "That is a job we need to do, no matter what is happening elsewhere. Idle talk will only waste time."

He gave specific orders, careful not to exclude those who had supported Atwyl. Elson assigned his defeated rival duties suitable to his position as JumpShip commander, but left Atwyl nothing of real importance. Mission command was transferred to the *Alexander*.

Elson's personal kit had already gone aboard.

23

The Wolf summoned me to his ready room on the main operations deck of the *Chieftain*. He was seated behind his desk, shoulders slumped. I saw him straighten as the door slid open, but his eyes were ringed with exhaustion. Motioning me in, he indicated that I sit. As I did, he picked up a packet of computer disks and held it out to me.

"Brian, I'd like you to carry this packet back with you when the *Chieftain* returns to Outreach."

I reached across and took the pouch. It was sealed and looked important. As this was not a formal situation, I presumed on my privilege as a member of his staff and asked, "What is it, Colonel?"

"Some instructions for the officer council. This trip has given me the opportunity to work out some of the details for the integration, force utilization, and defense plans. I don't want to risk transmitting them, so you'll have to hand-carry them."

The packet in my hands suddenly became very weighty. "Why, sir? You'll be coming back with us."

He smiled wearily. "Most likely, but I've learned to take as few chances as possible."

"Coming to Luthien was a chance."

"Yes, but it seemed worth the gamble to settle things with Takashi. It's time to bury the past. Next time you see Stan, tell him that I finally came around to his point of view." He swiveled his chair so that I could see only his profile. "I'd like you to take over communications with Unity Palace. Clearance for the *Chieftain*'s shuttle to land at the private field has just come in, but the flight paths need to be coordinated."

I didn't like the tiredness in his voice, the hints of resignation to a preordained fate. I had never before seen him like this. I liked less the implications of what he was saying. "The shuttle won't carry your *Archer*, Colonel," I pointed out.

"That's true," he said, nodding slowly. "But I won't need it. Takashi has a BattleMech ready and waiting for me."

"Isn't that risky, sir? I mean, using a machine they provide. It could be rigged."

He sighed, then rocked his head back and closed his eyes. "You would never think to question the equipment your Dragoon trainers provide."

"They're Dragoons, sir."

"And therefore honorable."

I thought about Kantov and how the Colonel had paid for that man's dishonor. "As much as possible. You wouldn't have them as Dragoons otherwise."

"Not everyone believes as you do."

"Not everyone is as honorable as you, sir."

He swiveled his chair back and stared at me with his hard gray eyes. "Implying that Takashi has some dishonorable motive in this?"

"He might."

"Ever met him?"

"You know that I have not, sir."

"But I have." The Colonel lifted a computer disk on which I could see the crest of House Kurita. "He didn't send the assassin."

"How can you be sure?"

"This is a personal message disk from him. He says that he had no part in that affair."

"And you believe him?"

"Yes."

"He could be lying, sir."

"Would you lie about it, Brian?"

"I wouldn't have sent an assassin."

"Neither would he. Not in this case." He put the disk down. "Takashi won't step outside his code of honor. He wants this duel. I think he feels that he *needs* it."

"What about you, Colonel?"

He swiveled the chair until his back was to me before saying, "I'm here, aren't I?"

That seemed to be all he wanted to say, but I was reluctant to leave. "When will we be leaving the *Chieftain*, Colonel?"

"*We* won't," he replied sharply. "*I* will. I will be the only passenger in the shuttle to the surface."

Steeling myself, I said, "No, sir."

The chair swung around. "What?"

I refused to be intimidated. I knew Founder William Cameron had died at the Wolf's side after insisting on accompanying Wolf into danger that William was not equipped to handle. I might be committing myself to the same fate. Back in the sibko I had adored the tales of the founder's unswerving courage and dedication. How often I had dreamed that I would be the same way, but now it was so much more than an abstract ideal. That didn't make me less scared, however. I felt that if I looked Wolf in the eye, he would see that fear and I would be lost. So I stared at the wall behind his head. "Hans and I will be accompanying you, Colonel."

The Wolf sat back, surprised at my refusal. His eyes narrowed. I saw the motion and knew I could not afford to meet his gaze. "I can order you to remain aboard the *Chieftain*."

"I hope you won't, Colonel."

We sat there for a long time. It seemed like hours, but I know it wasn't. At last, he said, "Stan put you up to this, didn't he?"

I wasn't surprised that he guessed. "Yes, sir."

"I could make it an order."

I was sure he knew where that would put me, but I told him anyway. "If you don't come back, I'll have to explain to Colonel Blake why I didn't follow *his* orders, sir."

The Wolf stroked his beard. "Do you expect me to lose this battle?"

I opened my mouth, but said nothing for a moment. How could he think I doubted his ability in combat? Takashi Kurita might be among the best of the Inner Sphere warriors, but he was not Clan-trained like Jaime Wolf. There was no comparison. "I have every confidence that you can defeat Takashi Kurita in combat, Colonel."

"Carefully spoken, Brian. We've trained you well, maybe too well." He was quiet for a moment, then he leaned forward a little. "The Dragoons need you. Whoever leads the Dragoons needs you. You are too valuable an asset to risk."

"I have been in combat with you, risking both my life and yours simultaneously. You did not shield me then."

Sitting back, he said quietly, "Times change."

"They may, but I have already been risked by coming to the Luthien system. So has the *Chieftain*, which is more important to the leader of the Dragoons than any individual commo officer."

"You'll be safe enough in orbit," he said as I drew breath.

"Respectfully, sir. I will not be in orbit. You are the leader of the Dragoons, and if I am an important asset to the leader, I am important to you. Wherever you are."

His eyes were hard and his tone angry, but something about his expression held a hint of another emotion. "Will you refuse a direct order?"

I didn't want to answer that question directly. Hoping I had the strength for it, I met his gaze and said, "It's not just duty, Colonel. This is a matter of honor."

It was the Wolf's turn to be silent. His eyes stared into mine until there seemed to be nothing left in the universe but him and me. I thought I would flinch, but I didn't. After what seemed an eternity, he found whatever he was looking for. Turning away, he sighed. I might have heard him whisper the word, "honor." I also heard the words, "Don't worry, son. I won't put you in the position of refusing a direct order. If you survive this, you still have a career with the Dragoons."

24

"Is this wise, husband?"

Jasmine's voice was neither imploring nor accusing, but Takashi's answer was gruff.

"It is my will."

"If you are to be obstinate and duel Jaime Wolf today, you must be rested. An athletic match will tire you."

"I am not so old as that. *Kendo* calms me."

"You never claimed that in your matches with Subhash-*kun*."

"Those days are gone."

The Coordinator busied himself adjusting the straps of his *do*. Silently, Jasmine helped him. Her fingers were more nimble than his, and no less sure. The body armor secure, he stooped for his gloves and mask.

"I shall see that your cooling vest and best uniform are laid out. You will wish a bath?"

"That would be good."

"Husband . . ."

"Say nothing, wife."

Tears welled in her eyes, filling them. Takashi reached a gentle hand to wipe away the fugitives that coursed down her cheeks. With a sudden, fierce move, she clutched one of his hands in both of hers and pressed it to her lips. Sobbing, she fled the chamber, her feet drumming on the veranda that led to the main portion of the palace. Takashi held a hand out to her, but said nothing. His hand fell to his side and he stood staring at the empty door.

From within the *dojo* where Homitsu waited, he heard all that was said between the Coordinator and his wife. Like any servant of House Kurita, he gave no sign that he had heard what was not his affair. Takashi finally stepped from the mats at the edge of the room and onto the polished wood. Homitsu, now a part of the Coordinator's world, greeted him with a deep bow. The Coordinator bowed in return, deeper than the proper response to a mere servant.

"I apologize for keeping you waiting, Homitsu-*san*."

"I am at your disposal, Coordinator."

Takashi chuckled at some private joke. "You know, I used to practice with the Director of the ISF. They were hard matches, well-fought. I did not always win."

"Does the Coordinator have a complaint?"

"Iie," he said absently as he slipped into his mask and secured the ties that would hold the *men* in place. "No complaint."

"If it would be the Coordinator's wish, I had thought to suggest *bokken* today."

Takashi's expression was hidden behind his protective mask. "*Bokken*? Yes, the wooden swords will be more appropriate than *shinai* today. You know what is to happen today?"

"*Hai,* Coordinator."

"Do not hold back."

Homitsu finished tying on his own *men*. He was glad his face was hidden. "I will not."

They donned gloves and Homitsu offered two *bokken* to Takashi, letting his *karma* choose his course. The Coordinator hefted the wooden sword he'd selected and nodded in satisfaction. Homitsu gripped the remaining sword, feeling its weight. He took a deep breath and let it out slowly. *Karma.*

They bowed and began. The Coordinator's form was sharper than usual as he pressed his attack. Homitsu gave ground, blocking only. He shifted balance, *bokken* canted away from the best line of defense. The Coordinator's weapon slipped through, striking Homitsu on the *do* with a resounding crack.

Takashi backed away. "You are holding back more than usual."

"It is so, Coordinator."

"Ha! You finally admit it."

"*Hai,* Coordinator."

"Why?"

"This will be the last time we fight," Homitsu said gravely.

Takashi stiffened. "I did not know you thought so little of my skills as a warrior."

"I respect you as a warrior, Coordinator." That was no lie. Takashi's skills as a warrior had no bearing on other matters.

"But you believe I will lose to Jaime Wolf."

"*Iie,* Coordinator. You will not lose to Jaime Wolf."

Takashi frowned, his puzzlement overcoming his emotional control. Then, as if suddenly sensing the threat Homitsu posed, Takashi snapped his *bokken* up between them.

Homitsu brought his own weapon up as he moved forward. Now that they were engaged, it must be resolved quickly. No one must interfere.

The Coordinator did not let him take the initiative. Takashi struck quickly, murderous strength in his blows. Homitsu parried. And parried again as the fury of the Coordinator's attack forced him to retreat. Takashi's blows shifted target from the restricted zones of *kendo,* darting for areas unprotected by armor. Wielded with lethal intent, a *bokken* could be as deadly as a sword, breaking bones and smashing muscles instead of slicing them.

Homitsu could not let himself be defeated. His life

would be nothing if he failed today; his honor would be wind. The fire of his need burned him clean and the flames filled his limbs.

Takashi snapped a feint to the *men* and twisted it into a rising cut from the off-side. Homitsu took the blow on his armor, flowing with it. The impact made his head ring, but the *bokken* was deflected and Takashi's rhythm was broken. Homitsu's *bokken* darted out, thrusting for the Coordinator's face. Takashi danced back, as Homitsu intended. Pressing forward, Homitsu rained blow after blow on Takashi, forcing him further back. Always the flat of Homitsu's weapon contacted the Coordinator's flashing *bokken*. Flaws appeared in Takashi's defense. His breathing became ragged, a sign of slipping concentration. Homitsu smashed the Coordinator's *bokken* aside, whirling his own weapon up for a pear-splitting stroke. Helpless, Takashi stood to take the blow, but Homitsu halted his weapon as it kissed the Coordinator's *men*.

He took a step back, allowing the puzzled Coordinator to raise his *bokken* to a warding position. Thought one with action, Homitsu struck at Takashi's *bokken*. This time, the edge contacted the Coordinator's weapon. Wood parted. The shining blade concealed within the wood burst free to slice through Takashi's *bokken* just above the guard. Homitsu completed the great circle, stilling his movement only when the blade's point hovered at Takashi's throat.

The Coordinator let the useless hilt of his *bokken* fall to the floor. The sound was loud in the sudden silence. Homitsu waited while Takashi mastered his ragged breathing.

"You could have killed me."

Homitsu said nothing.

"That you did not tells me that you have more in mind. Do you expect to torture me?" Takashi tugged loose the knot securing his *men*, releasing the mask to fall to the floor. "One shout will bring the Otomo.

Any suffering you inflict will be of inconsequential duration, and I assure you that you will be disappointed in my response. Even if you manage to kill me, you will die shortly thereafter.''

The Coordinator's baiting meant nothing. Holding his sword steady in one hand, Homitsu removed his own *men*. The Coordinator made no move to escape or cry out. Homitsu didn't care what Takashi's reasons were; he was grateful that the Coordinator remained calm. Perhaps Takashi sensed the importance of the moment.

Over the clatter of Homitsu's mask falling to the floor, Takashi asked, ''What is it you want?''

''Your death.''

''Why?'' Takashi demanded without hesitation. ''We have no quarrel.''

''With Fukushu Homitsu you have no quarrel, Takashi Kurita, but I am no longer Homitsu. He is a fiction, a tool.'' The man who had denied his own name reached to his face and peeled away his eye patch. A dead white orb was revealed. ''I am Michi Noketsuna.''

The pronouncement did not disturb the harsh set of the Coordinator's face. His stern expression neither lightened nor darkened. To that implacability, Michi said, ''You say we have no quarrel, and in a sense you are correct. I am justice for another man's quarrel, an innocent man you sacrificed to your personal hatred. Minobu Tetsuhara was my lord and mentor. I bring *his* quarrel to you.''

''Tetsuhara,'' Takashi said slowly. ''He chose his response and died a true samurai. I honor him.''

''You killed him. He would not see the truth, as I have.''

''You are mistaken, as he was not.''

''In ancient Japan, there was once a samurai forced to commit *seppuku* because he was caught in the machinations and intrigues of a noble of the court. His name was Asano, and he made the only decision he could, as did his loyal retainers. As have I.

"I have been as loyal to my master Minobu Tetsuhara as Oishi Yoshio was to his lord Asano. Oishi left his life as a samurai and pretended he didn't care about his lord's fate. But all the time, he was preparing vengeance in his lord's name. So for years, he and his fellows waited until they could confront Lord Kira, the man who had forced death upon their lord.

"I, too, have denied my heritage and hidden my goal. Though I am but one and not forty-seven, as the loyal retainers of Lord Asano, yet I will have justice done. You are in my hands now. As the forty-seven offered Lord Kira the way of honor, I offer you now the chance to commit *seppuku*. Atone for your failure as a samurai's lord."

Takashi's eyes were glacial ice. "If I do not?"

"I will kill you," Michi said, his voice as cold as Takashi's eyes.

"You say that you are justice, yet I tell you that there is no justice in what you are trying to do. It was never my will that Minobu Tetsuhara die."

"Warlord Samsonov was your man."

"Samsonov was a fool," Takashi snapped "Ultimately he was his own man, and he paid for it. But you know that, don't you? It was you who killed him, not one of Wolf's Dragoons."

"I killed him," Michi confirmed. "He was not enough of a man to end his life honorably. I expect better of Takashi Kurita."

"There is much I was blind to during those years," Takashi said. "Just as there was much that you could not see, or seeing, understand. Your vendetta is misplaced."

The Coordinator talked of the political maneuvering that went on around Wolf's Dragoons during their contract with the Draconis Combine. He spoke of Warlord Samsonov and the man's hatred for the Dragoons and for Jaime Wolf, in particular. He had not, Takashi declared, ordered Samsonov to do what had been done to the Dragoons; in particular, he had not ordered the attack on the Dragoon families.

If Takashi was to be believed, his concerns for the Combine had been misinterpreted by Samsonov. Michi felt the seeds of doubt begin to break the soil of his mind. If Takashi had not ordered Samsonov's actions, there was no reason for vendetta against the Coordinator. He was wrong in demanding Takashi's death.

Takashi enumerated the threats that had faced the Combine in those days. Emphasizing his paramount concern for the survival of the realm, Takashi asserted that no one person could put his own concerns ahead of the Combine. Michi could not disagree; he had set aside his own desires more than once in favor of the Combine's survival. Takashi believed that the importance of the realm's survival justified the actions necessary to ensure that survival. He spoke of manipulating the warlords, pitting them against one another and constantly testing their loyalty, as a tool to that end. Sometimes, regretfully, tools broke or were misused. The Coordinator implied that Samsonov had misunderstood, had usurped prerogatives reserved for the Coordinator.

Despite Takashi speaking of his own clan and the Combine as one, Michi found the Coordinator's arguments seductively persuasive, But what if all the arguments were merely another manipulation? What if they were simply lies?

Sounds impinged on his awareness. The scuff of a footfall on *tatami* mats. A soft mechanical whine. The rustle of cloth against flesh. Banishing his doubt, Michi dropped into warrior awareness. He felt the hardwood grain under his fingers and saw the flicker in the light that told of moving bodies.

He and Takashi were no longer alone.

═══ 25 ═══

Restoring the cache ships and organizing them into a convoy was a task unlike any Elson had ever commanded. He was surprised to find himself interested in the details and intricacies of coordinating the efforts of his command. His enemies in the council of officers seemed even more surprised, while his own faction simply took his abilities for granted.

The trip back to Outreach along a command circuit was as long as the trip out, but instead of drilling Elementals, Elson spent his time dealing with a wider variety of concerns. It was a different way of preparing for the future. Each time they lay over, recharging their drives or transferring to a waiting JumpShip, he visited some of the other DropShips and made himself known to the crews. Though he spent most of his time with the warriors, he did not neglect the techs or the scientists. Any good warrior understood the importance of those who designed and maintained weapons. By showing that he understood their roles, he won their loyalty with surprising ease.

By the time the convoy reached the Dragoon homeworld once more, Elson would have a strong cadre of people who believed in him and his vision. He knew that he would never convert Atwyl and his cronies; the oldsters were the most committed to the erroneous path of Jaime Wolf. Wolf commanded their respect and loyalty with such force that otherwise clear-thinking warriors ignored centuries of tradition. It was not something Elson could ignore, and it worried him constantly.

But he saw hope. Even at the funeral, some had spoken of MacKenzie Wolf's failings. The talk had not been public or in the recorded eulogies, but it was there. It became more common as the journey went on. Even some of the oldsters had been heard to speak of MacKenzie's corruption by easygoing spheroids. Jaime Wolf had not passed on his genius to his son, and now that MacKenzie was dead, there was no reason to pretend otherwise.

"The flaws of the offspring reflect the flaws of the parentage," said an old Clan proverb. Breeding rights went to those who performed, those who had proved themselves. Those who were disgraced lost all rights and privileges. The blood told the true story.

It was not hard to see that Jaime Wolf's bloodline was flawed, however successful he had been. Clanners understood that a flawed commander was a sentence of death, and no one wanted such a sentence. Clanners knew, too, that old men lose sight of the day they live in, preferring the past and its security. Such a commander would sooner or later fail his warriors, betraying them to an undeserved death or a disgraceful failure.

Fear is a warrior's constant companion, but the true warrior masters his fears. In doing so, he conquers and fulfills his destiny. Death is not a threat to a real warrior; he knows there is no escaping death. It is his job to deal in death, so he must understand its ways and, more importantly, the meaning of death. A death without meaning was the real fear of a true warrior.

But these Dragoons, Clanner or spheroid, misunderstood that reality. They had come to believe that life was their prize, that by excelling they could leave their warrior natures behind and go on to something else. How could they ignore the warrior's knowledge of the precariousness of life? They had fallen into an old man's way of thought. Jaime Wolf feared for his Dragoons and worried over their ability to survive. For years his actions had been directed toward reducing his fears, and this mission to recover the cache ships was only the latest step in Wolf's plan.

But Wolf's vision was clouded, distorted by his own rejection of his heritage. He had forgotten that a warrior's lot is death and dreamed that the cache ships and their technology could preserve the Dragoons. It was a foolish dream. Weapons are worthless without warriors to wield them, and warriors cannot ply their trade without death.

Wolf could not see the truth growing around him, but Elson could. He listened to the men and women who wore Dragoon uniforms. Occasionally he heard spheroids use Clanner arguments when they spoke of their fears. By spending time with them, he learned that they wanted to be warriors and how much they longed to walk the path of honor. Wolf was a fool to deny the Dragoons that.

Jaime Wolf's old man's ways would cost both him, and the Dragoons, if nothing were done.

When the Clans had returned to the Inner Sphere, life had changed forever. A new order was at hand. Elson was part of that new age, and those around him could see it. Soon all the Dragoons would know it.

26

From behind a concealed panel Subhash Indrahar's powered chair rolled into the chamber, the *tatami* mats crackling under pressure from the tires. The hated Ninyu advanced with him, stopping to stand behind his adopted father. Ninyu directed the squad of black-clad ISF troopers who followed him, coordinating their positioning with a second squad who entered by the doorway from the gardens. Each trooper held a Shimatsu 42, a short-barreled machine pistol made long-snouted by a sound suppressor.

While Michi stood gauging the new arrivals, the Coordinator took a step back, removing himself from the danger of Michi's sword.

"Your arrival is timely, old friend," he said to Subhash.

"So it would seem," Subhash replied, giving his famous smile.

Michi sensed confusion in the Coordinator and tasted the flavor of it in himself. Michi was armed and the Coordinator was not, but Indrahar was focused on Takashi.

The ISF Director spread his hands wide in a gesture of helplessness. "We find ourselves in a most regrettable situation, Takashi-*sama*. Saving you from this man will only preserve you for a short while. Jaime Wolf is already on his way down from orbit, fully prepared to meet you in a duel."

"As I intended," Takashi said in a cautious voice.

Subhash stopped smiling. "I warned you that this course held no good for the Combine. You chose not to heed me."

"As much as I value your advice, old friend, it is honor that compels my actions."

A brief frown flickered across Indrahar's face. "The Combine's survival is your honor, as it is mine. This duel with Wolf is counter to that survival. It should not take place."

"My life is of little consequence to the Combine's survival. If I fail, Theodore will succeed me. He will rule well."

"Well enough, when his time comes," Indrahar agreed, again with a smile. "I had hoped it would not be for some time, but even Theodore cannot save a Combine crippled beyond hope." The smile vanished as he added, "You did not have to accelerate matters to this point."

"I have followed the dictates of my honor and conscience."

"As a samurai?"

"Simply so."

"You are the Coordinator, not a simple samurai. You have concerns other than petty, insult-driven honor duels. This is no simple matter."

"No. It is not."

A wary look came into Indrahar's eyes. He folded his hands in his lap and said, "Regrettably, your decisions have forced the issue."

"I will listen to your argument," Takashi said calmly.

"I am not here for argument," Indrahar countered. "That time is past. *Any* outcome of this duel will be dangerous. If Wolf wins, the Combine's prestige is irreparably damaged. Theodore will most certainly be counseled to pursue revenge, and a small possibility does exist that he might choose that fruitless and costly path. Excuse my bluntness, Takashi-*sama*, but if you win, no one, especially the Dragoons, will believe that the fight was fair. There is a rising faction of Clan sympathizers within their ranks. Any antagonism offered by the Inner Sphere could play into the hands of that faction, forcing a change in loyalties that could well cost the Inner Sphere the support of the Dragoons. Such a course would likely result in the fall of the Inner Sphere, and thus of the Combine.

"Even should Wolf's faction retain control, they cannot be expected to deal kindly with the House responsible for their leader's death. Though they have withheld their services, they have not banished our military leaders from their anti-Clan strategy sessions or our scientists from the technology conferences. This would change were you to defeat Wolf. Without those advantages, the Combine cannot withstand the Clans.

"And what if you should you lose? Would our own people allow the government to treat with the Dragoons? Your own previous pronouncements have influenced their attitudes only too well. I doubt a victorious Wolf would be allowed to leave Luthien alive. Whether you are victorious or not, the result of your duel is the same in the end. The Combine will lose."

"Your assessment is overly pessimistic. The Combine is strong. Theodore is strong. We beat the Clans back from Luthien."

"Only with the aid of Wolf's Dragoons and other mercenaries," Indrahar pointed out. "Did you not once order death to all mercenaries?"

The Coordinator glared at him.

"Your foresight failed you then as it has now, Takashi-*sama*. The Combine cannot afford such a fallible leader any longer."

Takashi's manner hardened into rigidity. "I do not care for what you are suggesting."

"Nor do I. Your obsession has brought us to this impasse. Regrettable though it may be, I can see only one solution. For the Combine to live, the Coordinator must die.''

Takashi tensed, but said nothing. His eyes surveyed the room and the grim faces of the ISF agents. They were all obviously loyal to Indrahar, heart and soul. Indrahar continued to speak.

''I had hoped you might be persuaded to see the honorable solution, but you have resisted Noketsuna's arguments. You seemed, in fact, to weaken his own resolve. I will ask you to reconsider taking the path onward.''

''I am the Coordinator. *My* will is the will of the Combine. I have nothing to atone for.''

Subhash shook his head sadly. ''I had hoped you would see that the Combine is more important than any man. It is your dynasty that rules; that will continue, even if you personally do not.''

The chair pivoted a quarter-turn. Without looking at him, Subhash ordered, ''Complete your vendetta, Noketsuna. We will not interfere.''

Michi stared at the director of the ISF. This was not in the proper ordering of the universe. Vengeance, the death of Takashi Kurita, was not supposed to be a political solution of some kind. It was a matter of honor, a matter between samurai. Whatever else Michi had become during the long years of his vendetta, he was no one's political executioner. In preparing himself for this day, he had seen himself as a tool, a tool of honor. He did not care to be the tool of a faithless servant, a pawn in someone's games of power. Minobu Tetsuhara had been forced into death as the pawn of a power-hungry man.

But there were too many men, too many guns for one man to overcome. If he did as Indrahar demanded, Indrahar might allow him to live. But he doubted it. If he refused, the ISF men would simply cut him down. Whatever he did, Michi knew he would not leave the *dojo* alive.

He turned to the Coordinator.

"The right or wrong of my vendetta seems no longer to apply, Coordinator. I speak to you as samurai to samurai. My words shall not live long, for none other than you and these honorless dogs shall hear them."

"Get on with it, Noketsuna," Ninyu said irritably.

Michi ignored him. Staring into Takashi's eyes, he searched for understanding. He found the Dragon.

"I stand at a fork in the path of honor. Whichever way I walk, I abandon some of my honor in the course of fulfilling my honor. This is the lot of a samurai. My lord Minobu understood this. I now see as he saw." Michi raised the sword into *jodan-no-kamae* guard. "I am samurai, loyal to the Dragon. I, too, serve the Combine."

The Coordinator stared unflinchingly into his eyes. Michi steadied himself, reaching for the center of his *hara* and drawing strength. Calmed, he was ready for his death, which seemed inevitable this day.

He spun and charged Subhash Indrahar.

The move seemed to catch everyone off guard. The ISF agents failed to respond. Michi closed half the distance before Ninyu drew his pistol, another quarter before the man fired. Michi spun under the impact of the heavy slug, but managed another step toward the chair. His right arm hung limply at his side, blood pulsing out from his shoulder and pouring down his sleeve. The world was edged in spinning fireworks, but he still held the sword in his left hand. He took another step forward.

Ninyu fired again.

This time the pain flared in fire from his belly, disrupting his *hara* and shredding his resolve. He had gotten farther than he expected. No longer able to feel the sword in his hand, he wondered if it was still there. Tumbling backward, he slammed his head against the hardwood floor. There was no strength in his body and he felt his life pumping from him. His vision dimmed.

One of the ISF agents stepped forward. Slinging his Shimatsu, he retrieved Michi's sword from the floor, but did not attack. In the pause, Takashi knelt by the the fallen Michi and touched the warrior's brow. "He was a true samurai and understood *giri*. His loyalty to the Combine is stronger than yours, Subhash."

"He was loyal and loyalty is a great strength, but his understanding of *giri* was shortsighted, as you yourself pointed out to him, my old friend. He could not be expected to see the grand vision I work to attain. For you, I had greater hopes."

Takashi stood, his face was hard. "I am sorry to disappoint you."

"I am sorry as well."

"Will you announce that he killed me?"

"It would be a convenient story, but not one that would serve the Combine. To make public the story of the Coordinator's death at the hands of a Combine citizen would only weaken the Combine. Theodore will believe such a story, though, and he will agree to announce that you died in your sleep. You have had a long and full life, Takashi-*sama*. I wish you well in the next one."

The chair made another quarter-turn and began to roll back into the hidden room from which it had come.

"Agent Wilson." Ninyu addressed the agent with the sword. "Make the strike clean. Noketsuna was a master of the sword, after all."

Wilson bowed and, turning to Takashi, raised the sword high.

27

Takashi did not wait for the man to strike. Snapping a low kick, he shattered the other man's kneecap, but the effort cost him. He grunted involuntarily from the pain in his own wrenched knee. Being samurai, he put aside the fire in his leg and snatched the sword from the collapsing Wilson. The ISF agent's head left his body under the edge of the blade.

"No guns!" Ninyu called. "He must die by steel. First squad."

The agents who had entered with Ninyu slung their automatic weapons and drew swords from the scabbards lashed to their backs. Steel whispered against lacquered wood, the only sound in the chamber. The Coordinator raised the sword high over his head and slowly lowered it into *chudan-no-kamae* guard.

"A blade is too good for dogs such as you, but the curs are many and I but one. Come and die."

A burly agent, deceptively fast for his bulk, rushed the Coordinator. Their blades rang in belling parries until Takashi slid his sword along the agent's and turned the edge, slicing the man's neck as he withdrew. The dead man fell, a soughing moan coming from his slit windpipe.

The first encounter displayed the Coordinator's weakness to his opponents; Takashi's wrenched knee limited his movement. A second agent stepped up to fence at long range, trying to draw him out. Takashi stood firm, refusing to fall for the ploy. Instead, he sucked the agent into a trap of his own. Letting the agent's sword pass through his guard, he took a blow on his *do*. He had seen the lack of strength in what the agent had obviously intended to be a feint. The unexpected success of her unparried blow opened the agent to a counterstroke. Takashi's sword took her in the belly, gutting her. A second stroke cut upward across her torso and flung her back into her companions.

The others became more cautious and began to circle Takashi. He held his ground, keeping his back to the fallen Michi. The agents could not come at him that way without tripping over the body.

Two closed together, striking high and low. Takashi pivoted on his weak leg, dropping low as he did. The first agent's sword met his steel and the second's whistled over his head. Blade to blade, Takashi heaved himself up and threw his opponent back by sheer strength. The other agent's sword sliced through his kimono, scoring the flesh of his right arm. Takashi's single-handed return stroke caught the overextended agent on his own arm, but it bit deeper. The agent's sword clattered to the floor and he staggered back, spouting blood.

The first closed again and Takashi barely managed a parry. They exchanged a rapid series of blows, their blades a chiming gamelan of sound. To maintain the initiative, Takashi was forced to advance. With a sudden, sharp ping, the agent's sword snapped. Takashi ran him through with a quick thrust. Shoving the open-mouthed agent off his sword, Takashi retreated to his original position.

"Second squad," Ninyu said.

Five more swords were drawn as agents moved to reinforce the single survivor of the first squad. Ninyu stood at the edge of the room and watched. Takashi was tired, his swordsmanship beginning to falter. Even if the second squad was inferior to the first, they would likely kill the Coordinator.

Shouts echoed in the garden.

Ninyu cursed, and Takashi smiled. The agents stopped their advance. The closest backed away a step, retreating to a safer range while they looked questioningly to their leader.

"I will hunt you down," Takashi said.

Ninyu shrugged in exaggerated nonchalance. "You have no evidence, Coordinator. This was undoubtedly an attempt by a dissatisfied faction of renegades. Perhaps it was the work of Davion infiltrators. There will be evidence to that effect." His eyes kept darting to the garden entrance. "Let the matter go. Even you must know that the Combine could not survive if you decapitated the ISF at this point in history."

Takashi's voice was cold and unforgiving. "We have survived traitors before."

"The ISF serves the Combine, not the Kuritas. Who are the real traitors, you glory-bound samurai?"

Takashi took a step forward and his voice trembled with rage. "I will kill you myself."

Ninyu laughed at him. "If I thought that you would live to see another day, I might be concerned, Coordinator. But you will reap what you have sown, for you will die at Jaime Wolf's hand. A fool's death."

Hard footfalls slapped thunderously on the veranda. The Otomo would arrive in seconds.

"I must go. Enjoy your duel, Coordinator," Ninyu said.

The ISF agents slipped through the opening from which they had emerged. Ninyu slid the panel closed, apparently assured that he and his agents would be long gone before the Otomo could force their way through the wall.

Dead men dressed in black lay strewn about the chamber. One, only wounded, drew a knife from his

belt and joined his colleagues. Takashi was left standing alone within a ring of bodies.

A handful of men rushed into the *dojo*, a dozen Otomo and half again that number of Izanagi Warriors. Some were wearing the ceremonial armor of the palace guard, others wore duty uniforms or off-duty clothing, a few were half-dressed. All were armed. They halted just inside the doorway, stunned by the carnage surrounding the Coordinator.

Theodore pushed his way through them. He surveyed the room before holstering his pistol.

"Father?"

"I am barely wounded."

"No thanks to your bodyguard." His tone promised retribution for the breach in palace security. "Where is Shin Yodama?" There was no answer from the assembled guards. No one cared to speculate where the head of the guard could be. "He was on duty. Find him."

A woman in the uniform of Yodama's Izanagi Warriors dashed off. Still unsure, the other guards remained clustered at the door. Takashi knelt and laid his bloody sword on the floor. He looked exhausted.

"It will do no good."

"You killed them all?"

Takashi shrugged. "There might have been more. Perhaps it is a good idea to search the garden."

Theodore glanced at the guardsmen and nodded once. All but two rushed away. The pair who remained took up stations at the door. Theodore knelt at his father's side.

"You must see a physician."

"First you must hear what happened here."

A flash of puzzlement crossed Theodore's face. He leaned closer to listen to Takashi's whispered account of the confrontation with Indrahar. Takashi concluded, "For all that I do not care to have the decision made for me, Indrahar's evaluation of the situation has merit.

I was too blinded by my own concerns to see what a duel with Wolf would bring.''

"Perhaps a reconciliation with Wolf . . .''

"*Iie*. The Coordinator did no wrong. Wolf's public insult cannot be ignored.'' Takashi closed his eyes. "But I see what Michi Noketsuna saw before he spent his life for the Combine.''

"Surely we can find another course.''

"You never were comfortable with the code.'' Takashi almost smiled. "I am a samurai and I believe in the old ways. That may not be what is necessary to guide our realm into this new age. Certainly, you have shown me that new ways are necessary to deal with new problems. Perhaps in this I can show you that the old ways are not to be despised. In some circumstances, *bushido* is the answer to problems that no amount of flexibility can surmount.''

"Father, this is not the answer.''

"This is an old and tired samurai's answer.'' Takashi indicated Michi with a slant of his head. "Such strange *karma*. He put aside his personal honor for the greater good of the realm, defending my life against those who would take it unlawfully. He wanted my *seppuku* today, and today I will go onward. But I— we—cannot allow the truth to be known. My honorable passing must be cloaked in a dishonorable lie. For the good of the realm. Indrahar wanted the people to believe that I had died in my sleep. Let his lie serve us as well as him, let that be the tale. You must tell no one the truth, not even Jasmine.''

"I do not approve,'' Theodore said sternly.

"I am the Coordinator. In this, I do not need your approval.''

"I may not share your vision of the code, but do not forget that you had me soundly schooled in *bushido*. You cannot lie down in front of your enemies. Tetsuhara-*sensei* would not approve.''

"Perhaps you are right, but that old man is a stricter advocate of the code than I. Much as I am stricter than you. I believe he would tell you that a man's honor is in his heart, not in the eyes of other people. He understood the death of his son Minobu.

"Perhaps this course I choose shows me as weak, perhaps as strong. You may decide for yourself. I have made the decision to pass the fight to my heir. I will take the feud with the Dragoons with me, for the sake of the Combine. Though this means I die with my honor insulted, this lesser failing of honor serves a greater one. The realm must survive; it is our sacred duty as members of Clan Kurita to see that it does."

Theodore tried to argue, but Takashi ordered his silence. Resigned, Theodore left to obey his father's demand for writing materials. While he was gone, a physician arrived. Dismissing the man's attentions, Takashi directed him to attend to Michi, saying, "See that his body is treated with honor, for he was an honorable samurai."

Theodore returned, now dressed in kimono and *hakama* and wearing the paired swords of his samurai rank. His father was kneeling where he had left him. The Kanrei placed the tray he carried by his father's side. Lifting off a pile of white garments, he revealed a lacquered black box with an exquisite design of gold cherry blossoms.

"A good choice," Takashi said.

"Traditional," Theodore said.

"You honor an old man."

"I honor my father."

Takashi lifted the cover from the lacquered box and laid it to one side. Removing the tray of writing materials, he took a single sheet of rice paper and laid it before him. After preparing the ink, he selected a brush. He remained poised, brush in hand, for several minutes. Then he dipped the brush into the ink and held it for a moment before stroking bold characters onto the pristine paper.

He spoke as he wrote,

"Sunset, the dragon weeps;
Night to day as winter, spring;
Sunrise, the dragon roars."

Takashi put down the brush. It rolled from the lacquer tray onto the floor, splattering tiny drops of ink onto the rice paper.

"An untidy end," he said softly as he rose.

Taking the short sword Theodore offered him, Takashi retired to the garden.

Silent, Theodore followed.

28

Hans and I were in the shuttle two hours before its scheduled departure, so I was on hand when the Wolf boarded an hour later. He smiled ruefully when he saw us.

"Good morning, gentlemen. You're up early."

"We know our duty, Colonel," I said.

"Hmm. I've got a few things I need done. Hans—"

"I'll call a steward, Colonel."

"I see. Never mind. Is the crew ready?"

"Yes, Colonel."

"Then let's be about it."

The flight down was uneventful. We set down on the grounds of Unity Palace, well away from the main building and halls. I was concerned at once when I saw several BattleMechs prowling the edges of the tarmac. The Kuritans who greeted us assured us that the 'Mechs were standard security, but I knew otherwise from studying Stan's briefing.

The courtesy with which we were met was strictly formal. In Kuritan terms that meant a lot of flowery distractions and well-mannered delays. Colonel Wolf grew annoyed, though he hid it well. The hours crawled by but eventually the designated hour for the meeting with Takashi drew near. Meanwhile, our escorts seemed unaware of the passage of time.

Finally the Colonel's patience collapsed. Addressing

the old general who headed the escort delegation, he asked, "When will we be leaving for the meeting with Takashi-*sama*?"

The general stiffened, then bowed.

"My apologies, Colonel Wolf. I am most remiss. The schedule has been changed. Due to pressing business, the Coordinator is unable to meet with you at the agreed-upon time. Your understanding in this matter would be most appreciated."

"I thought Takashi wanted to get this over with."

The general looked very uncomfortable. "I obey the Coordinator's orders, Colonel Wolf. I am only authorized to say that you may meet with the Coordinator this evening."

"What about the duel?"

"That you must discuss with the Coordinator."

The Wolf folded his arms. "I was told that there was a BattleMech prepared for me. Do I at least get to see it?"

"A moment please, Colonel." The general held a hurried conversation with an aide wearing the black dress uniform of the Internal Security Force. Their whispers finished, he bowed to the Wolf and said with a smile. "If you wish. If not, other amusements may be arranged for you and your men."

"I'll see the 'Mech," the Colonel said bluntly.

"We are at your service, Colonel Wolf," the general said with another bow.

I doubted it, but they did lead us to a blue and gold *Archer* that mimicked the color scheme of Jaime Wolf's machine. We spent the afternoon checking it out and found it to be in almost perfect condition, though its ammo bays were empty. The Colonel seemed satisfied with the 'Mech, but I still worried about what the Kuritans had in mind.

Gobi Station maintains a geosynchronous orbit over a small island 160 kilometers off the east coast of Outreach's smaller continent. The orbital mechanics made for a short flight up from Harlech and a longer inbound trip. Useful for political reasons, useful now for Elson's reasons. He made sure he was in the bay when Alpin Wolf's shuttle arrived.

"I got your message," Alpin said as he walked up to Elson.

Direct. "I am glad you could come. I thought it best to give you the news first."

"News? The whole planet knows your news. You've—excuse me, *you have* come back with the cache ships."

"That is not what I am talking about." Elson turned slightly, letting the light shine on the rank insignia affixed to his collar, a colonel's star. The bright burnish of the longest point marked it as the insignia of the First among officers. Elson would not wear it much longer, but it would serve him now.

Alpin's eyes were drawn by the flash. Whatever he had been about to say died in his throat as he reached the obvious conclusion. His mouth hung open like that of a gaffed fish. Finally he stammered, "My father's dead?"

"I am sorry for your loss," Elson said solemnly. "He died in an ambush. There were looters aboard some of the ships. There were other losses as well."

Alpin shook his head slowly, brow furrowed. Several times he started to speak, then stopped before any words came out. Elson waited.

"Were you there?" Alpin asked tentatively.

"I was leading the capture of the looters' DropShip. When I realized there were ambushers on the ship he had boarded, we crossed to the *Alexander* as quickly as we could, but we were too late. His passing left a void."

In a bitter but unfocused voice, Alpin said, "So you stepped in."

Elson bowed his head. "The officers saw fit to name

me first among officers. I could replace him on the mission, but I cannot do that here. You still live, and Dragoon custom seems to decree that you are now Jaime Wolf's heir, since his only surviving son is far too young to command.''

''But that's not . . .''

''Was not MacKenzie to replace Jaime when his father stepped down? I've heard nothing else since the day I took my bondsman's band. It is only logical that you will now be Jaime's successor as leader of the Dragoons.''

''But I . . .''

''I know, my friend. I understand.'' Elson laid his hand on Alpin's shoulder. The boy was trembling. ''You are not yet ready for such responsibility, having been hidden for so long in the shadow of your father. But you will succeed; I have confidence in you. You will choose good men to aid you, men who understand what you have suffered at the hands of a jealous father. What honest man would not support your claim?''

Elson watched the slackness of Alpin's stunned expression stiffen into a grimace of calculation.

''You will help me?''

''I see no other course.'' Elson tightened his grip on Alpin's shoulder. ''Have you not felt that it is your destiny to command the Dragoons?''

''Yes,'' Alpin said softly. ''You know, I always thought it was.''

He seemed to look inward for a second. ''They knew it, too. My father and grandfather, I mean. I can see it now. They always made my tests harder so I wouldn't score well. It must have been to prevent jealousy among the others. Yes, that's what the old Wolf would do. He set it up to fool them all so they wouldn't hate me.''

''No one hates you, Alpin.'' *You are far too weak to deserve hate.*

''But they don't like me.''

"It is a commander's lot to be disliked. Most of the emotion comes from jealousy."

"Yes, you're right," Alpin said. "It's because they're jealous."

"They will be more jealous when you take Jaime's place."

Alpin looked up with a worried expression. "You won't be jealous of me, Elson, will you?"

"I have no reason to be, my friend," Elson said with an honest smile.

"Then you will help me, *quiaff?* You will watch my back when I am in charge. I will need loyal men like you, men who know the right of things."

"You will have my help, but you will need more."

"Just hearing you say that makes me excited and worried at the same time. I'm—excuse me—*I am* glad that I can count on you, but you are right. I will need more help. There are too many Dragoons who believe the results of those rigged tests. The old Wolf's plan has backfired. His old men think I am not fit to be a commander."

"They will not always be around. Among the Clans, such old men would have been retired long ago, letting the next generation keep the blood of the leadership fresh and forward-looking. It is the way of life, one generation yielding to the next, the better generation. Your own grandfather encourages the old ones in their selfish thinking by clinging to his own command."

Alpin nodded vigorously. "It *is* a bad example."

"As you say."

"But what can I do about it?"

Elson wrapped his arm around Alpin's slender shoulders. "Come," he said. "I have a few ideas."

29

Michi Noketsuna had not expected to live. He had thought that his decision to face the Coordinator was fatal, whether he fulfilled his vendetta or not. Then Indrahar and the ISF had intervened and, in electing to attack the ISF Director, Michi believed he had chosen a path to certain death. To awaken in the care of a member of the Physicians of the Dragon Brotherhood was a bizarre twist of fate, a peculiar reward for his chosen course.

Truly, his *karma* was strange.

The fact of his survival was a puzzle that he pondered as he drifted in and out of sleep. Once, he thought he heard a doctor whispering to another that Takashi was dead and that Michi had saved him from an assassin. How could both be true? His own recollections were muddled, his constant drowsiness only obscuring things further. Perhaps with time, the mist would lift from his mind.

He slept.

When he was aware again, he considered what he had heard the doctors say. If Takashi was dead, what more reason had Michi to live? The vendetta that had driven him was complete. Takashi was dead. That, he thought with sudden certainty, was true.

But the Coordinator had not died at Michi's hand or in atonement for wrongs done to Minobu-*sensei*, which left Michi a failure. The tubes and machines the

Brotherhood were using to sustain his existence made a mockery of him. His life was over. Why work to sustain a body when the reason for life is gone? His consciousness faded, but he remained tied to his body.

There was no release for him.

· *Karma.*

He woke again.

The room was full of light, far brighter than artificial illumination could make it. It was day. Someone had opened the drapes to let in the sun. And someone was still in the room, standing by the bed.

That person was not wearing the bright yellow of a Brotherhood physician. Though Michi was sure that he knew the man, the tall visitor's face refused to resolve into recognizable features. It was not until the visitor spoke that Michi saw that it was Theodore Kurita, the man who had chained Michi with the bonds of duty, who had demanded, rightfully, that Michi put service to the Combine before any personal desires.

Theodore nodded gravely when he saw that Michi's eyes had focused on him and said, ''My father told me of your decision in the *dojo.*''

Michi wanted to tell Theodore to go away and leave him to his search for hell, but his voice would not work. Theodore ignored the feeble sounds.

''He asked me to give you a command again, as a reward for your loyalty to the Combine. The health of the realm was much on his mind. He said that you would make a good warlord. Anywhere but Dieron, he said.''

An attempt at a head shake was thwarted by rebellious muscles. Michi's head simply rolled onto its side.

''I think Dieron would be the ideal place,'' Theodore said.

''No,'' Michi croaked, finding his voice at last. ''Not Dieron. Not anywhere. I never was a politician, just a soldier. Now, I am not even that. There is no place for me in your army.''

"You are tired and injured; do not decide hastily. I know what you did, and I remember how we met. You told me then that duty was the most important part of a samurai's life and that the duty to the Combine was the greatest burden a man could bear. That duty never goes away, Michi-*kun*. The Combine stills needs you, now more than ever. When you are ready, there is a place for you in the Ryuken. The command of Ryuken-*ni*, if you want it.''

"Fraser commands.''

"So you remember him? He would be pleased to hear it. Yes, he commands, but I have more need of him elsewhere. The Ryuken will need a commander, and I think you are the best man for the job.''

"The Ryuken are the past. It is dead, as I should be.''

"You are mistaken.'' Theodore walked to the window. The late afternoon sun cast his shadow across the bed and spared Michi's eyes from the glare. Staring out the window, Theodore said, "You saved my father's life by preempting those others. It gave him . . . a new perspective. He believed he had found an honorable death.''

Michi frowned. "I thought I heard a doctor say that he died in his sleep. A weak heart.''

Theodore's voice was almost inaudible. "The doctors say what they must say.''

"A warrior's death? I remember fighting.''

"No. He survived those others. He used your sword to hold them off long enough for the Otomo to arrive. Afterward, he told me what you had said about a samurai's choice. I think that your example is what turned his mind. In the end, he freely chose what others tried to force on him. He thought it wisdom.''

The twisted irony of the situation made Michi want to laugh, but the pain in his chest turned his amusement to agony. When the spasm subsided, he said, "He refused such a death when I offered it.''

"He never responded well to the younger generation," Theodore said ruefully. He returned to Michi's bedside. "I wish to reward you."

A fleeting burst of strength allowed Michi to rock his head back and forth. "It is inappropriate."

"Because you raised your hand against the House of Kurita?"

"*Hai.*"

"And if I, as head of that House, say that you were ever loyal, as a samurai should be?"

Michi met Theodore's gaze. He felt the strength in the Kanrei's spirit, the power to rule. But Michi had his own strength. "It would not change the truth. I have lived my last lie."

Theodore sighed. Bowing his head, he asked, "Will you become a monk?"

"Perhaps, in time."

They spoke no more for some time. Michi thought he must have slept, but when he was aware again, Theodore was still there, his position unchanged. Michi said, "If you have told me the truth, I have one more duty."

"On Awano?"

Michi shook his head. Awano, the ancestral home of his mentor Minobu, was as closed to him as Luthien and the inner circles of Kurita politics. Tetsuhara-*sensei* had cursed him from the family estate when Michi had brought him the head of Minobu's chief tormentor Samsonov. The old man had refused the validity of Michi's vendetta to restore the honor of his eldest son, Minobu. The old *sensei* had cursed him, but there had been a package waiting for Michi at the spaceport. A long slender box. That box now lay in a bank vault on the outskirts of Imperial City. The instructions he had left for its disposition no longer applied.

Theodore interrupted his thoughts. "Where will you go, then?"

"To fulfill my last duty," he said, but he would not elaborate despite the Kanrei's probing. This matter had nothing to do with Theodore, and everything to do with who Michi was and what he had become. Until that duty was done, he would not be free to go onward. "When will the doctors release me?"

"When you are able to travel. I will have a ship waiting for you."

"It is unnecessary."

"For you, but not for me. You will accept that at least."

Theodore's voice was firm, full of his conviction. Michi nodded. They understood each other at last.

30

The Wolf stopped short when he saw the man who stood at the window, back to the door. Even I knew enough to see that the tall man was not the stocky Takashi Kurita, with whom we were to meet. As we entered the room, the man turned to greet us and I recognized Theodore Kurita, Gunji-no-Kanrei of the Combine. He looked tired.

"Colonel Wolf, I am glad to see you."

"Good evening, Kanrei," the Colonel responded guardedly.

Theodore frowned, an uncharacteristically revealing expression from one schooled in Kuritan politics. Something was obviously upsetting him. I wondered if he approved of Jaime Wolf's duel with his father.

"Please take a seat," he said, gesturing to a group of intricately carved chairs near the center of the room. We took seats, but he remained standing. "I regret to inform you that your salutation is obsolete. My father passed on this morning. I am no longer Kanrei, but Coordinator."

Colonel Wolf stiffened, but his voice was steady and calm. "I did not know he was ill."

"It was sudden. The physicians say heart failure."

"Your circumspection suggests that you suspect otherwise."

"You are as perceptive as ever, Colonel Wolf. I am not sure whether you will find the news welcome or not, but I can assure you that my father did not die by treachery."

"I never wished him a dishonorable death."

"But you did wish him dead. Why else would you have accepted his challenge?"

"I came to end the feud."

"Ah yes, the feud." Theodore shook his head sadly. "Will my father's death bring an end to the hostilities between House Kurita and your Dragoons?"

"I came for the duel. It would have been a closure."

"There are many ways to reach an end, Colonel. What good is a vendetta prosecuted against innocents?"

The Wolf smiled grimly. "I could ask you the same thing."

"Your words are for my father, not me. We live in this world, Colonel Wolf. The universe is, now and tomorrow, what we make it." Finally, Theodore sat. He leaned forward, his expression earnest. "Will you not let the past go?"

Expressionless, the Colonel replied, "Too many Dragoons have died at Kurita hands."

"More deaths will not bring them back. Many Kuritans have died at the hands of Dragoons, and I do not hold you accountable. I thought you were offering a reconciliation when you invited me to Outreach."

"I called you, not your father. The Clans had to be stopped."

"And then you came and fought for Luthien. You might have stayed away and let the Clans settle your old debts."

"Hanse Davion invoked our contract with the Federated Commonwealth and forced us to come to Luthien, but I assure you it was against my wishes."

"You did not think it wise to defend Luthien against the invaders?"

"You should have met them in space and fallen back

with your ground forces. Benjamin was defensible."
The Wolf broke off then, dismissing the strategic considerations with a wave of his hand. "Now that Hanse is dead, I won't be forced into aiding Kurita again. My position remains unchanged."

"You will not help us against the Clans?"

"I won't fight your battles and have Dragoons give their lives for Kuritans. But if you offer no battles, I'll start none. We have no need to meet on the battlefield."

"If we did, you would not have the success you did against my father. My army is not so reckless as his."

"Start the fighting and you'll have more dead to bury than you can count."

Theodore sat back and a strange calm descended on him. "You speak much of death, Colonel. Is it death you seek? There are those who would be happy to arrange it."

"Threats aren't your style, Theodore-*san*."

"Are they yours?"

"I didn't start this feud," the Wolf responded hotly.

Ice to the fire, Theodore said, "But you are willing to finish it."

The Wolf nodded.

"I will not stand for a shadow war." Theodore leaned forward again, his face stern. "If you strike at me, you will reap the whirlwind. There will be no piecemeal attacks, no raids, no unorganized assaults for you to destroy at leisure. Your Dragoons have a permanent home now; they are more vulnerable than ever. Living in Davion's shadow, you must be more aware than ever of the Kuritan reputation for atrocities. Outreach is not so far from Kentares," he said ominously.

The threat was barely veiled, for the name Kentares was infamous. It was on that world that one of Theodore's forebears had perpetrated a massacre that amounted to planetary genocide.

The Wolf's expression hardened. "We Dragoons have dealt with threats to our families before, always harshly." He stared at Theodore for a long moment. "Besides, I don't believe you would start a war with the Clans at your back and the Federated Commonwealth on two sides."

"You are not Davion's people, for all you hide in his shadow. Who will cry for mercenaries when so much can be gained by picking their bones?"

Though Theodore's words were subtle, his meaning was crystal clear. I had seen the reports about the spies who attempted to steal our secrets. I had seen the results of the Capellans' raid. Since first arriving in the Inner Sphere, the Dragoons had fought in turn for each of the Great Houses, and in doing so, we had fought against each one as well. And by hiding our Clan origins, we had lied to the leaders of the Inner Sphere for decades. They could not trust us now, no matter how open we seemed. History has shown that what a Successor Lord does not trust, he considers an enemy. Outreach made a tempting target—so small, compared to the power of the leaders of the Inner Sphere, and so full of technological loot. We knew they envied our resources. History had also shown a distressing tendency for the lords of the Inner Sphere to take what they wanted if they thought they could get away with it. As Theodore implied, the other Great House lords might sit by while he dismembered us, but more likely they would fight each other over the spoils. But that wouldn't help us; once the fighting began, no one would want us working for another. Any one of the Inner Sphere leaders might decide to destroy us first, no doubt hoping to gain the prize of our technologies for his own state.

The Wolf's expression went dark. "Luthien is vulnerable as well."

"You have not the strength to stand before the regiments I can gather here," Theodore said confidently.

"I wouldn't have to." The Wolf leaned forward and bared his teeth. "Do you know what a warship, a *real* warship, can do from orbit? If not, go look up your records of the Clan attack against Edo. We came to the Inner Sphere with ships just like those of the Clans, but we have kept them hidden in the Periphery. We wanted no one to know who we were or where we came from, and the ships were too big a clue. Now that we're revealed as wolves, we no longer have need for sheep's clothing. We could bring those ships in; we needn't hide them any longer. The Dragoons have the power to obliterate your capital from orbit. What good are all your BattleMechs against that kind of threat?"

Theodore stood up and stalked away from the chairs. Taking up a position by the window, he turned slowly to face us again. His form was a dark shape against the dying light.

"The dragon might be wounded, but the wolf will die. Your force cannot be so great that you can stand against an entire star empire."

"Maybe not. But we'll bloody whoever tries."

"You would violate the Ares Conventions by using your warships against a planet?"

The Wolf's face remained impassive. "I will defend my people with whatever means I have to hand."

"If you used such ships, you would be outlawed."

"A small price, and one I have paid before." The Colonel settled back in his chair. "Are you willing to call my bluff?"

"Yes."

Theodore's reply brought silence. There was conviction in his voice that could not be denied. The two men stared silently at each another, and I felt cold sweat trickle down my sides. If the Wolf was pushed to implement his threat, I doubted we would leave the palace alive. Theodore would have nothing to lose.

At last the Colonel asked, "Why?"

Drawing himself up, Theodore folded his arms across his chest. "I will see this madness ended. My realm has fought on too many fronts for too long. We have a grave enemy now, one who demands all our attention. That enemy is yours, too, if your talk on Outreach was more than wind." I think he smiled slightly, but I couldn't be sure. "Would Minobu Tetsuhara have denied himself access to half the forces of his enemy merely to soothe dead grief?"

"That was low."

"If it was, I apologize, Colonel Wolf." Theodore bowed. "Your threat to Luthien was unbecoming of a warrior as well."

Slowly, the Colonel stood. He sketched a slight bow.

"We are practical men, Colonel Wolf. We each know that the other will do anything to safeguard his people. I gave up a fifth of my realm to save the rest. At the time, I thought it necessary, but the wheel turns, as it always does. Now the Clans have come and I see that the Combine's sacrifice may have been in vain. The invaders threaten to take the rest of the Combine away from me. If the Combine falls, what then? Will the Federated Commonwealth be able to stop the invaders? Will Marik's Free Worlds League? Will you? Is the tired lure of revenge worth the gamble?"

Jaime Wolf was quiet for a long time. "I will think about what you have said, Theodore-*san*."

31

Dechan Fraser stopped down the street from the mansion that had been a reward from Theodore Kurita for loyal service. At first he thought his tired eyes were confused, tricked by the evening light. He recognized the mane and beard of gray, the short, compact silhouette. Though he had not worn one in years, he knew the Dragoon dress uniform as well. He could not be mistaken. This unexpected guest waiting by his gate was Colonel Jaime Wolf.

He had heard a rumor that the duel had been postponed, but he never imagined that Wolf would make a visit to Dechan Fraser part of his itinerary. Curious, confused, and not a little angry, Dechan walked up to his former commander. "Looking for someone?"

Wolf turned and glanced up at him. "Dechan, you're looking well."

Ignoring the offered hand, Dechan said, "Receiving visitors in the street is bad manners. Please, come in."

Dechan palmed the lock and, when the door opened, gestured that Wolf should precede him. The Colonel entered and gave his cloak to the servant who appeared, then disappeared just as silently. Dechan led him into the common room where the servants had prepared tea and a tray of small cakes. There was a third cup beside his and Jenette's; the servants had known the visitor was waiting.

"I hope I'm not troubling you," Wolf said in pale

imitation of Kuritan politeness. He looked for a chair and, finding none, knelt awkwardly in the Kuritan fashion.

"*Do itashimashite*," said Dechan, kneeling too. As he did, he realized how easily he had slipped into the formal role of host and begun speaking in Japanese. The Kurita style had become a part of his own: politeness hiding personal feelings to make all smooth and to save face.

Wolf took Dechan's response as a cue and continued his pleasantries in Japanese. He was quite fluent and his standard remarks sounded more sincere. Dechan poured tea for himself and his guest. They spoke of the weather and Wolf's trip, but a disquiet underlay the formal conversation. Finally Wolf broke off the polite noise and said, "Will Jenette be here soon?"

"*Hai*. I would have expected her to be here already."

"Good. I wanted to talk to the both of you."

Seemingly satisfied, Wolf said nothing more. Dechan sat in the awkward silence, old pain gnawing at the shield of politeness. He reached for the kettle to refill his cup and misjudged. When his skin touched hot metal, he snatched his hand back. He wanted to suck on the burn, to cool it, but refused to show weakness before this man. Not now. Not after so long. Pent-up frustration burst forth in words.

"Why now? I had expected to hear something when you were last on Luthien."

If Wolf was surprised by the outburst, he didn't show it. Placing his cup carefully on the tray, he said, "We hadn't come to end the feud."

"But you fought for Kurita," Dechan accused.

"We were under contract to Davion."

Dechan shook his head in disbelief. "So a contract was more important than a blood feud."

"A contract is a sworn bond."

"More important than your sworn vow?"

"At the time," Wolf said quietly.

Dechan sneered. "Very convenient."

Wolf took a sip of his tea and returned the cup to the tray. The action placed Dechan's comment at a distance.

"You're not talking about our fighting for Kurita, are you?"

"Yes, I am. But you're right—there *is* more to it than that."

Wolf waited.

If Wolf was willing to take it, Dechan was ready to give it to him. "Like a lot of Dragoons, I idolized you. I thought you knew all there was to know about the mercenary business. Everyone believed that you were a man of honor. I'd have given my life for you. Hellfire, I *did*. I gave my life to Kurita to be a good little spy for you. To what end, Jaime Wolf? Are you a man to whom a handful of C-bills outweighs an honorable vow?"

"No one forced you."

"I was on Misery, remember? I saw the Dragoon dead. The sight cut to my soul the way the cold wind of that hellhole never could. I remember. I've heard the voices of the dead every day I stood before the Ryuken trainees, every time I led a Kuritan unit into battle. A lot of people died on Misery and not just Dragoons. Remember the Iron Man?"

"Yes."

"Well, I can't forget him. When we worked with the Ryuken, I admired him. No one could match his dedication, courage, and skill. Except you, or so I thought. On Misery the Dragoons fought the Ryuken and nearly lost. In the end, I fought him and watched him kill my lancemates. I thought it was the proudest day of my life when I brought his *Dragon* down. I was a kid. I didn't really understand the honor of observing his *seppuku* ceremony, but years of living in his world have taught me. Has the money washed your memories clean of Tetsuhara, too?''

Looking down at his teacup, Wolf said nothing.

''Well?''

Wolf remained silent.

''I thought you were an honorable man.''

Fire flashed in Wolf's eyes and his expression hardened. ''I acted as I thought best. I was commander.''

''Is that your excuse?''

''It's all the reason there is. I thought we needed someone close to Kurita who could warn us.''

''But then you beat up everything Takashi sent at you and got a whole world from Davion for your very own. Safe and sound. You didn't need to worry about old safeguards. You didn't have to; you could safely forget them.''

''You weren't forgotten. It wasn't safe to communicate.''

''Safe?'' Dechan chuckled bitterly. ''We used your Wolfnet codes, but we stopped getting answers. We were abandoned.''

''You weren't.''

''Weren't!'' Dechan rocked to his feet. He jostled the tray as he rose and his teacup tipped over the edge, shattering on the hardwood floor. ''Then why'd you send Lang to Theodore? Jenette and I were supposed to be in his inner circle. Why not tell us to get him to Outreach?''

''There were other considerations. I didn't think it was a good time to expose you. If the leaders of the Inner Sphere didn't agree to work together, we might still have needed you undercover. If Kurita had refused to cooperate, you could have been exposed to danger.''

''Might have. Could have. You could have told us what you had in mind instead of letting us stumble along, never hearing from the Dragoons.''

"It would have jeopardized you," Wolf said. He began to pick up the pieces of the broken cup.

"And your coming here isn't going to do that?"

"Not anymore." Wolf placed the shards on the tray. "It's not general knowledge yet, but there is something you should know. Takashi Kurita is dead."

Dechan thought of the much-publicized duel. "You killed him?"

With a shake of his head, Wolf said, "The duel never took place."

Takashi dead, and not in a duel with Wolf. It was not an outcome that Dechan had considered. "Then Theodore is Coordinator."

Wolf nodded. "There's no more need for you here."

"No need? I've served Theodore and the Ryuken longer than I did the Dragoons. No Dragoon need, you mean."

Wolf sighed and slowly got to his feet. "I understand."

"Do you?"

"Let me say that I was proud of your service with the Dragoons. I was prouder still when you agreed to go undercover with Kurita. I know what you gave up."

Dechan didn't believe it. "How could you?"

"I left my home once to live a lie. I lived my lie longer than you have yours."

"My apologies. I should have known that the great Jaime Wolf was better at anything I could do."

Wolf looked taken aback. "I'm sorry. I didn't mean it that way."

Dechan's ready retort was cut off by the slam of a door. Jenette rushed in from the entry, slinging off her uniform jacket as she came.

"Dechan, have you heard? Takashi's dead!"

She faltered as she noticed the visitor. The jacket dropped to the floor and she bowed quickly. "I'm sorry, I didn't realize—Colonel Wolf!"

She snapped to attention and saluted.

"This is informal, Jenette," he said.

Her eyes round with surprise, she asked, "Why are you here?"

Wolf glanced quickly at Dechan, then smiled for her. "I am here to ask you both to come home."

"Home?" Her expression was puzzled.

"Yes. To Outreach. There are places for both of you waiting in the Dragoons."

"There was no place for us at the siege of Luthien," Dechan said, still bitter.

"The times have been changing, and I have altered my view of certain issues since then."

"Oh? A new contract?"

"Dechan?" Unaware of the earlier conversation, Jenette was clearly confused by the harshness in Dechan's tone.

"It's all right, Jenette," Wolf said.

"No, it's not," she said. "He's being rude."

"Fair, by his lights."

"How kind of you," Dechan drawled.

"Dechan!"

"It's all right, Jenette. Dechan and I are not seeing eye to eye," Wolf said, putting a polite face on the disagreement. "I've made the offer, and I'm sure you two have a lot to talk about. I'm just getting in the way. If you want to come home, you can. You'll be welcome. If not, I'll understand. I would appreciate an answer, whatever you decide. The *Chieftain* is at the palace spaceport and I'll be staying aboard. We lift in a week, after the funeral."

"We'll—"

"We'll give it some thought," Dechan said, restraining Jenette with a hand on her arm. "Meshitsukai! Show Colonel Wolf out."

The servant came in a flurry of polite bows. Wolf followed him out of the room. Jenette waited until she heard the outer door close before rounding on her husband. Her face was flushed with anger.

"What was that all about?"

"I don't like being an untrustworthy cog in somebody's deep plans. Wolf said he couldn't trust us to know what was happening on Outreach."

"He didn't," she said in disbelief.

"He did. We gave him our lives and it's all been for nothing. He's just calling us back to ease his conscience."

Frowning, she said, "I'm sure that the Colonel did what he thought was necessary. It's not us that he didn't trust. The ISF has always watched us. A message, or even a messenger, might have been intercepted. Contact wouldn't have been safe."

"There are ways. He's found them before when he thought it was important."

She spun away and faced the wall. "You're overreacting."

"And you're defending him," he said just as harshly. Her back was rigid, full of defiance. He took a deep breath. They had been each other's only true friend for years, but now he saw her pulling away. He remembered all too keenly that she was one of the original Dragoons, a child who had come with them from the Clans. Fearing that her heritage was stronger than the love they shared, he turned away from her. Head hanging, he moved toward the door that led to the inner mansion, but then found himself unwilling to leave the room. He stopped in the doorway. His anger and sense of betrayal urged him on, but his love wouldn't let him walk away. He stood locked in his inner struggle.

He felt her hand tentatively touch his back. When he didn't shrug her off, she slid her arms around him and hugged him close. She was warm and shaking slightly. He felt a drop of wetness on the back of his neck.

"Dechan, I want to go home."

He turned to face her and put his right arm around

her. With his left hand he raised her chin until her eyes met his.

"And if I don't want to go?"

"Don't ask me to make that choice."

"You're asking me to make the same sort of choice."

She buried her head in his shoulder and hugged him fiercely. He knew what his decision would be. She was more important to him than anything Wolf or Theodore could offer. They would go.

But *he* didn't have to be a Dragoon.

Part 3

CRUCIBLE

═══ **32** ═══

"**M**ichi-*sama*!"

The path back from the edge of the abyss was long.

"Michi-*sama*!"

Insistent and demanding, the familiar voice burrowed through to Michi Noketsuna's awareness. There was no physical contact. There wouldn't be. For all his impropriety, the caller knew better.

"Michi-*sama*!"

Letting go of the cold embrace of the dark, Michi opened his eyes. Head bowed, his gaze fell naturally upon the honor sword on the ground before him. The gleam of its half-unsheathed blade promised release from the voice, from the burdens of the world, but for as yet unknowable reasons, he had taken a step back from the edge.

He raised his head, composing himself before bowing an apology to the memorial tablet. He thought to see the other sword of the pair held in the firm grip of a tall black man, but the *katana* lay where he had placed it, the gentle curve of its scuffed black scabbard stark against the sand. There was no samurai there, only the dull white stone. Absurdly, Michi was both surprised and relieved.

It is your son who calls, Minobu-sensei, but is it your voice I hear?

"Michi-*sama*?"

"*Hai*, Kiyomasa-*san*. I hear you."

"I was afraid I would be too late." Kiyomasa Tetsuhara stepped closer, moving around to face Michi. The young man wore a Kurita MechWarrior's dark gray uniform, the heavyweight material that served to protect him from the chill of the cavern making him look stout and clumsy. Despite the cold, sweat beaded on his smooth black skin. "I thought you would take this path, and I wanted to talk you out of it."

"Did you expect to have more luck with me than I had with your father?"

"I hoped to."

A smile flashed on Kiyomasa's face. With its easy promise of familiarity, that grin had undoubtedly made the young man many friends. Michi looked past it to the child he had known and, further, to the long-dead father of the child. Minobu's smiles had been rare. Shrugging off the memories, Michi spoke.

"Did you think they would help your argument?"

Kiyomasa's startled eyes flicked over Michi's shoulder, darting to those who had accompanied him. They offered him no verbal encouragement, but Michi sensed their agitation.

Nervous, Kiyomasa wet his lips and said, "I persuaded them that there are alternatives. So the least you could do is give us a chance. Talk with us. If we can't make you see that this is not the course for you, we will not interfere. Any one of us would be honored to be your *kaishaku-nin*."

"Very well."

Michi settled himself, drawing on his *ki* to strengthen himself for this last trial. Standing, he turned to face the small crowd whose breaths steamed in the frigid air. He bowed to them.

"*Konichiwa.*"

The group's return greeting was ragged, in keeping with their nature. Most wore Kurita military uniforms, although there was a wide array of unit patches. A few wore the uniforms of mercenaries, and one the white uniform of a ComStar Guardsman. The rest wore bits and pieces of military gear with no obvious antecedents.

They were of all ages. Some were young, too young to have been a part of the old battles. They would be the newest generation of warriors, raised on the tales of Theodore's revitalized Combine army. Others he recognized from his time in Dieron. Still others from the old Ryuken. He bowed to one of those.

"Kumban-*san*."

"Michi-*sama*." The man took a step forward and returned his bow. "I saw the stone for the old man. You?"

"*Hai*."

"He cannot thank you, so I will."

"Unnecessary. I was honored."

Kumban bowed again and retreated a step.

"You are the one we honor, Michi-*sama*," Kiyomasa said. "We know of your vendetta and what you did to uphold the honor of my father. Lord Takashi is dead, freeing us from our oaths. Before we could be bound to another Kurita, we decided to come to you. If you permit, we will join you. You are a man of great honor; we want you to lead us in what it means to be honorable warriors."

Michi gazed at the gathered Kuritans. He saw hope and fear and eagerness for glory in their eyes. His heightened senses let him feel the color of their *ki*. They were warriors, all of them, and embarked on a bold and daring course. Steeling themselves against the scorn of their fellows, they had run off to join a half-mad vagabond, no doubt believing him to be some sort of warrior saint. Yet they remained restive, troubled.

The great cavern and its eerie echoes was an unnerving place, but it should not cause a true warrior's heart to flutter. He considered the possibility that he was the cause of their nervousness.

He realized that he must present an appearance in accord with such fantasies. Like some ascetic defying the elements, he wore only a light kimono against the cold, and it was white, the color of death. The robe hung loosely on him and its open front and short sleeves showed the scars of a lifetime. The dead white orb that was his left eye made many of the younger ones unable to meet his gaze for longer than a moment. Even some of those who had known him before flinched as he turned his stare on them, each in turn.

There was no doubt that his physical appearance affected them, but the flavor of their agitation could not solely be accounted for by the reality of confronting their dreams in the flesh. Something else stirred them to apprehension. Michi extended his senses, searching for the source of the disturbance and found that among those present were others who represented another factor in the Kuritans' plans for the future. The presence of these others had been masked from his *ki* by the Kuritans' agitation, just as their bodies had blocked Michi's sight. Once alerted to their presence, Michi could only wonder how he had missed it at the start. They were not Kuritan, but they were strong. He recognized the fit of the pattern.

Michi nodded and said, "You may come forward, Colonel Wolf."

The Kuritans parted to let the three Dragoons pass through their midst. Jaime Wolf was flanked on the right by Hans Vordel. The bodyguard's years had etched deeper lines into his hangdog face and whitened some hairs, but had not weakened his warrior tread. The Dragoon on the left looked like a frozen moment from the past. He appeared to be William Cameron, Wolf's communications specialist, but he was not. Cameron had died on Crossing. This must be a son.

Wolf was smiling, as if amused at some joke. "Who told you I was here?"

''Your *ki* is strong.''

Wolf's smile vanished and he looked toward the memorial tablet. ''He said much the same thing when we first met. If you keep it up, you may yet persuade me about Kuritan mysticism.''

''You will believe as you believe, whatever I do or say.''

''Maybe so.''

Michi lifted an arm and waved it to encompass the rows of memorial tablets. Each was a plain white stone, engraved with the formal characters of a warrior's name and rank. ''Harumito Shumagawa is responsible for this. He was the officer in command of the forces remaining here when Warlord Samsonov ordered the Dragoon dead disinterred. Samsonov wanted the bodies left to the ravages of this planet's weather, to obliterate their presence. Samsonov said the Ryuken had failed, that their dead were not to be honored. Had he been more confident in his power, he might have ordered the same fate for their bodies as he had for the Dragoons, but he commanded only that their graves go unmarked. Those orders were among the last he gave before he fled. Shumagawa had survived the battle here; he only lost a leg. He knew what had happened.

''Minobu-*sensei* taught us that a warrior was to be honored; the warrior's gender, the color of his skin, or the uniform he wore didn't matter. Shumagawa felt dishonored by the warlord's order but, as a samurai, he was obliged to obey. Or at least appear to. He ordered a select group of his men to move the remains of the dead, Ryuken and Dragoon, to this cavern and then he swore them to secrecy. They were all Ryuken veterans; they understood. He could not let courage and valor go unremembered. After reporting the completion of his task to the warlord, he resigned his commission. His veterans dispersed among the Draconis Combine Mustered Soldiery while he came to live in this cavern and began to engrave these tablets. It took him twenty years. He died here by his own hand, atoning for his lie to the warlord.

"His spirit will be pleased to know you have seen this place."

Wolf stared out over the massed ranks of the tablets. "There are those who wouldn't understand this."

"Do you understand, Colonel?"

"I'd like to think so." Wolf turned his gaze to Michi. "Do you?"

Michi was surprised at the question. To evade the flutter of disturbance in his *wa*, he spoke. "Why have you come here?"

"I was asked to come by those who believe that I might do some good. Perhaps even prevent one more unnecessary loss in a tragic story."

"Kiyomasa."

Wolf smiled. "He is a persuasive young man."

"You hear another voice in his call. Do not delude yourself listening to the past."

There was a sudden wariness in Wolf's eyes. "Breaks with tradition are the sort of thing I've made a habit of. I know it doesn't come easy to your sort, but your teacher wasn't exclusively a stickler for tradition."

"He knew when tradition was important."

"Mostly. But he was human. I believe he made a mistake when it came to the end here on Misery. You believed it, too, or you wouldn't have vowed vendetta. And that didn't exactly turn out like you figured. Think about that."

"I have."

Wolf bent over and picked up the honor sword. He snapped the blade into the sheath. "Maybe you haven't thought about it enough. The dead have a lot to tell the living, but you can't just listen. You've got to do something about what they tell you." Wolf stepped to Minobu's memorial tablet and took up the *katana*.

He handed the pair to Kiyomasa. ''These were his swords. What do you Kuritans say about there being no future, no past? That only the present is real, and a lot can happen that can change unpleasant probabilities.''

Kiyomasa looked puzzled, and Michi felt echoing confusion among the Kuritans and Wolf's aides. But the words Wolf spoke were not meant for them; they were solely between Wolf and Michi.

Wolf looked at Michi. ''And what are you now, this instant, Michi Noketsuna? Alive or dead?''

''Alive.''

''Think about that, too. Once, I made you the offer of a place in the Dragoons, and you said you had other things to do. I took that as a 'talk to me later.' Looks to me like all the old business is finished. If you were really going to kill yourself at the end of it, you'd have done it by now. So what is it you're looking for, Noketsuna? It isn't death.''

No, Michi realized, it was not death he sought, but what it was, he didn't know

''Well, I've got things to do,'' Wolf said in a sudden display of impatience. ''Can't live in the past.''

Wolf turned and walked away. His Dragoons gave Michi brief bows, then followed their commander.

The Kuritans watched them leave, then turned to Michi, awaiting an answer.

''Michi-*sama*?'' Kiyomasa asked for all of them.

33

It was strange to have Kuritans aboard the *Chieftain*. In training I had studied their culture, perhaps a little more intensively than that of other Inner Sphere states because they were billed as high-probability opponents. But the reality was different from expectations, as it always is, I suppose. Though we were on a military ship, we were not in the midst of a military operation; perhaps that was part of the reason they did not behave as I expected them to.

Their clannishness was predictable, however. They were among strangers, some of whom had once been their enemy. Spheroids don't incorporate the losers of an operation into the winners' side like the Clans do. Well, it wasn't standard Dragoon practice, either. We had taken in Clanners, though, and in some ways they were stranger than these expatriate samurai and their families.

I wondered about those families. Not all of the Kuritans had brought theirs. Did that mean those who brought no one had no families? Might they be orphans, cast-offs, or even renegades? I didn't have the opportunity to seek out the answer because the families were billeted on the ships the Kuritans had brought with them. Since the ships were still the property of individual Kuritans, until proper transferrals could be made at Outreach, we Dragoons rarely visited them during the journey.

How many of those wives and children had voluntarily chosen to accompany their warriors? How many were forced into the journey? How did they deal with going among strangers to find a new life? I could have understood if they had all been sibkos. To see the unknown, to try new ventures together—that sort of comradeship was natural. How did families deal with it? I also wondered how similar this tiny exodus was to the departure of the oldsters from Wolf Clan.

I never worked up the courage to ask any of the officers who had regular conferences with Colonel Wolf. I just watched them come and go. Occasionally I overheard them speaking to one another of their families, but I could never be sure whether they spoke of someone on the accompanying ships or someone left behind. Maybe it was all part of the living in the present business that the Colonel had talked about with Michi Noketsuna. I didn't know.

I spent a lot of time on the bridge of the *Chieftain*, where I had set up my comm station to monitor Dragoon communiques and ComStar broadcast channels. The cluttered channels in space are odd: you're always having to sort out the past from the present, when it's all really the past. Since nothing arrives instantaneously, you have to put everything you get into perspective. That can be hard. Sometimes last week's news from one system is more important than today's from the system where you're sitting in a JumpShip getting its interstellar drives recharged.

Sometimes I'd look up and find Michi watching me. He never said anything, though. He'd just bow politely when I noticed him and then go wandering off about his business. I didn't really understand why he'd come aboard with the other Kuritans; he didn't seem quite the same as them. It wasn't just that he was distant and aloof—that was typical for a Kuritan. It was more that he didn't seem to be there all the time. He rarely spoke and then only when spoken to directly. There was something strange about him, something faintly dangerous. Sometimes I thought about him as an unexploded mine. An expert might handle it safely, but a green troopie would do something wrong and that would be the end of the troopie. If I was sure of only one thing when around him, it was that I was definitely a greenie. So despite my curiosity about why he watched me, I never asked.

It was probably just as well.

Dechan Fraser stayed aboard the *Chieftain* when Wolf, Vordel, and Cameron accompanied the Kuritans to the surface. He had recognized the cold blue face of the planet they were orbiting the moment he saw it on the bridge monitors. He had no desire ever to set foot on its ground again.

From snatches of conversation overheard among the Kuritans, he suspected he knew why they had come here, and it only gave him more reason to stay aboard. His suspicions were proven correct when the shuttle returned, bearing Michi Noketsuna alongside Wolf. Michi greeted Dechan and Jenette with a stiff formal bow, but he offered no spoken words. Though she said nothing at the time, Jenette had complained later. Dechan couldn't decide if he cared or not. Many years had gone by without words, what were a few minutes in a shuttle bay?

They saw little of Michi after that first encounter. He always seemed to be leaving a compartment just as they were entering, or vice versa. The other Kuritans were easier to talk to. After years in the Combine, Dechan found them more familiar companions than the Dragoons.

Still, it seemed strange to see Dragoon and Kurita uniforms sitting around the same conference table again. The byplay was slow at first, but the Ryuken veterans fell into it soon enough and the other Kuritans followed their lead. Dechan was reminded of the days when Iron Man Tetsuhara had sat across from Wolf. But Tetsuhara was dead and his son—well, his son wasn't the Iron Man. Michi Noketsuna had sat at the table in those days, too. He wasn't dead, but he wasn't at the table, either.

Dechan finally decided that the whole arrangement shouldn't be surprising. Things were different now. Even the Dragoons were different. That was obvious. every time he saw Pilot Grane. Her overlarge head and slight build marked her instantly as a Clan-bred aerospace pilot. None of the Clans' extreme phenotypes had been a part of the Dragoons when Dechan had worn the uniform. Hellfire, he hadn't even known the Dragoons had come from the Clans. As a recruit from the Inner Sphere, he hadn't been trusted with that knowledge.

Jenette had known, though; she was one of them.

But somehow he couldn't find it in himself to hate her. She had never really lied to him, she just hadn't told him the whole story. But he knew her. And loved her. Maybe that made it different.

Jaime Wolf, on the other hand, was an enigma. He was a man who played his own game and damned to hell anyone who got in the way. Sort of like Dechan's once-friend Michi.

Dechan was through being a pawn. Now all he wanted to do was stay out of the way and keep Jenette safe. It wasn't really possible to do anything really constructive until their journey was complete anyway. Then, well, then he'd see what could be done to build a new life.

34

The honor guard stood smartly at attention along the *Chieftain*'s ramp. They were all Elementals, and though not all had been part of the bondsmen transfer at Luthien, they all wore Nova Cat badges as prominently as their Dragoon unit and rank insignia. Elson wondered what Wolf would make of that.

Wolf's wife and children waited at the foot of the ramp, MacKenzie's widow and daughter along with them. Marisha Dandridge had applied to the officer council for permission to be the one to tell Wolf of his son's death. Elson had seen no reason to deny that request, even though it violated the standard chain of command. It was another sign of the decadent weakness of the blood families. Wolf's family making a public display of their grief would only weaken his standing with the Clanners among the Dragoons.

The DropShip's personnel hatch hissed open to reveal a knot of black-uniformed soldiers. Elson recognized the uniforms. They would be the Kuritans Wolf was hauling home with him. They walked slowly down the ramp, backs stiff. At the foot, they all took turns bowing to Wolf's family before stepping aside. They remained clustered in the shadow of the DropShip, apparently reluctant to approach the group of Dragoon officers among whom Elson stood.

Wolf and his bodyguard were the next to exit the ship, with the commo officer Cameron following almost immediately. Wolf's reunion with his family was full of emotion. Elson checked on Alpin. The boy fidgeted, but remained where he was.

The reaction of the Elemental honor guard was just what Elson expected. They kept their eyes fixed firmly ahead, their expressions stony. The Kuritans also found it expedient to ignore the scene being played out before them. Though their culture honored the emotions, it looked down on public displays of feeling, so their distaste was only for the impropriety of the expression. Some of the officers around Elson were making comments, noting that Wolf's behavior was unbecoming a military man. Elson was pleased. His upbringing made him want to sneer at the wanton display and blatant lack of control just as the others did, but it was important that he not appear biased against Wolf today. His control was more than sufficient for the task.

Cameron slipped past the family and tapped Vordel on the shoulder. He leaned down to whisper something into the stocky bodyguard's ear, then the two of them stepped away from the ramp and headed toward Elson's group. The whispering among the officers ceased as they approached.

"Why aren't you with your family?" Vordel asked Alpin.

"I'm an officer," Alpin snapped. "My place is here."

Vordel eyed him suspiciously. "What's going on?"

"You'll find out soon enough, old man," Alpin said. "They will be telling him any time now."

"Telling who? What?"

Cameron looked even more concerned than Vordel sounded. He snatched a glance back over his shoulder at Wolf. A tremor ran through his body, as though he was thinking of running back to his master. The reaction told Elson that the communications blackout had been successful.

"I don't need to answer your questions," Alpin sneered at Vordel.

Hans' face screwed down tight. Elson recognized the danger sign that Alpin missed. Cameron caught it too and forestalled Vordel's response by putting a hand on the bodyguard's arm. Vordel relaxed, ever so slightly. His voice was hard when he spoke, and Elson was pleased that the bodyguard directed his question to Alicia Fancher, one of the safer officers. Colonel Fancher remembered Wolf's dismissing her from command years ago; it had taken very little for Elson to fan the coals of her resentment. She would not betray the plan.

"What about it, Alicia? What's going on? Something's up or you wouldn't be here."

It was no surprise that the bodyguard noticed Fancher. As a member of Wolf's Command Lance, Vordel would have a good knowledge of all the combat unit assignments. Fancher's Beta Regiment was supposed to be engaged on Vertabren. Since he had not heard of any reassignments, Vordel had to assume it was something pretty important to pull a regimental commander away from her troops in the field. Colonel Fancher answered coolly.

"Like Alpin Wolf said, you'll find out soon enough."

She nodded her head to indicate the approach of Jaime Wolf. While Vordel had been digging, Wolf had been learning of the death of his son. The Colonel's cheeks glistened with the tracks of tears.

Cameron looked shocked and Vordel deeply worried. Wolf gave Alpin a brief glance as he walked past him. The gathered Dragoons parted before the Colonel as if he were some massive, threatening warrior rather than a slight man shorter by a hand span than the least of them and older by a good twenty years. Wolf stopped before Elson.

"Marisha said you ordered a commo silence."

"I did."

"Why?"

"I thought it best that the word not be spread across the Inner Sphere before you could return. The Dragoons have enemies who might have taken advantage."

"That was unnecessary."

A shrug would have been too cavalier. Elson stood still. "The necessity or lack was not as clear in deep space. A courier was out of the question due to our mission guidelines. An open broadcast could have been monitored. A ComStar communique would have entrusted sensitive information to a suspect organization. Is it not Dragoon policy to avoid trusting ComStar with any important information?"

Wolf sighed. "Maybe you were right. But I would have wanted to know sooner."

"It would have changed nothing, *quiaff*?"

Softly the Colonel replied, "I suppose not."

"He died in combat. What warrior could ask for more?"

"He was my son."

Elson nodded. "We have withheld the Remembrance for your return."

"We knew you would want to be there, grandfather," Alpin said.

Wolf looked at him blankly for a moment, then asked, "When?"

"Tonight, if you wish it," Elson replied.

"Tonight?" Wolf stroked his beard. "No. It's . . . I want a little time to let it sink in, to prepare."

"There are a few details," Elson prompted.

"I'll handle them," Cameron said in an unsteady voice. "There's no need for you to worry, Colonel. I'll take care of the technicalities."

He jumped when Marisha touched his arm. Obviously he had not heard her approach.

''Thank you, Brian. Jaime and I both appreciate it. We all appreciate it.''

She took her husband's arm in her own. He nodded to her absently, then looked around. Forcing a smile, he gathered Katherine into his free arm. She wept openly and sobbed on his shoulder.

''It'll be all right, Katherine. We'll get through this.''

''Come,'' Marisha said. ''It's time to go home.''

Hand in hand, they walked away. Rachel, Joshua, and Shauna trailed their parents. Vordel, the faithful and dutiful bodyguard, followed. Cameron stayed put, gaping at Alpin.

Elson stepped between them, shielding Alpin from the commo officer's stare. Sufficient demonstration had been made for this morning. This was not the time to let anything erupt on that front.

''The Wolf's come home,'' he said, lifting his voice to include the gathered Dragoons. ''We all have things to do, *quiaff*?''

''Aff,'' was the reply.

Elson smiled to himself. The voices might have been Clan voices.

=== 35 ===

Dechan tugged the formal jacket out of the closet and frowned. It hadn't looked so plain in the store when he bought it just yesterday. He slipped it on, settled the pads in the shoulders, and considered it again. It looked just severe enough and had enough hint of a martial cut. It would do.

When he had first heard about this thing the Dragoons were calling a Remembrance, he hadn't wanted to go. They hadn't bothered to let him in on such things when he'd worn their uniform, why should he care now? But Jenette had brought him around.

Dechan had known MacKenzie Wolf as Darnell Winningham during the years Wolf's son had spent learning the business. When MacKenzie's identity had been revealed, the official line was that the false identity was intended to prevent MacKenzie from receiving preferential treatment. From what Dechan had learned of the Dragoons recently, it seemed more likely that it was some sort of Clan thing, that MacKenzie had to earn the name or something. Or it might just have been more of Jaime Wolf's penchant for secrecy and duplicity.

Whatever, MacKenzie was dead now, and the Remembrance was being held in his honor. Jenette was right in insisting that MacKenzie was the issue, not the Dragoons' treatment of Dechan. Dechan had known Darnell as a good company commander. And

Darnell was one of the few who had not died during the time Dechan spent in the Periphery and in the Combine. A memorial service might be just the thing, a way to bury the dead past.

Jenette came out of the bathroom vigorously toweling the last drops of water from her short hair. "You're looking nice, but I wish you'd wear your uniform."

"We've been through that."

She frowned, then shrugged it away. She tugged on her tight uniform pants and slipped into her shirt and jacket with her usual brisk efficiency. Her belt hangers stayed empty; even dress weapons were inappropriate for a Remembrance. He helped get the dress cloak centered and snapped the wolf's-head clasp shut. She quickly brushed her hair into moderate order before setting her beret at a jaunty angle. Jenette looked dashing in her uniform, but then that was an effect carefully calculated by the uniform's designers.

She was uncharacteristically quiet during the trip to the city center, and Dechan felt disinclined to start any conversations. What was there to say? They emerged from the tube near the main entrance of Wolf Hall. The Remembrance was to be held in the great assembly chamber of the headquarters complex. Dragoons dressed in billowing dress cloaks and intent on the same destination accompanied them on the way to the Hall. Others approached singly or in small groups from all directions. The gathering crowd was unusually quiet, distant city traffic the only sound.

The great hall was raked down to a stage. Normally there were seats fitted to the stepped tiers of the chamber, but they had been removed. The audience would stand tonight. In reverence for the honored dead, Jenette had said. He followed her to a row a third of the way down and she led him to a place in the center. He looked down at the stage. Save for a simple podium sheathed in black plastic, it was bare. It bore the black wolf's head on a red disk attached to its front. The podium was miked so that a speaker's voice could be easily heard in the upper gallery. Dechan couldn't see the pickups on the stand itself, but they were evident in the enlarged image projected on the wall behind the stage. The screen, like the front of the stage and the walls of the hall, was draped in black bunting.

The hall filled quickly and with what Dechan thought might be called military precision. Once inside, the Dragoons seemed to feel the solemnity lifted somewhat. The soft buzz of hundreds of conversations filled the air. The snatches he heard seemed to be concerned with events and people of which he had no knowledge. He gave up listening and stared glumly at the stage.

Two figures stepped out from the wings. One was Jaime Wolf, his gray-maned head held high. In place of the standard cloak, he wore a sleeveless red gown over his dress uniform. The wide lapels of the garment were studded with badges and ribbons. The other person was swathed from head to toe in loose-fitting black robes that concealed his or her sex as easily as the head-covering hood concealed the face. That person too wore a wide-lapeled gown and the decorations matched those Wolf wore.

Wolf stepped to the podium and waited while the room gradually fell silent.

"I am the Oathmaster." He scanned the room as if taking attendance. "You came at my call. Listen as honor commands. Speak as honor compels."

He executed a brisk about-face and retired to the back of the stage, where he stood at attention. The black-robed person took his place at the podium. The voice was deep, a man's.

"I am the Loremaster, keeper of the *Remembrance*."

He must have touched a control on the podium, for the speakers began to ring with the sound of a tolling bell. When the sound died away, the black-robed man spoke again.

"Death is the warrior's lot, and we are all warriors. Seeking the flame that holds back the dark of oblivion, we walk the honor road and in honor, we find the light that we seek. Honor is the light in our hearts.

"The warrior who thinks to shine above others flares and ends a cinder. The warrior who holds the good of the trothkin above his own burns with an eternal flame. Let him be remembered in the halls."

The bell tolled.

A procession marched down the central aisle from the back of the hall. At its head was Alpin Wolf. Behind him were his mother Katherine and Marisha Dandridge. MacKenzie's daughter Shauna came next, and Rachel and Joshua Wolf followed her. All save Alpin carried lighted candles. Alpin held a folded uniform. They halted at the edge of the stage and Alpin laid the uniform down.

"Who has fallen?" the Loremaster asked.

"MacKenzie Wolf," Alpin answered.

"By what right do you address this assemblage?"

"He was my blood father," Alpin and Shauna said together. Shauna puffed on the candle she held and the light flickered out.

"He was my husband," Katherine said and blew out her candle.

"He was my son by law," Marisha said and did the same.

"He was my sib by law," Rachel and Joshua said in ragged chorus. Rachel had to help Joshua extinguish his candle.

In unison they all said, "We ask that he be remembered."

The Loremaster nodded solemnly. "You are the family of MacKenzie Wolf. You have the right."

The silence of the hall was marred by rumbling murmurs. Dechan noted that the loudest noise was from sections where the Clan adoptees stood. "What's their problem?'' he whispered to Jenette. ''Clan brain-washing,'' she whispered back.

''Who will speak of this warrior? Who was witness to his end?''

The raised voice of the Loremaster brought renewed quiet. For a moment nothing happened, then a large man, an Elemental by his uniform, stepped out into the central aisle. ''I am Edelstein, Captain. I was there when MacKenzie Wolf died. He died as a warrior should, his face toward those who sought his death. That is worthy.''

As Edelstein returned to his place, the crowd replied with the ritual response, ''Seyla!''

Dechan remembered when he had heard that word for the first time. It had been the beginning of the end for the Dragoons in the Draconis Combine. It had been the word uttered by the assembled Dragoons to signify their assent to the plan of escape from the Combine. Here, too, it meant assent. But though the circumstances were less dire, still he felt a chill.

''A death alone is not enough,'' the Loremaster said. ''Who will speak of the life of MacKenzie Wolf?''

A Dragoon standing in the front row stepped out into the aisle and walked around to the stairs that led to the stage. He was met at the top by a woman carrying a white robe. The Dragoon slung off his cloak and put on the robe. The Loremaster surrendered the podium to him. The white-robed Dragoon stood before the microphones in silence for a moment.

''Hear the words we carry with us. This is the *Remembrance*, our past and our honor. Hear the part MacKenzie Wolf played in our clan.''

The man began a chant. The phrases were archaic and the rhythm complex. Dechan was tempted to turn around and see if there was a prompter. When he noticed that the Dragoon's eyes were closed, the temptation vanished. The tale spun by the verses seemed to

be telling of the origin and history of Wolf's Dragoons. The highlights were there, but it was disjointed, as if the speaker were leaving things out. Dechan supposed the chant to be an edited version of something longer; if every detail were told with the intricacy of some of the verses, they would be here for days.

The speaker's recounting contained more and more of the detailed verses as he covered significant events in the life and service record of MacKenzie Wolf. The slant of the phrases and the choice of words made it all sound very heroic. Dechan had nearly tuned it out by the time the speaker reached the battle of Misery; then he paid attention and soon regretted it. Dechan's contributions went unmentioned. Instead his old friend Thom Dominguez was extolled as the one who had brought the Iron Man down.

"They had to keep it quiet, remember?" Jenette whispered in his ear. She had caught his arm and he realized that he was trembling.

"I thought the lie was over."

The speaker went on, telling of MacKenzie's heroics and the struggle to rebuild the Dragoons. There were verses about his service with the Black Widow Battalion and his ultimate leadership of it. Finally, the telling slowed to an end. The speaker stepped back and bowed to the Loremaster. The figure in black returned to the podium.

"MacKenzie Wolf has fallen. Shall his name be remembered in the halls?"

A silence descended on the chamber.

Hamilton Atwyl stepped into the aisle and shouted. "Aff! Let his name—"

Cries of "Neg! Neg!" cut him off.

Contradictory shouts erupted as the solemn dignity of the proceedings dissolved in turmoil. Dechan watched Jaime Wolf and was surprised at the stiffness of the man. Even when the Loremaster turned to him and said something that the microphones didn't pick up, the Colonel stood still and said nothing. The Loremaster tolled the bell and kept it tolling until the tumult floundered and quiet returned.

"The rule is clear. He died a warrior, he shall be remembered as a warrior, one among many. This is the rede of the Loremaster."

There was a pause, then a wave of grumbling and a few exclamations of satisfaction. But there were no objections.

"Seyla," the Loremaster intoned.

"Seyla," the sloppy chorus of the assembly echoed.

The dispersing crowd was much noisier than it had been when arriving. Dragoon jostled Dragoon in the exodus, and Dechan was cut off from Jenette by a squat tanker who seemed in no hurry. Jenette didn't seem to notice and pushed on ahead. He was sure she would be waiting for him outside, so he resigned himself to the slower pace. Soon enough he'd be out and they could go elsewhere.

Outside the hall, a fistfight broke out and stalled the crowd. Dechan leaned against the doorway, at once amused and irritated. Dragoon unity on display. Waiting on Dragoons seemed to be his life's work.

"You seem to have been forgotten, Dechan Fraser."

Dechan turned to look at the speaker, a sandy-haired giant of a man. Neither the face nor the deep voice were familiar to him, but the dress uniform bore a nameplate that gave him the giant's name.

"What would you know about it, Major Elson?"

"I was an adoptee, too."

"But now you're just one of the big happy family."

"I talk with many of the others who are not part of the circle of old-timers and sycophants surrounding Wolf. Some of them have told me that you were once a rising star with the Dragoons. Some even said you had the makings of a colonel, and that you might one day have commanded the Dragoons. But that was before Wolf sent you away. Many people say he will not give an outsider due reward."

"Yeah, well, whatever prospects I had, they're gone now."

"Look around you, Fraser. Not everyone cares for the way some officers take rank and make it privilege. The Dragoons are changing."

That was obvious, but Dechan didn't understand what this man was making of it. Maybe he'd been away too long to know the currents within the Dragoons, but he'd lived the Kuritan life long enough to know better than to commit himself to a stranger. "What are you suggesting?"

"I suggest nothing. I merely point out the obvious."

"Obvious to you, maybe."

"I was told that you were a perceptive man. You know what the old Dragoons did to your life. Look around you, see where things stand, then remember what you heard tonight."

"And what does that mean?"

If the man was annoyed by Dechan's stupid act, he didn't show it. His tone remained calm, and his voice stayed pitched to carry no further than the two of them. He smiled a friendly, almost conspiratorial smile. "True Dragoons welcome, and honor, true warriors."

"Look, Major, I'm in no mood for platitudes."

"I am sorry to disturb you then," Elson said with a dip of his head. "I will be about my business and no longer impose upon you. I wish you well, Dechan Fraser."

The big man vanished surprisingly quickly into the crowd that was finally breaking up. Jenette called to Dechan and he headed in her direction. Clearly, she had seen the man.

"Who was that?"

Dechan found himself surprisingly reluctant to talk

about what the big man had said. "Somebody who thought he knew me."

"I didn't know you knew any Elementals."

"I don't, but maybe I will someday."

Jenette wrinkled her brow at his obliqueness. She laughed in an attempt to change his mood. "But we don't need to play soldier tonight; that duty's done. I promised we'd have the night alone after the Remembrance and so I am at your command. What do you want to do?"

"I think I just want to go home."

36

Stanford Blake blew into Colonel Wolf's office like a whirlwind. I was glad to see him, and hoped he would shake the Colonel out of the strange lethargy into which he had fallen since learning of the death of his son. Blake was still in field uniform, which was worn and stained from the training maneuvers he had been conducting when I'd contacted him. I'd been worried that he would dress me down for not going through channels, but when he'd heard what I had to say, he had promised to come at once. He'd been as good as his word.

The Colonel looked surprised to see his intelligence chief burst through the door. Maybe it was because we were in the middle of an intel briefing that he took it in stride, but I had my doubts. Jaime Wolf had been been taking everything with a laconic indifference of late.

"You're a little early, aren't you, Stan?"

Blake started to say something and caught himself as he realized that the Colonel was not alone. Glancing at Captain Svados, Blake's intel second, he said, "Janey, you'd better go watch the store."

She nodded briskly. He stood slapping his bush hat against his thigh until she left. I started to follow, but Stan restrained me. "Just shut the door, Brian, then run a bugging check."

"But this is—"

"Just do it!"

I did. Stan appropriated a seat and waited silently until I was done. The Colonel humored him and waited as well. The scanners reported no active devices and I told him so. His response was, "Now, run a comprehensive check and match it against the last set in your personal commset."

Colonel Wolf lost interest as I followed Stan's orders. He called the morning's sitreps up on his screen and stared at them with more interest than he had shown when we were reviewing them. Still, I wondered if he was only feigning interest. Just as I started the tertiary checks, he spoke.

"Stan?"

"Soon enough, Jaime."

There was silence while I finished checking. When I reported that everything was normal, the Colonel said, "All right, Stan. Now maybe you'll tell me what this is all about."

"Maybe *you'll* tell *me*," Stan shot back.

The Colonel frowned. "Not the way it works, Stan. Start with why you chased Captain Svados out of here. If this is business, your second's got a need to know. When did you start keeping secrets from her?"

"Since she started keeping secrets from me," Stan replied, confirming what I'd feared.

Colonel Wolf's frown deepened. "What are you talking about?"

"It's what I've been trying to tell you, Colonel," I blurted out. I almost lost my courage when he turned his eyes on me. "Someone's been falsifying communiques."

"That's a dangerous accusation, Brian."

"I know, Colonel. That's why I've been trying to lock things down, but I haven't been able to. I see logs that say messages and orders have been sent and others that report them as received, but I hear people saying they never got them or arguing over just what the content was. It's why I contacted Colonel Blake. I thought he might have an explanation.''

Stan took up the argument. ''Jaime, I didn't even know you were back on Outreach until Brian punched a call through on the emergency net. And don't put him on report for misuse of the net; I think he has good cause. If he hadn't done it, things might be a lot worse. Svados reported you still incommunicado in deep space.''

''Incommunicado?'' the Colonel echoed in a puzzled voice.

''As per your orders,'' Stan added.

Jaime Wolf cupped his chin in his left hand. ''I never sent those orders.''

''Damn!'' Stan slammed his hat onto the floor. ''It *is* worse than we thought. Jaime, you should never have gone chasing that feud.''

Stan's outburst was cut off by a rap on the door. I don't know what I expected to see as Stan and I turned to see the door open, but it wasn't Colonel Carmody. The white-haired old man looked briefly surprised to see Stan, but he made no comment. He just said what he had come to say to the Wolf.

''It's time, Colonel.''

''I'll be there in a minute, Jason.''

Carmody nodded and closed the door.

''What's going on, Jaime?'' Stan said, voicing my own question.

''A council meeting,'' the Colonel said quietly.

That was news to me, and I was supposed to know the Colonel's whereabouts at any given time. ''It wasn't on your schedule,'' I said.

''Why wasn't I informed?'' Stan asked at the same time.

The Colonel looked at each of us in turn. ''I thought you were, Stan. I'm sorry, Brian, I forgot to tell you.''

''You *forgot*!''

''Stan, back off. I'm tired and I don't need a lot of

grief. I forgot. You'll just have to forgive me for being human.''

Stan wasn't buying. ''Unity, Jaime! What in Kerensky's name do you think you're doing? Why don't you just sell the 'Mechs for scrap and turn everybody out?''

''I'm trying to hold the Dragoons together.''

''This meeting is about naming a second-in-command,'' Stan said. There was suspicion in his voice, and I began to see what was happening.

''That's right,'' the Colonel said. ''I was planning to appoint Kelly Yukinov. He's done a good job with Alpha Regiment.''

''Scuttlebutt says that Alpin is expecting to be named your second,'' I said.

The Colonel shook his head. His voice was heavy, freighted with what I took to be regret. ''No. He's not ready now . . . if he'll ever be.''

Stan sighed, then wet his lips. He was nervous and I didn't blame him. ''Jaime, Alpin's been running with the Clanner faction. They've been touting him as your successor.''

''Alpin? He's no leader of men.''

''You've been a little out of touch. People change. He seems to have put together a coalition.''

''You're blowing things out of proportion, Stan. The Clanners don't like the idea of a family succession. Alpin couldn't convince them otherwise.''

''Then maybe you should put him in. The Clanners will have to shut up. Once he screws up, you'll have grounds to replace him, and in the meantime, there'll be time for some of the integration programs to do their work. We can't afford botch-ups like the cache mission.''

Stan realized his slip when the Colonel stiffened.

''I'm sorry, Jaime. I didn't mean that how it sounded. It's just that things haven't worked out the way we hoped. There's still too much friction within the Dragoons.''

Jaime Wolf's flare of emotion faded as quickly as it had come. The energy had fled and he spoke like a tired, old man. ''It's all right, Stan. It'll all work out. Yukinov is a good commander and he's done a good job with Alpha. Give it a year or so and then, well, who knows?'' The Colonel stood. ''The council is waiting.''

We walked down the hall to the meeting room. The council was made up of the commanders of each of the Dragoons' active regiments and the heads of the various commands and operational areas. There were thirteen members, fourteen including the Colonel as the head of the council. Most were present and, except for the Colonel and Stan, all had brought their two permitted aides. By tradition one aide was allowed at the table with the council member, while the other sat or stood around the edges of the room. I took my place at the Colonel's side. Stan sat alone next to me. His mouth quirked up in irritation, and I looked across the table to see Alpin Wolf seated next to Neil Parella of Gamma Regiment.

Of the other field commanders, only Alicia Fancher of Beta Regiment was present. Hanson Brubaker of the Contract Command leaned across his aide, deep in conversation with Gerald Kearne, the Blackwell Corporation representative, who was a non-voting member of the council. Jason Carmody was sitting bolt upright in his seat. The Outreach commander looked as though he didn't want to be present. I sympathized, but at least he had known this was coming. Next around the table from him were Chan, Nikkitch, and Grazier: BattleMech, Infantry, and Armored Operations heads. The last council member present was Hamilton Atwyl, head of the Aerospace Command.

Stan whispered to me. ''Maybe it's not as bad as I thought. Epsilon's on planet, and Nichole's a strong supporter. When she gets here, we'll have the numbers.''

I wished that he had let me in on his suspicions. I knew where Alpin stood. Parella was an open Clan idolator, and Carmody and Atwyl were staunch supporters of the Colonel, but I didn't know the politics of the others. How could I help if I didn't know who was safe?

The chamber door opened and Major Elson walked in with a quartet of junior officers, mostly infantrymen.

"What are you doing here, Elson?" Stan demanded.

"I stand for Epsilon," Elson said, drawing himself to attention. "Colonel Nichole and most of the command are down with an intestinal bug. It seems to have been something in the officers' mess. As I am the senior officer unaffected, Dragoon policy requires that I stand in for the commanding officer to fulfill all duties and responsibilities.''

Stan frowned, then gave the Colonel a sharp glance when Wolf invited Elson to take a place at the table. Elson motioned his allowed aide to the table, but he didn't sit. Instead, he walked around the circumference and held out a flimsy to the Colonel.

"Colonel Wolf, I was given this communique on the way in.''

The Wolf read what Elson offered, then passed it to me. I announced the contents. "Colonel Yukinov's DropShip has developed a drive malfunction. He is still in orbit.''

"We will have to begin without him," Fancher said.

"Now we are in trouble," Stan whispered to me.

Elson took his seat and the Colonel called the meeting to order.

"There's been a lot of pressure from certain quarters," he began. "I understand your concerns, and I share them. We really need to pull together and I'm hoping you will all stand behind my choice of second-in-command.''

"Come on, Jaime. Let's get on with it. I've got to lift for a contract this evening," Parella said. "Name your choice so we can get on with the arguments."

Other voices around the table echoed the sentiment. It was a sign of the confusion into which the Dragoons had sunk that some of those voices belonged to aides rather than council members.

The Colonel held up a hand for silence. When he got it, he said, "I name Kelly Yukinov as second. Considering the current situation, I expect he will turn over command of Alpha to his second and assume a position on my immediate command staff."

After the earlier reaction, I'd been expecting an outburst. No one said anything for a few moments, then Fancher stood up.

"You deny Alpin?"

The Colonel looked down at the table. "I must."

Elson spoke. "You break your own rules just as you broke the Clan's."

Atwyl's head snapped around and his face contorted. "You shut up!"

"I cannot. I am too concerned. Though I am not a medtech, I have eyes. What I see tells me that I must speak, even though others fear to say what they must know in their hearts. Jaime Wolf acts the part of a senile man. He withdraws from his responsibilities, letting others carry his burden. He will not relinquish his control over the Dragoons, yet he will not let the younger generation have its due. He is dangerous to all of us."

I was shocked that the Colonel said nothing in his own defense.

"He's your commander, Elson," Nikkitch pointed out.

Elson ignored him. "The council can act. Censure is an option."

"Not going to happen, Clanner," Atwyl said. "You can't get Jaime voted out."

"Perhaps not," Elson said. His confidence suggested that he didn't necessarily believe that Atwyl was correct.

"But we can challenge," Alpin said, looking to Elson like a trained dog checking to see if he'd performed his trick correctly.

"You'll lose, Alpin," Carmody said warningly.

"But *I* won't." Elson stood and faced the Colonel. "Jaime Wolf, colonel and too long the leader of Wolf's Dragoons, I call you unfit. You are old and have held your position beyond your time. Acknowledge your failing abilities. Acknowledge the truth and step down."

Still, Jaime Wolf maintained his silent stare at the table.

"Jaime won't step down for you," Stan answered for the Colonel.

"Then before this council, I challenge Jaime Wolf to a Trial of Position." Elson stared at the Colonel. "I will defeat you."

"This isn't permitted," Atwyl shouted.

"It is," Parella yelled back. "The council can sanction anyone's challenge."

"Only if the majority agree," Atwyl shot back.

Fancher slammed her fist in the table. "I call the vote."

"The council head must call for all votes," Carmody objected. His voice was bleak, as if he expected to be overridden. Fancher obliged him.

"Personal interest disqualifies the council head," Fancher smiled coldly at Carmody. "As Outreach commander, you must call the role at any member's request. And I so request."

Carmody cast an imploring look at the Colonel, but he got no support. The Wolf seemed turned inward on himself, uncaring. Reluctantly, Carmody asked each of the council members whether they would allow the challenge. Even though both Jaime Wolf and Elson were ineligible to vote, their presence meant that the council had enough members to enforce the ruling. Challenge was a part of Clan life, and I suspected that several council members felt that they had to allow it even though they might prefer a less martial solution. Too many votes favored the challenge.

With no one left to poll, Carmody quietly said, "My vote means nothing to the count, but let the record show I find the challenge inappropriate. The council allows the challenge by a margin of six to four."

"It is settled," Elson said. "We shall fight, Jaime Wolf."

At last, the Colonel looked up. "That does seem to be the way of it."

Elson grinned. "It must be. If you refuse the Trial, you lose. Your position is forfeited."

"I've lost that already," Jaime Wolf said in a barely audible voice.

"But even if you win the fight, Elson, you can't take over the Dragoons," Stan said. "You should have studied better. If you win, the council cannot sanction you as the leader of the Dragoons. You don't have enough time in uniform."

"I am aware of that, Colonel Blake. But, have no fear, for I have studied well. The challenger need not take the position for which he challenges, if he has a sponsor. That is, I believe, one of the improvements your freeborn council has made to the Clan way." Elson swept the table with his eyes. "I perform this challenge in the name of Alpin Wolf. He is of the leader's bloodline and therefore qualified to replace him, by your rules. Alpin shall lead the Dragoons when I win."

"You're a fool," Colonel Wolf said quietly.

His grandson Alpin rewarded his comment with a glare of naked hatred. Elson shrugged off the remark.

"I am a survivor, Jaime Wolf. Soon your opinions

will no longer matter. You have a decision to make which you cannot ignore: how the Trial shall be fought. You will of course choose to fight augmented.''

"No, I think not.''

"Jaime!'' Those who had stood by Colonel Wolf were shocked and incredulous. Fighting Elson unaugmented would be suicide. I suddenly feared that death was exactly what the Colonel was seeking. Since he had learned of MacKenzie's death, the fire had left him. Among the Clans, old warriors gladly accepted any chance to die in combat. Did Jaime Wolf see this as his opportunity?

The Colonel slowly pushed his chair away from the table, then stood. ''But I reserve the right to have a champion.''

Elson smiled confidently. ''Then name him, for mine is the right to choose the time and place of the Trial. I select now for the time, and this chamber for the place. Draw the Circle of Equals.''

37

"I will be the Wolf's champion!"

Elson turned his head to see the challenger. It was Pietr Shadd. Face full of grim determination, the young pup stepped away from the wall and strode up beside Wolf. He glared at Elson over Wolf's head. "If he will have me."

Wolf turned his head and looked up at Shadd. "This is not a sibko trial, Pietr."

Blake joined them. "Since you've accepted, you'd better let the boy fight, Jaime. He's got a better chance of beating that monster than you do."

"It will be better if I do this myself."

"Unity! Maybe you are going senile. Elson's a trained Elemental. Clan-trained. He'll tear you apart!"

"Let Shadd fight," Cameron advised. Other old-sters joined in, arguing that Wolf could not best Elson. Carmody suggested delaying the Trial to let Wolf find an even better champion, but Fancher quashed that proposal by pointing out that a delay would be a significant loss of honor. At which point, Shadd said, "You must let me fight for you, Colonel. I have the best chance of defeating him."

"This isn't what I wanted," Wolf objected.

"He's your best chance, Jaime," Carmody insisted.

Wolf folded his arms and hung his head, considering his options. He looked at Shadd. "I'm sure you can fight well, Pietr, but I don't want you to die here."

"I won't, sir. I will win for you."

"Listen to me, boy. This isn't worth your life."

"I will beat him."

Wolf gave Shadd a smile, but it was a sad, weak thing.

"You have already lost," Elson told him.

Elson's men moved forward to clear the center of the room of tables and chairs. He stripped off his weapons belt and his uniform jacket. Shadd did the same, while Carmody whispered urgently in the boy's ear. Elson almost smiled. If the old man thought he knew some tricks that would help Shadd, he was mistaken. This was not the time for learning; the Circle was where you proved what you already knew. There was no time for anything else.

The Dragoons formed a ring around the open space. Elson stepped into the Circle but stayed near the edge. Shadd stepped into the open space on the opposite side. There was no need for announcements or a rehashing of the rules.

They began.

For almost a minute, there was no combat. The two men circled, each watching the other for the slip that would offer an opening. Impatient, Shadd charged. He and the Elemental traded blows and battered at each other's guard. There would be bruises, but nothing significant was achieved in the first flurry. Or the next.

Elson moved in with a standard pattern designed to lift his opponent's ward into the high line, preparatory to an attack along the low line. Shadd flowed with the assault. He was well-trained, and his response to the shift in the pattern was fast. But it was also textbook-standard.

Elson let him take the next attack and shifted pattern again as a test. Shadd responded as before. Elson closed in to test his strength against the boy's. He broke away, having learned what he needed to know. Shadd was a little faster than Elson, but was unable to use his bulk to its maximum effectiveness. The boy was good, and showed the potential for developing into a truly formidable hand-to-hand fighter in time.

He would not have that time.

Elson closed, shifting for a high-line roundhouse kick. Shadd moved his right hand out to catch Elson's ankle and brought his left up in a move that would shatter Elson's leg if he resisted or tumble him if he did not. Elson didn't resist. Instead he continued shifting his weight into the kick, going with the throw. His hand snapped out and grabbed Shadd's ankle. Caught off guard, Shadd was pulled off balance. Prepared, Elson flowed with the throw. Tucking tighter, he spun faster and pulled Shadd down. The boy lost his grip on Elson and the Elemental took advantage by rolling away and to his feet. He spun and charged back.

Abruptly halting his charge, Elson lifted his foot for a downward stomp. Shadd threw himself to one side, taking his head out of line. Elson slammed his foot down on his intended target. Three of Shadd's fingers snapped as Elson's hardened heel came down on his hand. The boy screamed with the sudden pain.

Elson knew then that it was only a matter of time. He let Shadd get to his feet before attacking again. Elson launched pattern after pattern that forced Shadd to block with his injured hand or else take a more grievous hit. Each block shocked pain into Shadd's expression. By the fifth pattern, Shadd was slow. Elson's strike penetrated to the boy's body and cracked ribs. Shadd was even slower after that.

Elson moved closer, working harder against the boy's weak side. He got one in on Shadd's hip, then another to the ribs. The boy's defenses crumbled. Elson placed a fist into Shadd's solar plexus, doubling the boy over. A sharp elbow to the neck dropped him. Shadd's chin cracked sharply on the floor and blood spattered out onto Elson's feet.

Seeing that Shadd was defeated, Elson took a moment to gather oxygen. The boy had no more strength, yet he struggled to rise, with a courage befitting a true warrior. To reward that valor, Elson aimed a kick to snap Shadd's neck. The boy would die as a warrior should, in combat.

But Shadd's strength had fallen farther than either combatant expected, betraying Elson's intent and Shadd's determination. The boy slipped and Elson's foot caught him on the shoulder, lifting him up, before tumbling him backward. The kick became just another piece of punishment. Shadd sprawled, groaning.

Elson ground his teeth. The harmony of the Circle was broken, the purity of the fight tarnished. He moved in, determined to finish it with a swift knife-hand to Shadd's throat.

"Stop!"

Elson didn't listen. Catcalls, shouts, even orders from outside the Circle meant nothing. It was forbidden to violate the Circle. Thus, he was surprised to find the reedy Cameron stepping into his way.

"This fight's over," the commo officer said. His voice teetered on the edge of panic, but he had screwed up his courage to stand before Elson. It was almost too bad that Cameron was siding with the oldsters. He had promise. But promise unfulfilled was nothing, and Cameron would never fulfill any promises if he did not get out of the way.

"Not until one is dead." Shadd groaned behind his valueless protector, and Elson wanted to end the duel before it became more of a farce. Killing Cameron would only complicate the issue. "I will forget your violation of honor if you get out of my way now."

"No. Look at him." Cameron took half a step back and pointed.

Elson looked. Shadd's mangled hand stretched over the line of the Circle. The tip of one finger touched the floor. He had broken the Circle, escaping death at the cost of his honor.

"Seyla," Elson said as he pivoted away from his opponent.

Wolf would live, but it didn't matter. Wolf's champion was defeated, and the Trial was won. Maybe it was more fitting this way, Elson thought. The abandonment of the honor road had culminated with the abandonment of honor. The dethronement of Wolf was not as clean as he had wished, but, he realized, it would probably make the next stages go more easily, for who could cling to a dishonored ex-commander?

Cheers from his partisans rose around him.

38

The news of the successful challenge to Jaime Wolf's supremacy was the talk of Harlech. The Dragoons all knew, and the mercenary groups and Successor State representatives were beginning to get wind of it. As word spread, so did the controversy. Not everyone agreed that Elson's challenge and the subsequent appointment of Alpin as head of Wolf's Dragoons were legal. But Jaime Wolf made no public statements or appearances, having retired to his compound to the west of the city. He might have been in hiding. Or mourning. Or maybe he was just ashamed to show his face. Whatever the reason for his withdrawal, his silence sanctioned what had happened.

Dechan was confused, and the constant badgering from the various merc units courting him only made it worse. The news of Wolf's deposition should have been welcome, but instead he felt disturbed and unsettled. Restless and unable to sleep at night, he had taken to prowling the streets.

Nights in Harlech weren't quiet. The locals said it hadn't always been that way, except of course in the rowdy temptowns where the offplanet mercs hung out their shingles. Nightly celebrations or fights, or both, kept the townies awake late into the night. Dechan didn't like what he was seeing. Maybe Elson was right. Maybe the Dragoons *were* changing.

But what Dechan saw was not all of the Dragoons.

Several units were away on contract, but not Beta, the regiment in which he had served. He had a hard time imagining that they would serve under an upstart, but they were following the lead of their new commander, Colonel Fancher. Dechan had heard that she'd been dismissed, but somewhere along the line Wolf had recalled her. His mistake. Dechan had heard her speak on the news last night, saying that she was solidly behind Alpin.

Dechan's wanderings took him this night to the park across from the general headquarters. Wolf Hall, they called it. Would it soon be Alpin Hall, or did the young upstart's ego not extend that far? The moon cast a fitful light between the fast-moving clouds. Shadows danced across the squat outbuildings and up the sides of the tall towers, whence they leapt off into oblivion like the mythical lemmings.

Whatever the machinations in the command structure, Dragoon business went on. Lights burned in several offices. Even with Jaime Wolf no longer in charge, somewhere Wolf's Dragoons were on duty, and they needed staff support. That meant that here, someone was listening. Maybe things weren't so bad after all. Maybe different was all right.

"*Karma* brings us together again."

Spinning away from where he had stood, Dechan threw himself into the shadow of the wall and drew his sidearm. He couldn't see the speaker at first, but he could hear him panting as if he had been running. The man's dark uniform blended with the shadows, making it hard to see him though Dechan knew he was there. Soon the light blob that was his face became clear. Two smaller blobs, hands held out and open, were clear as well. There seemed to be no danger, however, and Dechan straightened from his crouch, holstering his weapon as he did.

"Michi?"

"I would wish you a good evening, but I doubt it will be one, Dechan-*san*."

"We don't speak for years and then you start with a riddle."

"I am sorry, Dechan-*san*. I would not have intruded on your life if it were not important. The plans are made. They will kill him soon."

"What are you talking about?"

"Jaime Wolf will not see the sunrise."

Dechan found it curious to realize that he believed Michi's statement without question. Jaime's death would certainly end any hope of seeing him restored. Dechan didn't know whose plot this might be, and he didn't care. He also didn't see how it involved him. "Why not tell him yourself?"

"I cannot." There was shouting on the far side of the building. Michi looked in that direction for a moment, listening. "There is no time for argument. There are others I must warn. As a Dragoon, the task to warn Wolf falls to you."

"I'm not a Dragoon anymore."

The shouting drew closer.

"You once said that being a Dragoon was like being a samurai," Michi said in a hushed voice. "A samurai serves until death. You have the opportunity to save your lord from dishonorable death."

"He abandoned me."

Michi took a step back into the shadows. Even to Dechan's dark-adapted eyes, none of the man was visible save for his face. "If you believe that, you can have your revenge. Do nothing and Wolf and his family will die."

Then the face was gone.

Dechan was alone, but not for long. A trio of Home Guard troopers came pelting along the avenue. One saw Dechan and covered him with a rifle while calling for him to stand still. Dechan didn't move.

"That's not him," a man wearing sergeant's stripes

said as he knocked the first trooper's barrel up. "Our man's wearing black."

"He coulda changed," the trooper whined.

"Not enough time." The sergeant turned to Dechan and squinted at him. "Say, citizen, haven't I seen you around?"

"Name's Dechan Fraser."

"Don't sound familiar. You haven't seen anybody lurking about, have you?"

"I saw a jogger in a dark suit down by the lake. I thought it was early for PE, but you know how fanatical some people are."

"That's gotta be him," the first trooper shouted and started off at a run. The other two guardsmen followed. As he disappeared into the trees, the sergeant shouted back, "Be a good citizen and report to the guard station at the Hall. Tell them what you saw."

Dechan thought about ignoring the sergeant's order, but he realized that the sergeant had his name. If he checked up and Dechan hadn't reported, it could raise suspicions that he had been a party to the fugitive's escape. Reluctantly, Dechan walked to the guard station. The guard captain wore the stylized wolf's-head favored by partisans of the new order. Though he seemed not to have much use for Dechan's circumstantial evidence, he spent a long time establishing it. During that time, Dechan thought about what Michi had said. Every time he went over the possible outcomes, he liked them less. He wanted to be away from Wolf Hall, but running out before the captain dismissed him wouldn't help anyone.

While Dechan waited for dismissal, Hamilton Atwyl exited the elevator bank. On his way across the lobby, he happened to glance at the guard station. Seeing Dechan, his face opened into a smile.

"Dechan? What are you doing here?"

"I could ask you the same thing, Ham."

Dechan made his remark with a jocular tone, but it

evoked a guarded look in Atwyl's eyes. "You're not under arrest, are you?"

With a shake of his head, Dechan said, "Just reporting a prowler."

"A prowler?" Atwyl frowned, then looked thoughtful. When he spoke, his voice was pitched so that anyone nearby would have no trouble hearing his words. "It's been a long time since we've talked. If you've got a few, I'll pop for the brew."

It was obviously an invitation, and one meant to be seen as nonpolitical. Under the circumstances, Dechan suspected that it was anything but. Still undecided about how to handle the burden Michi had placed on him, he realized that he knew too little of what was happening. Ham was an old friend, and high in the Dragoon command structure. At the very least, Dechan might get a better sense of the power balance. "A few. If I'm not home by dawn, Jenette'll wonder what happened."

"Wouldn't want to cause trouble between you two. You stuck together through a hell of a lot."

Atwyl laid his arm around Dechan's shoulders and started to lead him into the Hall. When the guard captain objected, Atwyl said, "That's all right, Captain. Mr. Fraser's a veteran. I'll vouch for him."

"You'll sign his pass?"

"Yes, I'll sign his pass." Atwyl scribbled his name on the datapad the officer thrust at him, then waited with obvious impatience while the captain processed a visitor's badge for Dechan. Wearing the plastic ID tag, Dechan allowed Atwyl to take him to the cafeteria. It was almost deserted and, once they had their beers, Atwyl selected a table well away from any of the other late-night customers.

Atwyl abandoned any pretense at joviality as soon as they were seated. "So where do you stand on the succession?"

"I'm out of the Dragoons, Ham. Remember?"

"Once a Dragoon, always a Dragoon."

"Somebody already fed me that line tonight, Ham."

"A prowler, maybe?"

"You know about that?"

"Don't know nothing, but I was hoping you'd tell me."

"There's a plot to kill Wolf."

Atwyl sat back in his seat, his beer bottle tilting in his slack hand and coming precariously close to spilling. "You're sure about this?"

"Fellow who mentioned it seemed to be very sure."

"You involved?"

"Would I be talking to you if I was?"

Atwyl laughed softly, bitterly. "I don't know anymore. There are too many two-faces for this old warhorse." He took a hit from his bottle. "When?"

"Before morning."

"That doesn't leave much time. Will you come with me to Carmody? Tell him what you know?"

"I don't know much."

"We'll need everything we can get. Will you help? For old times' sake?"

Heat burned under Dechan's skin. "I'll talk to Carmody."

"I didn't think they'd go that far," Carmody said when they told him. Significantly, he believed Dechan's unsupported statement. "But it all falls into place. That's why they sent the Home Guard out on maneuvers. Wanted me to oversee the whole thing, too."

"There's still a platoon in barracks besides the regular security forces, isn't there?"

Carmody nodded. "But Elson's got a Point of Elementals covering Wolf's place. They're supposed to be security against riots, but they're a guard. They won't let us in."

"Are they armored?"

"No. Even for him, that would be too blatant just now."

"Then we don't have to ask," Atwyl said. "Five Elementals won't stand up against a whole platoon."

"Then what, Ham? What do we do when we're inside?"

"We get Wolf out."

"It sounds so simple, but it isn't. Where would he go?"

Dechan looked at the clock. "If you're going to do something, you'd better do it soon."

"You're right. We'll have to decide what happens next after we make sure there is a next. Maybe Jaime ill have some ideas."

The night was fading into the half-light of predawn when the heavy hovervan whirred down the street toward the Wolf family compound. It might have been a transport truck carrying in foodstuffs from the surrounding countryside to fill the stalls of the fresh-food markets, but it wasn't. Better light would have revealed that its corporate markings were hastily painted and made its military lines readily apparent.

Dechan sat in the hovertruck's cab along with a pimple-faced kid who was supposed to be the best hover jockey in the Home Guard. Atwyl was elsewhere, doing things that were necessary if this scheme was to succeed. Through his earpiece, Dechan could hear the growling of the truck in which Colonel Carmody rode. The platoon of motorized infantry was approaching the Wolf family compound. Dechan popped the plug for a moment, then replaced it after confirming that it was the trucks' snarling engines he heard echoing in the predawn streets.

Carmody was with his platoon of Home Guard. He had to be; no one else could have gotten them out of barracks and persuaded them to face the Elementals guarding the Wolf compound. As it was, Dechan could tell by the colonel's haranguing that some of them were hanging back by the transports. The colonel's arguments shifted to a different sort when the leader of the Elementals confronted him.

Dechan turned on the hovervan's video deck and fumbled with the controls until he had it tuned to the channel from Carmody's truck. They had arranged that the video pickup would cover the gate area so that Dechan could observe as well as listen in to what was happening. He could see Carmody arguing with the Elemental leader. Suddenly, the colonel stopped talking and cocked his head to one side. Then he looked over his shoulder toward the center of the city.

It was painfully obvious to Dechan what was happening. The colonel's headset was spouting a report from one of the spotter posts they had set up on all the probable routes to the suburbs. The assassins were on their way.

The colonel's reaction must have meant something to the Elemental leader as well. He started calling orders to his Point.

"This is going wrong," Dechan told his driver. "Take the van in."

"I don't have orders," the kid objected. "We're supposed to wait for Colonel Carmody's signal."

Dechan slapped him on the shoulder. "Take the van in!"

The picture wobbled as the hovervan's engine gobbled power to spin the fans faster. The truck blasted from the alley where it was hidden and headed for the compound.

Carmody saw it coming and shouted. "Launcher on the gate!"

As the missile team jumped out of the lead transport, the Point commander reacted. He chopped Carmody in the throat and raced for cover, but he wasn't fast enough. The rocket roared past him, impacting slightly off-center on the iron gates. Fire flared over the gate, and the Elemental was flung away like a doll.

One valve was blown clear and the other hung drunkenly as the van barreled toward the gate. The Elementals had opened fire on the Home Guardsmen, who were returning fire erratically. Dechan caught a glimpse of Carmody sprawled awkwardly as the hovervan bucked over the debris and slammed into the hanging gate. Iron rang and the truck's fender crumpled, but the driver fought the slewing van and kept it on course through the gateway.

The hovervan roared up the drive, leaving behind the firing at the gate. With the house set so far back from the street, soldiers on foot would take some time to reach it. The van flashed across the parklike grounds in seconds. The van slowed as it climbed the slight hill, and the driver dropped the speed further as they took the last turn. The move was deliberate; a fast-moving vehicle would likely be taken as a hostile. The fans were muted to a purr by the time he spun the vehicle to a broadside parking position on the green in front of the mansion.

Wolf was waiting on the porch. Behind him, Joshua stood in the open doorway, a laser pistol cradled in both hands. The boy was probably more of a threat to himself than to an intruder. His mother obviously agreed; she appeared and appropriated the weapon. She joined Wolf as the hovervan settled, its fans idling.

Dechan was almost amused to see that Wolf seemed surprised to see him step down from the van.

"Is this a rescue or an assault, Dechan?" he asked.

"Both," Dechan answered perversely. "But I'm with the parties of the first part."

"And who's the other side?"

"I think you know better than me."

Satisfied that there was no immediate danger, the rest of the family boiled out onto the porch to sur-

round the little group. Dechan ignored their questions and spoke to Wolf.

"There's a plot against your life scheduled to be executed tonight."

Wolf looked at the graying sky. "There's not much night left."

"Exactly."

"There's no need for killing," Katherine said. "Don't we have enough dead? We could just leave."

"We could," Marisha said. "But Jaime can't."

"Why not?" Katherine asked.

"Because, whether he wants to be involved or not, he's too good a rallying point for those who oppose him." Marisha's expression was grim. "No one will rally around a dead man."

Katherine looked appalled. "You're talking about murder!"

Dechan snorted. "I don't think they see it that way. This is probably just a necessary precaution in the battle for supremacy in the Dragoons. Is it murder when you have one of your Trials? What about it, Wolf? If you'd fought for yourself in that challenge, Elson would have killed you then. Now, then. What's the difference?"

"There's enough of a difference that it will cause him problems," Wolf said.

"Only if he isn't the one to tell the story," Marisha said.

"There's truth in that," Wolf agreed with a sigh. "Maybe it's not too late to try and fix things."

A sharp series of explosions sounded from the gate, followed by increased weapons fire. "It won't be your choice if you stay here much longer."

Wolf nodded. "Get everyone in the van. We'll go out the back way. Riverview Parkway will put us on the expressway to the port."

There wasn't a lot of talking as the family boarded the hovervan. A loud explosion made Katherine jump and she nearly fell from the tail, but Rachel grabbed her arm and steadied her. Dechan sealed the doors and moved around to the front. The driver didn't let him get seated before he gunned the fans. The van howled away from the mansion, Wolf giving directions from the cargo compartment through the open panel.

The ride to the spaceport was tense, but they encountered no roadblocks, no ambushes. Men wearing Home Guard uniforms were manning the approaches to the spaceport. They waved the van through. Hamilton Atwyl and Brian Cameron were standing at the foot of the passenger ramp when they pulled up.

"I'm glad to see you, Colonel," Atwyl said as Wolf climbed out the back of the truck. "We were worried when we heard that Colonel Carmody was down."

Wolf's eyes flashed. "Another score to settle."

Cameron helped the women out of the van while Wolf talked to Atwyl. There was no luggage for the waiting crewmembers to carry. They scurried up the ramp ahead of the family. Cameron had a last word with Atwyl, before the aerospace colonel took off across the field in his hoverjeep. The great DropShip began to hiss and clang as the crew prepared for launch. A crewmember fretted, waiting for Wolf to board.

The Colonel held out his hand to Dechan. "Thank you."

Ignoring the offered hand, Dechan said, "I don't want your thanks."

"Well, you've got them anyway. I appreciate what you've done."

Dechan was distinctly uncomfortable. He couldn't look Wolf in the face. Staring off across the field, he asked, "Where will you go?"

"To the other side of the mountain."

"Why not just leave? Go to Davion?"

"Running away won't solve anything."

No, it wouldn't. "He'll come after you."

"He's welcome to try." Wolf smiled in the way Dechan remembered from years ago. It made him feel sorry for whoever got in Wolf's way. "Come with us. We'll need good MechWarriors."

"I won't leave Jenette."

Cameron called out from the top of the ramp. "Colonel, gate reports firing."

Wolf frowned. "There's no time to get her, Dechan. We can send a message for her to join us."

"And if they intercept it? No thanks, Colonel. I'll look after her myself."

"I wouldn't leave Marisha, either. Good luck, Dechan."

Turning his back on the Colonel, Dechan hopped aboard the van and ordered the anxious driver to pull out. Dust kicked out as the fans whirred to full speed, pelting Wolf as he ran up the ramp. Dechan didn't look back. The driver took the van around the bulk of the DropShip and away from the firefight at the main gate. They headed for a storage shed where technician uniforms and passes waited for them. While they changed, the *Chieftain* lifted for orbit.

39

When Colonel Atwyl woke me and ordered me to the spaceport without explanation, I was more annoyed then worried. Sudden assembly orders weren't standard in a safe zone, except during training. I had been dreaming about my sibko and, I suppose, I half-thought I was still in training. It wasn't until I reached the port and saw the frantic activity that I realized something serious was happening. Colonel Atwyl's briefing told me just how serious it was.

I was too busy to worry until some time after lift-off. Then, being mostly idle because we were running silent, I found the time. While I was glad that the Wolf had finally decided to fight back, I didn't see a lot of hope. Listening to the broadcasts, I heard the first lies. It seems a gas main had exploded near the Wolf family compound, causing casualties among the security forces. The public was being assured that no civilians—which currently included Jaime Wolf—had been injured. There was no mention of guns or rockets or escapes. I felt sure that the real news was being carried on tight beams or in coded transmissions that were, at present, unavailable to me.

The *Chieftain* was fleeing the sunrise, burning through a low orbit away from the day that was dawning in Harlech. I was encouraged that our flight was unopposed. No aerospace fighters or other DropShips were rising from the port or dropping from high orbit to oppose us. The *Chieftain* was powerfully armed, but a swarm of fighters or a group of DropShips could take her. We were too easy a target, hanging out here with only a pair of fighters for escort.

I longed to be on the ground where one could find cover from hostiles. A 'Mech carries a lot less armor and armament than a DropShip, but at least the jock is in control. Aboard a ship, someone else holds your fate hostage to his skills and luck.

I didn't know much about Colonel Wolf's plans at that point. I had been told where we were bound, the training ops center on the other side of the mountain. If all was well, we would soon be receiving landing clearance from the Home Guard forces stationed there. We had reasonable confidence that we would find a friendly welcome. After all, the usurpers had sent the Home Guard forces to the other side of the mountain to keep them out of the action in the World. Even if we weren't welcomed with open arms, we'd land. Some of the Guard had to be loyal. If we had to, we'd fight our way to a linkup with them.

Below and behind us, things were undoubtedly happening, but what? Once we'd established a base in the Outback, we'd have a chance to find out.

The dawn brought unwelcome news to the command center in Wolf Hall, but Elson took it calmly. Everything in his campaign had gone surprisingly well so far. Sooner or later there had to be a slip-up; but he wished it had related to a less important aspect.

Seventh Kommando was supposed to be the elite infantry of Wolf's Dragoons. They were very good, especially for non-Elemental 'pounders. But even the best commandos are at a disadvantage when they walk into a firefight after they'd been planning a quiet approach.

Somehow word had leaked and warning been given to Wolf's loyalists. They had arranged something more quickly than Elson had thought them capable, given Jaime Wolf's recent lethargy. The Wolf had escaped the trap.

The leak would have to be found and plugged, but there was no reason to punish the commandos, no need for harsh words or discipline. As much as Elson was disappointed by their failure, they were not at fault. At least they had eliminated one of Wolf's loyalists. Carmody's death would make it easier to isolate the forces of the Home Guard remaining in Harlech. In time, the forward-thinkers would be singled out from among them and reinstated in the Dragoon fighting elements. But there were more important things to accomplish first. He gave the orders to move on the Home Guard barracks. Fancher's picked team should handle that easily enough; the overwhelming force of the BattleMechs should cow the commanderless pensioners and trainees without need for battle.

"Unauthorized movement in Champaigne quadrant," the commtech reported.

Elson nodded to show he had heard. Despite the news blackout, word of Wolf's flight was spreading. The fight Elson had thought to see finished with the end of the night had likely just begun in earnest.

The city was still relatively quiet.

The spaceport was too far away; Dechan couldn't see if the fighting was still going on there. The early morning newscast babbling softly behind him had nothing to say about it.

The first of the morning commuters would be making their way into the city from the outlying suburbs. Some would be passing by the shattered gates of the Wolf compound. What would they think? Would they suspect what had happened in the predawn?

Spread below him, the city seemed still asleep, holding close to a dream of peace. It was an illusion, he knew, but he cherished it all the same. He wondered how much blood would spill in the day because he couldn't stomach seeing a little shed in the night.

To the north of the housing tower from which he watched, a familiar, ponderous motion caught Dechan's attention.

BattleMechs.

A lance of four was moving along Verban Avenue toward the city center: two heavies and two mediums moving at moderate speed. They spread out into a line when they reached the park. It was not an attack, else they would have charged right through rather than carefully avoiding small trees and the light recreation structures. Spaced evenly apart, they emerged on the side near Wolf Hall and halted facing the complex. He was too far away to see if any soldiers emerged to confront them. If the 'Mech pilots were siding with Elson, they would have turned their machines outward.

Dechan watched the motionless 'Mechs for some minutes. He debated waking Jenette, but was reluctant to tell her of the night's happenings. She would want to go to Wolf's aid, and he would have to try to talk her out of it. He wanted to put off that scene as long as possible.

A series of flashes lit up the front of Wolf Hall. They looked like gunshots, but the 'Mechs didn't react. More flashes. This time Dechan was sure it was gunfire. The lack of movement by the BattleMechs could only mean that their pilots had dismounted. He suspected that none of them would ever again sit in a jock's hot seat.

He turned away from the window and went to wake Jenette.

The commline buzzed for his attention. Michi reached out and tapped a button. The unit displayed the call code of the source, indicating that this was the summons he was expecting.

It had begun.

"Will you not answer it?" Kiyomasa looked older than his years, the dark circles of exhaustion under his eyes and slumped stance robbing him of his youthful appearance. Even so, the young MechWarrior had gotten far more sleep than Michi.

"Iie," Michi replied. "The words I would hear are unimportant, I already know the content of the message. I must leave now."

"You are determined, then?"

Michi let his actions be his answer. He stood. Taking up the duffle from beside his chair, he slung it over his shoulder. Kiyomasa stood also and stepped in his way.

"You must reconsider, Michi-*sama.*"

"I owe my loyalty to a new lord. Would you have me break faith?"

Kiyomasa frowned, clearly distressed by the dilemma. "Wolf is the real lord. He will need warriors."

Ready for that argument, Michi said, "If he rallies an army, he is in rebellion against the laws of the Dragoons."

"He is the rightful lord," Kiyomasa protested.

"He lost the Trial."

"He was tricked into it. It is meaningless."

"Are our customs meaningless?"

"Of course not."

"Then why do you think so little of theirs?"

Kiyomasa's glowered, frustrated. Finally he said, "You must come with us. You are why we came here."

"If that was the only reason, you are all fools and worse than fools." Stepping around the son of his master, he added, "You must do as I must. Follow the demands of your honor."

He left Kiyomasa standing in the room, staring at his feet.

40

We came down the ramps hot and ready, hitting the ground while the dust from the *Chieftain*'s landing was still rising. There were only four of us—there had been no time to fill the DropShip with its full complement without raising an alarm, so all we had were the 'Mechs still aboard from the trip to the Draconis Combine. I was in the lead machine and Grant Linkowski piloted the Colonel's *Archer*. Hans Vordel's *Victor* and Franchette's *Gallowglas* were only seconds behind us. Only the four of us to meet a full regiment of the Home Guard's armor and infantry.

When we weren't immediately fired upon, I allowed myself some hope that our landing clearance had not been a subterfuge, a ploy to bring the Wolf into a trap. In the distance I could see the ranked armor through the dissipating dust. I popped my magnification up a couple of grades and breathed a sigh of relief. Lieutenant Colonel Joe Garcia, Carmody's second, was standing in the open on the deck of his Rommel tank. Colonel Edna Grazier, armored ops chief, stood beside him. If it had been a trap, they would have been buttoned up in their vehicles.

As I throttled my *Loki* down, I noticed how hard my cooling suit was working and I realized how frightened I had been.

I opened communications with a laser link, making arrangements for setting up the Colonel's headquarters. In less than an hour, the command staffs were gathered in Garcia's mobile command trailer, listening to his explanation. Working as closely as he had with his boss, Garcia had suspected that there might be trouble. He'd put his forces on alert as soon as he lost communications with Carmody back in the World. He hadn't known what to expect and our arrival had been a surprise. He had decided to play it cautious: hence the assembled forces. Once he heard our account of the escape and Carmody's death, he knew where he stood.

"Colonel Wolf, we may be a bunch of downtesters, pensioners, newbies, and sibkids, but we're gonna stand by you. There's no honor in murder. I have to admit that I didn't understand about the Trial when I heard, but I thought that you must have had something in mind. Looks like I was right. You were just doing it to smoke out the rats so everyone could see them run, weren't you?"

"You're overestimating my abilities, Joe."

"If so, I'll be the first, Colonel."

"I'll do what I can to justify your faith."

"I'm not worried, Colonel."

"Maybe you should be, Joe. Lord knows we've got a lot to worry about."

"I've got confidence in you, Colonel."

"Thanks, Joe. I appreciate that. I haven't done a lot to deserve it lately." There was an awkward silence in the trailer for a moment, then the Colonel said, "But the past is dead, and we'll be just as dead unless we get rolling. So if we can get into the ops center, we can start getting serious about showing the upstarts who really owns the Dragoons."

The Colonel and the Home Guard officers took the train from the port to the training center complex. We took the 'Mechs cross-country, which was faster than following the rail line or the highway, both of which were confined to the long shallow grade around the northern hills. We couldn't have kept up with the train anyway. During the trip I was able to establish linkage to the ops center through my *Loki* and got a jump on my staff work. I was able to dump a map-update into the computer so that it was waiting for the Wolf when he arrived.

The command center at the Tetsuhara Training Facility didn't have all the sophistication of the main center at Wolf Hall, but it was superior to the *Chieftain*'s facilities. The advantage of space without concern for mass allowed better support for my *Loki* and provided more than adequate triple C for the forces at hand. The ground-based sensor array gave good coverage, but it was supposed to be part of a planetwide system. With the connective links cut, it wasn't operating at full efficiency, leaving holes in our coverage that bothered me. And with the satellite links down, we were also limited in the range over which we could control forces. With some work we could set up relay stations that would minimize the communications dead zones. Relay stations had some advantages; the commlasers and optical cable systems were far less vulnerable to intercept. As I finished my tour of the ops center, Grazier was reacting to the update map.

"This is all?" She looked horrified. "What happened to Yukinov?"

"Probably still on Ingersoll with the rest of Alpha Regiment," the Wolf told her.

We had learned that Kelly Yukinov was never actually on his way to Outreach, despite the intel report indicating that he would attend the fateful council meeting that had resulted in the Trial of Position. There was no doubt that Yukinov was loyal to Colonel Wolf and a report of his imminent arrival was surely meant to assure the Colonel that his partisans would have a majority in the council meeting. Those reports had been false, engineered by Captain Svados in support of Elson and Alpin's coup. I still didn't know if the

Wolf had been taken in by the subterfuge or if he had some other reason for letting the council meeting take place. Could Garcia be right when he suggested that the Wolf had planned it all along? Jaime Wolf hadn't exactly denied the possibility, but he hadn't confirmed it either. Whatever Colonel Wolf's plans had been, the meeting had taken place, he had been deposed, and we were all here in the Outback because of it.

"Alpha may be behind us," the Wolf said, "But they're not here. Since we're cut off from hyperpulse generators, we can't contact them. Even if we could, the situation on Crimond makes it unlikely that they could pull out in time to affect what will be happening here."

"Could the sitreps from Crimond have been falsified, too?" Garcia asked.

"Yes," I told him. "But it's unlikely. FedCom news media report Clan presence and that means combat."

"So we can't count on Alpha," Grazier said glumly.

"But neither will they be arrayed against us. Like Alpha, the Dragoon forces offplanet are engaged. They will be unable to affect anything in the immediate future. On either side. We can only count on what we've got here in the Outback to deal with Alpin's forces onplanet."

"And in orbit," Garcia grumbled.

"That doesn't look to be an issue," the Colonel said.

"What?"

"While we were on our way here, Ham Atwyl and his wingman peeled off for high orbit. They rendezvoused with the cache fleet. Ham's plan was to explain the situation. He seemed to think he could bring them around to our side or at least keep them out of any combat, and he seems to have had some success. Half an hour ago, Fleet Captain Chandra made a broadcast. She's declared the fleet neutral in any conflict. Gobi

Station and all orbital and deep-space assets in system are included in this neutrality.''

"Including satellites?" Grazier asked.

"Yes. All orbital scans are being withheld. Chandra says they will eliminate or disable any satellites used for unauthorized transmissions. The wording of Chandra's statement seems to omit any aerospace assets currently grounded. However, she is urging any disputants, her word, to minimize damage to Dragoon aerospace assets by minimizing use.''

"What's Ham doing now?" Cythene Martel asked. As captain of the *Chieftain,* she was a part of Atwyl's command.

"Nothing. They've cited him as a participant and interned him for the duration of the dispute. Chandra has taken over the Aerospace Command till then." The Wolf shrugged. "Looks like the Fleet Captain is playing for a bigger role for aerospace in Dragoon hierarchy, whichever side comes out on top.''

"So they're trying to force a strictly planetary struggle," Garcia said.

"You weren't listening," Martel said. "Nothing was said about anything sitting on the ground or anything that might come in. Specifically, there was no mention of action at atmospheric interface, am I right, Colonel Wolf?''

"You are. We can still expect DropShips and aerospace fighters operating on transorbital trajectories.''

"But no bombardments from the warships?" Garcia asked.

"It is possible that if the Fleet Captain sees an advantage tilting to one side, she might drop her neutrality in favor of ending up on the winning side," Wolf said. "But that is a problem for the future. We have more pressing ones at present. There are most of three regiments on Outreach. All units of Beta and Gamma are present, and from the performance of their commanders, I think we can be sure that Beta and Gamma regiments will be solidly behind Alpin.''

"What about Epsilon?" Grazier asked. Her hangdog look showed she expected an unpleasant answer.

"Only about half onplanet," I replied, "but Colonel Nichole's absence from the Trial meeting implies that she and her command favor Wolf."

"That's officers, Cameron," Grazier said. "What about the troops?"

"Dragoons are trained as a group and brigaded according to compatibility. It gives the regiments their character. Leaders promoted from within naturally have the group's personality. An officer posted to a regiment from another will strive to reflect his new regiment's character, that is, if he wants to keep the loyalty and respect of his troops. As a result, the troops tend to follow the leader's opinions as well as their orders." I thought I sounded like an academy lecturer, and Grazier's sour look confirmed it.

"I think we know where Epsilon's infantry stands, since they're Elson's boys and girls. You think the rest of Epsilon'll fight for you, Colonel?" she asked.

"If they can." No one thought it necessary to point out that Epsilon, like Beta and Gamma, was still in the World. It would be difficult for a single loyal regiment to take on two.

"If Elson doesn't have Nichole eliminated the way he tried to do with the Colonel," Garcia said.

"I don't think that's likely," said the Colonel. "Assassination is a tool of the dark, and this is in the light now. He wouldn't be able to disavow the action very easily, and he can't afford the dishonor."

"Then we need to establish contact with Nichole," Grazier said.

"As soon as we can," the Wolf agreed. "There are no other BattleMech units onplanet except for a few training units among the Home Guard. As Brian said, the combat units are pretty homogeneous, but the

Home Guard is more of a mixture. Joe, what's your best evaluation of the Guard's leanings?''

Garcia looked a little uncomfortable when everyone focused on him. He ran his hand through his hair and ended the pass massaging his neck. ''Mixture's a good way of putting it. I'd say the Guard is split. We're not getting a lot of info out of the World, but it looks like most of the units that didn't get sent out here are holding for Alpin as the legitimate head of the Dragoons. If Alpin and his cronies shipped the rest of the Guard out here to get your partisans out of the way, they've shown themselves to be fallible. We had a number of desertions when I broadcast your arrival. Tenth and Twelfth brigades, Viking Company, and three or four of the sibkos have pulled out of bivouac and are headed toward the Fortress complex. They're not talking, but we can assume they hold for the other side. That's a quarter of the Guard BattleMechs going out there.''

''The Fortress complex,'' I said, letting a question into my tone. I'd seen the designation on the map, but I'd never been there.''

''A war-game area,'' Grazier said. ''It's for assault scenarios. If they get in there, it'll cost the devil to winkle them out.''

''Have we still got command linkage to the Fortress, Brian?'' Colonel Wolf asked.

I checked. ''The computer is still accepting our passcodes.''

''Good. Order the computer locked down, priority alpha-omega-omega-three. That'll keep them from the arsenal and shut down the simulated defenses. If they want to hold it, they'll have to do it themselves.''

''Still a tough nut,'' Grazier observed.

''With any luck, they'll just sit tight. If Elson didn't trust them enough to keep them in Harlech, he may not trust them to fight for him.''

''He may not need them,'' Garcia said. ''Colonel, is there going to be any help from outside?''

At the Wolf's nod, I answered. "At last report, Delta Regiment and Zeta Battalion were heavily engaged. They'd have to pull out, breaking contract, to get involved. Colonel Paxon has always been a strong supporter of the Colonel, as has Jamison. However, Paxon's record suggests that he won't voluntarily break contract, so we can forget about Delta. Jamison's anybody's guess. He'd be living up to Zeta tradition if he headed home."

"That would be a blessing; we could use Zeta's firepower. A battalion of assault 'Mechs is something the bad guys couldn't ignore. And if Zeta pulled out of the contract, Paxon'd be hanging with too few forces to complete the ticket. Maybe he'd break contract then," Grazier said. "On the other hand, FedCom might just let them all go if you asked, Jaime. We'd owe them, but with Delta and Zeta, we'd have enough to force the rebels down."

The Wolf shook his head. "We can't afford to owe the Federated Commonwealth at this point. They're already implying we owe them a lot. If we accepted help from them, we'd end up like the Horsemen."

Mention of the Eridani Light Horse touched all the oldsters present. The Horsemen were fine soldiers and believers in the ancient Star League virtues, who had slowly been absorbed into House Davion's military. Officially, they were still mercs, but their contract was so long-term that it left them little leeway to move around or pick assignments. Colonel Wolf had fought hard to keep the Dragoons independent, to keep them from that kind of domination. It seemed he'd rather face dissolution than have the Dragoons become a House-controlled mercenary unit like the Eridani Light Horse.

"All right," Grazier said. "So we can't count on them. What about Spider's Web Battalion? They were Mac's guys. Won't they side with us?"

"There's been no reliable contact with them for

days,'' I said. ''Every report for the last week or so has come through Captain Svados. MacKenzie's second was John Clavell; he's a strong antiClanner, but he was injured last month. Gremmer was next in line; he's a Nova Cat adoptee. The battalion's loyalty and cohesiveness are unclear. Remember, Alpin is Mac's son; loyalty to the family could go either way. The only thing we know for sure is that we don't know where they are.''

''Maybe Elson had them taken out,'' Grazier suggested.

''Stanford Blake would know,'' Martel said.

I gave her a hard look. I knew that I wasn't Stan, but I wasn't an intelligence officer either. ''Stan gave us everything he could before we left Harlech. Svados has been hamstringing his operation for months. If he were here, he'd tell you the same thing.''

'And where is he?''

''I wish we knew,'' the Colonel said. ''He insisted on staying in the capital. He said he could be more valuable there.''

''A spy in the enemy camp? Not when he's so well known as your man, Jaime. He won't get anything but shot.'' Grazier sighed. ''Too bad. I liked him.''

The Wolf glowered at Grazier, who appeared not to notice. Garcia did, and tried to shift the mood into something more positive.

''What about the Kuritans, Colonel? They came to join up with you, specifically, didn't they?''

''Some of them did. But as a fighting force, they're a wild card. Since they haven't been formally inducted, it's likely they'll sit it out. It would be the wiser course for them.''

A priority call cut in to the flow of traffic on the commo net. I passed it on at once.

''Colonel, command center reports a DropShip overflight of Orange Sector.''

The Wolf's hand snapped down to the map-table

console and the picture dissolved, to be replaced by a command-sector representation of the continent. Orange Sector, one of the four color-coded divisions of the Outback, was a wide wedge stretching away from the Tetsuhara Proving Grounds to the east. The terrain was rough, mostly badlands. Farther away the land started sloping down toward the sea in a rocky desert that was bounded by a range of mountains that met the sea in a crazy maze of islands. Orange Sector was an unlikely avenue for a major assault by the usurpers; supply lines to the World would be more complicated than those running through any of the other three sectors.

"Vector," the Colonel demanded.

"Came in from the north, then cut west," I said, simultaneously routing the datafeed to the map-table. "Now moving on over the mountains and out of range."

Martel offered a suggestion. "Recon flight?"

"Negative," I said with the authority of a new report. "Multiple contacts on downward vectors. They've laid eggs. We've got BattleMechs coming in, estimated two to three companies."

"Scramble the 'Mechs," the Wolf ordered. "Half the armor to form a second line, Joe. The rest, and the infantry, stay in position. If we can, we've got to meet them before they organize."

=====41=====

Elson sat staring at the holotank wherein rotated a green globe representing Outreach. The greater continent of the Outback slipped from view as the wide Argyosean Sea filled most of the visible surface. Then little by little the smaller continent crept into sight. Elson called up the force display. Blue dots winked into existence on the sphere's surface, marking the locations of forces loyal to Alpin. Other dots appeared, red for the forces loyal to Wolf and amber for those still undecided about which side to support in the struggle for control of the Dragoons.

The first stage of the battle, he reminded himself. Once Jaime Wolf was taken care of, the next phases could begin. Alpin would not lead the Dragoons for long.

Foolish, self-important Alpin.

Alpin was styling himself the Khan of Wolf's Dragoons. Enamored of anything to do with the Clans, perhaps the boy thought using Clan designations would make him more popular with the Clanners in his faction. If so, he was ignoring the sentiments of those who sided with him for other reasons, having no particular love for the Clans. Indeed, many of those were already offended just when Alpin needed all the support he could get right now.

Elson had been unintentionally drawn into the light by Alpin's sudden declaration that the position of saKhan was to be revived and that Elson would hold it. The intent, a return to proper Clan forms, was laudable. The last Dragoon saKhan had been Joshua Wolf, one of the original Dragoons. When Joshua was killed, Jaime Wolf had amalgamated the position into his own, a move that had been the Dragoons' first overt step away from their heritage.

The timing of the change had not been Alpin's first blunder. No. That unfortunate move had come hard on the heels of the failed attempt on Jaime Wolf. The panicked Alpin had ordered security guards to fire on Patrick Chan and his lance after they had dismounted from their 'Mechs. It was a bad choice. The crusty old 'Mech jock was chief of BattleMech operations and a potential ally because he professed belief in the honor road. Chan might have been talked around, brought to see that the future lay with a revitalized Clan organization for the Dragoons. Still, Elson had been able to hide the truth beneath a story that Chan and his MechWarriors had attacked Alpin. Not all believed, but no one openly contradicted the tale.

Then, in unconscious mockery of Elson's plans, Alpin's awkward and flustered announcement of the restoration of the Khan ranks had come. Elson's refusal to support and accept the move would have embarrassed Alpin and weakened the boy's tenuous hold on the position of commander of the Dragoons. Elson was not yet ready for that. Neither was he ready to step into the light as the power behind the changes. He knew he should welcome the return of proper Clan command structure, but the move had cost, alienating some Dragoons whose allegiance to the new leadership was wavering. Tapping the code for Epsilon Regiment, Elson watched as the updated data made some of the lights change from blue to amber. A few, several BattleMech companies and the majority of the support elements, went all the way to red.

Elson brooded over the development as the holographic globe continued to turn, bringing the Outback back into view. Whereas the smaller, developed continent was lit primarily with blue and amber lights, the Outback was mostly amber, spotted with tiny clusters of red and a few scattered spots of blue. Admittedly, most of the units represented by the amber lights were Home Guard and not as combat-capable as the line regiments, but only a fool would discount them. If they sided with Wolf, there would be serious fighting. The cursed neutral position taken by Fleet Captain Chandra prevented him from ascertaining the loyalties of far too many of the Home Guard units. The sooner he acted, the smoother things would go.

The door to the office opened and let in the bustling noise of the command center. Annoyed by the interruption, he snapped, ''What is it?''

''Delta call, sir. The Kuritans are reported moving out of their encampment in the Provence Sector. There is a convoy with the BattleMechs.''

Although unwelcome, the Kuritan move was not unanticipated. ''Have they opened fire?''

''Neg. The 643rd Home Guard infantry was on watch. They decided to withdraw.''

''Bring the big tank on line. I'll be out in minute.''

He had been expecting something from the Kuritans for some time now. The convoy was interesting, though: it would be the MechWarriors' dependents. Clearly, the Kuritans were finished with Dragoon hospitality. But where were they going? Home, or to Wolf?

The possibility that they might be heading to join Wolf could not be discounted. Jaime Wolf had partially equipped the Kuritans with Dragoon machines, possibly engendering some kind of honor debt. But the machines were Dragoon property, not Wolf's. The Kuritans could not be allowed to leave without surrendering that equipment.

Elson stalked into the ops center. As he had ordered, the holotank was up and running. A glance told him the number of BattleMechs in the column, and that figure revealed that the Kuritans were taking the Dragoon equipment. He walked around the tank, passing Fancher and Parella, to confront the short Kuritan who stood there staring into the holotank. As usual, the small man showed no sign of being intimidated by Elson's bulk or demeanor. It was an admirable, if irritating, trait.

"Well, Noketsuna, they are your clan, what are they doing?"

"Leaving," was all he said.

Elson found that insufficient answer. "To fight with Wolf?"

Turning an impassive face to him, Noketsuna said, "Wolf is a rebel by your law. Kuritans despise rebels. Those who transgress against the bond of duty are outcasts."

"They are already outcasts, *quiaff?*"

"Some would call them so," the Kuritan said blandly.

"Does that mean you think they will run to Wolf?"

"I cannot know their minds."

Fancher stepped around the tank to join them. "If we hold their DropShips, the Snakes won't be going anywhere."

"I do not advise that," Noketsuna said. "Those ships are their property. I believe that, given what is occurring, they will have their armament ready for defense. If you initiate a battle for the ships, you will force the ground forces to fight you."

Grimacing in annoyance, Fancher said, "The DropShips are too big an asset to give up, Elson. If we can take them, we augment our available force. We can put almost another battalion on the other side in the first wave. Send the commandos after the ships. The Snakes won't make a fight of it when they see they're stranded."

"I do not advise that," Noketsuna repeated.

Elson looked around the center until he spotted Major Sean Eric Kevin of Seventh Kommando. Calling him over, Elson brought the commando officer up to date on the situation. After considering the options, Kevin said, "It's possible, but we would need command codes to lock down the weaponry and take control of the computers."

Elson turned to the Kuritan. "You had access, Noketsuna, *quiaff*?"

"Yes."

"You can supply those codes, *quiaff*?"

"Yes."

"Then give them to us."

"As you command."

Noketsuna's words were subservient, but his attitude was defiant. It didn't matter. The Kuritan would not dare put false codes into the computer.

"Kevin, get your commandos out to the port and put them on standby. I want two Stars of Elementals ready to supply backup." Elson gave some more deployment orders, then said, "Noketsuna, you're coming with me. I want to talk to your fellow Kuritans."

The bolt from the particle projection cannon crackled past the hoverjeep and splashed into the building behind them. Steam and debris erupted from the wall, pelting the jeep with stone and mortar chips. One flying chip cut Elson's cheek. He gunned the engine, sending the jeep scooting out of the 'Mech's field of fire.

"What is going on? What did that guy say before he dogged down?"

"He said that the DropShips were under attack."

Elson cursed. Someone had taken the initiative at the wrong time, and he had a good idea who it was. Fancher was far too impatient.

"I warned you," Noketsuna said.

"And you were right. I'll remember that."

Elson headed the jeep down the street at high speed. It would not take the first of the Kuritan 'Mechs long to reach the corner behind them. Fortunately the street was not wide enough for two of the giant machines to get clear fire lanes; they would only have to dodge fire from one. A 'Mech appeared in his rearview mirror, the *Warhammer* that had fired before. Particle beam, then. It could have been worse; a missile spread would have been harder to avoid. As soon as he saw the faint glow of the charging elements in the blackness of the muzzle, Elson turned the wheel hard. Cutting power to the starboard fans, he let the jeep spill air out the port. The starboard skirts dug into the pavement with a spray of sparks, nearly jarring both passengers from the vehicle.

Blue lightning crackled overhead, barely missing them. Elson rebooted the fans and gunned the engine. Bullets followed the jeep as it screamed toward the safety of a side street. Gouts of asphalt erupted as heavy-caliber slugs chewed their way toward the jeep. Elson floored the accelerator, using the jeep's speed in an attempt to out-race the machine gun's tracking mechanism. Metal screamed as the first slugs caught the back of the jeep, then they were safely behind a building.

Running flat out in a city was dangerous, but Elson had little choice. He needed speed to get away from the Kuritan force. The light hoverjeep was not armed, and if it had been, it would still be no match for the 'Mechs. Noketsuna reported that the *Warhammer*'s shots had taken out the radio.

Elson decided to head for the port. He could get there well before the heavy 'Mechs like the *Warhammer* that had tried to kill them. Even the lighter elements, if the Kuritan commander decided to send them in, would be slower than the hoverjeep. But any lead he gained would be precious little and he would need every second he could get to regain control of the situation.

He could hear energy weapons before they cleared the approach road. The gates were abandoned, open to whoever would use them. In his haste Elson nearly crashed the jeep after one skirt brushed against a gatepost. As the tops of the Kuritan DropShips came into view beyond a row of hangars and maintenance sheds, he slowed, looking for a safe zone to stop. He turned the jeep into an open hangar and stopped it just short of the far door. Noketsuna was right with him as he jumped out and dashed to a window.

It was as bad as he had feared. The Elementals were pinned down by fire from the DropShips and there were dead commandos on the tarmac. One Point of five Elementals was crawling up the side of a *Union* Class DropShip. Their position on the hull protected them from the guns of the ship to which they clung, while the ship itself shielded them from the fire of the *Union*'s three sister ships. The Elementals were advancing, clearly determined to capture at least one of the ships.

It was hopeless. The arrival of the Kuritan BattleMechs would be the Elementals' deaths.

Elson located one of the other Points sheltering in the lee of a blast wall, and dashed across the field to them. He crouched next to a trooper and ordered him to open his suit. Using the man's commo equipment, he connected with the ops center. He cursed when he heard that Fancher had ordered Beta into action. Two battalions were headed for the port and the third to intercept the main Kuritan column. Elson immediately countermanded the order. Within seconds, Fancher was on the line, screaming at him.

"What do you think you're doing?"

"Protecting our assets, Colonel Fancher. We do not need to lose BattleMechs in fruitless combat, and we need the port facilities more than we need to stop the

Kuritans from leaving. A battle here will cripple our campaign.''

''So you're just going to let them go?''

''Aff.''

''And if they run to Wolf?''

''Then they will be running to their deaths.''

42

In a BattleMech you always have copilot fear. You don't always think about it; but sometimes you think about nothing else. But whether you're thinking about it or not, the fear is always there, coiled in your gut.

A BattleMech may be the single most formidable fighting machine ever designed by man, but it is not invulnerable, especially when confronted with another 'Mech. As a MechWarrior, you've been trained in simulators and the harsh school of combat until you're very good at what you do, but your opponent may be better. Equipment, skill, and courage may improve your chances, but they cannot always save you. Sometimes it's just a matter of luck and, no matter how good you are, your luck can run out.

I couldn't help wondering if luck was with me as the 'Mechs of our ad hoc battlegroup scrambled from the hangar outside the ops center. I had an OmniMech, Franchette had one of our new machines, and Hans and Grant were running in upgraded classic designs, but the tech in the rest of the 'Mechs was not as good. We didn't know who we'd be facing, but their tech was probably higher. They were definitely more numerous. We were not quite four lances, a reinforced company, facing about twice our number.

I knew my own training and experience, and I wasn't happy about those odds. A few of the other jocks had seen combat before, but this was going to be the first time for most of the MechWarriors in this battlegroup. Those we were heading to meet were almost certainly veterans; greenies are rarely assigned to orbital drops. As far as equipment and skill went, we were on the downside of the equation, but I couldn't fault the courage of our old warriors, sibkids, and trainees. They knew the score, and they never hesitated.

Hans and Franchette took command of two lances and moved wide on the left flank. Grant and I were in the forefront of the rest. Two of our machines were piloted by veterans, but they were jockeying *Chameleon*s. The *Chameleon* is a training 'Mech, intended to simulate a variety of opponents by mounting a wide variety of weapon systems. A *Chameleon* is a medium 'Mech, but it doesn't always look like one. It can be fitted out with extra plates to modify its appearance, and carries special electronics to falsify its signature; these special abilities let it look and scan as something other than what it is, hence the machine's name. Ours were configured to appear as heavies; we wanted to be as threatening as possible. I only hoped the machines would make it into combat; *Chameleon*s aren't really designed for long-distance travel.

Because I outranked Grant, I was in command of our contingent. When our channel to ops suddenly started to break up, my invisible copilot grabbed me by the balls. It's bad enough when you only have to worry about yourself.

Our 'Mechs ate up the kilometers. Because of the superior terrain-handling capability of the Battle-Mechs, we outdistanced the Home Guard armor units in short order. I didn't worry too much. We were expecting the opposition to be spread out, so we wouldn't have to face their whole force at once. They'd also be suffering from the same lack of intelligence as we were and would need to do recon, further splitting their forces. If we ran into trouble, Hans would sweep in from the flank. If it was too much trouble, the whole force would fall back on the armor.

We had intercepted no transmissions from the incoming 'Mechs during or after their drop. I hoped that meant they were a recon force and would be mostly, if not all, light 'Mechs. If the tonnage of the two forces were equal, their greater numbers would be less of an advantage. The lack of transmissions suggested something else as well: that the 'Mech force out there was hostile; friendlies would have called in.

We'd been moving through the Hannovassian Highlands for a quarter of an hour when Jeremy in the *Griffin* reported a contact on his scope.

"Bogey, boss. A klick off left flank. He's lying low. There may be a couple more, but I'm not sure. Too much iron in the rocks."

"Anyone confirm?" There were no affirmative responses. "You got any motion on that bogey, Jeremy?"

"Neg."

"We'll keep on then."

There was a lot of scrap metal in the Highlands. I didn't think it was an enemy unit; we were still a good way from their drop zone. Besides, an enemy would have reacted to our presence. I hoped I was right and that Jeremy was just being jittery.

Twenty minutes later, Jeremy reported another bogey, but this time he had plenty of confirmation. We had five BattleMechs moving on an intercept course. As they cleared a bluff, I punched up my magnification to get a visual ID and felt my stomach roll.

The approaching 'Mechs were all black with red trim, each one painted with the emblem of a black widow spider on a white web. The Spider's Web Battalion. And they hadn't called in their arrival.

I wasn't queasy just because this unit—which had been MacKenzie Wolf's—was apparently hostile, or because two of the machines were OmniMechs, though either was more than enough to get my copilot in an uproar. My concern was more personal: Maeve had been a part of the battalion. I wondered if she was still with them, a member of the lance approaching us now.

I entered them into my battle computer, tagging each with a target code. My *Loki* beeped at me when the first one entered the outer effective zone of my long-range missiles. On our side only Grant's *Archer* and Jeremy's *Griffin* had LRMs, but I was sure the Omnis on the other side could match us. I expected them to open fire, but they didn't. Instead they halted.

"Open up the formation," I ordered as I throttled down. As soon as I had dropped behind the line of our advance, I ordered the lance to slow down too. Grant had followed my lead, throttling back even before I gave the order to slow. That put two of our long-range platforms into support position. Whether the Spider's Web warriors were spooked by our response, or just didn't like the odds, I didn't know. But they started to move again, pulling back.

Did they know about Hans and the rest of the company moving out of sight on the flank?

"Follow up," I ordered. Withdrawing without even an attempt at an engagement was curious—too curious not to investigate.

We followed them deeper into the canyon lands, their vector bringing them closer to Hans and his lances. My fears about a trap subsided a bit, but didn't go away. How could they? The tall mesas and narrow valleys between the eroded mountains offered too many places of concealment, too many blind alleys where we might be trapped. I watched my maps and monitored the progress of the rest of the company. Soon Hans would be in position to cut across the path of the retreating black 'Mechs. Once we'd cornered them, we would get some answers out of these warriors.

That was when they turned the tables.

A rumble like distant thunder echoed through the

badlands. As if on cue, the black 'Mechs we were chasing closed up their extended formation, gathering in the shade of a tall bluff, where they turned and faced us. More black 'Mechs appeared from canyons to either side of our position. I was ordering a reverse and Jeremy was screaming on the same channel that we had bogies behind us. At least twenty 'Mechs were surrounding us. All the 'Mechs from the drop might have been there, but I couldn't be sure. The black 'Mechs held their fire, though a single combined volley from them would have devastated our ranks. A voice cut into our commo channel.

"Welcome to the web, jocks. Hans won't be here for a while. The canyon he entered used to have an opening in our rear, but not anymore. It's just you and us, and it's time for a talk. If we don't like what we hear, you won't be seeing your friends again."

I recognized the voice at once although I hadn't heard it in months—at least not outside my dreams.

"Maeve."

"Hello, Brian." She didn't sound surprised, nor particularly pleased. "Where's the Wolf?"

I wasn't sure I was pleased either. "That's his *Archer* beside me."

"I can see that, but he's not in it."

"What makes you think that?"

There was a pause, as if she were considering what to say. Maybe she was just annoyed. I almost expected to see the protective covers on her 'Mech's weapons begin to open. When she finally responded, her voice was cool, almost conciliatory. "The machine's not moving like the Wolf's. So where is he?"

I wanted to tell her. I wanted her to be on our side, but I had a responsibility not to let my personal feelings endanger Colonel Wolf. Until I knew where she and her comrades stood, I couldn't trust the Colonel's location to her. Our position was too precarious. My throat was dry as I said, "Somewhere else."

She laughed. "Very cautious, Brian. Would you be so cautious if I said we were here to fight for him?"

"Are you?"

"Answering a question with a question. You've been hanging around with Stan Blake too long. By the way, is he with the Wolf?"

"Colonel Blake stayed in the World."

"Spy stuff?"

Her tone was conversational, and the restraint shown by the warriors in the black 'Mechs was in itself a statement. I decided to take a chance. "We don't know what happened to him."

"Sounds like things are pretty grim."

I didn't need to be told that. "Have you come to fight for the Colonel?"

"Could be."

"Now *you're* being cautious."

"With good reason. We got the notice of Mac's death over the net, but there was nothing from the Wolf. That's not his style. Then we got the word that Alpin was the new boss of the Dragoons and styling himself Khan. That got a few people suspicious, but we got no good answers to our queries, nothing quite clear enough to tell us there really was a problem. When we heard Elson and Fancher were running a lot of the show and that Kelly Yukinov wasn't even on Outreach, a few people got excited. We had a . . . a false start, but we got that straightened out and headed in. We hadn't been insystem for thirty seconds before we had Fleet Captain Chandra on the horn, telling us that we'd better stay clear of the planet. She tried to talk us into linking with her ships in orbit, waiting till matters were settled, but that's not the way we do things in this battalion. We made our drop out here because I knew this is where the Wolf would go if he made it out of Harlech."

"But you dropped in like you were coming to battle."

"I didn't know that we weren't."

"You could have transmitted your intentions. Or at least your questions. We could have told you what was going on and had you land at the ops center."

"Sure we could have," she said sarcastically. "In case you hadn't noticed, not everybody involved in this thing has been telling the truth. If we came in broadcasting who we favored, and the Wolf hadn't made it here, we wouldn't have been real popular with the people in charge. Dropping in like this, we could always claim caution and not reveal favoritism for any side."

I wanted to hear her say it. "Then you *are* here to fight for him."

"You're fighting for him, aren't you?"

I could imagine the smile that went with that question. I was grinning myself when I answered, "We are."

"Hah! I knew he'd make a challenge to the Trial." There was exultation in her voice. Faintly, I heard other voices, leakage coming through her microphone from the channels to the other black 'Mechs. "I guess we are, too."

I can't tell you how relieved I was. There are no words to express it. It was all for the Colonel's sake, though. The Spider's Web Battalion was a significant addition to our fighting capabilities. Personally, I was a bit befuddled. Maeve was back in my life and I wasn't quite sure how I felt about it.

"Hadn't you better give Hans the word, before he comes charging in here, guns blazing?" she suggested.

I did. Within the hour we had linked up and were heading back toward the ops center. As soon as we got within line-of-sight of one of our relay stations, I beamed the good news in.

43

Elson stalked into the command center, already angry. He had not cared for the peremptory tone of the summons from Alpin. He cared even less for the fact that the boy seemed to think he was really in command.

All of the command council loyal to the Dragoon organization was there. Neil Parella and Alicia Fancher were sitting on opposite sides of the table, eyeing each other with ill-concealed hostility. Their rivalry made it easy to play them off against each other. Elizabeth Nichole, the other combat regiment commander, was working at a console near the door to one of the offices lining the ops center. For all his initial fears about her, Nichole had turned out to be a supporter of the new regime. Sean Kevin of Seventh Kommando sat in one corner. He was a quiet and competent officer who had no interest in the strategic positioning of the Dragoons; he only wanted someone to point him in the right direction so that he could use his skills. Elson found him very valuable. Rebecca Ardevauer of the Fire Support Group was less tractable, but she was valuable, too. She was well-liked and vocal about the necessity of avoiding conflict and holding with the outcome of the Trial of Position. Douglas Piper of the Support Battalion was more of an enigma. He said little except to voice his votes, and those had always been what Elson wanted.

Though not of the council, Noketsuna was there,

too, talking quietly with Svados. The Kuritan was proving valuable for his insights concerning the reaction of the local populace, gleaned through the exercise of his somewhat dubious investigative skills. He was working well with Svados, recently promoted to head Wolfnet in the absence of Stanford Blake.

Of course, Alpin Wolf was also present. He stood leaning against the main table, intent on the images flickering through the holotank. His MechWarrior's jacket, with its motley collection of unit-recognition patches, was tossed over a chair.

Elson ignored him and stepped up to Nichole. "Things quiet enough at Epsilon, Nichole?"

Alpin looked up when he heard Elson's voice. His face was pinched into a frown that deepened when he saw who Elson addressed. He slapped his hand on the table.

"My grandfather is gathering troops in the Outback. I am convinced that he means to make a strike against the capital. He will assume that he can unseat me and retake command."

Parella snorted. "He can't best three regiments of BattleMechs with full support, when the best he can field is a bunch of old men and kids."

"There's no proof he's actually doing anything," Nichole pointed out.

Alpin stabbed a finger at the holotank. "Then explain the drop by the Spider's Web Battalion. There was no fighting when they landed."

"That's the report, but we don't have positive confirmation," Svados said.

"There doesn't have to be," Alpin snapped. "The Spider's Web flushed out anyone who supported the legitimate succession before they left Wing. Of course they came to support my grandfather's rebellion."

"Chandra says Captain Maeve is in command of the battalion," Svados said.

"Maeve? She's a good jock, but she's just a pup."

Fancher chuckled. "She's not ready for command. If that's the best Wolf can rally, we've nothing to worry about."

"She is in my ageframe," Alpin said. He tried to make his tone a warning, but it came off as more of a whine.

Fancher looked disgusted and about to say something, so Elson spoke up. "There are many battalion commanders of her age among the Clans. In the current circumstances, her age is not the issue, but her politics are. The lack of fighting between Wolf's loyalists and the battalion is a strong sign that the Spider's Web will side with Jaime Wolf."

"If he has a side," Nichole said. She might have accepted Alpin as leader of the Dragoons, but she was still struggling with the concept of having to send troops against Jaime Wolf.

Parella shook his head. "Liz, if Wolf were simply going to give it up, he would have left the system."

Folding her arms across her chest, Elizabeth Nichole chewed her lip. "Maybe. Maybe not."

"Jaime Wolf has demonstrated his rebellion by running," Alpin said loudly. "I propose a first strike, before we lose any more sympathizers."

Surprised, Elson turned to him. "What do you mean *any more*?"

Alpin smiled, apparently pleased that he was ahead of Elson on something. "Graham took the Special Recon Group out last night. They left Camp Dorrety just after midnight."

Elson turned to Svados. "Is that true?"

She nodded and Noketsuna reported. "All contact with them has been lost. Some vehicles were noted moving toward the strait at Jormenai, suggesting they're headed for the other side of the mountain. However, that could be a feint. Some or all of the group might remain on this continent to form a harassing force. In either case, I think it is clear that their sympathies lie with Jaime Wolf.''

"Like your damned Kurita friends," Alpin snapped.

"Then they've gone over, too?" Nichole looked unhappy.

Shoving her chair back so that it screeched across the floor, Fancher stood. "Once Elson called off the attack, they loaded their people onto the DropShips and lifted. They never even made a pretense of going anywhere else. They lifted and made straight for the Outback. They only touched down long enough to unload their 'Mechs, then their DropShips lifted again and took up a geosynchronous orbit over Green Sector, becoming high cover for the training ops complex.''

Elson ignored Fancher's venomous stare. "It is a negligible shift in the dynamic.''

"And we can make it less," Alpin said, tapping on the holotank's control board. The imaged globe shrank and orbital paths burned into neon existence around it. A formation of four DropShips over the Outback blinked on and off. Vector arrows leapt out from various orbital assets, showing how the position could be approached. "Only the 'Mechs got off, which means that the families of the MechWarriors stayed on the DropShips. There are no port facilities to worry about in orbit. If we blast the ships out of the sky, we will teach those Snakes a lesson they well deserve. We can make their families pay for the MechWarriors' foolishness.''

Elson walked around the table and backhanded Alpin without a word. The boy flew across the room to land sprawling over a desk. Alpin stared up at Elson with sheer hatred. All Elson felt was his own contempt.

"I gave you position, I can take it away!" Alpin snarled.

Icily calm, Elson responded, "Not by the laws of the Khanship."

"I can make the council do it!"

"Go ahead."

Alpin stood, smearing blood from his cut lip across his cheek as he rubbed the jaw that was already angrily red. He looked around the assembled group. The only unreadable face was that of Noketsuna. The Dragoons looked stern, offering no sympathy. That was as Elson had expected. The families, blood or sibkin, were sacred; they were not objects of war. Only the debased warriors of the Inner Sphere made war on civilians.

Alpin screamed, "You are all dismissed!"

When no one moved, he stared at them a moment longer, then stalked into his office. The door slammed.

Elson turned at once to the holotank's console, returning the image to a depiction of the Outback. "Do we have any information about where the Kuritans will be deployed?"

"None, sir," Svados said.

"They are not a coherent unit," Noketsuna said. "They have no specialties or organization."

"Are you saying that they will not fight well?"

"They will fight. They have given their loyalty and will die for Wolf. Do not discount them, but do not expect to divine how they will be used either."

"Sounds like they're about as stable as Little Al," Parella put in.

"Yeah," Fancher agreed. "When are you going to dump that collection of bad genes?"

Elson looked through the holotank and met her gaze. "When the time comes."

"We need a real commander if we're going after Wolf."

"Jaime Wolf is exactly the issue, Colonel Fancher." Elson stepped around the tank to Fancher's side. "How strong do you think your claim to legitimate leadership would be while he is still alive?"

"Stronger than yours," she replied. "I could challenge Little Al to a Trial of Position."

"The Dragoons can't take another Trial right now," Nichole said.

"She is right, Fancher. There is talk in some quarters that Jaime Wolf is challenging the results of the Trial."

Fancher snorted. "He'll lose the challenge like he lost the Trial. We're better equipped and there are a lot more of us. Even the Spider's Web and the Kuritans won't shift the balance in his favor. There'll just be more blood. It won't matter in the end."

Elson had known that Fancher lacked the foresight for command and now she was damning herself with her own words. "If you think that the amount of Dragoon blood shed will not matter in the end, I would not care to serve under you as Khan."

He noted with satisfaction that Piper, Ardevauer, and Nichole nodded in open agreement. He was not surprised when Parella said, "Nor I." Elson had hinted to Fancher that she might be the best person to replace Alpin once things had settled. He had done the same with Parella. They could not both have the top slot. From observing Parella, Elson guessed that the MechWarrior had divined that Elson had been offering the same carrot to Fancher. Parella was working to undermine his rival colonel before she could become a threat. The man was clearly a more subtle player than Fancher and would have to be watched. Elson had no intention of backing either of them. Jaime Wolf had proved that one of his innovations had merit: a single Khan was a powerful Khan. Elson intended to be a powerful Khan.

"For the moment Alpin is necessary to the elimination of Jaime Wolf," he said. "A problem to which we must put our minds, warriors."

44

At first Dechan thought that the struggle for control of the Dragoons would erupt in open warfare immediately, but days passed and there were no large-scale confrontations. Beta, Gamma, and Epsilon Regiments remained in their quarters on the public continent. If it was a public relations ploy designed to convince outsiders that nothing was happening, it met with only limited success. The news of Wolf's departure and rumors of impending conflict circulated widely in Harlech.

Dechan was questioned about the brewing trouble by every interviewer with whom he talked. Telling them all the same thing—nothing—wasn't a difficult feat: he knew little more than that. When Jenette packed up and headed for Camp Dorrety the night the Special Recon Group slipped away, his inside line to the Dragoons went with her. He didn't miss the information, but he missed her. His refusal to join her and her refusal to stay might have been their final disagreement. A conflict was coming and it was very possible she would not survive to return from it.

Dechan knew the lull was coming to an end when Elson started visiting the Hiring Hall. Alpin had put out a call for Dragoon auxiliaries, promising that good performance would mean a permanent slot with the Dragoons. A lot of the mercs thought they were being offered a free ride down easy street. Dechan watched the boards in the Hall and noted the names of those who signed on. Some of them he'd never heard of, but others he recognized by reputation. They weren't the sort of troops the old Dragoons would have hired. The big-name freelancers were conspicuous by their absence, and so were less well-known but effective units like the Black Brigade. Scuttlebutt said it was price, but Dechan suspected other, more important reasons.

Dechan was heading up the steps to the Hall when Elson and a covey of mercs came through the door. The big Elemental noticed him almost at once and said a few words to his companions. With a flurry of nods and jovial remarks, Elson left the mercs and headed directly toward Dechan.

"Good day to you, Dechan Fraser."

The smile on the man's face looked sincere, but something about Elson's attitude seemed forced, making Dechan uncomfortable. Reluctantly, he said, "Hello."

"I have heard that the Federated Commonwealth has made a substantial offer for your services."

"I turned them down; they just want to pump me for intelligence on the DCMs. In the old Dragoons, we didn't betray a former employer to a new one."

Elson didn't react at all to Dechan's implication that the Dragoons were not what they had once been. Continuing to smile, he said, "Then you are still in need of work."

"I'm not one of them," Dechan said, canting his head in the direction of the mercs standing nearby.

"I know you are not," Elson said earnestly. "That is why I left them to speak to you."

"Looks to me like you've got more than enough mercs in your bag today."

"When did a mercenary care how many others there were, as long as the paymaster had enough C-bills?"

"When he was smart enough to worry about what he was getting into," Dechan replied.

"You are an astute man, Dechan Fraser. I believe you can see what is happening. The more forces arrayed on our side, the less chance of armed conflict with the Wolf loyalists. You know Jaime Wolf for a practical man. Do you not think he will realize he has no hope of winning?"

Dechan shrugged. The Jaime Wolf who had forgotten him was not the one with whom he had hired on. Or maybe he was, and a snot-nosed kid just hadn't known any better. Who could say what such a man would think of long odds? "And if he fights anyway?"

"He will lose, and the cost to the victors will be less than it might have been if the odds were more even."

"A cost borne mostly by the mercs," *And maybe by Jenette.*

"As I said, you are perceptive, Dechan Fraser. I *do* expect Wolf to fight because he is foremost a warrior, and no true warrior surrenders without a real fight."

"Like he did in the Trial?"

"His champion fought." A shadow passed across Elson's face. "Perhaps Wolf wished to lose the Trial. Perhaps, at the time, he saw a strategic advantage in appearing to lose, expecting to use the power shift to some hidden advantage. But his next loss will be very real, whatever his devious plans. When this is over there will be real openings in the Dragoons, and more than just a few. Men who have proven themselves could become well-positioned."

The bait was obvious, but Dechan found it tempting all the same. He had trained and led the Ryuken, but they hadn't been *his.* Logic pointed out the problem. "Dragoons won't follow me."

"Your troops wouldn't have to be Dragoons, to begin with. Raise your own unit of warriors. You are a good judge of men, select good ones. I feel confident that any you choose would be worthy of the new Dragoons."

From his experience with the Ryuken in the Combine, Dechan thought Elson was right. He was confident that he could create a good unit and that the MechWarriors he chose would be worthy of the Dragoons. Or at least the Dragoons as Dechan remembered them to be. But there was a major problem that made Elson's offer easy to ignore. "I don't have the cash to start a unit."

Elson waved away that argument. "The money is available."

Still wary, Dechan tried to provoke him. "Money you won't have to pay when such worthy men prove their worth by dying for you."

Elson's smile vanished. "I do not waste valuable resources. It is not the way of the Clans."

Dechan was favorably impressed by the vehemence of Elson's last remark. He might not actually waste good troops. Did that apply to the other side? Would Elson spare Dragoons, like Jenette, who sided with Wolf? Did they deserve to be spared? She'd left him, after all. Confused by his feelings and worried by the trend of his thoughts, Dechan found himself nodding to Elson and mumbling, "I don't suppose it is. Will you let me think about it?"

"A while only, as you can surely appreciate." The smile returned. "Leave word at Wolf Hall. Until then, Dechan Fraser."

"Yeah." Dechan watched as the Elemental strode away. The mercs reformed around him and the group headed across the square toward the entertainment district, no doubt for the traditional contract closing. As he stood bemused on the stairs, a tall man with a salt-and-pepper beard approached him. Dechan recognized the face and the uniform as he turned to face the man, but needed to check the name flash to put a name to him: Major Norm Carter of Carter's Chevaliers.

"Elson trying to recruit you?" Carter asked bluntly.

"Yeah."

He looked disappointed. "I expect I won't be able to match his offer. With Wolf out of the picture, I guess you'll take the uniform back."

"Would you?"

"I've never been a Dragoon so the question doesn't exactly apply. But my people have been taking Dragoon subcontracts for decades, ever since my dad hooked up with Wolf. It's always been a square deal. Not always easy, but fair." He frowned in thought for a moment. "Yeah, I guess I might, if they offered. But I'd have to make sure my people were taken care of first."

"Lots of opportunities on the Clan frontier."

"I would've agreed with you yesterday but the market's gone cold. This new Dragoon regime's dropped the A list of recommended mercs—where, I might add, the Chevaliers had a good place—and the House recruiters are putting a lot more emphasis on individual contracts. Then there's all this open recruiting the Dragoons are doing, almost in direct competition to the Houses. It's shifting the way the market works, and I haven't decided if that's good or bad. I suppose it depends on how this mess comes out."

"What mess?"

Carter gave him a look of mock annoyance. "Don't be coy, Dechan. Everybody knows Wolf's holding out on the other side." He shook his head sadly. "Never thought I'd see a Dragoon civil war. You guys were always so close-knit."

Dechan had never thought he'd see one, either, but his view of the Dragoons, as well as of individual members, had gone, and was going, through some changes. "Things changed."

"Don't they always."

"Wolf won't start anything."

"He won't have to. How long do you think it'll be before Alpin and Elson send their bought boys out to play? Time may not favor Wolf, but it doesn't favor the new regime, either. If they don't prove they're in complete control, they won't have any control at all.''

Dechan looked at him and wondered. "Would you do something to affect the outcome in your favor if you could?''

"I might.''

"Then I think we should talk.''

"I think we should talk.''

It took all the nerve I could muster to say that to Maeve when I waylaid her outside the barracks. She looked up at me, her expression guarded. I thought I saw a shadow in her normally clear gray eyes.

"About what?''

"About what?'' I echoed. "Us!''

My shout turned heads among the people passing by or simply idling time in the area. Maeve flashed an uncomfortable glance around, grabbed me by the arm, and dragged me around the side of the building. She shoved me against the wall and I was too numbly embarrassed to object.

"Look, we got to know each other pretty well, but it was fast, intense. It was—'' She broke off her breathy rush and turned away. She tossed her head back and shook it to straighten out her hair. She sighed and I ached at the pain I heard in the sound. "Look, I'd never say this in front of the troops and I'll call anyone who repeats it a liar, but . . . but you're the reason why I'm here.''

My hopes soared. I hadn't dared believe that she still cared about me, but here she was about to say so. If I hadn't felt the harsh surface of the foamed 'crete against my back, I would have been sure I was dreaming.

I knew it was hard for her; it was hard for me. Love, real love, wasn't one of the emotions commonly experienced by someone raised in a sibko. At least not love for people outside the sib group. We were both wandering in strange territory. She took a deep breath and seemed to consider what she was about to say. Her eyes fluttered to me, then away again. She shuddered, clearly wracked by the intensity of her emotions. Her back stiffened as she gathered her control before speaking.

"You're loyal, Brian, but you know what the Dragoons mean, what the forms mean. I knew that if you were still with the Wolf, Alpin's claim to the succession couldn't be right. Your being out here told me immediately that either the Wolf had been tricked or this whole thing was a trick of his own. Either way, I knew where I'd have to stand."

I saw at once what an idiot I was. She hadn't meant her comments personally. She'd left, hadn't she? Without a word. I'd been a fool to think I might have stayed in her thoughts as she had stayed in mine. She'd sent no communiques—but then, neither had I. She had never considered us to be more than warriors sharing what warriors shared. I gathered together the shards of my ego and tried to put on a good face. Too bitterly, I said, "So you came back for the Wolf."

"Of course. Did you think I'd have done anything else?"

There was a strange tone in her voice. She seemed to need reassurance that she had made the right decision. What did I know? She was a warrior and I was a lovesick boy too addled by hormones to know a convenient affair from something else. The Clanners were right, I decided, with sudden conviction. Emotions had no place in a warrior. When I made no answer, she said, "I'm back now."

"But you left."

Her eyes clouded and she swallowed hard. "I had to."

What kind of an answer was that? Of course she did, orders were orders. "I thought that I—"

She hushed me with a quick touch to my lips.

"It wasn't you, Brian. It was me." Her words didn't make sense to me and I must have looked as stupid as I felt. She laughed nervously, then said, "I was afraid, Brian."

I couldn't imagine her frightened of anything. "Of what?"

"I thought you were sympat, like a sib. But you weren't like my sibs and I didn't understand what that meant. When I was with you, I felt different. Strange. It scared me and I didn't know what to do. I thought at first it was because you were the first outside my sibko and that I was just confused by the outside world. I thought that once I'd seen more and done more, I'd be able to handle it. But I don't know, Brian." She stared away into the sky. "Look, meeting you in the field told me one thing. When we're just Dragoon officers, I can deal with it. I can let the uniforms take the strain. Here in person, it's different."

I hung my head. I wasn't going to let my fantasies gain control again. "I understand."

"No, you don't." Her strong fingers touched me under the chin. Yielding to their pressure, I raised my head until I met her gaze. "Brian, I'm still scared."

I didn't know what to say and I knew I looked like an idiot.

"What are we going to do?"

We? My resolve was blasted and my mind was a whirlwind. Fortunately, my body had an answer. I put my arms around her. She was soft and warm and she melted into my embrace.

"I'm sorry if I pushed you too hard," I babbled.

She laughed. The sound was strained, strangled, and muffled against my chest, but delightful. "You know, for a bright boy you can be really slow."

"Do I get a second chance?"

"How many do you want?"

"I don't expect to need more than one."

"Look, it's yours if you want it."

"I do."

She pulled back just a little. "Maybe it's a bit premature to get to that line."

I flushed when I figured out what she meant. I hadn't thought about the vows that were sealed with that expression, and I was appalled and thrilled to realize that she had. "I guess we should talk about it for at least five minutes," I said teasingly.

"At least." She laughed. Then, her expression went suddenly serious. "This may not be the best time to talk about this kind of thing. There'll be fighting soon."

There didn't have to be. Despite the tension that came with the absence of combat, I found the lack encouraging. It might mean that we wouldn't have to fight our former friends. I knew the Colonel held similar hopes because we had been working out evacuation plans, along with the contingency plans for combat. "The Colonel won't start anything."

"He already has. The challenge started when he didn't lie down and die before the usurpers' assassins. They can't let him live."

I knew she was right and I held her tighter. For the first time in my life, I wasn't sure that I wanted to be a warrior.

=== 45 ===

By the time Dechan Fraser arrived on the other side of the mountain, the perimeter of the landing zone had been secured by Fancher's Beta Regiment. Beta had met no resistance, but that was expected. Jaime Wolf's forces were too small to cover more than a fraction of the continent's area.

The first of Wolf's forces arrived as Dechan was supervising the unloading of his new unit's tech-support equipment. Norm Carter had the routine down, so Dechan was really just looking on to see that nothing was disrupted when he went haring off to the command trailer. He almost missed all the action.

A lance of light hovertanks had come into the valley, apparently without knowing what they were heading into. Moving at cruising speed, they were easy targets for the 'Mechs of Beta's Second Battalion, who were on guard in that sector. Half the hovercraft brewed up in the first volley. The other two reacted quickly and turned to run at flank speed. A third vehicle was crippled before it had covered a hundred meters. Ten seconds later, the lance commander reported a kill on the last hovercraft. The schismatics never got off a shot.

What they did get off was a screech transmission from the crippled scout craft.

"Kill it!" Alpin's face was red. "They'll know where we are!"

Fancher gave the orders to smoke the crippled craft.

Alpin watched the holotank display avidly until the blinking light that represented the craft went dark.

"We'll have to move up the schedule," he said. "Fancher, put out your scouts. I want Lee's Iota Battalion in the slot behind the recon screen and Fraser's Kappa Battalion in line behind them. I want one company from each of Beta's battalions to remain at the base as guards, the rest will be reserve for the advance. We move out as soon as tactical can feed the maps to the 'Mechs."

Dechan thought the move hasty, but he knew better than to say anything. Corley Lee, commander of Iota, grinned at him and said, "Going huntin'." He whistled as he walked out of the trailer.

Stepping over to Fancher, Dechan asked. "Are there estimates of the local forces?"

"Not really." She shrugged. "Should be just Home Guard. Armor and infantry. He'll be keeping the good stuff back until he knows where we're coming from."

"Are the other regiments in?"

She eyed him suspiciously. "It's not like you need to know."

"My butt's on the line, too," he said calmly. "I don't want to find it hanging in the breeze."

"That's fair. They're in, but don't expect to see much of them. We've got Green Sector to ourselves, Khan's orders."

"Right."

"Right," she agreed sarcastically.

Dechan saluted and left the trailer. He found Carter where he had left him and told him the news. They had a staff conference, passed their readiness check on to headquarters, and saddled up. They had to wait an hour longer until Lee and the less professional hireons of Iota Battalion were ready.

Once moving, Dechan had his comm officer feed him constant updates from the scout reports. He noticed that one lance missed the 1500 report, but nothing from command indicated that they suspected trouble. The Hannovassian Highlands were notorious for causing erratic breaks in communications. Dechan remembered that the lance in question was on the right flank and thought the communications break entirely too convenient. He called up a map on his battle computer. Knowing that the Dragoon command had edited the tactical display, he hoped it didn't leave out anything vital. What he saw was worrisome enough. The missing lance might be dead and gone; their advance would have taken them into prime ambush terrain.

When Wolf's armored formations were reported just to the right of Iota's line of advance, Alpin ordered the recon elements to withdraw toward the column. The map already before him, Dechan spotted a route to a strong support position and gave the necessary orders to his command. He barely noticed Alpin ordering Iota into battle formations.

Dechan moved his 'Mech into a position from which he could watch the mercs of Iota deploy. Their formations were ragged and sloppy. Were he feeling charitable, he might have attributed the disorderliness to insufficient practice; the battalion was only recently assembled from a number of smaller, previously independent units and individual mercenary Mech-Warriors. Many of the pilots didn't understand tactics beyond those of a lance; many more had never experienced actions on a scale larger than a company or two.

One lance surged forward suddenly and Dechan had to increase his magnification before he could make out the target toward which they raced: Wolf's tanks. The mercs engaged at long range, their missiles falling among the tanks to send up gouts of dust and, once, a billowing column of oily smoke. Apparently lacking the armament to reply, the tanks bore in. The 'Mechs added PPC and laser fire to their barrage as they closed. When the tanks finally replied, it was to little effect. Their weapons chewed at the 'Mechs, but the faster, more agile battle machines were difficult targets. The tanks were forced to withdraw after heavy losses when Iota began a general advance.

Dechan brought his battalion forward into another over-watch position. Iota was well engaged with Wolf's armor. In closer, where their heavier tanks could catch the 'Mechs, the tankers were doing better. Dechan watched as a *Demolisher* tank rolled out of a concealed position to blast a merc *Warhammer* in the side. The volley from the heavy tank's massive twin autocannons rocked the seventy-ton 'Mech onto one leg. Smoke and flames streaming from the gaping cavities on its torso, the 'Mech crashed to the ground, Iota's first loss. The *Demolisher* crew paid for their victory with their lives as the *Warhammer*'s lancemates concentrated their fire on the tank.

When black BattleMechs appeared on the right flank, Dechan knew that the recon lance would be making no more reports: they had walked into the web and the spiders had gobbled them. The black 'Mechs were moving at high speed when they opened on Iota Battalion.

"Frak!" somebody said over Kappa's command channel. "They've got Clan tech."

Dechan saw that it was true. The black 'Mechs danced at the fringes of the effective ranges of Iota's 'Mechs. While Iota's shots were falling short or striking with insufficient energy to penetrate a BattleMech's armor, the black 'Mechs were scoring hits. In short order Iota's right flank crumbled under the assault.

Dechan scanned the terrain between his battalion and the black attackers. It was rough, some of it even classified as impassable. It would take time for his battalion to get into an effective attack position. By the time they did, the Spider Web would just as likely have pushed Iota back, or even broken them. He was more

worried by the fact that he could not confirm enough black 'Mechs to account for more than half a battalion. He was sure there had to be more ambushers.

Alpin was on the command channel screaming for information. Iota's commanders seemed to be too busy with their battle, so Dechan reported the situation. Describing the approach Kappa Battalion would have to take, he made it clear that adding Kappa to the battle would imperil the unit without any guarantee of success. He was surprised when Alpin agreed.

"Beta's Second Battalion is moving up to engage," the Khan told him. "You will hold while Third Battalion moves behind you to take their flank."

"Affirmative," Dechan replied. He had no desire to lead his battalion into the teeth of a Clan tech trap.

Alpin's strategy might have worked, given time, but Iota was the wrong unit for buying time. As Dechan watched, the battalion, broken into its constituent parts, streamed away from the battlefield. The Schismatic forces didn't pursue. Instead, fast hovercraft skimmed around the field, searching for surviving crewmen. Several black 'Mechs raced in and inspected the downed mercenary BattleMechs. They selected three of the least damaged ones and began to drag them away, including one that had apparently shut down from heat overload. The pilot ejected when a Spider's Web *Grasshopper* grabbed his machine, but a hovercraft was waiting for him when his parachute drifted to earth. The retreating Wolf forces had claimed him. The Spider's Web was through fighting for the day, and that suited Dechan just fine.

I didn't want to be where I was. Outside of my *Loki*, I felt cut off, out of touch with everything. I knew Alpin's forces had landed in the Outback and were making their first probes. Maeve's battalion had been sent to reinforce the Home Guard forces in Green Sector.

I was worried. Green Sector would be a high-priority target for Alpin's forces. The fighting would get hot there. It was where I should have been, but the Wolf had other plans, as always. I prayed that my reunion with Maeve wouldn't be over before it had a chance to blossom.

I worried so much that I forgot where I was.

A cardinal sin for a warrior.

I nearly walked into the guard pacing his watch along the perimeter of the Blackwell facility. Blackwell Corporation, despite the long association with Jaime Wolf and all the success they owed to him, had taken Chandra's path. They were officially neutral in this conflict, cutting both sides off from supplies and new equipment until the matter was settled. The Wolf was unhappy about their stance, but Blackwell's president was livid. Gerald Kearne was an ardent Elson supporter, who tried and failed to persuade Blackwell's board of directors to back Alpin with full support.

The guard reacted by rote when he saw me. He called for me to stand still as he raised his rifle. I complied, but I wasn't sure he would hold his fire. He looked very nervous, and I looked like a black-suited saboteur carrying a bomb.

He didn't shoot.

His mistake. A massive, dark blur suddenly roared out of the culvert twenty meters behind me. It rocketed into the guard, spilling him into the electrified fence. The man's body convulsed when it hit, muscles jerking spasmodically as the current jolted through him. Brilliant red laser fire seared from the culvert and cut through one of the fence posts. The post collapsed and wires parted. As the power died, the guard slumped to the ground.

The dark shape was Pietr Shadd in his battle armor. I imagined his disapproving face behind the viewplate of the armor's headpiece, but he said nothing. He fired his jump jets again and was gone.

I dropped the black box I was supposed to have attached to the fence. It was useless now. The element of surprise had been lost when the fence's power went out. No longer afraid of setting off an alarm, Shadd's Star roared over the fence and began bounding toward Assembly Buildings 4 and 5. Each Elemental's battle armor had been repainted especially for this raid. Snarling Nova Cats leapt across each pauldron.

In the distance I could see Blackwell guards boiling out of their barracks to the accompaniment of the bleating alarm. The duty guards were wearing vests, but half of the suddenly activated reserves had only their uniforms. They all carried light weapons, nothing that would be a significant danger to the Elementals' battle armor. Had the guards guessed they'd be facing Elementals, they might have spent a little time in the armory first.

My electronics expertise no longer needed, I left the infantry to their battle and headed back to my *Loki*. At a full run, it took me ten minutes. I was panting as I climbed the ladder into the cockpit, and more winded by the time I hit the button that retracted the ladder while I shrugged into my cooling vest. But I was happier; as dangerous as battle is for a man in a 'Mech, it is worse for everyone else.

My commo board was lit with incoming calls and the open channel to my lance was full of Grant's voice.

"What happened?"

"I fell asleep. Now shut up and let me find out how bad it is."

Amazingly, it wasn't bad at all.

The Blackwell bosses were just beginning to react to the jamming. I cut in Program Two, randomly punching in variations to keep the waves locked. Shadd reported reaching the buildings, and I released Grant to launch long-range volleys against targets that the

Elemental ground team designated. When the first whooshing roar was accompanied by the acrid scent of rocket propellant, I realized I hadn't sealed the *Loki*. There was so much else to do that I was coughing steadily by the time I could spare a moment to button up.

I was wondering if we'd have to take the 'Mechs in. The Wolf hadn't wanted that. He wanted a fast, clean strike with minimal damage and all the hallmarks of a pure Elemental raid. Once BattleMechs got into it, we'd blow our cover—and blow up a lot of property.

Shadd's channel beeped with the Go code. His team had reached and secured the objective. Soon they'd be roaring back to join us and we'd be out of there.

Other channels carried even better news. Maeve had met the enemy and their forces were on the run.

$\equiv$ 46 $\equiv$

We got a breather after our transfer to Green Sector, and we needed it. Our Battlegroup G—no, we were D after the transfer; the shifting of designators might be masking our forces from the opposition, but the practice caused us a few problems as well—had survived a number of encounters with Gamma Regiment's probes and needed repair, resupply, and refit. Although we would never say it in front of them, we were glad to see the conventional forces go in to hold the line for a while. I hoped they'd do as well as those ranked against Epsilon Regiment in Blue Sector.

Over in Blue, the Home Guard forces were having a relatively easy time of it. Neither side was being aggressive. Battlegroup H met any attempts to thrust through or around the Guard positions, and Nichole's MechWarriors usually backed away as soon as the Kuritans put in an appearance. The pattern had led the Colonel to believe that Nichole was not wholeheartedly behind the assault. He played into that, willing to keep things at a simmer as long as she was. Naturally, the Kuritans kept requesting permission to go over to the attack against such an obviously weak-willed enemy. Fortunately, they obeyed the Colonel; he was not about to send them against such a numerically superior enemy, no matter how weak-willed.

We had replaced Maeve's Battlegroup A in Green Sector as part of the Colonel's policy of shifting us around to keep Alpin's forces guessing about who they were facing. That's when we became Battlegroup D and Maeve's strike force had gone from A to N.

It was lucky timing, for almost as soon as the transfer was complete, Parella's Gamma Regiment had started a serious push in Red Sector. His initial success brought Alpin in on top of him; no doubt the self-proclaimed Khan was urging Parella to accelerate the assault. They hit Battlegroup N, Maeve's reinforced Spider's Web Battalion, and a couple of battalions of armor, but Maeve stalled them as she had Beta. The drive stopped, dissolving into the raiding we'd lived with for almost a week.

Dragoons in the field were used to full support. Our haphazard supply arrangements in this action meant going without a lot of the things we'd all become used to. The privations made life in the harsh Outback even more rigorous. Complaining didn't make it any better, but we all complained just the same. It made us *feel* better.

Battlegroup D's sector had been quiet for several days now and we'd been able to operate out of this base camp for almost a week. It was beginning to have a few of the amenities.

One of our advantages was Master Tech Bynfield. She was a crusty old wrench jock, but she knew battle machines, even the Omnis, like she was one of them. I'd heard that she'd cross-trained with the scientists to learn more about man-machine interfaces. With the help of our chief medtech, Gaf Schlomo, she had all our machines responding superbly. The two of them made an unbeatable team, even when they weren't working together to fine-tune our neurohelmets. If it hadn't been for her, we would have been short on operational 'Mechs, and if it hadn't been for him, we would have been even shorter on operational soldiers.

Techs don't normally spend their free time with

MechWarriors, but Bynfield and Schlomo were such a part of our group that none of the warriors, even the old-timers, objected when they joined us around the cook fires after the evening meal. It was only the lack of aerial surveillance that made the luxury of those fires available to us. That lack was something we bitched about when we needed to know where the hostiles were, but nobody complained about it on those cold nights. Naturally, we talked about what was going on around us. And of course no one wanted to suggest that we might lose this war being fought to restore the Colonel to his rightful place. So we also talked about what we'd do after things were settled, even knowing that some us might never have an after. Grant, as usual, was the most talkative.

"When we get back to the World, I'm gonna do what comes natural. That's for sure. Gonna take me a Dragoon's right and make myself a replacement. That's what I'm gonna do." He grinned all around. "Howzabout you, Brian boy? That Maeve you're so sweet on has got the right kind of terrain. You and her gonna make some little Dragoons and fill up the ranks?"

I was saved by the fire, which made everyone's face look flushed, but I didn't trust my voice. Giving only a shrug, I tried to make my expression wry enough to be an answer.

"Need to check her bloodline," Circoni said.

"Hey, old-timer, we ain't Clan anymore. Freeborn is fine among the Dragoons."

Circoni laughed. "And a damn good thing, too. I meant that you'd have to check the records and make sure there's no inbreeding. I think she's a sibkid and I know our fearless leader Brian is, even if he did earn back his bloodline name."

"I ain't no scientist, but I don't see a problem," said Captain Slezak, my battlegroup second. He had been one of the children who'd left the Clans with the Dragoons. "Just use your eyes. That tall drink Brian can't have many genes in common with the feisty little she-wolf.''

"What ya see is what ya get," Grant added.

Schlomo dropped his cup. Hot liquid splashed the old man, and Slezak as well. The two of them leaped to their feet.

"A touch of the palsy, Schlomo?" Grant grinned. "I thought you scientist types had cleaned up the gene pool."

"Many genotypes have similar phenotypic expressions," Schlomo said stiffly. He might be a medtech now, but he still talked like a scientist.

For a moment Grant looked puzzled at Schlomo's response, then he shook his head. "I don't know why we let you sit around with us. All you scientists wanta do is lecture or fiddle around in your labs. And since we ain't got a lab, ya lecture. I thought I'd left that kind of excess mass behind when I qualified for 'Mech duty. If I'd known that's what I was in for between fights, I'd have volunteered to be a groundpounder. Nobody cares enough about them to bother giving them lectures."

Almost everyone laughed at that and the tension broke. The spotlight on him again, Grant rambled off into an anecdote about an encounter with a squad of infantry and a one-legged BattleMech. I had heard it before, but him telling gave me the opportunity to tune out and think about what Grant had said about children. Until he mentioned it, I hadn't given the matter any thought.

Even before Grant finished his joke, the perimeter guard passed the word that a Dust Rat was coming in, cutting short my revery. I got up and wandered away from the fire, looking for the six-wheeled recon vehicle. I guessed that it would be Greevy's Rat. He was our Special Recon Group liaison, part of the detachment that had crossed over to the Outback while the majority of the unit stayed in the World to make life interesting for Alpin's supporters. Greevy had already been by earlier and given us the latest intel from the other sources. If this Rat was his, he had found a spot from which to beam his findings back to the Colonel in record time.

The Dust Rat pulled up twenty meters from our campfire. Even before the scruffy scout unlimbered his lanky frame from the vehicle, I knew it was Greevy's from the vehicle's paint scheme.

"Yo, Greevy. What's the word?"

"Coffee first."

When he walked past me, I could smell his stink from being cooped up too long in his car.

"The news," I said, falling in beside him.

He stopped and turned his head slowly until he was staring at me. His long face was drawn into a frown. "I've rolled without coffee before."

I didn't really expect him to leave, but the members of the Special Recon Group were all a little strange. I thought it best to humor him. People sometimes got weird from humping around the edges and behind battlefields all alone. They tended to forget about things like chains of command. I got him a cup, then went back to the fire.

Once he'd knocked back half the coffee, he sprawled beside the fire, his nonchalance belying the import of his words.

"Back in the World they tapped a patch into Chandra's commo. Report of a JumpShip convoy appearing insystem two days ago. There are DropShips on the way in. Zeta Battalion."

"Zeta!"

"Unity! That's good news," Circoni said. "We could use Jamison's assault 'Mechs."

"Fancher's freakos better look to their butts," Grant was saying when suddenly the camp speakers began to howl.

"Bandit!" was the cry that went up, but the news

was too late; the *Stingray* was already diving on the camp.

The incoming aerojock must not have been sure who we were; he didn't start firing until he was halfway through the first pass over the camp. When he finally decided to shoot, his lasers sliced furrows into the ground and anything else that got in their way. Wind created by the *Stingray*'s passage ripped through the camp, and the sonic boom knocked several people off their feet, including me. But I was up and running again while the *Stingray* climbed for altitude before another pass.

To get to my 'Mech, I had to run among the pads set up for the VTOL fighters. The fighters were only *Guardian* atmospheric craft, but I knew that the aerojock would consider them prime targets because they had the best chance of meeting him on his own terms.

Cursing the luck that put the pads between me and my 'Mech, I continued to run as fast as I could.

Dust billowed from beneath one of the *Guardian* fighters. The pilot must have been ready for a night patrol if he could scramble that quickly. Hot air and sound buffeted me as the fighter took off. He wouldn't have much chance against the *Stingray,* but on the ground, he'd have none at all.

I couldn't hear a thing over the roar of his jets, but the wild arm-waving of the people in front of me was warning enough. I hugged dirt. A crackling particle beam dug through the ground a few steps ahead of me.

Laser bolts clawed into the fighters still sitting on their pads, one ruby beam cutting into a fuel tank and igniting it. The aircraft vanished in a trio of explosions and a ball of fire. In minutes the night was a scene from hell as the flames lit the rising smoke.

The *Guardian* intercepted the *Stingray* as it came around for a third pass, but our fighter's cannon was pathetically unable to track the fast-moving aerospace fighter. The *Stingray*'s PPC and lasers flickered briefly and the *Guardian* disintegrated.

But its pilot had bought us some time.

I scrambled up the ladder to the cockpit of my 'Mech. The *Loki*'s fusion reactor was on damped idle. The risk of being spotted was high, but the danger of being caught with cold engines was worse. I was glad I'd decided to chance it. I popped the dampers and prayed as the engine pumped power to the machine.

My computer acquired the *Stingray* as it swooped in for its next pass. Lasers flickering from its wings and blue lightning erupting from its nose, the aerospace fighter roared across the camp, explosions erupting as it passed. It was obscured briefly by the rising cloud from an obliterated ammo dump, but then I had my sights on it. The seven-centimeter Blackwell lasers glowed, sending their scarlet energy to crisscross behind the *Stingray*'s forward-port canard wing. I thought my shot had missed, but the forward speed of the fighter was so great that it swept through the pulse of my lasers. Shrapnel littered our camp as armor peeled away from the fighter's main wing.

The *Stingray* wobbled as it screamed away into the darkness.

I hoped we had seen the last of it, but my radar screen showed it banking around for another pass. My cockpit was full of sound. Warriors firing up their 'Mechs. Ground troopers screaming for vectors to aim their antiair. Calls for medics and firefighting equipment. I watched the aerojock maneuver on my screen.

I thought he'd come around the heavy column of smoke from the ammo dump, but he came through it instead. My lasers raked empty sky. He was a better shot, pummeling my *Loki,* which rocked as coherent light savaged its armored shell.

Other 'Mechs and some of the antiair emplacements fired at the *Stingray*. Some hit, but the fighter's armor held. When he finally roared away into the night, heading south, my radar told me that he wouldn't be back. I passed the word over the battlegroup channel as two friendly fighters streaked across the perimeter of our encampment.

"Those are ours, folks. The bird's going to have to burn it if he's not going to smoke." I didn't know if our aerospace boys would catch him, but I hoped so. The *Stingray*'s pilot had done more than enough damage. "Now, everybody saddle up. We're going to have ground forces moving on us soon. The big bad bird squawked."

47

In the week since the *Stingray* had caught us off-guard, we did a lot of skirmishing with Gamma Regiment. Per Colonel Wolf's plan, we were trading ground for time, trying to bloody Alpin's forces as much as possible, while minimizing our own losses. We'd been laying a lot of ambushes and were getting very good at it.

Now we were deployed in and around Silone Lake. Hidden underwater, I waited and watched.

My *Loki* wasn't hot, but the other 'Mechs in the detachment were sure to be. They were old tech and had been in battle while I had been waiting in the lake. They wouldn't be a lot of help till they'd had a chance to let their heat sinks vent for a while.

The video feed from the pickup floating above me came through the optical-fiber line. The quality of the image wasn't great, but it served to show me the 'Mechs approaching the lake. Most cut to their left and raced along the beach. A *Vindicator* and two *Wasps* fired their jump jets and sailed over the water. The 'Mechs were pretty badly beat up.

A *Fenris,* the first of their pursuers, came over the rise. The OmniMech was moving flat out, and rapidly closing the distance separating it from its prey. I let it go. There would be more.

Two *Blackhawks* were next and I would have taken them, but they fired their jets and sailed high above the lake. The detachment would have to handle them as best they could. Although I was unhappy that all three of the Omnis we had identified with Ansell's company were still operating, I was pleased to see that they had also taken a beating.

Another half-dozen 'Mechs came into sight, the rest of Ansell's company. I was relieved to see that they were older designs; our limited intelligence hadn't told us what sort of replacements Gamma Regiment was getting. The charging 'Mechs moved in the tight formation we had come to expect from the warriors of Gamma Regiment, especially those under Major Ansell. Keeping their spacing required some of the 'Mechs to enter the lake; there wasn't enough space for them on the beach.

It was time to trip the switch for the *Loki*'s jump jets, which sent me and my 'Mech boiling out of the lake in a cloud of steam. The spy cable ripped away as I rose, but I didn't need it anymore. As soon as the *Loki*'s arms cleared the water, I triggered both the big lasers at the most massive of the hostile 'Mechs. It was a tricky shot, but nothing for which my targeting computer couldn't compensate. Twin scarlet beams sliced into the rear of a *Marauder,* cutting in beneath the port heat sink. The carapace of the *Marauder* erupted in a chain of explosions that blew the left arm out in an arcing trajectory. Even before the seventy-five-ton 'Mech had collapsed to the ground, I moved on to another target.

Grant's *Archer* rose from its crouching position in the depths of the lake like some leviathan seeking prey. The armored covers for the twenty missile launchers opened like jaws as the *Archer* vomited forth a double salvo of long-range missiles. Grant held the big machine steady under the vibrations of the ripple launch, improving his chances of hits. Forty missiles screamed toward a sixty-five-ton *Axman* that was the deadliest in-fighter of the enemy company. The 'Mech rocked under the impact, then toppled in slow motion, arms flailing as the pilot struggled to reassert control. The missiles that missed banked in a tangle of contrails, each searching for a secondary target. Flashes from impacts on the two 'Mechs nearest the falling *Axman* told me that the swarm warheads had been a good choice for this ambush.

I landed uphill from the beach along the tree line where the dense woods would mask my silhouette. Dodging among the smaller trees at the edge, I swiveled the *Loki*'s torso back to keep the firing arcs of both arm-mounts on target. Whenever I could, I put a shot into the *Axman* struggling in the mud at the lake's edge.

Our *Vindicator* and *Wasps* were back as per the plan, their return sparking confusion among Ansell's jocks. Their formation broke, but they didn't run.

The pinging of the *Loki*'s antimissile system warned me I had incoming missiles. A glance at the threat-assessment screen pinpointed a *Sentinel* as the launch platform. A standard *Sentinel* carried only short-range missiles. I modified my firing pattern to compensate for the heat the antimissile system would generate and prayed that it would catch them all. The AM ammo bar shrank and I felt none of the sharp raps of SRM impacts. The antimissile system was not good against the *Sentinel*'s autocannon. Shells pocked the front of the *Loki*, ripping shards off armor in a vain attempt to reach my 'Mech's inner structure.

Reluctantly, I abandoned my attack on the *Axman* in order to deal with the *Sentinel*'s more immediate threat. I triggered the left-arm laser and watched its beam boil away the last armor remaining on the *Sentinel*'s right thigh. Sparks leapt from the wound and the *Sentinel*'s pilot shifted his machine's course to the right to shield the exposed area. Trailing smoke, he raced past me along the beach. I tried another shot, hoping to take him down, but the heat levels in my

Loki were rising and affecting the targeting systems. I missed.

Grant had the *Axman* covered. Slogging ashore, the *Archer* swiveled back and gave him another double dose. Explosions blossomed across the *Axman*'s right arm and chest, shredding ferro-fibrous armor and opening craters to the vulnerable innards. The missiles that had failed to target the stricken 'Mech screamed around it, seeking in vain for other targets.

"Ken's down! Somebody help him!"

The call was on the command channel. Ken Shiamatsu was piloting a *Dervish,* the heaviest of the machines in our decoy element. If he was down, they were in trouble.

A laser cut across my *Loki*'s leg as I tried to assess the situation. I lost armor, but there was no warning of a breach. I snapped a shot in return, but with all the steam and smoke, I didn't know what I'd fired at, let alone whether I'd hit.

Wu's *Vindicator* was landing from a jump on my right. It hit ground poorly, its right leg collapsing under it. An enemy *Jenner* came through a smoke bank a hundred meters away, ripping at the fallen *Vindicator* with a quartet of lasers. The beams gnawed armor, then broke through to vaporize the myomer pseudo-muscle that moved the machine's foamed titanium bones. The *Vindicator* was out of the fight.

We'd done damage. The *Marauder* was a definite kill and the *Axman* a probable, but we had too many down.

"Break off! Break off!"

The hostiles continued their fire as we retreated, but they used only energy weapons. Fed by the fusion reactor that powered a BattleMech, such weapons had inexhaustible ammunition supplies. Ansell's jocks did not use their other weapons and that worried me. Typically, they would have dumped everything they had in hopes of taking down a few more of us, but they were saving their ammo for something.

At least they didn't follow us. Maybe they were afraid of another trap. Or maybe they were finally learning respect.

Iota Battalion's losses were being made for by more down-and-out mercs eager for a chance at the Dragoon name. Dechan doubted that they had heard what happened to their predecessors; Elson had a tight rein on the news that got back to the World. Iota's jocks soon found out why there had been openings.

Spider's Web Battalion had shifted away from Fancher's line of advance through Green Sector, to be replaced by another force of BattleMechs that some reports claimed was led by Jaime Wolf himself. The shift made Alpin and Elson reconsider their plans. Svados' intel people predicted that Jaime Wolf was lairing somewhere in Red Sector, but the famous blue and gold *Archer* had been seen among the enemy 'Mechs in Green Sector.

No matter who was leading Wolf's forces, they were effective. Their tricks and traps were taking a toll, and not just on the front-line troops of Iota Battalion and Beta Regiment. The morale of the rest of the forces was hit hard as well. What was supposed to have been a lightning campaign had been bogged down for too long. Wolf, for all he was on the defensive, had stolen the initiative. The so-called hunters were dancing to his tune.

Hunters.

The nickname had come into use when we'd learned that the rebels had taken to calling themselves the Wolf Pack. Dechan supposed they'd adopted the name as a show of loyalty to Jaime Wolf. Dechan didn't think it coincidental that the name simultaneously flouted their rejection of Alpin. Referring to the forces under Alpin as hunters had started in Beta Regiment. The Khan legitimized it when he put a bounty on his grandfather's head.

That bounty excited a lot of the mercs. They talked about hunting Wolf themselves, but their talk was as disjointed as their tactics. They couldn't agree on anything, each one trying to outdo the others. Elson had really scraped up the dregs.

Dechan had heard similar talk among some of his own Kappa Battalion. He cut it off whenever it started, going so far as to prohibit the topic from staff conferences. But he knew he couldn't keep a lid on it forever. Now that word was out that Wolf himself was leading the forces of our opposition, even relatively disciplined mercs like the Chevaliers were feeling the lure of a lucrative bounty.

Dechan doubted that Wolf was present in Green Sector. It wasn't that his troops weren't well-led; they were. It was just that he was sure Alpin would never have left to spearhead Parella's force in Red Sector if he'd believed that Jaime Wolf was here in Green. Then again, Elson hadn't left, even when Gamma Regiment moved to relieve Beta and started pushing past the ground Beta had gained. When it came down to it, you never knew who was in the BattleMech till you checked the cockpit.

Carter tossed aside the flap of Dechan's tent.

"We've got orders."

"Elson or Alpin?"

"Elson."

"A briefing in ten."

Carter nodded. Reaching up, he tugged the flap and let it drop closed. Dechan listened to him crunch across the gravel, passing among the other tents and rousing the officers as he went.

So far, Kappa Battalion had been held back from the fighting. Dechan had taken it as a sign that Elson had something special in mind for them. If Elson was abandoning the facade of working through Alpin, the decision point was coming soon.

Michi knew he was being followed, but he had no time to do anything about it. He walked down Lafayette Avenue among the midday crowds. There were too many eyes here for his pursuers to pose a threat, but that was a temporary condition. Soon he would have to leave the avenue. They might try to take him then, if they knew; or they might wait, if they only suspected. He could not tell their numbers. If there were too many, and they *did* know, they might take him.

He turned off the avenue.

Once around the corner, he began to run.

He had covered two blocks by the time he heard the curses telling him that the pursuers had turned the corner. They would run now, too.

He was fortunate that he did not have far to go. They were younger, more fit for running. He heard their footfalls growing ever closer.

The ComStar acolyte was startled when Michi burst through the door—too startled to stop him, which was good. He heard the woman shouting for guards as he ran down the corridor to the inner court. The guards arrived in time to stumble into Michi's pursuers; he heard the scuffle start as the door closed behind him.

He was the only disturbance in the peace of the garden as he raced across it. But only for a moment. Shouts shattered the tranquillity; the ComStar guards had only been able to delay the pursuers. It was to be expected; the guards were not prepared and the pursuers were professionals.

Michi ran along the row of small cottages. He reached the one he sought and, without pause, he turned his last stride into a kick. The door flew open, bouncing off the wall and returning to strike him as he moved through the opening.

The air inside was warmer than that of the garden, the only light streaming in from the open doorway. The only furnishings were a chair, a bed, and a nightstand that held a computer work station. The bed was occupied.

The man grabbed a gun from behind the computer monitor, rolled off the bed, and took aim at Michi. In sync with the flash of recognition in the man's eyes, Michi tossed him the silver cylinder.

"GO!" he ordered.

Stanford Blake caught the cylinder with his free hand, then shouted, "Look out!"

Michi wheeled, drawing his sword and striking all in one smooth motion. The keen blade sliced the pursuer in half at the waist. Major Sean Eric Kevin looked surprised as he died.

Blake fired through Kevin's fountaining blood, dropping the second man.

There were more running across the garden.

"Go," Michi said again as he closed the door. "Now!"

Blake nodded curtly. He stuffed the cylinder into his waistband and pulled open the back door. "Thanks," he said as he bolted through. Michi watched him run across the garden. The house would shield him from the pursuers' sight once he left the direct line between the front and back doors. Michi swung the front door closed, then stooped and took the pistol from Kevin's holster. He stepped against the wall beside the door, well away from the frame.

He waited.

They were cautious, perhaps believing him trapped. He hoped that they would stay cautious; every second they wasted was useful. He knew they would not wait long, however. If they had suspected before, he had confirmed their fears.

A fusillade of shots splintered holes in the door and the wall on either side of it. Michi was moving forward as the door slammed open, this time dropping free from its abused hinges. He cut at the first commando as the man came through, the sword biting deep into his arm. Screaming, the man twisted away, ripping the sword grip from Michi's hand. Two shots dropped the second commando, but another one came crashing through the front window as her companion died. Forced back by fire from the two still outside, Michi was unable to halt the woman as she rolled to her feet and sprang through the open back door.

He could not know if he had delayed them long enough. He started to run after the woman, but his move was not enough of a surprise. Her companions fired on him as he cleared the edge of the house. Feeling a shock to his arm, he spun under the impact of the shot, then fell to the ground. He rolled aside and fired as one of the commandos came around the building after him. The man took the first slug and two more before he collapsed.

Michi knew that he had succeeded in his mission when he heard the mighty hyperpulse generator thrum with the sound of an outgoing pulse.

His relief almost cost him his life. The last commando had circled around the other side of the building, and only a scrape of gravel betrayed his presence. Michi was rolling before the man fired the weapon, and the slug slammed into the ground instead of into Michi. His answering shot went wide, but the man ducked back. Unfortunately for him, he moved into the path of Michi's last, unaimed shot.

Karma.

A gunshot boomed from the direction of the generator building. Michi forced himself to his feet. The gun in his hand was empty. Dropping it, he stooped to take another from one of the commandos. He nearly fainted as he straightened up. Too much blood loss and not enough concentration. He fought down the pain, banishing it beneath clarity of purpose.

He ran toward the sound of gunfire.

The door to the generator's control chamber was open when he reached it. He went in low, intending to roll into a firing position. He froze.

It was too late.

ComStar guards had weapons trained on him. They were very nervous. One attended to an acolyte who had been shot in the leg. The female commando and Stanford Blake lay in separate pools of blood that were slowly spreading toward each other.

"Drop your weapon," a guard ordered.

Michi complied.

Stanford Blake had managed to transmit the plans for Elson's final assault. Jaime Wolf would have the information he needed to unhinge those plans. Michi's part in this was over.

He fainted.

48

As I had feared, Ansell's men had been conserving their ammunition for a reason. Two days later, as our last units were moving into night laager, a bombardment began. Radar and telemetry interception told us that Arrow missile systems were being used to supplement the normal artillery, which meant that Fire Support Battalion had been brought in. At that time, they were the only Dragoon unit with that kind of firepower. Elson was getting serious.

Reports began to come in from the Home Guard units holding the front. A major attack was developing on the hinge between Twelfth and Fourteenth Armored. Elson's BattleMech forces were pushing into the gap to take advantage of the split in command zones.

"Unity! Zeta better get here soon," Grant said.

I didn't bother to answer him. Whether Zeta arrived or not, we had a lot to do. I was sure that there was action all along the front, though I had heard nothing from the other battlegroups.

Our first contact with the enemy came shortly after midnight, just outside the mock village of Potterdam. A short lance of three BattleMechs was moving along the dry river course. They were well ahead of the furthest reported thrust and that wasn't good. There being only three, we hit them hard. I didn't want them around if there were more hostiles on the way, and our numerical superiority made taking them out easy. One blew apart in an ammunition explosion created by several volleys of missiles. The second was crippled, and the third broadcast his surrender and popped his hatch after taking cover from our onslaught. They called themselves members of Iota Battalion, but they were just hired guns. I called base to send a fast hovercraft out with one of our dismounted jocks; we could use the merc's 'Mech.

The merc was talkative. He confirmed that Elson and Fancher were the commanders in this part of the front. He also told us that another 'Mech unit, Kappa Battalion, had been transferred to Orange Sector. It had to be the unit that recon had spotted in reserve during the early phases. Fancher wasn't the sort to weaken her command just before a major offensive. If she had dispensed with a unit now, it was likely because the main thrust would be falling elsewhere. Sending reinforcements to Alpin's forces in Orange Sector, where Maeve was defending, suggested that Alpin was leading the principal attack.

We pressed on.

Fourteenth Armored's command was in turmoil. Most of their tanks were out of commission, but they had succeeded in relinking with Twelfth Armored. Twelfth was in better shape but not by much. Beta Regiment had come forward and was pounding on the tankers. Our strategy of isolation and traps was faltering against this strategy of vigorous assault. It wouldn't be long before the enemy 'Mechs crumbled our shaky defense.

I sent my battlegroup in to blunt a thrust that was probing along Fourteenth Armored's right flank. If that flank came unglued, Alpin's troopers would have an open field and be able to slice through our scattered infantry positions and into Orange Sector behind Maeve's lines. The battlegroup turned back the enemy 'Mechs, but had to withdraw when Stars of Elementals were spotted moving into attack position along a ridgeline.

I gave the order to fall back.

On the way to our second line, I was able to break through to the Colonel. He assured me that Maeve was aware of our new position. She was under heavy pressure from Parella's Gamma Regiment, but so far had managed to hold them off by constantly shifting her battlegroup to where the fighting was hottest. I knew what a toll this must be taking on the Spider's Web; they wouldn't be able to keep up that pace forever.

There had been no sign of the Kappa Battalion in that sector.

Over in Blue Sector, there had still been no major engagements, but that was likely to change soon. The Kuritans were moving to counter a two-battalion thrust by Epsilon.

"We're doing fine," the Colonel assured me.

I wanted to believe him.

I knew that BattleMech combat was not the drawn-out affair that had been a soldier's lot for so much of history. 'Mech battles couldn't be sustained for long periods of time. Too many machines carried limited supplies of ammunition, and lost effectiveness when those were gone. Even 'Mechs armed exclusively with energy weapons had limited duration; the combat was too brutal and even a BattleMech's armor can take only so much punishment. And the machines were too expensive, too hard to replace. Once a warrior's machine got mauled, he pulled out, if he was smart. Refitted and resupplied, he'd be a threat again; staying in was just asking for death.

So the battles ebbed and flowed, rarely seeing the commitment of all a unit's forces. With each engagement, the 'Mechs would be worn down and the forces would grow smaller. We had to put our warriors in more often and that worried me. People wore down, too. Tired people make mistakes, and the price of a mistake on the battlefield is often paid for with lives.

And so it went. Like Maeve's, my battlegroup rushed back and forth plugging holes in the line and sideswiping the units that managed to punch through our positions. The tankers had the hardest job. Less mobile than the 'Mechs, they had to do an infantry-man's job and hold ground. There were times I wished we had infantry, that I could pull the tanks back and regroup them for a counterattack, but the arid waste-lands of Green Sector were not an infantryman's ter-rain. An armored Elemental's, maybe, but I didn't have any under my command.

I couldn't complain about the troops that I did com-mand. They were magnificent. What had begun as a motley group of old warriors, trainees, and sibkids had become a lean, hard machine. It gave me a glimpse of what the old Dragoons must have been, what the Colonel had wanted from the new ones. I was damned proud to be part of it.

As rough as the fighting was, I'd begun to believe that the Colonel was right, that we were doing all right. Then recon reported DropShips landing on the left flank: three *Leopard* Class and two *Union*s. 'Mech transports. I feared the merc we had captured had lied to us, and we had just found the missing Kappa Bat-talion.

I ordered the battlegroup disengaged, taking Grant with me. Our two-'Mech Command Lance was going to be more useful in the field than in the command camp. It took us time, too much time, to cross behind Twelfth Armored. The newly arrived 'Mechs would be deployed and moving before we could get to them.

When we came in sight of the distant Luma Moun-tains that owned the skyline on the far side of Grem-mer Canyon, we got the updated scout reports. The new force had deployed and was moving toward us. They had passed at least two bunker complexes without opening fire. I knew why the men in the bunkers hadn't opened up; there were too few, having been intended mostly as an outpost screen to watch moving hostiles and report positions. But the 'Mechs? That confused me.

Dust announced their arrival well before we could actually spot them, even at maximum magnification. The size of the cloud meant at least two companies, probably more.

Captain Jenette Rand, out on point a klick forward of our positions, reported two *Stalkers*, a *King Crab*, and a *BattleMaster* in the first lance she spotted. Assault 'Mechs all. She observed a variety of color schemes but no unit markings. I called her back. Her *Mongoose* wouldn't last a minute against that kind of firepower.

The approaching 'Mechs were moving in a tight formation. They were still several minutes away, so I gave orders to take up ambush position. We might be outnumbered, but if we could get in a few shots before having to retreat, I figured we'd be ahead of the game.

Rand's *Mongoose* burst out of the dry streambed she'd been using for cover from the approaching assaults. "More incoming," she radioed. " 'Mechs to the southeast."

I moved my *Loki* along the ledge to where I could command a view in that direction. She was right. Half a dozen light 'Mechs, mixed Omnis and old tech models, were racing toward us. There was no doubt who they belonged to; bold black betas decorated their sandy camo patterns. Several launched long range missiles at Rand's 'Mech and started hammering away with their light autocannons.

I alerted Corwyn's lance and gave them license to engage. They were in the path of the Beta 'Mechs, but the rough terrain between them and the approaching assaults would mostly screen them. I fired a seven-centimeter laser at the lead light, a *Puma*. The beam ripped across the broad shell of armor that shielded the boxy hunched torso. Having gotten the jock's attention, I also took a hit from a PPC, whose manmade lightning chewed armor from the left side of my *Loki*. The *Puma*'s second bolt missed.

Then Corwyn's lance opened up, and the *Puma* jock had a lot more to think about. He'd shown he was dangerous, and Corwyn's people gave him their best. Armor disintegrated under the barrage. The *Puma* staggered, then hopped a couple of steps to the side under the pounding. A jet of steam erupted through a crack in the *Puma*'s right-arm armor. Joint seals blew, and the arm dropped from its extended firing position. Rand's *Mongoose* turned and blasted three laser beams into the crippled Omni. The *Puma*'s cockpit blew open as the pilot ejected, his 'Mech crumpling to the ground.

The second of the Omnis, another *Puma* but with a different weapons configuration, caught Rand's *Mongoose* with a heavy laser, the beam of coherent light punching straight through her 'Mech's left torso. The pilot followed up with a salvo of autocannon fire that slammed the *Mongoose,* twisting it around. The arms of Rand's *Mongoose* arms flailed as it fell heavily. I didn't see her eject.

Grant moved his *Archer* up beside me and opened up on the Beta 'Mechs. The combined fire from Corwyn's lance and our two heavies from a superior position made the Beta warriors reconsider their position. In minutes they had gone from chasing a lone scout to a full-blown firefight against superior numbers.

They had just started to pull back when long-range missiles began to explode along the cliff face above Grant and me. A second barrage arced over the lights to impact beyond them.

The assault 'Mechs had come into range and we were exposed. I had halted and dust was starting to settle on the motionless 'Mechs. Another lance, two

*Daishi*s and two *Mad Cat* OmniMechs, was taking up position to the left of the first lance while another lance of mixed heavies and assaults moved into position on the right.

The quality of the 'Mechs told me that this wasn't the missing mercenary battalion. I didn't need to hear the commander's announcement to know that Zeta Battalion had arrived at long last.

"This is J. Elliot Jamison of Zeta Battalion. This has gone on long enough."

"Yeah," Grant crowed over our lance channel. "We're gonna kick some butt now!"

"Cease now, Wolf."

"What? They're supposed to be on our side!" Grant's tone was more affronted than confused.

"Why?" I asked on an open band.

"I didn't come to talk to you, Cameron. I don't know why you let the Trial of Position take place, Jaime, but now it must be upheld. So what's it going to be, Jaime Wolf?"

I realized Jamison thought he was communicating with the Colonel. Grant, in the Colonel's old *Archer*, was silent.

"If that's the way you want to play." There was a short pause. "I sincerely regret this. Zeta, attack."

The Zeta 'Mechs disappeared in billowing clouds of missile exhaust. The blue lightning of PPC beams and the ruby spears and eye-searing pulses of laser weapons burned through the smoke, raining onto our position.

The barrage flayed Grant's *Archer*, the main target of the attack, but my *Loki* caught many of the shots that missed Grant. Alarms shrieking of failing systems, the *Loki* began to topple. The ammunition explosion that vaporized the *Archer* picked my machine up and tossed it away. I don't remember my *Loki* hitting the ground.

49

The night march had been long, but accomplished with surprising ease. But afterward Dechan Fraser still could not sleep. He was tired and needed rest, but his tent was so stifling and confining that he got up to walk among the sleeping BattleMechs. In the gray light of predawn, the plain should have been quiet. Instead the million soft sounds of a MechWarrior camp buzzed, clanked, rattled, scraped, hummed, and hissed around him. It was almost as if the 'Mechs stirred restlessly in their sleep, but it was only the tech crews tending to the machines after their long march.

Dechan was staring at the sky, pondering the coming day, when a bright flash—like a shooting star but stationary—caught his attention. It was no natural phenomenon; he'd seen enough combat to know that. Making for the command center, he resisted the urge to run, as though hurrying would add too much weight to what might already be a portent.

Dechan had the tech on duty patch him through to Gamma Regiment's headquarters. When Parella finally came on the line, he didn't bother with politeness.

"What's happened?"

"Chandra's taken down a satellite," the scratchy-voiced Parella told him gruffly.

"Ours or theirs?"

"What a stupid question. Since Khan Alpin wants

us to play along and be nice to Chandra, it sure wasn't ours. The transmission was beamed to somewhere in Orange Sector.''

Somewhere out beyond their lines, presumably directly to Wolf. Dechan's stomach churned. ''Any idea what it was about?''

''We are nosy today. What's the matter? Can't wait for the morning briefing?''

''It would be nice to have some warning if we're going to be walking into more of Wolf's traps.''

''And it'd be nice if Wolf laid down and died, but he ain't going to do that unless we help him along. That's what we bought you for, merc. Now you just go get your folks ready to roll.''

''Let me talk to Alpin.''

''That's Khan Alpin to you and he's busy,'' Parella snarled. ''Just do your job.''

The line went dead. The commtech tried but was unable to reestablish contact, though she assured Dechan that the line had not been cut. Dechan's stomach began to churn. It was never good when headquarters wouldn't talk to you. Walking to the mess tent, he began to wonder if Elson had been holding Kappa Battalion back so that he could use it up it in the grand finale. He spent two hours trying to convince his stomach to hold down some oatmeal so the acid would have something to work on, but he had no more success with that than the commtech had in raising Parella again.

The mess tent was half-full with other, more successful, diners when Alpin made a general broadcast.

''This is the morning when all we have worked for will come to pass,'' Khan Alpin began. ''Wolf's force is on the ropes. Early this morning Zeta Battalion arrived onplanet in support of the rightful succession. Jaime Wolf and his followers are doomed. Already the forces blocking our progress in Green Sector are in retreat. Already the lead elements of Gamma Regiment are moving into position for the final assault.

"Soon you will be moving out." Groans and complaints filled the tent. Kappa had been promised a day's rest. "I know it is much to ask, but I also know you are warriors and so will understand. We must rise to this effort and strike now. We must strike hard and fast. I expect no less from the warriors of Kappa Battalion. I will meet you on the other side and we will walk the honor road together.

"Seyla!"

There was a courier waiting for Dechan with a sealed packet of orders when the broadcast ended. The last mouthful of oatmeal went down hard, plummeting into his stomach to sit like a lump of lead as he read the orders.

Dechan saw immediately what his unit had been saved for. Gamma Regiment was to open a breach in Wolf's line, then wheel right. As they advanced, a gap between Gamma's left flank and Epsilon's right would appear. Kappa was to move through that gap, flanking the enemy Battlegroup M. Once past the forward battle area, they were to race for the Tetsuhara Proving Grounds and occupy its command center before Wolf's forces could retreat there.

Tetsuhara Proving Ground. *Tetsuhara.* The name was back to haunt him. Outreach wasn't cold like Misery, but their objective would provide its own misery. The proving ground was full of automated defenses, and Dechan was sure Wolf would have them operating. The place would be a maze of booby traps. Those defenses might have been designed simply to test warriors, but he was sure they were also capable of lethal force. Even the promised artillery support of Fire Support Battalion wouldn't make it much easier, if they ever got such support. Kappa Battalion was being assigned a mission of unusual lethality.

So much for Elson's promises of a place in the Dragoons. Maybe in the Dragoons' cemetery.

Then again, maybe this was the Elemental's way of making Dechan and his warriors prove that they were truly Dragoon material, that they were strong enough for what Elson had in mind. Taking the proving ground wouldn't be easy, but it would be a vital stroke. If they could take the control center before Wolf's forces got there, the campaign would be over quickly. The proving ground control complex was the last defensible position for an organized force. Without it, Wolf would have to surrender or go guerrilla. If he took the latter course, his bid to retake control of the Dragoons was finished. Dragoon custom demanded that challenges to Trials be fought as stand-up combats.

Dechan shoved aside his concerns in the work of getting the battalion ready to roll.

Despite his fears, the initial advance met with little resistance, because Wolf's forces were far too busy elsewhere. The arrival of Zeta Battalion on Alpin's side had shifted the balance. Jamison was even claiming that they had killed Jaime Wolf, but the cohesiveness of the enemy forces put the lie to that. Though reeling from the hammer blows of Beta and Gamma Regiments' assaults, Wolf's troops were pulling back in good order. The only place Alpin's forces weren't advancing was in Blue Sector, where Epsilon Regiment was still in place. The Kuritans had blunted Epsilon's attack, taking minimal losses.

Nichole pulled Epsilon back to its jump-off position, ceasing offensive operations and informing the commanders of the attacking forces that the battle plan had been transmitted to Wolf. Dechan failed to get through to Alpin or Elson for confirmation, but Alpin responded to Nichole's assertion with a commanders-only broadcast admitting that the satellite destruction earlier that morning had been Fleet Captain Chandra delivering on her promise to eliminate any satellites used by the combatants. He pointed out Beta's and Gamma's success, but never actually denied Nichole's statement about the battle plan having been given away. Dechan took the failure to deny it as an admission that Nichole was right, at least partially.

But despite the intelligence coup by Jaime Wolf's partisans, Alpin's attack was proceeding well. The enemy was falling back on two fronts, converging on the Tetsuhara Proving Ground. The proving ground was where Jaime Wolf had put spine into the lords of the Great Houses of the Inner Sphere. There, with staged tests and contests, he had shown them and their gullible children how to stand up to the fierce warriors of the marauding Clans. For Wolf, the proving ground had been the place where the Inner Sphere's answer to the Clan invasion had begun. Unless Wolf had some surprises in store, it would be the place where his answer to Alpin and Elson ended.

Kappa Battalion reached the outer boundaries almost on schedule, still ahead of the retreating Battlegroup M. But less than a hundred meters past the boundary marker, Kappa's advance slowed when a *Vindicator* detonated an unexploded shell or a mine. Kappa moved on, leaving the *Vindicator*'s pilot to contemplate his footless 'Mech. But they moved slower.

The proving ground was a huge area with a wide variety of terrains, simulated structures, and clusters of buildings. Dechan kept Kappa moving cautiously, not wishing to lose any more 'Mechs to unnecessary damage. The flash and rumble of battle to the northeast grew closer as they probed to find the headquarters' location, a detail curiously missing from the maps provided them.

The lance scouting Dechan's right flank reported seeing 'Mechs and armor approaching from the battle. He ordered a halt and moved his lance over to investigate. The scouts were correct; the first elements of

Wolf's forces were arriving. Dechan directed his battalion to take up positions across their line of retreat.

Then they sat and waited.

The lead hovertank must have had an active probe. Just out of missile range, it swerved and headed back to its fellows. The rest changed course as well, ducking into a simulated town. Dechan held his unit in place, refusing a request to flush the tankers with a probe by a light lance.

Battlegroup M was coming, with at least a battalion of Gamma Regiment in hot pursuit. The enemy forces were executing a classic leapfrog retreat, using alternate fire and movement with precision and élan. Fascinated, Dechan watched his commo officer make tentative identification of the battlegroup's leader from the radio activity. That commander was piloting a *Thunderbolt,* fighting with admirable efficiency while simultaneously controlling her troops' retreat. It was a bravura performance.

The main body of the opposition had almost reached the town when a fresh charge erupted from Gamma's lines. Heavy 'Mechs led the way, taking the punishment that Wolf's people were dishing out and sending it right back. In the forefront of the charge was a Star of OmniMechs. Dechan only knew of one unit in Alpin's forces that was organized that way: Alpin's own Command Lance. The Khan had come to settle matters personally.

A close-fighting melee developed on the outskirts of the town. Wolf's troops fought hard, but they were outnumbered and the outcome seemed inevitable. Then, in one of those lulls that unaccountably occur in battle, a 'Mech stepped into the open. The battered *Thunderbolt* raised its arms and spread them wide.

"I, Maeve of the Wolf Pack, make my challenge!" The pilot's voice boomed out on external speakers and a spread of open frequencies. "I challenge the leader of the usurpers to meet me. Alpin Wolf, are you a coward that you will not face the one who has held you at bay for a month? Are you afraid of a warrior with no surname?''

Dechan snapped his eyes to the position where he had last seen the Command Lance. Alpin had been in the thick of a battle that had cost him two of his lance. His *Thor* took a step toward the *Thunderbolt*.

"What are you doing, you fool?" Parella shouted over the command channel.

"I will fight her. Her death will end this battle sooner," Alpin replied. He sounded eager. "She *is* the one who has cost us so much."

"Then clear the line of fire, and we'll all waste her."

"Neg! I forbid it! It's not the Clan way. What would Elson and the Clanners think?"

"Elson would tell you to waste her. There's more battle to fight. There's still Wolf."

The *Thor* stopped its steady progress toward the *Thunderbolt*. It seemed to Dechan that Parella's words had struck a chord with Alpin. A hearty laugh cut across the channel. Somehow Maeve had found Gamma's command frequency. Maybe it had been in the transmitted plans. How didn't matter; what she said did.

"Poor little Alpin, maybe you should listen to tough old Parella. But I can tell you what Elson would say. He's a Clanner. He'd tell you that you aren't man enough to do the job."

"Bitch!" Parella screamed as Alpin's *Thor* lurched forward into a run.

"You're mine!" Alpin screamed, then launched his *Thor* on a tail of superheated air.

The *T-bolt*'s top-mounted launcher swiveled, tracking the incoming Omni. A spread of missiles streaked out toward it, but no laser pulse went with them. Those were not standard tactics for a *Thunderbolt*. Dechan expected the rebel warrior to do all she could at long range, but the big arm-mounted laser was the *Thunderbolt*'s main gun. If she wasn't using it, it must be damaged.

He admired her courage. Going up against an Omni was tough enough in a fully functioning BattleMech. She must have seen the challenge as the only chance she had to strip the enemy of its leader.

Alpin's own launcher vomited a spray of missiles as the *Thor* landed on flexed legs. Charged particles streamed toward the *T-bolt*. The PPC beam blasted rock from a bunker housing, but missed the racing 'Mech. Missiles crashed around its feet, a good half-dozen cratering leg armor.

The *Thor* raced after the *T-bolt*. They were closer now, less than a hundred meters apart. The *Thunderbolt* dodged among the buildings and bunkers, keeping the distance open. Occasionally it appeared, triple lasers flashing out to strike the *Thor*. Mostly they failed to penetrate, but sometimes one burned away a bit more of the *Thor*'s torso armor. The *Thor* rained down missiles, doing more damage to the landscape than to the *T-bolt*. Alpin blasted with his PPC, too, but did more damage to the surrounding buildings than to Maeve's 'Mech. He did score occasionally, though, tearing away chunks of armor.

Slowly the *Thor* worked its way closer to the *T-bolt*. Still relying on the *Thunderbolt*'s missiles for her big punch, Maeve fired her launcher again and again, the missiles striking with little spread, suggesting that the *T-bolt* might be armed with a Clan-tech launcher. Dechan realized that Maeve's *Thunderbolt* was not an Inner Sphere model and wondered if Alpin had noticed the discrepancies. Perhaps she was not so desperate as he'd first thought.

Alpin's PPC caught the *Thunderbolt*'s left leg. The weakened armor over the shin gave way, exposing tatters of pale myomer. Electrical discharges sparked and crawled along the exposed structural members. The

Thor's autocannon fired, its cluster rounds cratering openings in the *T-bolt*'s upper torso. Missiles screamed in, impacting all along the *Thunderbolt*'s left side. The blocky 'Mech staggered away, placing a brick structure between it and the oncoming Omni before crashing down.

Alpin closed in for the kill.

By the time he came around the corner, the *Thunderbolt* had gathered itself into a crouch. The 'Mech was clearly mauled, its right arm lifting out toward the advancing *Thor* as if in supplication for mercy. Alpin raised his own 'Mech's right arm, its PPC crackling with the sparks one sometimes sees before the capacitor discharged.

The *Thunderbolt*'s laser fired in eye-searing pulses, the beam striking just beneath the *Thor*'s missile rack. Armor bubbled and flowed, exposing the inner structure to the laser's ravening hunger. The *Thor* doubled over at the waist like a man kicked in the belly as the launcher ammunition exploded. Flames and smoke shot from the 'Mech's back as the CASE safety system released most of the devastating force. But it was too little, too late for the *Thor*.

The explosion had gutted most of its interior. Its left arm tumbled away, the autocannon coughing unaimed fire for a second before its ammo cooked off as well. Through the smoke the victorious *Thunderbolt* rose on jump jets of its own.

It came down behind the stricken Omni, its left arm raised. Slamming the limb down, Maeve forced Alpin's *Thor* to its knees. The Omni landed hard, rocking back and forth. The *Thunderbolt*'s right arm swung around, caving in the armor protecting the *Thor*'s shoulder coupling, then sliding up to crash against the cockpit housing. The Omni canted over and crashed to the ground on its left side.

The *Thunderbolt* reached down and dug its mechanical fingers into the armor below the *Thor*'s cockpit.

Smoke poured from within as the armor peeled away. Maeve tossed the canopy away and, in a dazzling display of BattleMech control, reached into the open cockpit and delicately lifted out her defeated opponent.

Then she lifted her *Thunderbolt*'s arm high and held up the limp and bleeding form of Alpin Wolf for all to see.

50

Even though Jamison was holding back, Elson decided that the assault was going well. The threat of Zeta's assault 'Mechs was enough for now. Nichole was proving reluctant to fully commit her forces, but that was not a serious problem, either; Wolf's main forces were engaged north of her. Epsilon remained a threat to the rebels, tying down badly needed forces. Sometimes threats could be as good as the presence of frontline troops; certainly they forced a poorly supplied commander to spread his forces thin. Such a commander simply couldn't know where his enemy would come from.

Elson wished he could be sure that Wolf was in the position of the befuddled commander. The theft of the battle plan from the main tactical computer at Wolf Hall and its subsequent transmission was distressing, but there was no evidence that Wolf had received the transmission. Certainly, there'd been no drastic change in the battlefield activity of his troops, no sudden shifts to hit vulnerable points in the attacker's forces, such as could be expected if Wolf had access to their plans. Even with Nichole's reluctance, the battle was proceeding as Elson had anticipated; he had not been expecting much from her Epsilon Regiment anyway.

Under the pressure from Beta and Gamma Regiments, Wolf's forces were collapsing. And despite Alpin's interference, Parella was making progress against the Spider's Web Battalion and the Home Guard forces supporting it. Fancher's MechWarriors had routed the Home Guard in Green Sector and were in pursuit of the ragged remains of Battlegroup B. Of the rebel forces, only Wolf's Elemental units remained uncommitted. Earlier in the conflict, they had shown themselves more effective than Elson had expected, making lightning raids up and down the front, but today's battle had yet to see them on any front. Wolf's options were diminishing quickly.

It was time to strike the final blow.

Elson reached up and lowered the lid of his battle armor suit. The soft hiss of the seals engaging was comforting. As his displays came online, varicolored lights glowed to life in the darkness of the helmet. The systems check was positive. He stepped out, the other four members of his Point falling in behind him.

Fancher's Command Lance was waiting outside the command bunker. Three other Points of Elementals were already clambering up the OmniMechs toward the carry positions on the torsos of the 'Mechs. They would ride to the battle hugging the armored machine. That was how it was done in the Clans when a fast assault was necessary or when great distances had to be covered.

Unfortunately, there were not enough OmniMechs to mount all the Elementals. Elson had ordered the techs to weld crude grab-irons to standard Battle-Mechs, but the system only allowed a 'Mech to carry two or three armored infantrymen. Still, enough makeshift carry positions had been created to mechanize the force. Elson's troops would be involved in the battle. Decisively, he was sure.

His Point mounted Fancher's personal 'Mech, a *Gladiator* and a favorite model for combined operations. The standard Clan tactics for coordinated combat would not be in use for today's battle. The 'Mech jocks did not have the proper training.

That would change.

A lot would change today.

Elson was confident as the *Gladiator* stomped forward, the other Omnis forming up around it. They marched forth, headed for the battle at over sixty kilometers an hour, passing burned-out tanks and the occasional BattleMech hulk as they went. Nearly all were rebel vehicles.

Elson's forces were exclusively BattleMechs and battle-armored infantry. True, some of the Home Guard forces professed to support Alpin, but Elson had not deemed them trustworthy enough to deploy in the Outback. For the same reason, he had not included the forces holding the Fortress complex in his battle plans. The 'Mech forces and his Elementals, with their expendable mercenary supplement, would be enough for the job.

They passed through an area with a high concentration of broken 'Mechs—the site of this morning's battle. Elson was mildly perturbed to count more Beta Regiment machines than rebel; he opened the channel to Fancher.

"There are more BattleMechs on the field than you reported."

"Don't build up a sweat, Elson. Most of them are just damaged; easily refitted when the shouting's over. The warriors got out."

"My plans were based on the expectation of higher numbers of BattleMechs."

"So were Wolf's." She laughed. "We've still got them outnumbered."

An encounter with the rebels ended the conversation. The skirmish was with a combined unit, 'Mechs and what had to be their last few tanks and armored vehicles. The battle was brief, ending shortly after the Elementals dismounted among the conventional forces. Tanks were no match for trained battle armor.

As expected, the BattleMechs retreated when the

skirmish turned against them. Perforce they abandoned the tankers; it was the strategically sound solution. Elson ordered the crippled tanks ignored. Finishing them would take time and he wanted to pursue the 'Mechs; they were the prime objective. Once the 'Mech force was eliminated, Wolf's challenge would have no heart.

The troopers remounted their BattleMechs and set out in pursuit.

Long-range exchanges between the two forces were the only action for the middle of the day, but Elson was satisfied. The rebels were retreating toward the Tetsuhara Proving Ground, just as he wanted.

At 1310 hours Fancher's forces crossed the outer boundaries. The rebels were little more than a couple of klicks ahead, the open ground offering a good view of their fleeing 'Mechs. In the distance the smudge of a building appeared on the horizon. Elson tapped Fancher's computer and noted that it was a training center intended to simulate a factory complex with a defensive ring of bunkers. Those bunkers would have weaponry able to support the Wolf's people.

Fancher's 'Mechs accelerated when the rebel 'Mechs turned toward the facility. Small dark dots could be seen bouncing among the buildings. Elementals. There seemed little doubt that the Wolf force would make a stand among the buildings.

The attacking 'Mechs crossed the line of what Elson estimated was the outer range of the defensive weapons. No shots were fired. The lack of defensive fire could only mean that Wolf had been denied the opportunity to turn the simulators into real weapons. The rebels began jamming, forcing a crackling static into the commo channels. It could not drown out short-range transmissions, but Elson lost contact with the rest of his loyal forces. It mattered little; he and Fancher had brought the northern forces to bay here, and Gamma was cornering the rest of the enemy's mobile forces in a similar facility.

Elson was satisfied. They would do battle here. It would be BattleMechs and battle armor; a combat in the grand style. This was what a warrior trained for, lived for, died for.

As Fancher's 'Mechs began evasive maneuvers, they came within range of the rebels' weapons. The defensive barrage exacted a toll on the attackers. Only one 'Mech went down, but many took damage. Some Points reported casualties.

Elson gave the order to dismount at the first line of bunkers. They were so close now that the Elementals' own jump jets could carry them into the facility. Riding on the 'Mechs only made them targets, and no sane trooper would hold on and let himself be armor for some incompetent 'Mech jock.

Fancher sent a unit wide on the flank to cut off escape, but the enemy commander had anticipated her and blocked the move, ambushing the lance and sending it back with enough damage that Fancher ordered the survivors out of battle.

The fighting among the buildings was fierce, mixing 'Mech and infantrymen and costing all dearly. Elson's Point was back from the fighting, getting reloads for their launchers, when he noticed a pattern in the reports from the Points still in combat. They were losing contact with the rebel Elementals. Elson tried to get Fancher on line, but the static was too great among the buildings. He spotted a tower and raced for it. If the higher elevation did not let him communicate, it would at least permit him a view of what was happening.

He was halfway up when he saw the Wolf 'Mechs regrouping on the far side of the complex. Instead of returning to battle, they were heading out of the facility, racing away to the south. Fancher's orders broke through the static in bits, the jamming becoming erratic. Elson heard enough to tell him that she was aware of the enemy 'Mechs and was organizing a response.

Elson could not see any Elementals clinging to the fast-disappearing rebel 'Mechs. They had left their armored infantry behind, presumably to delay Beta's 'Mechs and allow their own to escape once more. But Fancher's quick reaction was spoiling that. Elson told her to take her 'Mechs out of the facility the way they had come in. He did not want her walking into Elemental ambushes. The abandoned Elementals would be his. He directed his troopers forward to sweep the facility.

Fancher's 'Mechs would deal with the rebel 'Mechs while his troopers took their Elementals. That it would be two separate battles rather than one would not matter in the end.

The first Points to hit likely ambush spots reported no hostiles, not even any harassing fire. Elson ordered the sweeps to pick up speed.

The two BattleMech forces were growing smaller as they raced into the distance.

The static stopped completely.

Grant's Point was the first to report on the suddenly clear comm channels.

"We are hearing engines, sir. Fusion."

Tanks would not be a problem in the built-up areas, that was an infantryman's domain. The command channel took his attention away from his immediate surroundings.

"Elson! Elson! Damn it! Where the hell are you?"

"Calm down, Parella. I am here. Report."

"Everything's coming apart."

"What do you mean?"

"Alpin's dead. The fool dueled the rebel commander and got himself killed. Half my troops are pulling—"

Parella's channel broke up into static again.

The sound of missile launchers from the edge of the

facility announced what Elson assumed was the resumption of the battle. He was wrong.

Small hovercraft shot from behind the screen of buildings, then zoomed out across the open terrain. Missiles from Elson's troopers chased them but impacted well short of the fast-moving craft. Elson tapped his magnification up and stared at the things. Each vehicle—if such skeletal structures could be called vehicles—was little more than an open framework wrapped around a fusion engine and ground-effect ducting. Each carried a Point of Elementals. He remembered seeing plans for the things, but he had not known any had been completed. Blackwell Corporation was only in the prototype stage. Then he realized that these must be the prototypes and knew what Wolf had done.

Wolf had raided the Blackwell facility, taking the prototypes for his own use and creating a fast-strike force. There were not more than six Stars worth of Elementals, a far smaller force than Elson had estimated. The fast hovercraft explained how so few Elementals could seem like so many. Using these vehicles the Elementals had mobility far beyond the norm, allowing them to shift up and down the battlefront with ease.

Elson wished that he had thought to raid the Blackwell facility. But wishes did not win battles. Even though there was no way his Elementals could pursue effectively, he gave the order as he clambered down to join his Point. He led them out across the arid terrain, bouncing in pursuit of the vehicle-borne troopers, themselves closing rapidly on Fancher's forces.

He would not be left out of this battle.

Static-chopped communications told him when the zooming hovercraft had reached the Beta 'Mechs and deposited their passengers among them. The fleeing 'Mechs had turned to fight as well. Wolf had effectively separated the Beta 'Mechs from their Elemental support. What might be the last battle of the campaign was underway, and Elson was too far away to affect it.

He raged and cursed. But neither made him feel better.

"We've got another 'Mech force approaching," Fancher reported. Her voice was faint, almost unintelligible through the jamming, but even so Elson shivered when he heard the next words. "Frak! It's Wolf!"

The Wolf had come out of hiding and committed his last forces.

Elson pushed his suit's jump jets to maximum thrust. This surely was the final battle.

51

Dechan watched as Maeve displayed her victory. Her own troops were cheering on the open frequency. Snatches of outrage, frustration, and confusion came through on the Gamma frequencies. One officer was insistently calling for his unit to back off, claiming that the battle was over.

Carter's *Caesar* stomped up beside Dechan's *Black Knight*.

"Well, is that decisive enough for you?"

"Not yet."

Beyond the *Thunderbolt*, Dechan could see the remainder of Alpin's command Star shifting. Parella's *Mad Cat* strutted forward toward the site of the duel. In a few minutes he would have the *T-bolt* within range of his long-range missiles. Sparks danced around the muzzles of the fully charged PPCs in the *Mad Cat*'s bulky forearms.

The duel had ended with Maeve at such a distance from her troops that they wouldn't be able to aid her against the oncoming Omnis for at least ten minutes. Kappa Battalion was closer; they could be on her as fast as the Omnis. If she went down, the rebel resistance would collapse.

Dechan throttled up the *Black Knight*, heading it down the slope toward the *Thunderbolt*.

"Give the order, Major Carter," he said into the microphone. One hand tapped last-second corrections into his battle computer while the other adjusted commo frequencies. The jolting run of the *Knight* made him miss several codes on the first try, but he kept punching until he got it right.

Behind him, the 'Mechs of Kappa Battalion started to move.

The *Thunderbolt*'s torso rotated until it faced Kappa, then stood motionless for a moment. Had the 'Mech been a human soldier, Dechan would have said it stood still in shock at the sight of a new threat approaching. Its pilot was no novice, though. More likely, she was assessing her position, noting how far she was from the other 'Mechs of her battlegroup. The *T-bolt*'s upper structure tilted as the arm holding Alpin's body reached down. The limp form rolled from the battle fist and onto the ground next to the wrecked *Thor.* Then the *Thunderbolt* crouched down.

Dechan lost sight of Gamma's Command Lance as he hit the lower reaches of the slope; he no longer had the height to see over the buildings. He estimated no more than a minute before they cleared the outer fringes of structures and got an open field of fire on the *Thunderbolt*. Parella wouldn't be accepting any challenges; he would finish Maeve off with the massed firepower he and his companies would apply.

But Dechan would be there first.

The fluttering tone of the frequency searcher merged into a clear, single note.

"Company coming," he transmitted. "Run, if you can."

The *Thunderbolt* shifted to the left, moving slightly behind the downed *Thor.* Poor cover at best. Dechan shook his head, or would have had there been room for it inside the neurohelmet.

Parella's *Mad Cat* appeared, a *Thor* by its side.

Dechan opened fire. The *Knight*'s twin torso-mounted McCorkel lasers lanced their beams in deadly coordination with the manmade lightning from the

Magna HellStar PPC on the pylon mount along the 'Mech's right arm. Heat suffused the cockpit, instantly evaporating the sweat from Dechan's exposed arms and legs. The pumps circulating cooling fluid through his vest whined in protest as they kicked into high gear. It was dangerous, unloading with all the *Knight*'s heavy armament at once, but this was no time for subtlety.

All three weapons scored on the *Mad Cat*.

The solid shot from the Gauss cannon on Carter's *Caesar* boomed past the *Mad Cat* and slammed into the *Thor*'s right arm. Armor cracked and the arm swung down, broken and useless. Carter's PPC blast crackled harmlessly past.

Dechan cut right, away from the *Thunderbolt*, to avoid the *Mad Cat*'s return fire. He mostly succeeded. Two particle beams caught him, devouring armor from the *Knight*'s left side. There was no breach, but Dechan couldn't afford to take another hit there.

The lead 'Mechs of Kappa opened fire on the rest of the Command Star as it came into view. The damaged *Thor,* exposed the longest, took crippling damage. The *Mad Cat* took a pounding as well, but Parella was a superb pilot. He kept the 'Mech on its feet despite the vicious barrage assailing it. Parella was no fool, either; he knew a hopeless fight when he was in one. The *Mad Cat* backpedaled into cover while he screamed for his Star to retreat.

"Keep on them," Carter urged Kappa.

Dechan fired a few more shots at the retreating Beta 'Mechs, but he didn't join the pursuit. There were more than enough 'Mechs to handle Parella and any impromptu defense he could throw up. The Beta frequencies were in chaos; there would be no organizing them for a while. Kappa's shift in sides was fatal to the battle plan. Dechan turned his attention to the *Thunderbolt*. It was standing upright and facing in his direction.

"Are you all right?" he asked over the battlegroup's tactical frequency.

"Well enough," she replied. "You sure know how to make a flashy entrance, stranger."

"Dechan Fraser."

"Fraser?"

"That's right." Dechan didn't know whether to laugh or cry at the total mystification in her voice. "Don't you have a battlegroup to run or something?"

"I thought you didn't want to get involved."

"I didn't."

"Then why?"

That's what he'd been asking himself. "If I figure it out, maybe I'll let you know."

The sounds of the BattleMech combat grew fainter as the combatants moved further away.

"You saved my life."

"In the Combine that would make me responsible for you."

"Don't know about that, but you just became responsible for quite a bit. I hope you get a fair reward."

Whatever that meant. The only thing Dechan was sure he wanted was to see Jenette again. But that wouldn't happen until the battle was over. Mustering his composure, he said, "You just get your people together. We've got work to do."

"Turncoats don't make very trustworthy allies."

"Neither do spies. Sometimes you've got to take what you get, if you want to win. You want my help or not?"

"Like you said, sometimes you just take what you can get."

52

Even as a peacetime maneuver, the withdrawal from the mock factory would have been a tricky feat of co-ordination. With the 'Mechs of Beta Regiment and El-son's Elementals pressing us, I had not expected it to succeed. But the Wolf knew our capabilities better than we did; both phases had gone well.

Our 'Mechs fled the built-up area in apparent, and near real, disarray. Taking the bait, the BattleMechs of Beta Regiment pursued, catching us when we slowed among the gulches and low buttes to the south of the complex. It was prime in-fighting territory, something we couldn't afford to do for long against the fresher machines and more experienced pilots of Beta. They knew it, too; they came charging in after us. We lost three 'Mechs in the first ten minutes of the en-gagement.

I think the only thing that kept us from falling to them was the knowledge that we wouldn't have to face those odds for long. There were cheers on the tactical channels when Rand reported the first of our zoomers screaming in behind the Beta 'Mechs.

The Wolf had called this part of the battle "phase two," a prosaic name for the whirling snarl of laser beams and rocket exhausts that was our Elementals' assault on the surprised 'Mech pilots of Beta. Shadd's Elementals caught them from behind, completely un-aware.

In the close confines of the gullies, the 'Mechs had a hard time getting away from the Elementals. The battle-armored infantry swarmed individual 'Mechs, clambering over light models and ripping through their armor. I watched one *Hornet* rise on billowing clouds of jet exhaust in an effort to shake off its tormentors. Some debris fell away and, after an instant, the trajectory shifted slightly. Smoke began to taint the exhaust, then there was a flash of light and the *Hornet* started to wobble. It tilted toward the ground, finally shaking off three armored infantrymen when it was less than twenty meters from the ground. The troopers used their jump packs to cushion their landing. For the *Hornet*, there was only fiery oblivion.

The *Hornet* was a mere twenty-ton BattleMech, the lightest of our opponents. The Elementals didn't fare so well against the bigger machines, whose armor withstood their attacks long enough for a beleaguered 'Mech to free itself or have a comrade come to the rescue.

The surprise attack of the Elementals gave my battlegroup a chance to collect our wits. Seeing the Elementals throw the Betas into such confusion gave us enough hope that we rallied. When we saw that the armored troopers had exhausted their missiles, we charged. We pushed hard, but not hard enough to knock Beta out of the fight.

I saw Hans Vordel's *Victor* take a hit from a 200-millimeter autocannon in the midst of a punishing salvo of missiles. The eighty-ton 'Mech shivered under the impact, then froze. I thought the old beast had only shut down from overheat and shifted my *Loki* in its direction, hoping to provide cover so the enemy wouldn't rip it apart before the pilot could restart the fusion reactor. I hadn't covered fifty meters before the *Victor* shuddered again. The oscillations increased with frightening speed, and then the 'Mech's right arm disintegrated in a shower of shrapnel. The machine toppled backward, twisting to fall on its left side. Even amid the roar of combat, I heard the thunder of its fall. Searing beams reached for the fallen 'Mech, ravening over its surface and boring into the gaps in its armor. It blew apart as one of those beams found its ammunition bay and the remaining missiles detonated in a storm of fire. I throttled back. There was nothing I could do for the fallen warrior. I sent one of his killers a beam from the seven-centimeter laser in the *Loki*'s right arm and retreated. Warriors in my battlegroup were still fighting and they needed me more than did the dead man.

I didn't take too much damage escaping from Vordel's slayers. They pulled back when I ran through a position held by our Elementals, allowing me to rejoin one of my lances.

I moved the remnants of the battlegroup into an area of low gravel mounds near the remains of the processing machinery, a position that gave us a commanding view of the highway leading south into the heart of the Tetsuhara Proving Ground. Somewhere down that road lay the Colonel's command post and the last of our reserves. Further down and away to the east, Maeve was leading the resistance to Gamma Regiment's advance. The jamming we were using against the enemy was also preventing us from keeping in close communication with our scattered forces. I prayed she was doing better than I was.

Down among the gullies, Beta was gaining the upper hand. I watched as a pair of heavy 'Mechs ganged up on a *Wolfhound*. The pilot in the light 'Mech fought back valiantly for the two minutes it took his bigger opponents to burn, crater, and crack enough armor to expose the *Wolfhound*'s inner structure. I saw the pilot eject just before the smaller of the two heavies slammed into his 'Mech.

I intercepted a tight-beam communications laser between two of Beta Regiment's units flanking our position. The sender was reporting what I already knew: BattleMechs were approaching from the heart of the Tetsuhara Proving Ground, Wolf Pack 'Mechs.

The Wolf himself was coming.

If Wolf was coming out of hiding, the decisive battle was underway. Elson only wished that the battle was unfolding as he had planned rather than as Wolf had. But there was no use in complaining, or cursing. The jamming made coordinating the attacking forces impossible; only direct action could shift the initiative back in his favor.

The 'Mech battle was several kilometers away, but there was no choice but to continue toward it. He urged his troopers to greater speed. Elementals launched on steamy clouds to go bounding away across the plain, following the trail of the Beta 'Mechs.

Elson hoped they would reach the battlefield in time to make a difference.

The arms of Alicia Fancher's *Gladiator* moved in an awkward parody of a traffic cop. Without reliable radio communications, she was using hand signals from her 'Mech to direct her units. It was moderately effective, as long as her MechWarriors remembered to make visual checks on their commander. At least one company responded to her attempts; they headed out to block Colonel Wolf's advance.

But such a mechanism required her to expose her position, allowing us to see her, too. With most of the battlegroup well out of effective range, she was relatively safe until some of our 'Mechs could get closer.

Rand's *Mongoose* flashed from among the buttes, leading the remains of her company. There were only six of them, all lights and mediums and all damaged, but they raced brazenly toward Fancher's 100-ton monster. Firing on the run, they didn't score as many hits as they might have, but they distracted Fancher nevertheless. She retreated from her hilltop. Rand's crew closed in, spreading out to ring the *Gladiator*. It was a rash maneuver; once Fancher's support arrived, Rand would only prove that light BattleMechs could not stand against heavies and assaults. But Rand had been fighting the whole battle as if she had something to prove.

I had no time to worry about her. The Colonel's force was engaging the company sent to stop him and he needed help. I backed my *Loki* down a few meters until I reached a point where I could turn it around. The other warriors followed me down the hillside.

We reached level ground in time to see the company from Beta recoiling from the Colonel's 'Mechs. The Beta machines were heavily damaged and the onrushing opponents were barely scratched. There were more Wolf Pack machines than I expected, and it took me a moment to realize that the Kuritans were accompanying the Colonel. No wonder the Beta company had taken it so hard.

This first skirmish for our reserves would not be the whole battle. Colonel Wolf had clearly staked his chance of winning this battle on success here on the northern flank. Pulling the Kuritans up here jeopardized the whole defense by stripping the southern flank of its mobile element. If Nichole's Epsilon Regiment stayed put, we might be all right. If not, we were lost.

Either way, we were committed.

An Elemental vaporized in the ravening hell of a PPC beam.

Elson sent his last two SRMs at the killer *Clint*. One punched into the 'Mech's left shoulder, and the other dug a bright metal scar into the *Clint*'s upper right chest. A bad spread, but at least both missiles had scored.

In open terrain, Elementals were rarely a match for MechWarriors who knew what they were doing. These rebels were no fools. They kept their distance, forcing the Elementals to keep moving or die. Some choice. Even moving, Elementals went down, pounded by weapons with greater range.

The end of the jamming made coordinating his Stars easier. It also made it easier to hear their dying screams.

A laser blasted the ground at his feet. Elson shifted away, ready to fire his jump jets, but another beam caught the battle armor just above the knee. Pain screamed through his leg, but the suit was already pumping healing gel in to flood the area, soothing the pain. Heat flooded him, and he cursed. The suit's automatic damage control was taking over, its auto-injector had just filled his veins with the nerve dead-eners and synthetic adrenaline that Elementals called hero juice.

He wanted to think clearly.

He had to.

The *Locust* that had wounded him fired again, but he was faster this time, juiced up. He shifted away; leaving the beam behind. The laser gouged only the ground. Dodging and weaving, Elson closed on the light 'Mech.

He had to take it down before it got him.

Then, then he would have time to think. He would have time to plan, and find a way of this disaster.

The *Locust* fired again.

Pain seared his chest, spreading faster than the gel.

He tried to keep moving, tried to raise the suit's laser to show the jock what an Elemental could do to a 'Mech.

The suit didn't respond. Sparks flashed before his eyes as the heads-up display winked out. Systems lights went dark and blackness filled his helmet.

The Wolf was slow but elegant. He was old, no lon-ger possessed of lightning reflexes despite what some would tell you of Clan-bred vitality. But his cunning and experience compensated for much. He handled his 'Mech as if it were a part of him, almost like the fabled blend of man and machine so popular in holovids.

Missiles flew from the *Archer*'s bulky shoulders, trailing smoky clouds after them as they sought out targets. Each volley impacted with an accuracy that surpassed mere computer-aided targeting. The Wolf guided his munitions with an instinct that could not be quantified.

My ragged lance joined the Colonel's column in time to receive another thrust from Beta. The Kuritans responded faster than we did. Then we learned that we were not the only ones capable of ruses.

A company of medium 'Mechs swarmed out of a dry streambed screened from us by an iron-rich mesa. Another lance rocketed over the top. They were on us in seconds.

A *Wasp* caught a full barrage from the Colonel and disintegrated before it could land. It was the only one of the attackers to be silenced before they opened fire. The Colonel's *Archer* was screened from the attackers by two of our reserve 'Mechs, which took a lot of fire meant for him. The lance that had come over the top had clear lines of fire, and they used them. They rained missiles down on us and stabbed at us with energy beams.

I sidestepped the *Loki*, soaking up some of the enemy's fire. My *Loki* shook like a rag doll in the hands of an angry child. System-status lights went from green to amber to red almost faster than I could see. Smoke filled my cockpit with an acrid smell and I knew I was losing electrical lines somewhere.

Through the armor of my cockpit I heard the roaring thunder of a ripple launch from the *Archer*. Missiles tore holes in the torso and limbs of a *Javelin* just as its own launchers were recycling for another volley. The *Javelin* crashed over backward, a leg gone.

The rebel lance pulled back, lifting up and jetting away as fast as they had come. As if they were a signal rocket, a lance of Kuritans came pounding back. Outnumbered, the Beta 'Mechs disengaged.

It was another skirmish in our favor, but the battle was not over yet.

Hours went by. The fighting was hard, but the Kuritans made a difference, a vital difference. Where we would have had only one 'Mech, now we sometimes had two. Over the course of the small encounters that make up a 'Mech battle, we slowly gained the upper hand. In a fusillade here, a physical attack there, we shifted the odds. The battle began to turn once more in our favor.

The cat-and-mouse game between Rand's company and Fancher's Command Lance changed mode suddenly when a Kuritan *Panther* appeared on a ridge and sent a crackling blue beam of charged particles into the shoulder of Fancher's *Gladiator*. Fancher turned the 'Mech to face the new threat, and Rand and her crew swarmed in. Short-range missiles burned in on sooty tails. Beam weapons lit the hazy field, turning it into a hellish scene where BattleMechs stalked and fought like mythical demons. Fancher's *Gladiator* fell, a lion pulled down by wolves.

The loss of Beta's commander might have been enough to decide the battle, but at almost the same moment, the static filling the channels of Elson's people peaked and vanished. Our jammer linkage had been destroyed somewhere, the network broken and rendered useless. I didn't need to hear the sudden activity on Beta's channels to know we were in trouble; they were reorganizing very quickly. No less could be expected from those who wore the Dragoon wolf's head.

Our own scouts used the absence of jamming to report more bad news. Zeta Battalion was moving up.

The news soon spread through Beta. Reed, who had taken command, ordered his battered BattleMechs to fall back. After the mauling Beta had given us, he knew we'd have a hard time handling Zeta. A renewed assault by Reed's 'Mechs, coming while we were engaged with Zeta, might be just enough to break us.

The Colonel was on the line as soon as the scouts finished reporting. He told them to route all further reports through me, then he addressed our surviving units. There weren't a lot of them, and all were operating well below strength. As I scanned the status data, I wondered how much longer we could last.

The Wolf called out orders, making the most of our depleted forces. He sent the Elementals' zoomers scurrying around the battlefield to collect armored infantry into effective Points and Stars. With an uncanny eye for the strength of positions, he positioned BattleMechs across Zeta's probable line of advance.

Then we waited.

As always on an arid battlefield, we saw the dust before we saw the approaching 'Mechs. Zeta was spread wide. Besides providing a broad sensor scan range, the formation let them hide their main force behind a screen of dust. If we'd had access to aerial recon or satellite telemetry, we would have known their disposition, as they might have known ours.

Zeta's Jamison and the Colonel were old friends, well familiar with each other's style. I had no doubt that each was trying to outguess the other, trying to pit his force's strength against the other's weakness. In such a contest, I had no doubt the Wolf would come out on top, but even so, the battle would not be a sure thing. We were tired, our machines damaged and low on expendables.

Do you remember what I said about fear? My cockpit was very crowded on that late summer afternoon.

The leading 'Mechs of Zeta resolved out of the dust clouds. They advanced at a steady pace, well below their maximum. I didn't see a single machine below seventy tons. They advanced slowly, as if reluctant to begin the battle. Maybe they'd heard about the breakup of Gamma Regiment. Maybe they were having second thoughts.

I hoped so.

The only thing in our favor was that Zeta was as understrength as we were. But machine for machine, they outmassed and outgunned us. Maeve's success against Gamma Regiment would go for naught if we were defeated here and Jaime Wolf was killed. Our whole cause would be lost.

"Hold your positions," the Wolf ordered as he moved his *Archer* forward.

I objected, as did other Dragoon officers, but Jaime Wolf ordered us to silence. We watched as his BattleMech moved through our forward positions and into the open space between us and Zeta Battalion.

I had heard it said that a wolf will win every fight but one, and in that fight, it dies. I suddenly wondered if this was what the Wolf intended. Did he hope to stake it all on a single combat, a duel in the style of the Clans? Was this going to be the Wolf's last fight? I hoped, I prayed, that it wasn't.

Across that open area a single BattleMech of Zeta Battalion began to move. A *Stalker*. Though the machine was more battered than the Colonel's 'Mech, it outmassed Wolf's 'Mech by fifteen tons, a formidable opponent. An open channel broadcast from the advancing *Stalker* told me who the pilot was. J. Elliot Jamison, commander of Zeta Battalion.

"Is it really you this time, Jaime?" he asked

"It's me," the Wolf replied

"Single combat won't settle it, Jaime. This is a Trial of Refusal."

Jamison's referring to the conflict as a Trial of Refusal told us where he stood. As the Wolf had predicted from the time he learned that Zeta had gone to Alpin's side, Jamison saw this as a battle of honor.

"If you didn't think we could settle it, J. Elliot, why'd you come out alone? Did you think I was coming to surrender?"

"I had considered the possibility." Jamison said nothing for a moment, then, "But I thought it unlikely. You never really give up, Jaime."

"I'm not giving up now. Alpin is dead. Elson's down, as is Fancher. Parella's missing. Their leadership is gone. You're senior commander now, J. Elliot. This doesn't have to go on."

"Forces remain on the field," Jamison responded promptly. "The Trial of Refusal is not yet complete."

"The point's been made. More bloodshed won't prove anything."

"The Trial must be completed," Jamison repeated stubbornly.

"Damn it, J. Elliot! This isn't an extermination war. Enough people have already died."

"That is not the issue." Jamison's voice was cold. "Zeta came back to Outreach to fight to uphold our laws and traditions. And we will continue to fight until there is no more hope."

"You always were too confident, J. Elliot." Jaime Wolf sounded almost regretful. "I'd never deny the quality of Zeta, but you're not fresh and neither are your troops. Your force may be heavier, but we outnumber you."

"The odds are not so uneven," Jamison replied calmly. "Beta remains nearby"

"But Reed's in charge of Beta now. His Elementals have been scattered and his BattleMechs have been whipped hard. He's scared. Half of Zeta will be gone before he commits. Combined, you might destroy my force, but you know the cost will be high. And what will be left? If we fight today we will do what no foe, not even Kurita, has been able to do to us. We will destroy the Dragoons beyond redemption.''

Jamison's tone was deadly calm as he replied, ''We have recovered from worse devastation. A true warrior has no fear of death in honorable battle.''

''A good commander worries about his forces, J. Elliot, not just honor.''

''The time for worries is after battle.''

''But who will lead, J. Elliot? Not you.''

''Threats are inappropriate, Jaime.''

''I'm not threatening you, J. Elliot. I'm just telling you what I know about you. You'd hate the job. It's not like running a battalion, or even a regiment. You remember when you took over Alpha? That was a cakewalk.''

''I'm not doing this for myself.''

''I know you're not, J. Elliot, and I understand why you sided with Alpin. That's why I came out here to talk with you. Honor can be served without battle. The issue can be decided by agreement. Even if the battle isn't lost, the cause is. Give it up, J. Elliot. We don't need to fight.''

''The Trial is not yet concluded.''

The *Stalker* backed away from the *Archer*.

''Will my death satisfy your honor, J. Elliot?''

Jamison made no reply. His *Stalker* turned and moved to rejoin his unit.

''There's been too much death,'' the Wolf called after him.

The *Archer* stood unmoving on the field. If the Wolf did not soon start back, his 'Mech would be caught in the open, unsupported. Zeta's charge would destroy him.

I started my *Loki* forward. ''Colonel Wolf!''

''Hold your position, Brian. No one is to move.''

Throttling back, I wondered if the Colonel was going to sacrifice himself to stop the battle? If I had correctly understood Jamison's slavish devotion to tradition, the Wolf's death might indeed buy the lives of our surviving forces. As the principal in this challenge, Jaime Wolf was pivotal in its prosecution; he could end it instantly by admitting defeat. Yet, that was the one thing he would not do. He was a Dragoon and would fight on as long as there was any hope.

The *Stalker* moved through the forward positions of Zeta Battalion and mounted the small rise from which it had previously surveyed the field. The lead elements of Zeta Battalion began to move again.

I looked at the *Archer* standing alone on the field. Jaime Wolf's death would automatically negate a Trial of Refusal in his name. Even if we fought on, the end would be the same. Jaime Wolf would no longer lead the Dragoons. Our victory, should we achieve it, would be hollow.

The air around us suddenly filled with the sound of thunder, the noise washing over us in waves as the badlands erupted in columns of smoke and fire. The ground shook beneath the feet of our 'Mechs. At first I thought that Fire Support Group had backed Zeta's attack with an awesome artillery barrage, then I saw that the approaching assault 'Mechs were in as much disarray as we were. More, several of the assaults in the front rank were down and smoking.

· The thunder rolled across us again and the moon came down from the sky. But it was no moon; it was a gigantic DropShip. The vessel hovered between the contending forces on pillars of flame while aerospace fighters buzzed around it like angry protective angels. More fighters swept between us and Zeta, furrowing the ground with their energy weapons. All comm channels were blanketed by the same message from Fleet Captain Chandra.

"There has been enough dying. I take upon myself the role of Loremaster and arbiter. The challenge is over, the decision made.'' She paused. I think no one on the battlefield breathed while we awaited her next words.

"Welcome back, Colonel Wolf.''

53

Colonel Wolf spent the first night and day after the battle making sure that all fighting ceased and all casualties were picked up. He got no sleep that night. Neither did I, but I was able to do my own job with an easier heart when Maeve arrived with the remnants of her Command Lance. Once we got confirmation that hyperpulse messages had gone out to Alpha and Delta telling them that everything was settled, the Colonel ordered me to get some sleep. I disobeyed him, of course; my reunion with Maeve did more to refresh me than mere sleep.

When the evening shift changed, Schlomo came to the command center. Though primarily a research specialist, he had been using his medical skills to assist the overworked regimental surgeons. Like the rest of us, he was tired almost beyond exhaustion.

"Colonel Wolf?"

"Yes, Schlomo."

"He's awake."

"His condition?"

"Bad, but stable. His kind are tough. He might recover."

Schlomo was referring to Elson. The Elemental had been found in dysfunctional armor and brought in nearly dead. The Colonel had left orders to be informed when and if Elson regained consciousness. The fact that the man had rallied at all made it seem that the Elemental must have battled death even harder than he had fought the Wolf.

The Colonel nodded to his staff. There was no need for words; all the words had been said in the heated conference with which we had brought up the sun. Commanders from both sides were there. The challenge was over, and the results of the Trial overturned. Now was the time for healing the wounds. Chandra, Jamison, Nichole, Atwyl, Grazier, Maeve, young Tetsuhara, and Graham of Special Recon Group fell in behind us as we headed for the recovery ward.

The officers trailing us were serving as an emergency council for the Dragoons, serving as extensions of the Wolf in the grueling business of picking up the pieces. It was an unusual procedure, and only partly defensible by Dragoon custom. Though the Colonel could make decrees as commander and expect them to be obeyed, orders went down smoother with a council of officers backing him, especially when those backers included some who had recently opposed him. The emergency council was a makeshift arrangement, but a lot of what the Dragoons would do for some time would be makeshift.

The formal Dragoon council was, of course, in shambles. Several members had died, and the Colonel had not yet approved replacements. Fancher was among the dead, leaving Beta Regiment without representation. Gamma Regiment was in a similar position, although Parella was classified as missing, not dead. The offworld members would be coming to Outreach as soon as their contracts permitted. Until they did and the formal council was reformed, the Colonel would operate with the counsel and approval of the emergency team.

The main complex of the Tetsuhara Proving Ground was a hive of activity. I had thought it busy before the battle, but now it was more so. Cratered and battered BattleMechs and tanks were parked in haphazard arrangements, while techs scurried about dragging or driving repair equipment from one repair job to another. Damaged battle suits were stretched out on repair racks, being fussed over by the armorers.

But machines weren't the only casualties of the fighting, and they were certainly not the most important. The gigantic *Fortress* Class DropShip that had arrived to end the fighting now pumped power to the hospital and operating chambers to ease the drain on the complex's facilities. The warship's shadow shaded the operating wards where the doctors fought to save the injured. To deal with the influx of wounded, the field hospital that had been serving our forces had quadrupled in size. Buildings that were normally barracks had been pressed into service as convalescent and recovery wards. Schlomo led us toward the one where Elson had been taken.

I glanced around as we went, seeing the color blue everywhere I looked. No one had given the order to do so, yet everyone seemed to be wearing the blue Dragoon coveralls, even the civilians. Many of the Kuritans had acquired coveralls, too. I wasn't going to object; they had proved themselves.

I know that for some, wearing the normal Dragoon undress uniform was a physical relief. I certainly was glad enough to be free of my cooling vest and the sticky biosensors of its feedback system. Others, I believe, wore the coveralls as a sign of solidarity, a statement that we were all Dragoons again and not loyalists or rebels or whatever fast-talk slang one faction had favored to designate the other. Some, especially those who had fought for Elson and Alpin, were probably grateful for the anonymity the ubiquitous blues provided.

When our little cavalcade reached the entrance to the former barracks, Maeve stepped up to open the door. The handle pulled away from her hand as someone inside tugged on the door. Dechan Fraser nearly knocked her from her feet as he rushed out. Catching her arm to keep her from falling, he apologized in Japanese. At least I assume it was an apology; it sounded like one.

Colonel Wolf stepped up to Fraser and said, "I was hoping to see you soon, Dechan. We have much to talk about."

"I'm not here to see you. They told me this is where I could find Jenette."

"Ward Three," Schlomo said. "This is Ward Two."

"We can talk later," the Colonel said.

"Yeah, sure." As Fraser looked around the people in our group, he forced what was obviously an uncomfortable smile. "Looks like a lot of changes, Colonel. I suppose I can at least stick around for introductions. I've been away for a long time and if I'm going to stay, I'll need to know these people. You might even introduce me to your daughter."

Rachel wasn't with us, and I was momentarily confused. When I realized that Fraser was looking at Maeve, I suddenly saw what he did. The Colonel and Maeve were of a height. Both were compactly framed. He was wider across the shoulders, but not by much. They had the same gray eyes, the same dark complexion, and her hair was as raven black as his had once been. I remembered that Maeve was of a mixed-line sibko and did not know her parentage. But everyone knew that the Wolf had always refused to donate to the sperm banks, maintaining that his blood family was all he needed. It felt like I'd taken a PPC shot to the brain.

While I stood there stunned, Maeve was introducing herself. "Colonel Wolf's daughter is working at the hospital with her mother. My name's Maeve. I'm acting commander of the Spider's Web," she said.

Fraser looked confused. "The *Thunderbolt*?"

"Mine."

Schlomo broke in with, "Captain Rand is in Ward

Three. I can take you there if you wish.'' Fraser shook his head like a man starting awake from an unwanted sleep. ''This way,'' Schlomo said, giving him a tug on the arm.

I watched Schlomo hustle Fraser away while the rest of us entered the ward. I'd never seen the old man so pushy, and I wondered if he knew something he wasn't telling.

I was the last to reach Elson's bed and his appearance startled me. The Elemental looked shrunken; his brush with death had exhausted his body. He lay limp in his wrappings of bandages and burn dressings. Bruises and lacerations covered much of his exposed skin and one of his eyes was swollen shut. Despite the punishment he had taken, his spirit was unbroken, as I learned when he addressed the Colonel.

''I thought I'd be hearing from you, Wolf. Is this your council of execution?''

''Hardly,'' said Jaime Wolf.

Elson managed a mangled chuckle. ''Is the prognosis that bad?''

Shaking his head, the Colonel replied, ''The doctors say you're a fighter, and they give you a fair chance. I want to do the same.''

Elson said something under his breath, but I didn't catch the words. I doubt anyone else did either. The Colonel looked at him silently for a moment, then cleared his throat.

''We fought over the Dragoons because they weren't what either one of us wanted them to be. I gave up on them for a while because I was tired. I let my personal feelings get in the way of my judgement, my duty.''

''I am not your counselor, Wolf.''

''You're wrong, Elson.'' The Colonel walked from the foot of the bed to the head and sat down on a stool Atwyl handed him. ''The Dragoons are going to be different now. We've both been part of making sure of that.

"Once I thought I was keeping the Dragoons alive by changing them as they needed to be changed, but I didn't have it quite right. I'm a strategist, not a sociologist. I was operating in a field I didn't know, and I botched it. I didn't really understand some of what had happened to us, some of the changes we had already been through. We had come a long way from our Clan heritage, but I forgot that some of us didn't have the same history, might not even want to have that history. You opened my eyes."

"I would have opened your throat," Elson said weakly.

"And that was only what you considered to be right. I know that in your eyes I had failed as a leader. In some ways, you were right. Some of my policies were wrong. I can see that now. I didn't take enough account of how we had changed or how little we were doing to make our newcomers at home. Poor treatment of those who were not born of the elite is a standard complaint the freeborn have about the Clans, but we made the same mistakes. Nobody wants to live as a second-class citizen. I thought we'd get past it, though. I thought that with enough time things would smooth out, but there wasn't enough time. There's never enough time."

"I will not absolve you."

"I'm not asking you to. Things can't be what they were, but then I don't suppose anything ever stays the same. Life means change, and if you don't change, you aren't alive, *quiaff*? I think you understand what it means to try to make things right and fail."

Elson rolled his head so that he faced away from the Colonel. "I am prepared to accept the fate of those who fail," he said softly.

"Are you still prepared to fight? I want to change what went before, I want everyone who wears the Dragoon patch to be a part of the Dragoons, and I want to see that everyone earns his or her place and that no one gets a place unearned. Isn't that a lot of what you were fighting for? Do you still have the strength to fight for it?''

Facing the Colonel again, Elson asked, ''What do you mean?''

''It was distrust and misunderstanding that brought us to this point.''

''And not a little ambition,'' Atwyl interrupted.

''No one's denying that, Ham,'' the Colonel said without looking at him. ''Ambition is not necessarily bad. Sometimes it's exactly what's needed. I have ambitions, too. I intend to make what we went through a crucible from which a better organization will emerge. It's clear now that we can't be what we were. We're not Clan any more than we are Inner Sphere; we're a blend of the two. More than that, we're what our lives and battles have made us. We won't find our future by clinging to the past; we've got to chart a new course.''

Elson squinted his good eye at Wolf. ''You cannot be suggesting that we abandon the honor road.''

''The path of honor is a concept older than the Clans' honor road. It's meant a lot of different things to people over time, but I think there are certain basics. I'd never ask you, or anyone, to abandon those. If you've got to have an honor road, we need to find one that will also be the Dragoons' honor road. We're not a Clan, and we're not the resurrected Star League Army, either. We hire our warriors out, but we're not *just* a mercenary company. We're something different, something new. Are you willing to help me find a new road, Elson?''

''I cannot be part of this.''

''Why not? Scared?'' Maeve taunted.

''I am born of the Clans,'' Elson said, frowning in his pride. ''Their heritage is in my blood. Though I was freeborn, I knew I was part of something when I was with the Nova Cats. I must *be* part of something. I cannot be a mercenary.''

"You are part of something," the Colonel insisted. "Us."

"Wolf Pack," Maeve said with a grin.

"That's not a name I approve," Jaime Wolf said.

"Too late." She grinned wider. "It's gonna stick."

"We're the Dragoons," he insisted.

"Yeah, *Wolf*'s Dragoons. We're the Wolf Pack, too."

"I am neither," Elson said.

"You were rebellious, but you are a warrior," the Colonel told him. "Warriors of the Clans sometimes fail a challenge. That does not make them outlaw. The testing that you provided has strengthened the Dragoons. Though it was a testing harder than I would have liked, I think we will be the better for it. Especially if you will see that we can make it better together."

"I no longer understand you."

"The Colonel is offering you a restoration to the ranks," Nichole said.

"You're being honored, lout," Atwyl said.

Elson's good eye flashed anger at Atwyl, but it was a momentary flare. He looked calmly at the Colonel. "You have mastered me, Jaime Wolf. I can accept you as my Khan."

Shaking his head, the Colonel said, "No Khans. That's the Clan way. But I do think I will need a position other than colonel. This first-among-officers arrangement will not bear the weight of planetary administration. I'll be taking the title of Commander."

"I do not care what you call yourself. The arrangement is the same."

"Then you accept?" Nichole asked anxiously.

Again Elson said, "I will loyally serve the man who has proved my master."

Epilogue

Secrets are curious things. You never know when they really are secrets, although you usually know when they are not. How can you be sure that your buddy doesn't know the secret and isn't telling you because he's promised somebody else that he'll keep his mouth shut? It has also been said that three can keep a secret when two are dead, but that old saw doesn't take into account the value of the secret to those who hold it. If you benefit from something staying secret, or if you'll be harmed if word gets out, you're much more likely to stay quiet.

Being a member of Commander Wolf's staff makes a person privy to many secrets. Most are military secrets, usually fleeting information on positioning and available forces. But some involve other matters, more personal matters. Some of the secrets are kept on what is called a "need-to-know" basis; you're only told if you "need to know." Being a member of the Commander's staff, however, sometimes means that you can find out more than you "need to know."

I had been puzzled by Schlomo's behavior outside the recovery wards and had promised myself to look him up as soon as things calmed down around the general headquarters. The move back to Wolf Hall was chaotic, and the business of reuniting the Dragoons was time-consuming. New officers had to be assigned, old officers checked for loyalty. Surprisingly, Elson was useful in pinpointing those of his former faction who were unable to accept the changes and the new order. The Dragoons lost a lot of personnel even after the fighting was over. When I finally had some time to myself, I couldn't find Schlomo, so I decided to use my rank to do some of my own digging. He found me as I sat fussing over the med center computer.

"You won't find anything about her in there."

I looked up, startled by his silent approach. The old man was haggard, his face showing the deep tiredness of a long-carried burden.

In a brilliant response, I asked, "What are you talking about?"

He sat down beside me and gave me a weary smile. "The others didn't catch on. They only saw what they expected. But I saw your face when Fraser called Maeve Jaime Wolf's daughter, and I knew you'd come looking sooner or later. Does she mean something special to you?"

"She means everything to me," I said. "That's something you ought to understand. Even though you're an old-timer, you know what love is."

"Yes. I'm an old-timer, but I never was a warrior. The other castes didn't abandon love for honor. We weren't so foolish." He sighed. "At least not that way. She means everything, you say. Is that why you want to ruin her life and destroy the Dragoons?"

"How can knowing who Maeve's parents were destroy the Dragoons?"

"Don't pretend to be stupid, Brian. You know what would happen if she had the parentage you suspect."

I did, and the thought sent a slight shudder through me. To placate certain factions, Wolf had sworn that all officers of the Dragoons would be tested and evaluated for their positions. There would be no favoritism, he had promised. As a gesture of good faith, he stipulated that none of his children or grandchildren could hold a major command within the Dragoons. Maeve hadn't tried out for the command of the battalion in which she served; she hadn't wanted to take that away from Gentleman Johnny Clavell now that he had recovered. Instead she had entered the competition for the new Dragoon rank of general. Some said she was too young, but a lot of old-timers pointed out that she was the same age as Jaime and Joshua Wolf when they had first led the Dragoons into the Inner Sphere. Commander Wolf had supported her, saying that a young leader was what the fighting forces needed. The Clanners didn't object, but, then, they were used to young commanders, as long as they tested well enough. And test well enough she had. Once the scores were adjusted for ageframe and experience bias, she held the highest rating and became the first general of Wolf's Dragoons.

But who would support General Maeve if it became known that she was Jaime Wolf's sibko daughter? Who would believe that Wolf hadn't lied or that the tests had not been rigged? The factionalism, quiescent now, would flare, and we would be plunged again into civil war. The Dragoons could not survive another.

"Then she is Jaime Wolf's sibkid," I said, throat dry.

"No."

"What?"

"But the danger you fear is there nonetheless. The warriors would find the truth less palatable and less believable even than assuming her to be Wolf's true-born child."

Dreading the answer, I asked, "And what is that truth?"

"Aren't you afraid it will change your feelings for her?"

"No."

"You should be."

His calm sparked the worry that he had expected to find. "Tell me. You obviously want to."

"I *want* to?" He chuckled at some private amusement. "Yes, maybe it is a question of desire. You probably already think that I only do what I want to do. Well, that's not quite the situation. I'm talking to you because I think it necessary, because I believe it's the right thing to do, the necessary thing. I think you should know the truth, but not for my sake. For yours. And hers.''

"So tell me already."

"All right. You know about the genetic sampling of the heirs of the leaders of the Great Houses of the Inner Sphere. That was not Jaime Wolf's first attempt to add Inner Sphere genes to our gene pool. For years he had us collecting samples from captured soldiers, civilians who were treated in our medical units, and every single one of the nobles and politicos who sought us out for our so-called advanced medical knowledge. He had us create a sibko using the best specimens of the Inner Sphere and the best of the Dragoons seed. It was his belief that such a sibko could produce multi-talented children, a new generation to face the threat of the Clan invasion.

"The scientists considered the move unethical and ill-advised, or most of them did. Officially, the plan was rejected, but there were a few of us who saw the plan as a chance to do what we thought was necessary to achieve the same goal. We went to Wolf and offered to secretly replace the seed for an already planned sibko with the parental contributions he desired. He was frustrated by the science council's refusal and took us up on the offer, helping us bury the records. The secrecy he helped us create allowed us to perform the experiment we deemed necessary. However, Jaime Wolf contributed more to Maeve's sibko than he knew.''

I could hardly speak for a moment. "So you used his genes without him knowing. I thought you said she wasn't his sibdaughter."

"She isn't, in the strict sense. But in the broadest, she might be considered so."

"You're confusing me, Schlomo."

"I'm sorry. I don't mean to. You see, Jaime would never contribute to the Dragoon gene pool. He was freeborn and believed that the old ways were the best in that regard. For him anyway. It was hard enough for him to order the creation of any sibkos at all, but he had to bow to the necessity of filling Dragoon ranks with soldiers of quality genetic heritage. He knew the Clans were coming.

"All the children of Wolf's first marriage except MacKenzie had been killed and MacKenzie had yet to reproduce—or even to prove his genetic heritage enough for his seed to be entered into the sibko program. Our group of scientists believed that the Dragoons needed Jaime Wolf's heritage to survive, and MacKenzie was too slender a thread. Don't you agree that subsequent events have proven us correct on that last point?"

I didn't want to even begin trying to respond to that last question. Maybe Schlomo didn't really want an answer either. When I shrugged, he went on as though his thread had never been broken.

"Well, we believed that the Dragoons needed more than just his heritage; we needed Jaime Wolf personally, but he was getting older every year like the rest of us. When his blood offspring didn't show enough of the right aptitudes, we conceived, if you'll pardon the expression, a plan.

"A direct reiteration would have been too obvious, even to the uninitiated. Though it took us to the edge of our capabilities, we were able to manipulate some of his cells, deleting the sex determinate from the Y chromosome. The resulting genetic blueprint was superimposed on an egg from which the nucleus had been removed. Mitochondrial matter from the donor was introduced to the egg as well. Most of the recombinants failed to multiply. Only one thrived."

"Maeve."

He nodded slowly. "For all practical purposes, she is a female Jaime Wolf. Genetically speaking, of course. Her upbringing and education are substantially different."

"Why?"

"Because the raw material was there. The Dragoons needed another Jaime to get them through the change that was coming."

"So you *made* her." She was almost what the sibs called a retread, what a layman might call a clone. I was terrified. We had all been taught that the reuse of a genetic blueprint was not moral. But it had been done.

"She is no less human than any womb-born individual."

He was right. She was a person. My terror abated when I remembered just how human she was, and suddenly his revelation really didn't make any difference to me. She was Maeve. My Maeve. "Oh, I know how human she is."

Schlomo smiled indulgently. "I know you do. I've seen you two together. That's why I am trusting you. I believe you have the strength to carry the knowledge and keep it to yourself. The other scientists of my group are dead, and I won't live forever."

"Then the Wolf really doesn't know? He didn't set up the rank trial to favor her?"

"I don't believe so. He knew the preliminary scores and he saw her in battle. He would have known she was a prime candidate. I do not believe that he would have let her compete if he had known her origin."

"Should I tell her?"

"That I will leave to you."

"Schlomo, you can't put this on me."

But he did.

In many ways I was thankful that the next weeks continued to be full of duty for both Maeve and me. I had to handle an enormous volume of communications traffic, and I saw more of the ComStar Precentor than I did of Maeve. She was overseeing the restructuring of the fighting units, putting us in shape to hire out more than just Alpha and Delta, who had missed the fighting on Outreach. The Dragoons needed the income.

I saw a lot of Jaime Wolf, but I never dared bring up the subject of Maeve.

In late September, the council forced a resolution on the Commander. Over his objections, the name Wolf was added to the Honornames of the Dragoons. He and his surviving offspring would of course retain the name, but the council wanted competitions to be held in MacKenzie's and Alpin's ageframes now and in all succeeding ageframes to come. The council believed that the institutionalization of the name Wolf would help heal the wounds. Jaime protested, but to no avail. The call went out announcing the competition.

When the day of the competition came, I stood outside Wolf Hall and watched the crowd assemble for the final naming of the competitors. As was my place, I stood beside Commander Wolf. The rest of his staff stood with us. Ranked several steps before us were the Honornamed. The Loremaster stood on a podium and faced the crowd as he read the proclamation establishing the new Honorname.

As he finished, Maeve stepped out from the front row of the crowd and shouted, "I call to challenge! The name Wolf shall be mine!"

A stir swept through the crowd as Elson shouldered his way forward. He was at the upper limit of the eligible ageframe. What he said surprised me. I even saw the Wolf raise an eyebrow.

"I support the challenge of Maeve. I withdraw."

Voices roared in agreement.

Tolling his bell for silence, the Loremaster called for other competitors. MechWarrior Jovell stepped forward and shouted, "I withdraw from the challenge.'' Lydia came forward and said the same, then Harold, his broad Elemental shoulders square, withdrew as well. One by one all the contestants advanced up the steps, announced their withdrawal and retreated back to the crowd.

For a long minute, the Loremaster waited. The word spread through the amazed crowd. Never had an Honorname gone uncontested.

"You must finish the ritual," the Loremaster said to Maeve.

"I call to challenge!" she shouted. Her expression was in turmoil. I knew how much she wanted the name, and I knew she was prepared to fight for it. She *wanted* to fight for it.

But no voice rose in challenge.

Maeve shouted for a third time. "I call to challenge!"

And again no one spoke.

"Let it be known that none stand to contest Maeve," the Loremaster said. He called her to the podium. Once she was at his side, he addressed her, "Maeve, you are the sole contender in the ageframe of Alpin Wolf. None are willing to oppose you for the name. You are Wolf."

The cheers and chants of "Wolf! Wolf!" boomed and echoed across Harlech. Maeve stood stunned by the roar of approval. I stood silent as well. Only I and one other knew how truly she had been named.

Under Commander Jaime Wolf and General Maeve Wolf, the Dragoons have been reorganized in both lifestyle and military force, taking full advantage of what we learned from the infighting that almost destroyed us. Our units are well under-strength for our new table of organization because we lost many who could not accept the new order. Their departure weakened us, but the effect is only temporary. We have new recruits in training and new sibkos on the way up. All

will be carefully, and fully, made to understand that we are something new. The Dragoons are not just mercenaries, not just warriors, we are a family. The Wolf Pack nickname has become popular with astonishing rapidity, sticking even as Maeve had predicted it would.

Until we reach full complement, we'll make do. And why not? We're all veterans now. The Dragoons are tougher and stronger than ever. We started as the best the Inner Sphere had ever seen, and we have become better. To my thinking, we're hardier and more skilful than any of the Clans. What can we do now except keep on getting better?

The Hiring Hall is open again, friends.

The Wolf Pack is on the prowl.

Glossary

CULTURAL/POLITICAL TERMS

After the fall of the Star League General Aleksandr Kerensky, commander of the Regular Star League army, led his forces out of the Inner Sphere in what is known as the first Exodus. After making their way beyond the Periphery, more than 1,300 light years away from Terra, Kerensky and his followers settled in a group of marginally habitable star systems near a large globular cluster that hid them from the Inner Sphere. Within fifteen years, Civil War erupted among these exiles, threatening to destroy everything they had worked so hard to build. In a second Exodus, Nicholas Kerensky, son of Aleksandr, led his followers to one of the worlds of the globular cluster to escape the new war. It was there on Strana Mechty that Kerensky first conceived and organized the system that would one day become known as the Clans.

Though Wolf's Dragoons originated among the Clans, they have repudiated their allegiance to the Wolf Clan. Nevertheless many Clan traditions, concepts, and customs still prevail among the Dragoons, as described below.

BLOODNAME

The Clans have approximately 760 Bloodnames. These are the surnames of the 800 warriors who stood with Nicholas Kerensky during the Exodus Civil War. These warriors were the first contributors to the elaborate eugenics program by which the Clans create their elite warrior caste in each generation. A warrior earns the right to bear one of these surnames only if he succeeds in a series of grueling competitions known as the Trial of Bloodright; only twenty-five warriors are permitted to bear any one Bloodname at a given time.

When one of the twenty-five Bloodnamed warriors dies, a Trial is held to determine who will assume that Bloodname. A contender must prove his Bloodname lineage, then win the Trial of Bloodright against the other contenders. Only Bloodnamed warriors may sit on the Clan Councils or are eligible to become a Khan or ilKhan. Clan Bloodnames are determined matrilineally, at least after the original generation. Because a warrior can only inherit from his or her female parent, he or she has a claim to only one Bloodname. Forty of the original 800 Bloodnames were eliminated after one of the Clans was annihilated for committing a grievous crime against the Clans as a whole.

BONDSMAN

Clans can keep prisoners taken during combat. These are called bondsmen, and are considered members of the laborer caste, unless and until the capturing Clan releases them or promotes them back to warrior status. A bondsman is bound by honor, not by shackles. Custom dictates that even Bloodnamed warriors captured in combat be held for a time as bondsmen. All bondsmen wear a woven bracelet called a bondcord. The base color of the bondcord indicates to which Clan the individual is now bound, and the striping indicates which unit captured him.

CASTES

Clan society is rigidly divided into five castes: warrior, scientist, merchant, technician, and laborer. Each caste has many subcastes, which are based on specialties within a professional field. The warrior caste is based on a systematic eugenics program that uses the genes of prestigious current and past warriors to produce new members of the caste (see **Sibko**). These products of genetic engineering are known as trueborns. Other castes maintain a quality gene pool by strategic marriages within each caste.

CODEX

The codex is each Clan warrior's personal record. It includes the names of the original Bloodnamed warriors from which a warrior is descended. It also records background information such as the warrior's generation number, Blood House, and codex ID, an alphanumeric code noting the unique aspects of that person's DNA. The codex also contains a record of the warrior's military career. Many Clan warriors wear their codex as a kind of bracelet; Wolf's Dragoons members wear their codex as tags around the neck.

COMSTAR

ComStar, the interstellar communications network, was the brainchild of Jerome Blake, Minister of Communications during the latter years of the Star League. After the League's fall, Blake seized Terra and reorganized what was left of the communications network into a private organization that sold its services to the five Successor Houses for a profit. Since that time, ComStar has also developed into a powerful secret society steeped in mysticism and ritual. Initiates to the quasi-religious ComStar Order commit themselves to lifelong service.

ELEMENTALS

Elementals are the elite, battle-armored infantry of the Clans. These men and women are giants, bred specifically to handle Clan-developed battle armor. The Inner Sphere military has recently captured samples of these battle suits and have developed their own versions, but they do not breed 2.4-meter-tall Elementals to wear and fight in the battle suits.

FREEBORN/FREEBIRTH

An individual conceived and born by natural means is freeborn. Because the Clans value their eugenics program so highly, a freeborn is automatically assumed to have little potential.

Freebirth is an epithet used by trueborn members of the Clan warrior caste, generally expressing disgust or frustration. If a trueborn warrior refers to another trueborn as a freebirth, it is a mortal insult.

HONOR ROAD

Clan society is a warrior's society in which honor is a key important concept defining behavior and obligations. Honor road is a Clan code of conduct that is analogous to the Japanese *bushido*, the way of the warrior.

HONORNAME

Among Wolf's Dragoons an Honorname is analogous to a Clan Bloodname (see above). The surnames descend from the warriors who originally arrived with Jaime and Joshua Wolf when the Dragoons came to the Inner Sphere on an extended intelligence mission for Clan Wolf. To be eligible to compete for an Honorname, a Dragoon must be of the proper ageframe and neither under disciplinary ban, nor the holder of another Honorname. In contrast to the Clans, only one individual in each ageframe, or generation, has the right to bear a particular Honorname. All eligible Dragoons with a known genetic link to the Honorname bloodline are honorbound to compete in the Honorname Trial. It is unusual for an individual to lose the right to bear an Honorname he/she has won, but it could happen as a result of a particularly heinous crime or breach of honor.

INNER SPHERE

The Inner Sphere was the term originally applied to the star empires that joined together to form the Star League in the mid-2700s. The states, kingdoms, and pirate domains just beyond the Inner Sphere are known as the Periphery, the great unknown. When Aleksandr Kerensky led his exiles out from the Inner Sphere, they traveled even beyond the Periphery in search of a life that would remove them irrevocably from the destructive wars of the Inner Sphere.

JUMPSHIPS AND DROPSHIPS

JumpShip

Interstellar travel is accomplished via JumpShips, first developed in the twenty-second century. These somewhat ungainly vessels consist of a long, thin drive core and a sail resembling an enormous parasol, which can extend up to a kilometer in width. The ship is named for its ability to ''jump'' instantaneously across vast distances—up to thirty light years per jump. Before it can make another jump, however, the ship must recharge its interstellar drives by gathering up more solar energy. This can take up to a week.

The JumpShip's enormous sail is constructed from a special metal that absorbs vast quantities of electromagnetic energy from the nearest star. When it has soaked up enough energy, the sail transfers it to the drive core, which converts it into a space-twisting field. An instant later, the ship arrives at the next jump point, a distance of up to thirty light years. This field is known as hyperspace, and its discovery opened to mankind the gateway to the stars.

JumpShips never land on planets. Interplanetary travel is carried out by DropShips, vessels that are attached to the JumpShip until arrival at the jump point.

DropShip

Because interstellar JumpShips must avoid entering the heart of a solar system, they must "dock" in space at a considerable distance from a system's inhabited worlds. DropShips were developed for interplanetary travel. As the name implies, a DropShip is attached to hardpoints on the JumpShip's drive core, later to be dropped from the parent vessel after in-system entry. Though incapable of FTL travel, DropShips are highly maneuverable, well-armed, and sufficiently aerodynamic to take off from and land on a planetary surface. The journey from the jump point to the inhabited worlds of a system usually requires a normal-space journey of several days or weeks, depending on the type of star.

KHAN

Each Clan elects two leaders, or Khans. One serves as the Clan's senior military commander and bureaucratic administrator. The Second Khan's position is less well-defined. He or she is second-in-command, carrying out duties assigned by the first Khan. In times of great internal or external threat, or when a coordinated effort is required of all Clans, an ilKhan is chosen to serve as the supreme ruler of the Clans.

LOREMASTER

The Loremaster is the keeper of Clan laws and history. The position is honorable and politically powerful. The Loremaster plays a key role in inquiries and trials, where he is often assigned the role of Advocate or Interrogator.

OATHMASTER

The Oathmaster is the honor guard for any official Clan ceremony. The position is similar to that of an Inner Sphere sergeant-at-arms, but it carries a greater degree of respect. The Oathmaster administers all oaths, and the Loremaster records them. The position of Oathmaster is usually held by the oldest Blood-named warrior in a Clan (if he or she desires the honor), and is one of the few positions not decided by combat.

PERIPHERY

Beyond the borders of the Inner Sphere is the Periphery, the edge of the vast domain of known and unknown worlds stretching endlessly into interstellar night. Once populated by colonies from Terra, the worlds of the Periphery were devastated technologically, politically, and economically by the fall of the Star League. At present, the Periphery is the refuge of piratical Bandit Kings, privateers, and outcasts from the Inner Sphere.

QUIAFF/QUINEG

These Clan expressions are placed at the end of rhetorical questions. If an affirmative answer is expected, *quiaff* is used. If the speaker expects a negative answer, *quineg* is the proper closure.

REMEMBRANCE, THE

The Remembrance is an ongoing heroic saga detailing Clan history from the time of the Exodus from the Inner Sphere to the present day. *The Remembrance* is continually expanded to include contemporary events. Each Clan has a slightly different version reflecting its own opinions and experiences. All Clan warriors can quote whole verses of this marvelous epic from memory, and it is common to see passages from the book lovingly painted on the sides of OmniMechs, fighters, and even battle armor.

SEYLA

This word is the ritual response voiced in unison by those witnessing solemn Clan ceremonies, rituals, and other important gatherings. No one is sure of the origin or exact meaning of the word, but it is uttered only with the greatest reverence and awe.

SIBKO

A sibko consists of a group of children produced from the same male and female geneparents in the Clan's eugenics program to create its warrior caste. The members of the sibko are raised together, then begin to undergo constant testing. Those who fail are transferred to one of the lower castes. A sibko consists of approximately twenty members, but usually only four or five remain at the time of the final test to become Clan warriors, the Trial of Position. These tests and other adversities may bind the surviving ''sibkin'' together.

STAR LEAGUE

The Star League was formed in 2571 in an attempt to peacefully ally the major star empires of human-occupied space, or the Inner Sphere. The League prospered for almost 200 years, until civil war broke out in 2751. The League was eventually destroyed when the ruling body, known as the High Council, disbanded in the midst of a struggle for power. Each of the Great House leaders then declared him or herself First Lord of the Star League, and within months, war had engulfed the Inner Sphere. This conflict continues to the present day, almost three centuries later. This era of continuous war is now known simply as the Succession Wars.

SUCCESSOR STATES

After the fall of the Star League, the remaining members of the High Council each asserted his or her right to become First Lord of the Star League. Their star empires became known as the Successor States and the rulers as the Successor Lords. The Clan invasion has temporarily interrupted the centuries of war—the Succession Wars—that first began in 2786. The battleground of these wars is the vast Inner Sphere, which is composed of all the star systems once occupied by the Star League's member-states. The Successor Lords have temporarily put aside their differences in order to meet the threat of a common foe, the Clans.

TRIAL OF BLOODRIGHT

A series of one-on-one, single-elimination contests determines who wins the right to use a Bloodname. Each current Bloodnamed warrior in that Bloodname's House nominates one candidate. The head of the House nominates additional candidates to fill thirty-one slots. The thirty-second slot is fought for by those who qualify for the Bloodname but who were not nominated.

The nature of the combat is determined by "coining." Each combatant places his personal medallion, a *dogids*, into the "Well of Decision." An Oathmaster or Loremaster releases the coins simultaneously, so that only chance determines which coin falls first to the bottom of the well. The warrior whose coin lands on top chooses the manner of combat ('Mech versus 'Mech, barehanded, 'Mech versus Elemental, and so forth). The other warrior chooses the venue of the contest. Though these Bloodname duels need not be to the death, the fierce combat and the intensity of the combatants often leave the losing candidate mortally wounded or dead.

TRIAL OF GRIEVANCE

When two warriors cannot resolve a dispute on their own or with the aid of their superiors, the parties may call for a Trial of Grievance. A Circle of Equals is defined, and no one but the opponents may enter the Circle unless invited. Leaving the Circle before the contest is ended is a shameful defeat. All such trials are defined as to the death, but they usually end before either party is killed.

TRIAL OF POSITION

The Trial of Position determines whether a candidate will qualify as a warrior in the Clans. To qualify, the candidate must defeat at least one of three successive opponents. If he defeats two, or all three, he is immediately ranked as an officer in his Clan. If he fails to defeat any of his opponents, he is relegated to a lower caste.

TRIAL OF REFUSAL

The Clan councils and the Grand Council vote on issues and laws that affect the community. Unlike Inner Sphere legislation, however, any decision can be challenged and reversed by a Trial of Refusal. This trial allows the losing side to demand the issue be settled by combat.

The forces used in the Trail of Refusal are determined on a pro-rated basis. The faction rejecting the decision declares what forces they will use. The side defending the decision (the attacker) can field a force equal to the ratio of winning to losing votes. For example, if the contested vote carried by a three-to-one margin, the attacking forces can field a force three times the size of the force challenging the decision. Bidding usually results in a smaller attacking force, however.

TRUEBORN/TRUEBIRTH

A trueborn is a product of the warrior caste's eugenics program.

MILITARY/POLITICAL TERMS

AUTOCANNON

An autocannon is a rapid-firing, auto-loading weapon that fires high-speed streams of high-explosive, armor-piercing shells.

BATTLEMECH

BattleMechs are the most powerful war machines ever built. First developed by Terran scientists and engineers, these huge, man-shaped vehicles are faster, more mobile, better-armored, and more heavily armed than any twentieth-century tank. Ten to twelve meters tall and equipped with particle projection cannons, lasers, rapid-fire autocannon, and missiles, they pack enough firepower to flatten anything but another BattleMech. A small fusion reactor provides virtually unlimited power, and BattleMechs can be adapted to fight in environments ranging from sun-baked deserts to subzero arctic icefields.

BATTALION

A battalion is a tactical military unit usually consisting of three companies.

BINARY

A Binary consists of two Stars and is roughly equivalent to an Inner Sphere company.

CLUSTER

A Cluster is a Clan-style military unit that consists of three to five Trinaries and is the rough equivalent of an Inner Sphere battalion.

COMPANY

A company is a military tactical unit consisting of three BattleMech lances or, for infantry, three platoons with a total of 50 to 100 men. Companies are generally commanded by a captain.

GALAXY

A Galaxy is a Clan-style military unit composed of three to five Clusters. It is the equivalent of an Inner Sphere regiment.

LANCE

A lance is a BattleMech tactical combat group, usually consisting of four 'Mechs.

LASER

Laser is an acronym for "Light Amplification through Stimulated Emission of Radiation." When used as a weapon, the laser damages the target by concentrating extreme heat on a small area. BattleMech lasers are designated as small, medium, and large. Lasers are also available as shoulder-fired weapons operating from a portable backpack power unit. Certain range-finders and targeting equipment also employ low-level lasers.

LRM

This is an abbreviation for Long-Range Missile, an indirect-fire missile with a high-explosive warhead.

PLATOON

A platoon is a tactical military unit typically consisting of approximately twenty-eight men, commanded by a lieutenant or a platoon sergeant. A platoon may be divided into two sections.

POINT

A Point is a Clan-style military unit consisting of one 'Mech or five armored infantry.

PPC

This abbreviation stands for Particle Projection Cannon, a magnetic accelerator firing high-energy proton or ion bolts, causing damage through both impact and high temperature. PPCs are among the most effective weapons available to BattleMechs.

REGIMENT

A regiment is a military unit consisting of two to four battalions, each consisting of three or four companies. A regiment is commanded by a colonel.

SRM

This is the abbreviation for Short-Range Missiles, direct-trajectory missiles with high-explosive or armor-piercing explosive warheads. They have a range of less than 1 kilometer, and are accurate only at ranges of less than 300 meters. They are more powerful, however, than LRMs.

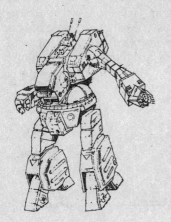

ARCHER

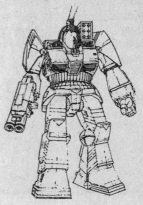

BATTLEMASTER

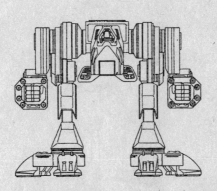

BLACKHAWK

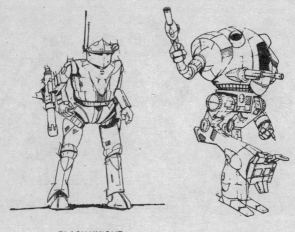

BLACK KNIGHT

CAESAR

DERVISH

GALLOWGLASS

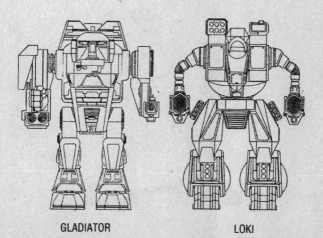

GLADIATOR   LOKI

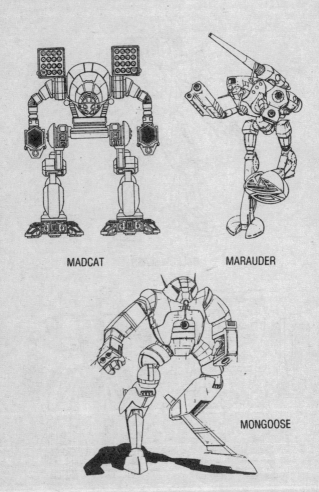

MADCAT

MARAUDER

MONGOOSE

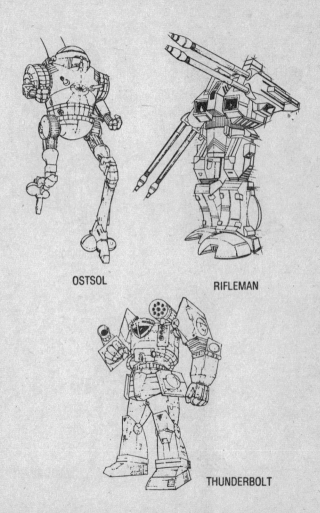

OSTSOL

RIFLEMAN

THUNDERBOLT

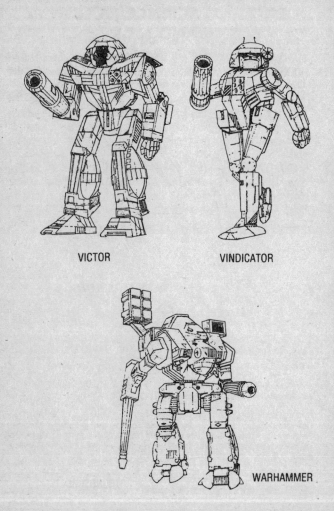

VICTOR

VINDICATOR

WARHAMMER

THE FUTURE IS UPON US . . .

(0451)

WORLDS OF WONDER

If you and/or a friend would like to receive the *ROC Advance*, a bimonthly newsletter featuring all the newest and hottest ROC books and authors, on a complimentary basis, please fill out this form and return it to:

ROC Books/Penguin USA
375 Hudson Street
New York, NY 10014

Your Address
Name _____
Street _____ Apt. # _____
City _____ State _____ Zip _____

Friend's Address
Name _____
Street _____ Apt. # _____
City _____ State _____ Zip _____